HER REAL FAMILY CHRISTMAS

BY
KATE HARDY

CHRISTMAS EVE DELIVERY

BY
CONNIE COX

MILLS &
BOON®

Kate Hardy lives in Norwich, in the east of England, with her husband, two young children, one bouncy spaniel, and too many books to count! When she's not busy writing romance or researching local history she helps out at her children's schools. She also loves cooking—spot the recipes sneaked into her books! (They're also on her website, along with extracts and stories behind the books.) Writing for Mills & Boon® has been a dream come true for Kate—something she wanted to do ever since she was twelve. She's been writing Medical Romances™ for over ten years now, and also writes for Mills & Boon® Romance. She says it's the best of both worlds, because she gets to learn lots of new things when she's researching the background to a book: add a touch of passion, drama and danger, a new gorgeous hero every time, and it's the perfect job!

Kate's always delighted to hear from readers, so do drop in to her website at www.katehardy.com

Praise for Kate Hardy:

'A spellbinding novel
which you will want to devour in a single sitting.'
—*www.cataromance.com* on
A CHRISTMAS NIGHT

Connie Cox has loved Harlequin Mills & Boon® romances since she was a young teen. To be a Harlequin Mills & Boon® author now is a fantasy come to life. By training, Connie is an electrical engineer. Through her first job, working on nuclear scanners and other medical equipment, she had a unique perspective on the medical world. She is fascinated by the inner strength of medical professionals, who must balance emotional compassion with stoic logic, and is honoured to showcase the passion of these dedicated professionals through her own passion of writing. Married to the boy-next-door, Connie is the proud mother of one terrific daughter and son-in-law and one precocious dachshund.

Connie would love to hear from you. Visit her website at www.ConnieCox.com

Praise for Connie Cox:

'RETURN OF THE REBEL SURGEON is an emotionally packed reunion story…I would definitely recommend reading [it].'
—*HarlequinJunkie* on
RETURN OF THE REBEL SURGEON

HER REAL FAMILY CHRISTMAS

BY
KATE HARDY

MILLS & BOON

First published in Great Britain 2013
by Mills & Boon, an imprint of Harlequin (UK) Limited.
Harlequin (UK) Limited, Eton House, 18-24 Paradise Road,
Richmond, Surrey TW9 1SR

© Pamela Brooks 2013

ISBN: 978 0 263 89925 2

Harlequin (UK) policy is to use papers that are natural, renewable
and recyclable products and made from wood grown in sustainable
forests. The logging and manufacturing process conform to the
legal environmental regulations of the country of origin.

Printed and bound in Spain
by Blackprint CPI, Barcelona

Dear Reader

I rather like stories where the hero and heroine teach each other to trust again and/or love again.

My heroine doesn't think she'll ever fit into a family, because she's never had one—except in-laws who didn't ever accept her for who she was. This is where my hero and his daughter come in. They need to learn to love again and open their hearts—which is what she does for them.

This idea actually started last year, when I got my twice-yearly cold. It *always* turns into a horrible croupy cough, nobody in the house gets any sleep for about a week, and I can't nag about homework because I lose my voice (that bit is popular and almost makes up for the lack of sleep). I was having a bit of a pity party on Facebook about it when one of my readers e-mailed me and suggested I got checked out for reactive airways. I looked up the condition (which I don't have, by the way—I'm just prone to croup), and I thought it would be a great way for my hero and heroine to meet... (A special thank you to Pat Amsden for the lightbulb moment.)

I also love writing about Christmas. The season's one of my favourites, with its chance to spend some real quality time with my family. (And I admit I love all the sparkling lights and the special ornaments on the tree. And now my littlest is old enough she helps me find the perfect presents for her dad's and brother's stockings.) When my children were really small, one of our favourite Christmas traditions was taking them to see Santa. So I couldn't resist getting my hero and heroine to take his daughter to see Santa—and that, of course, led to finding out what she really, really wanted for Christmas...

Oh, and then there are the scallops. My daughter and I discovered them while I was writing the book, played around with different ways of cooking them, and thought it should be this book's recipe! Enjoy!

I'm always delighted to hear from readers, so do come and visit me at www.katehardy.com

With love

Kate Hardy

DEDICATION

To Pat Amsden, with thanks for the lightbulb moment.

Recent books by Kate Hardy:

A DATE WITH THE ICE PRINCESS*
THE BROODING DOC'S REDEMPTION*
BALLROOM TO BRIDE AND GROOM**
ONCE A PLAYBOY…*
THE HIDDEN HEART OF RICO ROSSI***
DR CINDERELLA'S MIDNIGHT FLING*
THE EX WHO HIRED HER***

*In Mills & Boon® Medical Romance™
**In Mills & Boon® Cherish™
***In Mills & Boon® Modern™ Romance

CHAPTER ONE

'IT'S ALL RIGHT, darling.' Daniel stroked his daughter's hair, and hoped that the panic seeping through his veins didn't show in his voice. 'Don't try to talk. Just breathe. In for two, out for two. Good girl. And again. In for two, out for two.'

How could Mia have got so much worse in one short hour?

The old trick of a steamy bathroom helping to calm a child's airways wasn't working. She couldn't stop coughing; and it was a horrible, barking, croupy cough. He'd just bet that if she were wired up to a pulse oximeter, her oxygen stats would be way too low.

He had to act. Now. He needed to take her to hospital.

Should he call an ambulance? No, it'd scare her too much. And in any case he could drive her there quicker than an ambulance could get to his house and back to the hospital.

Except that meant Mia would be on her own in the back of the car, in her seat, with nobody to hold her hand and calm her down. Sure, he could call his mum or his sister and they'd come straight over to help—but that would mean waiting for them to get to his house. And right now he didn't think waiting was an option.

Not for the first time, Daniel wished he wasn't a single dad. If that stupid, selfish elderly driver who'd mown down his wife on the footpath hadn't been so stubborn and had taken a taxi that day, instead of driving a car she really hadn't been capable of handling any more.

But wishing wasn't going to bring Meg back. It was pointless and self-indulgent, and he was only letting himself wish it now because he was panicking that he'd let his daughter down. Panicking that he'd lose his precious girl because he hadn't kept a close enough eye on her and realised how bad her symptoms were getting.

What kind of useless father was he?

What kind of useless *doctor* was he?

He scooped Mia up into his arms. 'I think,' he said softly, 'we need to get you some special medicine for that cough. And we don't have any indoors. So I need to take you to where I work, OK?'

Mia nodded, her brown eyes huge. So like Meg's. Guilt spiked through him; right now he was letting Meg down as well as Mia.

'Good girl. Let's go.' Daniel grabbed a blanket from her room on the way, along with her favourite teddy, and closed the front door behind him. 'Daddy's going to be driving so I can't hold your hand, but Fred Bear's going to give you a special cuddle for me so you don't feel lonely, OK?' He strapped her into her car seat, put Fred Bear into her arms, and arranged the blanket quickly so she wouldn't get cold.

He talked to her all the way to the hospital. All the way from scooping her out of her car seat until they got to the reception of the emergency department. And, all the way, the only thing that he could hear from her was that dreadful deep cough.

To his relief, the triage nurse saw them immediately, and sent her straight through to the paediatric assessment unit.

The doctor on duty wasn't one he knew, but that didn't matter—just as long as she treated his daughter right now.

'Hello, Mia. I'm Dr Stephanie Scott,' the doctor said, crouching down so she was at the child's height.

Mia managed the first syllable of a reply before she started coughing.

'It's OK, sweetheart, you don't have to talk,' Stephanie said. 'I can hear exactly what's wrong with you. What I'm going to do now is put a special mask on your face, which will help you breathe a bit better and not cough quite so much, and I'd also like to put a special sleeve on your finger. It won't hurt. It just shines a light through your finger and tells me some numbers that will help me to make you feel better. Is that OK?'

The little girl nodded.

Daniel knew what Stephanie Scott was checking for when she put the oximeter on Mia's finger: pulse and oxygen saturation. Good. Just what he would do.

Stephanie looked at the readings and smiled at the little girl. 'That's what I thought it would say. Mia, I'm going to give you some special medicine through another mask that will *really* help with that cough, and then I need to talk to Daddy for a little bit because I think he's going to find it easier to talk to me than you are, right now. Is that OK with you?'

At the little girl's nod, she glanced over at Daniel. 'I'm going to give her a medicine called adrenalin—it will help a lot with her breathing. And I'm going to do it through a nebuliser so all she has to do is breathe it in. It looks a lot scarier than it is, but she's going to be absolutely fine, OK?'

'OK.' Daniel was holding it together. Just. But he found himself relaxing as he watched her work. Stephanie Scott clearly knew what she was doing and she was really good with Mia, talking her through what she was doing as she hooked the little girl up to the nebuliser, and reassuring her all the while. And that smile—she had the kind of smile that lit up a room.

Daniel caught his thoughts and grimaced. What on earth was he doing, thinking about that sort of thing when his daughter was desperately ill? Especially when he hadn't been involved with anyone since Meg's death, four years ago, and had concentrated on his daughter and his job rather than his social life? Hot shame flooded through his cheeks, mingled with guilt. Right at that moment, he was at the end of his tether and his head felt as if it was going to implode under all the pressure.

'Mr Connor?' Stephanie asked.

He shook himself. 'I'm so sorry. I didn't catch what you said.'

'I was asking if Mia has any family history of asthma or any kind of allergies.'

'No, none.'

'Does Mia wheeze at all or say her chest feels tight or hurts?'

'No.'

'OK. Do you ever notice that Mia's a bit short of breath or her nostrils flare?'

Daniel realised swiftly that Stephanie was running

through a list of asthma symptoms. 'No. Is that what you think it is? Asthma?'

'It's quite a strong possibility,' she said.

He shook his head. 'Mia just has a cold. They always go to her chest and she ends up with a bad cough—she had bronchiolitis when she was tiny and she was in here for a week on oxygen.'

Stephanie nodded. 'Colds are often worse for little ones after they've had RSV. And I guess seeing her here on oxygen is reminding you of that? It's tough.'

'Yes,' he admitted. It brought back all the nights when he and Meg had taken turns to sit at their tiny baby's bedside, feeding her through a nasogastric tube because the virus had left Mia too exhausted to drink normally. 'I guess I panicked a bit.'

'No, you did exactly the right thing, bringing her in,' Stephanie reassured him. 'She wasn't getting as much oxygen as I'd like, so the medication's going to help a lot. Though I'd also like to admit her overnight and keep an eye on her. So she's had a cold recently?'

'For three or four days. And yesterday it went to that croupy cough.' He sighed. 'Usually a steamy bathroom helps. I get her to drink warm blackcurrant or something like that, and keep her sitting upright on my lap.'

'Which are all exactly the right things to do to treat a cough,' Stephanie said. 'Colds are viral infections, Mr Connor, so antibiotics won't do anything to help and I won't prescribe them, but liquid paracetamol will help to keep Mia's temperature down.'

Daniel thought about telling Stephanie that he was a doctor and he was well aware of the problems with antibiotic resistance, but that wouldn't help Mia—and his daughter was a lot more important than his professional pride. 'I last gave her some of that about four hours ago, so she's due some more now anyway,' he said. 'The steamy bathroom didn't work this time.'

'Does she get many coughs like this?'

'Too many,' he admitted. 'She hates having time off school when this happens, but she gets so tired and the cough just won't stop.'

Stephanie looked thoughtful. 'Has your family doctor prescribed corticosteroids for her?'

'No.'

'It's usually a treatment for asthma, but it's also very good for reducing inflammation in airways when children have this sort of virus. And I should explain that corticosteroids are the same kind of steroids that the body produces naturally, not the sort you associate with bodybuilders.'

Yes, it was way, way too late now to tell Stephanie Scott that he was a doctor; it would just embarrass them both. But Daniel liked the clear way she explained things. It was a pity she was on the emergency department team, as he had a feeling that she'd be good with neonates. Unless she was a locum, maybe? He'd check that when he was back on duty and, if she *was* a locum, he'd get Theo to add Stephanie to their list. She'd be a real asset to their team.

Mia's breathing started to ease as the medication did its job. Stephanie glanced at the readout on the oximeter. 'I'm happier now. She's responding nicely. Mia, I'd like you to stay here tonight just so we can make sure that cough's getting better or give you more of the special medicine if it doesn't. Daddy can stay with you if he wants to—' she looked at him '—or maybe Mia's mum might like to stay with her?'

Daniel was pretty sure that Mia's mum would be there in spirit; but, oh, how he wished she could be there in body, too. He'd had four years now of being a single parent, and it didn't get any easier. Missing Meg hadn't got much easier, either. Though, between them, Mia and his work kept him too busy to focus on how lonely he felt. He had to swallow the sudden lump in his throat. 'I'll stay with her,' he said gruffly.

Stephanie took him up to the children's ward, settled Mia in and made sure that Daniel was comfortable, then sorted out the paperwork. 'I'll see you both tomorrow before the end of my shift,' she said. 'If you need anything, just go and have a word with the nurse. If it's an emergency, then you press that button there and someone will be straight with you.'

He already knew all that. But he appreciated the way she was looking after them and it would be churlish to say anything. 'Thank you.'

'No worries.' She squeezed Mia's hand. 'You try to get some rest, sweetheart, OK?'

The little girl nodded tiredly.

'I'll see you later.'

Stephanie was almost tempted to call in and see the Connors on her break. Mia's father had looked so tired and worried. And it was unusual for a dad to be at the hospital with a child on his own; in her experience, mothers usually took over when a child was ill. Unless maybe Mia's mum wasn't well herself, or had been working a night shift. Or, given the way Mr Connor had flinched when she'd mentioned Mia's mum, maybe he was a single dad and he was worried about the fact his daughter had become ill so quickly when he was looking after her.

No. She needed to keep some professional distance. Besides, she knew better than to get involved—especially given the way her world had imploded the last time she'd got involved with someone else's medical problems. It had put her marriage on its final crash-and-burn trajectory; although it had been four years now since the divorce, it still hurt to think about the way things had gone so badly wrong. The way all her dreams had blown up in her face. The way she'd managed to lose a second family. And all because she'd put her job first.

Now her job was all she had. And that had to be enough.

She shook herself. Enough of the self-pity. She needed to concentrate on what she was supposed to be doing: working the night shift on the paediatric assessment unit. Though her shift was reasonably quiet, and that gave her time to research her hunch on Mia Connor's condition.

When she'd done the handover at the end of her shift, she called up to the children's ward to see how Mia was getting on.

Mia's dad looked as if he'd barely slept and, although Mia was sleeping, the little girl was still coughing in her sleep.

'Hi,' he said, giving Stephanie a tired smile.

'Rough night?' she asked sympathetically.

He nodded. 'But I'm glad I could be here for her.'

'I've been thinking about Mia. Given that you don't have a family history of asthma, I think she has reactive airways. Whenever anyone gets a cold, their airways tend to get a bit swollen, but if someone has reactive airways their systems really overreact.' She drew a swift diagram on a piece of paper.

'Basically, these are Mia's lungs. They work a bit like a tree, with her windpipe as the trunk and the smaller airways like branches. The airways are covered in muscle—a bit like the bark of a tree—and inside they have mucous membranes, which produce mucus to keep the lungs clean. When she gets a cold, her muscles tighten and the mucous membranes swell and produce more mucus than usual. That makes her airways narrow, which in turn makes it harder for her to breathe.'

She glanced at him to check that he was following what she'd said; it was the clearest way she could explain things, but he obviously hadn't slept much overnight in the chair next to his daughter's bed and she wasn't sure how much of this he was taking in.

'Reactive airways.' He looked thoughtful. 'So can you give her something for it?'

'Yes. Corticosteroids, an inhaler and a nebuliser. I'll write the prescription, but as Mia's asleep at the moment I don't want to wake her. One of my colleagues will show you how to use them when she does wake. The corticosteroids will stop the swelling in her throat, so if you get her to use the inhaler and nebuliser as soon as you spot the symptoms, hopefully she won't end up with that really croupy cough next time.'

'Thank you.'

'Though there are sometimes side effects,' Stephanie warned. 'She might have a headache or an upset tummy, or be sick. If that's the case, your family doctor can review the treatment and prescribe a slightly different medication, but this one should do the trick.'

'I appreciate that.' He raked a hand through his hair. 'And thank you for being so reassuring last night. You were really good with Mia.'

His praise warmed her—and that was dangerous. She never let herself react like this to anyone. She was good at her job and she did what needed to be done; but she didn't allow anyone too close, patient or colleague. She'd learned after Joe that she was better off on her own. Nobody to get her hopes up, and nobody to let her down.

She shrugged off his praise and gave him a small smile. 'No worries. It's what I'm supposed to do.' She wrote on Mia's chart. 'Do you have any questions, or is there anything you're not clear about with her condition and the treatment?'

'No, it's all fine. Thanks.'

'OK. Well, good luck.' She shook his hand, and left the department.

Four days later, Stephanie was called in to the maternity department to check over a baby after an emergency Caesarean section.

The obstetric surgeon was still in the middle of the operation, so Stephanie introduced herself to the midwife and the registrar and waited for the baby to be delivered.

'So what's the history?' she asked.

'The mum had pre-eclampsia—it came on really suddenly,' the midwife explained. 'She was fine at her last check-up; her blood pressure was a bit high, but she'd been rushing around all day. And then today she started feeling really rough, had a headache she couldn't shift and swollen ankles. Her community midwife sent her in to us, and her blood pressure had spiked and there was protein in her urine. Daniel wasn't happy with the baby's heartbeat and so he brought her straight up here.'

Daniel, Stephanie presumed, was the surgeon. She knew that the only cure for pre-eclampsia was to deliver the baby. 'How many weeks is she?' she asked.

'Thirty-six.'

So there was a good chance that the baby's lungs had matured enough, though the baby might still need little bit of help breathing and some oxygen treatment after the birth.

'Is there anything else I need to know?' she asked.

'That's the only complication,' the midwife said.

Though, as complications went, that one was more than enough; Stephanie was aware of all the potential problems for the baby, from low blood sugar through to patent ductus arteriosis, a problem where the blood vessel that allowed the blood to go through a baby's lungs before birth didn't close properly and caused abnormal blood flow in the heart. She'd just have to hope that the baby didn't have a really rough ride.

Once the baby was delivered and the cord was cut, Stephanie quickly checked him over. His heart rate and breathing were both a little on the low side, and his hands and feet were slightly bluish, but to her relief his muscle tone was good and he grimaced and cried. And he was a good weight, too; that would help him cope better.

She wrapped him in a clean cloth and brought him over to his mother.

'I think you deserve a cuddle after all that hard work,' she said. 'He's a beautiful boy. Now, I do want to take him up to the special care unit for a little while, because he needs a little bit of help breathing—but that's because he's a bit early and it's really common, so please don't start worrying that anything's desperately wrong. You'll be able to see him in the unit any time you like, and I'll be around if you have any questions.'

'Thank you,' the mum whispered.

By the time Stephanie had sorted out the baby's admission to the special care unit, the surgeon had finished sewing up the mum and she'd been wheeled off to the recovery room.

The surgeon came over to her, removing his mask. 'Sorry I didn't get a chance to introduce myself earlier. I'm Daniel—'

'Mr Connor,' she said as she looked up and recognised him.

He was the last person she'd expected to be here. And to think she'd been so careful to explain his daughter's condition. What an idiot she'd made of herself. As a doctor, of course he would've known the biology—especially as he was clearly senior to her, being a surgeon.

She shook herself and switched into professional mode. 'How's your little girl?'

'She's fine, thanks.' He blew out a breath. 'I feel a bit ashamed of myself now for panicking as much as I did. And I'm sorry. I really should've told you I was a doctor.'

So he felt as awkward as she did? Maybe this was salvageable, then. Which was good, because the chances were that they'd have to work together in the future. She wanted to keep all her work relationships as smooth as possible. 'It's not a problem. I think any parent panics when their child can't breathe properly, and it's probably worse when you're a doctor because you know all the potential complications—it's scary stuff.' She gave him a rueful smile. 'But I *am* sorry for drawing you that diagram. It was pretty much teaching you to suck eggs.'

He laughed. 'Don't apologise. It was a great analogy, and I needed to hear it right then. Actually, I'm glad you're on the paediatrics team. I wondered at the time if you were a locum.'

'No, I was rostered on the paediatric assessment unit. Rhys Morgan had it moved to the emergency department at about the same time that I joined the team.' She looked at him, surprised. 'Why are you pleased I'm in paediatrics?'

'Because, if you were a locum, I was going to ask Theo Petrakis—my boss—to put you on the list for Neonatal. You're good with panicky parents,' he said simply, 'and I can say that from first-hand experience.'

'Thank you.'

'Perhaps I can buy you a coffee later today?' he said.

Coffee? Was he asking her as colleague, or as a grateful parent, or as a potential date? Stephanie couldn't quite read the signals and it filled her with panic. Especially as she didn't know what his situation was. No way did she want to get in the slightest bit involved with a colleague who wasn't free.

Actually, she didn't want to get involved, full stop. Once bitten, definitely twice shy. It was safest to keep people pigeonholed as patients or colleagues, the way she'd done ever since her divorce. 'There's no need, really. I was just doing my job.' Flustered, she added, 'I'd better get back to my department.'

'Sure. Nice to see you again, Stephanie,' he said.

'You, too,' she said, and fled before she made even more of an idiot of herself.

CHAPTER TWO

'STEPHANIE? YOU'VE GOT visitors,' Lynne, one of the senior paediatric nurses, said. 'They're waiting at the nurses' station for you.'

Visitors? Stephanie wasn't expecting anyone. Everyone she knew in London either worked with her or lived in the same block of flats. And Joe definitely wouldn't have come down to London to see her, to check she'd settled in OK to her new job and her new life. After the wreck of their marriage, they couldn't even be friends.

She'd walked out on him because she'd seen the blame in his eyes and his contempt for her every time he'd looked at her, and she just hadn't been able to live with it. That, and the knowledge that he was right about her. That she was a selfish woman who wouldn't know how to put a family first because she was useless at being part of a family.

Well, hey. Now wasn't the time for a pity party.

She saved the file, then headed out to the nurses' station. As she drew nearer, she recognised Daniel Connor and his daughter waiting there.

'Hello, Dr Scott,' Mia said shyly, and handed her a hand-drawn card and a paper plate covered with cling film. 'I made these for you and the nurses to say thank you for looking after me.'

Cupcakes, painstakingly decorated with buttercream and sprinkles.

Gifts from patients weren't encouraged, but a home-made card and cupcakes from a little girl were definitely acceptable. Especially as Stephanie could see that these were meant to be shared with the other staff who'd helped to look after her.

Stephanie crouched down so she was nearer Mia's level. 'Thank you very much, Mia. The card's beautiful and the cakes look lovely. Did your mummy help you make them?'

'No, Nanna Parker helped me.' There was just the tiniest wobble of her bottom lip. 'My mummy's in heaven.'

'I'm sorry,' Stephanie said softly. She'd hurt the little girl with her assumption, and she'd misjudged Daniel. He'd clearly been through the mill. She wasn't going to ask whether he'd lost his wife to illness or accident; either way would still have left a gaping hole in his and Mia's lives.

And now she understood exactly why he'd flinched when she'd asked if Mia's mum wanted to stay overnight with the little girl. It explained why he'd been so frantic about his daughter's deteriorating health, too; clearly Mia was all Daniel had left of her mother. Her heart bled for them. It would be bad enough losing someone you loved; how much worse would it be, losing someone who loved you back?

'I've still got Daddy,' Mia said, almost as if reading her mind and reminding her that life had light as well as shade.

Stephanie nodded, and looked up at Daniel. 'Sorry,' she mouthed.

He made a brief hand gesture to tell her it was OK, but she knew it wasn't. Yet again she'd messed up when it came to dealing with other people. Dealing with patients and colleagues, she could do; other kinds of personal interactions were much, much trickier. Which was why she usually managed to avoid them. Especially since the way she'd messed up with Joe and his family.

'I'd better get this young lady home,' Daniel said, as if he knew how awkward she felt and had taken pity on her.

She nodded. 'Well, thank you very much for coming in to see me, Mia. It's lovely to see that you're so much better. I'll put your card up on our special board, so everyone can see it, and we'll all really enjoy these cakes.'

'Good. I put extra sprinkles on yours,' the little girl said, pointing out one that was extra pink and sparkly.

'It looks gorgeous. Thank you.'

Stephanie waved her goodbye and shared out the cakes with the rest of the team on duty. But that evening, as she ate her cupcake, it struck her how a stranger could be so much kinder than family. And it made her feel really alone. She didn't have a family at all now, not even the in-laws who'd barely accepted her in the first place but had been the nearest she'd had to a real family. And the previous month she'd moved from Manchester to London, so she didn't have any really close friends nearby either.

She shook herself. Enough whining. Things were just fine. There was no problem at work; she'd fitted in easily to her new role and already felt part of the team. Though she knew that was probably thanks to growing up in an institution; it meant that she knew exactly how to fit in to an institution, whether it was school or university or the hospital. Whereas, when it came to family...

OK, so Joe's family had refused to accept where she'd come from and had always treated her as an outsider; but at the same time Stephanie knew she had to accept the lion's share of the blame for the wreckage of her marriage. She hadn't exactly made it easy for Joe's parents and sister, either. Not being familiar with a family dynamic, Stephanie simply didn't know how to react in a family. She'd never been quite sure what had been teasing and what hadn't; so she'd never really joined in, not wanting to get it wrong and hurt someone.

Was it any wonder they'd tended to leave her on the sidelines? And of course Joe would take their part over hers. They were his family and, despite the promises she and Joe had made in a packed church, she wasn't.

And now she was being really maudlin and pathetic. 'Stop feeling so sorry for yourself, Stephanie Scott,' she told herself fiercely. Her new life was just fine. She liked her colleagues, she liked her flat and she liked the hospital. She had a great career in the making. And she was *not* going to let a cupcake throw her. Even if it had been made with extra sparkles.

Everything was fine until the inter-departmental quiz evening on Friday night. Almost as soon as Stephanie walked into the pub and was hailed by her team, she noticed who was sitting on the maternity department's table.

Daniel Connor.

And the prickle of awareness shocked her. She wasn't

used to noticing men on anything other than a patient-
or-colleague basis. She hadn't been attracted to anyone
since her break-up with Joe. And Daniel Connor definitely wasn't the kind of man she could let herself get
attracted to. He came with complications. With baggage. *A family*. The thing she'd wanted all her life, but
had learned the hard way that it just wasn't for her.

So she damped down that prickle of awareness,
ramped up her smile, and threw herself into full colleague mode as she headed for the paediatric department's table.

Katrina Morgan patted the chair next to hers. 'I saved
you a seat, Stephanie.'

'Thank you.' Stephanie smiled at her and slid into the
seat.

'Did you do this sort of thing where you were before?' Katrina asked.

'In Manchester? Not as often as I'd have liked to,'
Stephanie admitted. 'Our team nights out tended to involved Chinese food, ten-pin bowling, or going to a gig.'

'It's pretty much like that here too,' Katrina said,
'though there's the annual charity ball. My cousin helps
organise that and it's the highlight of the hospital social calendar. It's a shame you'll have to wait until next
year's now.'

'It's something to look forward to,' Stephanie said.
Being positive. The way she'd always taught herself to
be, even in those dark days before she'd walked out on
her marriage. Smile with the world, and they'll all smile
with you. Most of the time, anyway.

She accepted the glass of wine that Rhys Morgan
offered her and thoroughly enjoyed taking part in the
quiz; she'd always enjoyed trivia games. Each round,

the team with the lowest score was knocked out; and the last round saw the paediatrics team going head to head with the maternity ward's team.

And the subject was history. The one subject that had almost tempted Stephanie away from doing a medical degree.

'How do you know all this stuff?' Katrina asked when Stephanie scribbled down their answers, naming Henry VIII's fourth wife and what happened to her.

'We learned a rhyme at school,' Stephanie said with a smile. 'I liked history. But I'm glad there are others in our team who know about sport. I'm hopeless when it comes to sport, and I would've lost the quiz for us.'

'You were good on literature, too,' Katrina said. 'And general knowledge.'

'Well, I read a lot.' Stephanie shrugged off the praise, but inwardly she was pleased. Here, at the London Victoria, she fitted in. And life was going to be just fine.

The question papers were finally marked by the emergency department's team. 'And the winner—by a clear ten points—is the paediatric team,' Max Fenton announced. 'Well done. You get the tin of biscuits this month. But don't think you're going to make it two in a row, Morgan,' he informed the paediatrics consultant. 'We're still in the lead overall.'

'By all of two quizzes. Don't count your chickens.' Rhys laughed. 'We have a secret weapon now.'

'Who could just as well be on our team,' Max said, 'given that the PAU has such a crossover with the emergency department.'

'Hands off. She's ours,' Rhys said.

Stephanie was pretty sure that it was just friendly bickering, but even so she judged it politic to disappear to the toilet until any ruffled feathers had been smoothed over.

On the way back, she discovered that all the teams had merged and groups of people were sitting at different tables. Not quite sure which one to join, she paused and scanned the room.

'Hey, Stephanie.'

Relieved at not being totally deserted, she turned towards the voice.

Daniel Connor.

He smiled at her. 'Seeing as you wiped the floor with us, will you let me buy you a celebratory drink?'

Did he mean as a colleague?

If she could pigeonhole him just as a friend and colleague, and ignore the way her heart seemed to do a backflip every time he smiled, it would be fine. OK, so she knew he was single, which meant there was no reason why he shouldn't ask her to have a drink with him as more than just a friendly gesture from a colleague; but she was pretty sure that he had as much emotional baggage as she did. She had no idea how long ago he'd lost his wife, and she wouldn't dream of asking, but for all she knew he could still be healing. Just as she was. Neither of them needed any complications.

'Stephanie?' he prompted.

She had to answer now. 'A drink from a colleague would be lovely.' Just to make the terms clear. 'Thank you.'

'What would you like?'

'Sparkling water, please.'

'I'll just go and get our drinks. Have a seat.'

She noticed that he, too, was drinking mineral water when he returned with their glasses. Because he was on call, so he needed to keep a clear head in case of an emergency? Or because he was a single parent, and couldn't afford the luxury of a couple of glasses of wine, in case his daughter woke and needed him in the night?

Not that it was any of her business.

'So how come your general knowledge is so amazing?' Daniel asked.

She smiled. 'Misspent youth.' Which he could interpret how he liked. She wasn't going to tell him that it was from growing up with her nose in a book to keep the outside world at a safe distance. She'd read and read and read, and absorbed everything.

'I'm impressed. And I'm trying to work out how I can annex you for our team, next time round.'

This time, she laughed. 'Sorry. Max Fenton's already suggested that to Rhys and got short shrift.'

'I'm not Max.' He tapped his nose and grinned.

'I still don't rate your chances.' She turned her glass round in her hands. 'I meant to say, I'm sorry about your wife. It must be hard for you.'

'Yeah, it was very hard when she was killed.' He grimaced. 'I might as well tell you now and get the pity party out of the way.'

Oh, no. She hadn't been fishing. 'You really don't have to say anything,' she backtracked hastily. 'I'm sorry. I didn't mean to be nosey.'

'It's natural to wonder. And I'd rather you heard it from me than from anyone else.' He looked sad. 'It was a freak accident, four years ago. Mia was only two at the time. An elderly driver panicked when she was parking her car and she hit the accelerator instead of the brake. She ended up driving over the pavement and mowing Meg down. We were lucky that Mia wasn't killed, too—Meg had the presence of mind to shove the pushchair out of the way when she realised the car wasn't going to stop.'

Stephanie stared at him, shocked. 'I'm so sorry. What an awful thing to happen.'

'Not just for me. Meg's family lost their daughter, Mia lost her mum, my family lost Meg…and the old lady who killed her probably still has nightmares about it. She was in bits at the inquest—but it *was* an accident. It's not as if she meant to run Meg over like that.' He shrugged.

'Sometimes I wonder what would've happened if she'd given up driving when her family asked her to, instead of being stubborn and insisting that she could still do it and they were trying to take away her independence. Meg would probably still be alive. Mia might have a brother or sister. We'd probably have a dog.' He blew out a breath. 'But it's pointless torturing myself over it because nothing I can do will ever make a difference. And I have a lot of good things in life. I have Mia and my family and Meg's family.'

Yeah. He was definitely lucky there. Not that Stephanie intended to say that. It would be too crass.

'And they all chip in to help with Mia.' He smiled. 'Mum does the school run for me in the mornings if I'm on an early shift. My sister, Lucy, happens to be a teacher at Mia's school, so she'll take Mia home if I'm on a late, provided she doesn't have a meeting. If she's got a meeting, then Meg's mum picks Mia up and gives her dinner. I'm really lucky.'

'And so is Mia, having so many people who really care about her.'

'Absolutely.' He smiled at her. 'So what's your story?'

The question threw her. 'I…er…'

'Married, children?' he asked.

Once, and almost, she thought. 'No story.' At least, not one she wanted to tell: a failed marriage; a failed surrogate pregnancy; and a failure at being part of a family.

'In other words, back off and stop being nosey,' he said.

She winced. 'Sorry. I didn't mean to be that sharp. You weren't being nosey. I've noticed that everyone's very close here, at the London Victoria, and they look out for each other.'

'And at your last hospital it was a bit more private?'

It was a let-out, and she took it gratefully. 'Something like that. And there isn't a story. I'm just a boring divorcée.'

Oh, there was a story, all right. Daniel recognised the barriers Stephanie was busy putting up; he'd spent enough of the last four years doing something similar. Keeping people at a little more of a distance, except for his family, and evading all the attempts by well-meaning friends and his mother to fix him up with a date to help him move on from the past. And if he pushed Stephanie too hard right now, he had a feeling she'd do exactly what he'd done in the past and make an excuse to leave early. It took courage to join in with inter-departmental events when you had a past to live down.

'Message received and understood,' he said easily.

Stephanie looked relieved that she didn't have to explain any further, especially when Daniel steered the conversation back to more normal things—how long she'd been in the department, how she'd settled in and what the differences were between the London Victoria and her old hospital in Manchester.

'I do hope you're not trying to poach our new quiz star for the maternity team, Dan,' Rhys Morgan said, coming to stand by their table.

'If you are,' Katrina said, 'then I'll be having a word with my cousin.'

'Cousin?' Stephanie looked at her. 'You have family working in the maternity ward?'

'Maddie Petrakis,' Katrina confirmed. 'She's part time at the moment. You might have met Theo, her husband.'

'My boss,' Daniel said. 'Who's not here tonight, or you lot might've been buying us the celebratory drinks.'

'In your dreams, Dan—you know the last round's always between us and Max's lot,' Rhys said with a grin. 'Actually, I'm seeing Theo on Monday about a cross-departmental project. Stephanie, I want to talk to you about that, too.'

'And you can talk to her on *Monday*, Rhys,' Katrina cut in. 'You're both off duty right now.'

'I know. And we have a babysitter to relieve,' Rhys added. He kissed Katrina lingeringly. 'I get the message. I'll shut up. Let's go home. See you later, Stephanie.'

'See you on Monday,' Stephanie said with a smile, then turned to Daniel. 'You must have a babysitter to relieve, too.'

Well, of course she'd know that. She'd treated Mia. But Daniel was intrigued by the difference between the bright, confident doctor in the PAU and this slightly diffident woman who'd drawn such huge barriers round herself. At the same time, it worried him that she intrigued him. OK, so it had been four years since Meg had died, but he wasn't ready to think about another relationship—not when he had Mia to put first—and he was pretty sure that Stephanie had emotional baggage, too. So it would be much more sensible to keep things to strictly colleagues.

Though he could still be kind to a new colleague.

'My parents are babysitting,' he confirmed. 'But I can give you a lift home, if you like.'

'No, you're fine, but thanks for the offer. See you later,' she said, and beat a hasty retreat. Just as he did, he thought wryly, when anyone tried to get too close to him.

Daniel filled Stephanie's thoughts as she walked home. If she was honest with herself then, yes, she did find him attractive. She'd already warmed to his personality, and his smile and cornflower-blue eyes could make her heart skip a beat. Now she knew for sure that he was single, there were no barriers to her acting on that attraction.

Apart from the fact that he came with complications. Daniel was a widower who'd lost his wife in incredibly tragic circumstances. OK, so it had been four years ago now, but that didn't mean he was in any way over what had happened, even though he was able to talk about it.

And he had a daughter. Mia seemed a very sweet child, but no doubt she missed having a mum; she was the odd one out at school. Stephanie could relate to that. Mia had lost her mum at the age of two, and Stephanie hadn't been much older than that herself when her own mum had died. Though Mia still had her dad. Stephanie had had only herself to rely on.

And, more to the point, Daniel had a close family. *Including in-laws.*

Her own in-laws had never really been able to accept her; Daniel's in-laws would no doubt find it hard to see him dating anyone else, feeling that she was trying to take their late daughter's place, so they'd have extra reasons not to accept her on top of the ones that Joe's family had had.

So it would be better to stick to being just colleagues. And she'd be sensible and keep a little bit of distance between herself and Daniel Connor in future.

CHAPTER THREE

'DR SCOTT. JUST the person I wanted to see.' Rhys smiled at Stephanie. 'I wanted a quick chat. Can you come into my office for a minute?'

'Sure.' This had to be the project Rhys had mentioned on Friday night after the quiz, she thought.

'So how are you settling in?' he asked, gesturing to her to take a seat.

'Fine. Everyone's been very welcoming. And I'm enjoying the work—it's really good that we can work with the emergency department staff in the paediatric assessment unit.'

'I'm glad. Actually, that's what I wanted to talk to you about. I'm working on another cross-departmental project to see how we can improve liaison between teams and give better patient care.'

'Which sounds perfectly sensible to me,' she said. 'Having the PAU in the emergency department works well.'

'And obviously we work closely with the maternity department.'

Where Daniel worked. Stephanie's pulse leapt. Stupid. She forced herself to concentrate. This was work, and Daniel was purely a colleague. 'Of course. We need to check the baby immediately after a complicated birth, and do the standard early postnatal checks, as well as following up any issues. Once the mum's been signed off, then the baby would come to us if there's a health problem.'

'Exactly. I'd like you to be part of the team working with the maternity department. Apart from anything else, it means you'll get to know a few more people a bit more quickly, too. Is that OK with you?' Rhys asked.

'That's fine,' she said with a smile. 'Thanks for the opportunity.'

'Good. I'll give Theo a call, and whoever's on his team can liaise with you.'

Stephanie was writing up her notes after a ward round when there was a knock on the open door of her office. She looked up to see Daniel.

Oh, help. Her stomach really wasn't supposed to be filled with butterflies like this. Even if he did have the most amazing blue eyes and a smile that made the room feel as if it had just been lit up. He was her colleague—*just* her colleague—and she'd already told herself that enough times to know better. She knew that relationships didn't work for her. How ridiculous was it to let herself react to him like this?

She took a deep breath and willed herself to calm down. 'Hello, Dr Connor.'

'Dan,' he corrected her. 'I can see you're busy, but can I have a quick word? Maybe later, if you're up to your eyes?'

'Now's fine. You know how it is with paperwork; it's always going to be there. What can I do for you?'

'I believe Rhys has talked to you about the team liaison project?'

'Yes.' Suddenly it all fell into place. 'Does that mean you're on the maternity team for the project?'

He nodded. 'So it looks as if this one is down to you and me. Are you busy at lunchtime?'

Which was her let-out. She opened her mouth to say yes, but the wrong words came out. 'If you call having a sandwich and going for a walk busy.'

'How about we have a sandwich and a walk together?' he suggested.

Oh, help. This was beginning to sound like a date. And she could feel the colour rising in her cheeks to betray her.

'We can talk about the project and work out what we need to do.' He wrinkled his nose. 'I know it's a bit of a cheek, asking you to give up your lunch break for work.'

Work. Of course it was just work. She seized the excuse gratefully. 'No, it's fine. Otherwise we're going to have to fit in a meeting between patients—and one of us is bound to be needed in the middle of it.'

'Or just before a shift starts or after it ends, and we might not be rostered on at the same time. I thought we'd both be more likely to be around at lunchtime,' Daniel said.

'Good idea. OK. I'll see you at lunchtime, then.'

'Great. I'll call for you.' He smiled and was gone, leaving her to her paperwork.

Odd how that smile made her feel warm inside.

Stupid, too. This was about work, and nothing but work. They were having lunch together simply because it was the easiest way to fit in a meeting. And her common sense had better come back, pronto.

* * *

For once, the ward was quiet, so Daniel was able to call for Stephanie as they'd agreed. They picked up a meal from the hospital canteen; he noticed that she chose a healthy chicken salad wrap, fruit and water. Clearly she was someone who looked after herself, rather than a lot of the medics he knew, who grabbed a chocolate bar for quick energy because they didn't have time for a proper break and a proper meal. Then they walked out to the park opposite the hospital and found a seat.

'So how was your morning?' she asked.

She really did have an amazing smile, he thought. Crazily, although they were outside and it was already sunny, the whole park felt brighter when she smiled. 'Fine. Yours?'

'Fine. Well, full of paperwork,' she said ruefully. 'And I guess this is going to be more of the same.'

Daniel found it hard to concentrate on talking to her about the roles of their departments and where they could work together to give their patients better care. He wanted to reach over and touch her dark hair, see if it was as soft as it looked. Which was insane; he never normally acted this way towards anyone.

But Stephanie looked so cute, all serious and thought-ful as she made notes on her mobile phone while they discussed the ins and outs of their respective departments.

For a mad moment, he itched to lean over and touch his mouth to hers. Just once. Just to see what it felt like.

'Dan?' she asked.

'Uh.' He felt the betraying heat crawling into his face. 'Sorry, I was multi-tasking. I should know better. I don't have enough X chromosomes to do that sort of thing.'

She laughed and the seriousness in her face vanished. She really *was* pretty, Daniel thought. He liked the way her green eyes crinkled at the corners, even at the same time as it scared him. He didn't notice things like this about women. He didn't think of women in terms of anything other than family, colleagues or patients. This woman could be seriously dangerous to his peace of mind.

'Don't do yourself down,' she said. 'Or do you normally hang around with totally sexist women?'

He laughed back. 'Would a bossy little sister count?'

Her smile faded then, and he wondered what he'd said to change her mood.

Not that he could ask. There were suddenly barriers a mile high round her, and she kept the rest of their conversation on a totally businesslike footing. By the time they'd finished their lunch, she had enough notes for the basis of a report. 'I'll type it up and email it over to you, so you can see if I've missed anything.'

'Thanks, that'd be good.'

And he couldn't get the easiness back between them when they walked back to the hospital. He had no idea what he'd said to upset her, but he'd definitely rattled her cage.

'Daddy, Ellie in my class is going to be a bridesmaid,' Mia said, when Daniel had finished reading her bedtime story that evening.

'That's nice, darling,' he said.

'She's going to have a really pretty dress. A purple one.'

Where was his daughter going with this? he wondered.

'I'd like to be a bridesmaid.' Her brown eyes were earnest.

Daniel relaxed and ruffled her hair. 'I'm sure you'd make a lovely bridesmaid. Maybe one day.'

'Maybe Aunty Lucy will get married,' Mia said.

Given that his sister was still recovering from the break-up of her first marriage, he wasn't sure that'd happen any time soon. Not that it was a topic he wanted to discuss with a six-year-old. 'Maybe.'

'Ellie's going to have a new mummy,' Mia added thoughtfully. 'Because her daddy's getting married. That's why she's going to be a bridesmaid.'

Oh, help. Now he could see where she was really going with this.

'And she's not like Snow White's nasty stepmother. She's really nice. She taught Ellie how to draw cats.' Mia bit her lip. 'Ellie's so lucky. She's going to have two mummies.'

And Mia didn't even have one.

Had he been selfish, avoiding everyone's attempts to fix him up on a date? Should he have put his own feelings aside and tried to find someone who'd fit into their lives and be a mother to Mia? Guilt seeped through him.

'Yes, she's lucky,' he said softly. 'But you're lucky, too. You have two nannas. And Aunty Lucy.'

'Ye-es.'

But he knew that having two grandmothers and an aunt weren't the same as having a mum. And now he felt really bad because he'd effectively stopped his daughter talking about her feelings. He could see that she was hurting.

'Your mummy loved you very much,' he said, stroking her hair. 'And so do I.'

'Love you, too, Daddy,' Mia said.

'Sleep tight, angel.' OK, so he was being selfish again, backing away from the conversation—but he didn't know what to say to her. How to make it right. Because this was something he couldn't fix. 'See you in the morning.'

'Night-night, Daddy.' Mia snuggled under her duvet after he'd kissed her goodnight.

Daniel thought about it for the rest of the evening.

He was still thinking about it, the next day. A mum for Mia.

Could he do this? Find her a mother? Replace Meg in his life as well as in hers?

After all, he had met someone. The first woman he'd been attracted to since Meg's death. Though that in itself made him feel horribly guilty, as if he were betraying Meg's memory. Mia had made it clear that she wanted a mother figure in her life; or was it just a phase? How would she feel if he started seeing someone? Would she feel as if she was missing out on time with him?

And then there was Stephanie herself. She'd been cagey about her past, and Daniel was pretty sure that someone had hurt her. Badly. Like him, she might have filled her life so she didn't have space for a relationship. And, even if she did have space, would she want to get involved with someone who already had a child?

He brooded about it all the way home.

His sister was curled up on the sofa, reading, when he walked in; she looked up and frowned. 'Tough day?' she asked.

'I'm fine,' he lied.

'Dan, I've known you long enough to see the signs. Come and sit down in the kitchen. I saved you some pasta. While it's heating through, you can talk.'

'Lucy, you're being bossy.' But he followed her into the kitchen and sat down at the table anyway.

'I'm worried about you, Dan.' She put the pasta in the microwave and sat down opposite him. 'Tell me.'

'I don't know where to start.' He sighed. 'Mia was saying yesterday that one of her friends is getting a second mum.'

'That would be Ellie.' Lucy nodded. 'Her new step-mum's very nice.'

'Mia, um, kind of hinted that she wants a mum.'

'And that's upset you?'

'Thrown me.' He grimaced. 'Lucy, do you think it would be wrong of me to see someone?'

'That depends. If you're doing it just to give Mia a mum, then yes. That wouldn't be fair to any of you.' She paused. 'But if you've met someone *you* want to see, that's different. Mum and I have been saying for ages that you could do with some fun in your life. We all love Mia dearly, but it's hard being a single parent, and the only things you ever do are if you go out some-where with us or if it's a team night at work.'

'Which makes it sound as if I don't have a social life.'

'You *don't* have a social life,' she said gently.

He rubbed his jaw. 'I feel guilty. It's—well, it feels as if I'm betraying Meg.'

'Rubbish,' Lucy said roundly. 'Think of it the other way round—if you'd been the one killed in the accident, would you have wanted Meg to be on her own for the rest of her life?'

'I'm not on my own,' he said. 'I have Mia, I have you, I have Mum and Dad, and I have the Parkers.'

'Having a daughter and a supportive family who love you,' Lucy pointed out, 'isn't the same as dating someone. You're still young, Dan. You're only thirty-five, but you're acting as if you're an old man.'

He had no answer to that.

'Would you have wanted Meg to stay on her own?'

He sighed. 'No. I would've wanted her to find someone who'd love her as much as I did. Someone who'd treat Mia as his own and love her, too.'

'Exactly. And Meg was my friend as well as my sister-in-law. I knew her well enough to know how she would've felt—and she would've felt the same as you do.' She paused. 'So have you met someone?'

He didn't answer. Not that it made any difference.

'Why don't you ask her out?' Lucy asked.

He gave her a speaking look. Wasn't it obvious?

Lucy spread her hands. 'What's the worst that could happen?' When he didn't answer, she said it for him. 'That she says no. And then it's no different from the situation you're in now, not going out with her. Ask her.'

He wrinkled his nose. 'It might be a bit awkward at work.'

'She works with you?'

'Sort of,' he hedged.

'In the same department?'

He had to be honest. 'No.'

'Well, then. It won't be awkward. You always put patients first and you're professional. OK, it might be a *little* bit awkward at the first team night out afterwards, but it'll soon smooth over.' She leaned over and squeezed his hand. 'You're scared, aren't you?'

Trust his sister to work that out. 'It's been a long time since I've dated. I have no idea what I'm doing.' He dragged in a breath. 'And it's not fair to Mia. Or to this woman.'

'Whoa, you're really building bridges to trouble here. Look, there's a world of difference between going out with someone and enjoying an evening in each other's company, and asking the woman to marry you and become Mia's stepmother.'

'I guess.'

'Mia doesn't have to know anything about this, so she's not going to get hurt. If it doesn't work out between you and the mystery woman, then it doesn't work out, but you've still had a couple of nice evenings out and had some fun, for a change. And if it does work out—well, you've already said Mia wants a mum.'

How easy she made it sound. 'You make it sound so easy,' he said lightly.

She laughed. 'It sounds easy, but we both know it isn't always. Don't forget I made a pretty good mess of my own love life. Dan, you don't have to be perfect. You just have to be yourself.'

'Harvey was an idiot, you know.' He'd never liked her ex.

'And so was I, for choosing him, but I've forgiven myself for that.'

Daniel felt his eyes widen as he absorbed her words. 'Lucy, are *you* seeing someone?'

'I might be.'

He folded his arms and waited.

She gave in and groaned. 'If you tell Mum, you're toast. I don't want her getting her hopes up, not until I know where this is going.'

He laughed. 'OK, this is just between you and me. What's he like and where did you meet him? Did Karen finally talk you into doing that online dating thing?'

'No, he's a parent at the school—not the parent of anyone I teach,' she added swiftly. 'I met him at a school governor meeting.'

So the man had a social conscience and was happy to do his bit for the community—unlike Harvey, who was the most selfish man Daniel had ever met. That was a good start. 'You deserve someone nice—and you can tell him that your big brother—'

'I'm telling him nothing of the kind,' she cut in, 'and, much as I love you, Dan, I don't need you to fight my corner every second of the day. Just as you don't need me there every second, fighting your corner.' She softened her words with a smile. 'But I'm glad we talked about this. Mum worries about you, and so do I. You need to do something for *you*, Dan. You're more than just Mia's dad and a busy doctor.'

He didn't quite see how he could fit anything else into his life. But he smiled at his sister, knowing that she meant well. 'The same goes for you. You're more than just a brilliant teacher and aunt.'

She laughed. 'I know. And I'm doing something about it. So maybe it's time for you to do something about it, too. Ask her out, Dan. You'll never know what she'd say unless you do.'

He thought about it for the next couple of days, and decided that maybe his sister was right. The next time he saw Stephanie, he'd ask her out.

But their shifts were clearly out of sync, because she didn't attend any of the births where there were enough

complications for the midwives to involve him and need
a paediatrician on standby.

He made the decision when she emailed him the report. He emailed back.

Can we have a quick discussion? When's good for you?

The reply came.

Lunch today or tomorrow, patients permitting?

Sure. I'll ring down and see if you're free.

He spent the rest of the morning doing the ward
rounds, reassuring the nervous first-time mums and
double-checking the obs for one of his mums with suspected pre-eclampsia before asking the midwives to
step up the frequency and call him the minute anything
changed. And then he called Stephanie's extension.

'Paediatrics, Stephanie Scott speaking,' she said.

'It's Dan. Are OK for a lunch meeting about the project today?' he asked.

'Yes. I'll meet you at the canteen. I think we'll have
to give the park a miss today.'

He glanced out of the window and realised that it was
absolutely bucketing down outside. It looked more like
November than September outside. Definitely not the
right weather for lunch outdoors. 'OK. See you there.'

Funny how his heart skipped a beat when he walked
down the corridor and saw Stephanie waiting for him
at the door to the canteen.

He kept himself in check and steered the conversation over lunch to her report and his suggested amend-

ments, agreeing them with her point by point. And then, at the end, he looked at her. 'Stephanie, before you rush back to the department, are you free any evening this week?'

She looked started. 'Free?'

Oh, help. How was he going to ask her without it sounding sleazy or needy? It had been ten years since he'd last asked someone out. He was way out of practice in the dating game. Then he remembered what Lucy had said. Just be himself. The worst that could happen was that she'd say no.

'I, um, thought might be nice to have dinner together. If you're not busy,' he added swiftly.

And he didn't dare look at her. In case he saw disgust—or, worse, pity.

Would she say yes?

Or would she make a polite excuse and then be cool with him from here on after?

CHAPTER FOUR

STEPHANIE COULDN'T QUITE believe this. She hadn't dated since she'd been a student—since she'd met Joe—and it really wasn't something she was good at. She'd married the last man—ha, the *first* man—she'd dated; and that had turned out to be a complete disaster.

She shook herself. Daniel was asking her out to dinner, not shoving an engagement ring at her and asking her to spend the rest of her life with him. But, even so, panic flooded through her. 'If this is about me looking after Mia when she was ill, there's really no need—I was just doing my job, the same as you do with your mums and babies.'

'It's not about Mia. It's about you and me, and—' He stopped. 'Sorry, I'm hopeless at this. I haven't asked anyone out for a long time.'

Was she the first person he'd asked out since his wife had died? Oh, help. That was extra pressure she didn't need. How could she be mean enough to knock him back, under those circumstances? Then again, how could she be mean enough to say yes, knowing that she was an emotional mess and totally hopeless when it came to relationships?

'I really should've gone on one of those online dating site things and brushed up on how you ask someone out,' Daniel said wryly.

His candour made her feel a lot better and she smiled at him. He was obviously feeling as out of his depth as she was, right now; and he obviously wasn't taking anything for granted. 'That makes two of us. I mean, not that I ask people out. I just haven't dated for a while and—oh, dear.' She grimaced. 'I think I'm digging a hole for both of us.'

He smiled back at her. 'I think we need to start this one again. My sister said I should just be myself and be honest.'

He'd talked to his sister about her?

Stephanie went cold. Clearly Daniel was close to his sister; he'd already told Stephanie that she babysat for him and sometimes picked his daughter up from school. But Stephanie had been there before with a man who was close to his sister. It had ended in tears—and not just hers.

Then again, there was no reason to assume that Daniel's sister would be anything like Joe's sister. Besides, why was she assuming that he'd even introduce her to his sister? She really was putting the cart before the horse here, and she needed to stop this right now. What was her best friend always telling her about never troubling trouble until trouble troubles you? She dragged in a breath to help damp down the panic, but she still didn't have a clue what to say.

Daniel didn't seem to let her silence throw him, though. 'Stephanie, I like you and I'd like to get to know you better outside work. Would you have dinner with me one evening?'

That was as clear as it could get. Almost. She knew

that Daniel came as a package, so there was just one tiny thing to clarify. 'Just you and me?' she checked.

He nodded. 'Look, you know I'm a single dad. It wouldn't be fair to Mia to introduce her to anyone I date until we know exactly where the relationship is going and we're both sure it's the right thing to do. So for now this is just you and me, and—um—we'll just see how it goes?'

No expectations. No pressure. Just getting to know each other. That worked for her. 'OK. I'd like that. Thank you. Well, I'm on an early shift on—' She grabbed her phone and checked the calendar function. 'Wednesday and Thursday.'

He checked his own calendar. 'Sorry, I'm on a late. How about next week?'

'My early shifts are Monday and Tuesday,' she said.

He nodded. 'I can do Tuesday.'

'Great. We can sort out when and where—well, some time before Tuesday.' She bit her lip, knowing that she was being a total coward but unable to stop herself. 'I'd better get back to the ward.'

'Me, too,' he said. 'And I'll look forward to Tuesday next week.'

Stephanie found that her concentration was shot to pieces for the rest of the day. It was fine when she was with a patient—she could focus on keeping her patient calm, doing any tests and carrying out any treatment needed, and explaining any treatment to the patient's parents. But once it came to sorting out the paperwork, she found herself wool-gathering. Thinking about Daniel. Wondering if they were doing the right thing. Wondering if it was twenty years too soon for her to date again.

She needed to talk to someone about this.

And there was only one person she trusted enough to talk to. So when she got home after her shift, she called her best friend.

'Hey, Steffie. How are you?' Trish said, sounding pleased to hear from her.

'Fine,' Stephanie fibbed. 'Trish…are you busy? I mean, I know you are, but is now a good time to talk?'

'Harry's asleep and I'm just flicking through the channels while Jake's at the gym. So now's absolutely fine.' Trish paused. 'What's wrong, sweetie?'

'Nothing's *wrong* exactly. Just…' She blew out a breath, not sure what to say.

'I really wish you were still just round the corner instead of a couple of hundred miles away. I'd tell you to come straight over with a bottle of wine and we'd talk.'

Which was exactly why Stephanie was calling her. Because right now she really needed to talk. Get the confusion in her head straightened out. 'I've, um, been asked out to dinner.'

'And you don't want to go?'

'I do—but it's complicated. He's a widower.'

'Much older than you?'

'Three or four years, maybe. He has a six-year-old daughter.'

Trish was silent.

'You think this is a bad idea, don't you?' Stephanie asked.

'I think,' Trish said carefully, 'a date could be good for you.'

'But?' Even though her best friend hadn't actually said the word, Stephanie knew she was thinking it.

Trish sighed. 'Steffie, it sounds like everything you've always wanted. A ready-made family. And, yes, that does worry me.'

Stephanie knew exactly why Trish was worrying. Because of Joe. Because of the way her marriage had imploded. Because of the baby she hadn't been able to carry to term for Joe's sister. On paper, this was the promise of having everything she'd lost: a partner and a child. A family. Like she'd never, ever had.

She bit her lip. 'It isn't quite like that. Mia doesn't know about me. Well, obviously she knows I exist, because I treated her at the hospital—that's how I met Daniel—but he isn't telling her that we're dating. Right now we're taking it slowly and seeing what happens.'

'If you were sitting here right now on the sofa with me, you'd see the relief in my face,' Trish said.

'So you *do* think it's a bad idea.'

'Dating someone? No. All I'm saying is don't rush into it. Have some fun.' Trish paused. 'But don't build your hopes up. Don't take it too seriously. Don't put the cart before the horse.'

'Or trouble trouble. I know. It's not going to be another Joe situation,' Stephanie said.

Trish blew out a breath. 'That wasn't your fault, Steffie, and you know it.'

Stephanie loved her friend for her loyalty, but she also knew it wasn't a completely fair comment. 'I have to take my share of the blame for it going wrong. I'm not very good at families.'

'You're good with mine,' Trish pointed out.

'Mmm. But that's different. Your family's *nice*.' And they'd accepted her for who she was; Joe's family had been judgemental right from the start, never quite accepting her as one of them.

Trish laughed. 'You have a point. So when are you going out on this date?'

'Next Tuesday night.'

'Doing?'

'I don't actually know, yet. Dinner, probably.'

'Good. Have fun. And call me when you get back so you can tell me how it went.'

The phone was the next best thing to going over to Trish's house and talking about it, but it wasn't the same. Stephanie realised again just how much she missed her best friend. 'I will,' she promised. 'Anyway, enough about me. How are you, and how's my godson?'

Just as she'd hoped, Trish was happy to chatter about her son and how he was doing at nursery. And it helped to distract Stephanie from the worries about whether she really was doing the right thing.

Dinner. Was that too intimate for a first date, Daniel wondered, especially given that Stephanie had admitted to being divorced, which meant she probably had scars? Should he have suggested something else?

Which was all fine, but he had no idea what. He was well out of practice when it came to dating.

He waited until Mia was in bed, then looked online to see if he could find any suggestions about first-time dates. His first attempt netted him an article with ten suggestions, and he skimmed down them. The problem was, he didn't know her well enough to know her tastes, and he certainly wasn't going to ask around at work. He didn't want any speculation.

He was about to give up when he saw the last suggestion. Play the tourist. Actually, that might be a nice idea, because he knew she'd moved here from Manchester and didn't know the city that well.

This time, he typed in 'London attractions'. Museums, the London Eye, the Tower of London... And then he saw a link to an exhibition that sounded intriguing. When he clicked onto the site to read more, he loved the sound of it: a room where you could walk through it with rain falling down, but you didn't get wet because the rain was controlled by a computer that could sense your movement and stopped the rain from falling on you.

He texted Stephanie before he lost his nerve.

Tuesday, fancy doing something mad before dinner?

The reply came back sooner than he'd hoped.

Such as?

He typed in the link to the website of the exhibition. If she hated the idea, he had plenty of time to look for something else.

There was a long pause and he thought he'd blown it. He should've suggested something more sensible. Now she was going to think he was totally flaky; he was out of his depth, who was going to want to date a single dad and face all the complications that went with that?

When his phone eventually beeped, he felt sick as he opened the text message. He had to read it three times to make sure it really said what he thought it said.

Sounds great. How fantastic that you found it :)

Relief flooded through him. This might just work out.

Meet you there at seven?

Mia would be in bed by then, so he wouldn't miss out on any time with her; plus the queue for the art installation would probably have died down by then.

Seven's fine. Thank you :)

It felt like months until Tuesday finally arrived. But Daniel was standing outside the exhibition hall at three minutes to seven. He had a feeling that Stephanie wasn't the type to be 'fashionably' late, and he was relieved to discover that he was right.

'You look nice,' he said. She was wearing flat shoes and a pale turquoise dress that made her dark hair look almost black.

She laughed. 'It's rainproof.'

'Rainproof?' The material didn't look remotely shiny or waterproof; it looked like soft, soft jersey. As soft as her skin might be.

'Well, not rainproof *exactly*. But I found a couple of articles about the installation online. They said if you wear dark clothes, you're more likely to get wet.'

He glanced at his own dark trousers and dark-coloured casual shirt and gave her a rueful smile. 'You could've told me that.'

She grinned. 'They might not be right. Given the colour of my hair, I hope they're not!'

He laughed. 'Let's go and find out.'

The queue wasn't too long, so they were soon in the exhibition. They walked very gingerly through the room.

'This is amazing. I can feel the moisture in the air and hear the rain falling, but you're right, we're not actually getting wet.'

'I did wonder if we ought to bring an umbrella, just in case,' he admitted.

She laughed. 'I'm glad you didn't. I love this. Doesn't it make you want to do that Gene Kelly routine?'

So she liked musicals. Maybe they could go to one together. He started humming 'Singing in the Rain', then gave her a sidelong look. 'Dare you.'

She wrinkled her nose. 'I'm not quite brave enough.'

'Neither am I,' Daniel said, though he knew he probably would've done it with Mia. Then again, he could get away with behaving playfully when he was with his daughter.

'This is amazing,' Stephanie said. 'I'm not normally one for modern art, but this is really clever. Thank you so much for suggesting this.'

'My pleasure.' Daniel found himself relaxing again. 'Look, there's a couple over there dancing.'

'And a bunch of students obviously trying to find out how fast you have to move before the computer gets confused and lets you get wet,' she said, pointing them out.

They found themselves chatting easily as they walked through the installation—and neither of them got in the slightest bit wet.

Afterwards, they went to a nearby pizza place for dinner. Daniel discovered that they both loved Italian and Thai food, and Stephanie was a keen cook.

'My stuff tends to be simple,' he said. 'Mia's pretty good at trying new things, but she's at the age where she still prefers plain food to fancy stuff.'

'Nothing wrong with that,' Stephanie said with a smile. 'And she makes great cakes.'

'Yeah.' Daniel had to swallow the lump in his throat. At the end of the evening, he said, 'I'll see you home.'

'Thanks, but there's no need. I know Manchester's not as big as London, but it's still a city, so I'm used to looking after myself in a city.'

'Sorry. I didn't mean to be patronising. Just I was brought up—'

'—to be a gentleman,' she finished. 'Which is sweet. But I'm fine.'

So now they'd go their separate ways. What now? Did he kiss her goodnight? Or would that be too much pressure? It had been so long since he'd dated, he'd forgotten all the rules. 'Well—I guess I'll see you at work.'

'Yup.'

Would she take that as a brush-off? He could ask her out again; or would that be too pushy? He decided to take the risk. 'I, um, enjoyed this evening. Maybe we could do something like this again?'

She smiled. 'I enjoyed it, too. And, yes, I'd like to go out again.'

Her reaction gave him courage. 'Let's synchronise our off duty,' he said.

'OK. I'll text you my schedule when I get home.'

'That'd be good.' He wondered if kissing her cheek would be OK. But then he realised that he'd dithered too long. Doing it now would be awkward. 'I'll talk to you later, then. Goodnight.'

'Goodnight, Dan. And thanks for this evening.'

CHAPTER FIVE

WHEN STEPHANIE WENT onto the maternity ward, the next day, Daniel was there; he smiled at her and she could feel herself blushing. 'Hi, there. I've come to do the rounds and the newborn checks.'

He walked with her to the midwives' desk. 'We have three newborns for you this morning—it was a busy day, yesterday.'

Iris, the senior midwife, said, 'I'm a little worried about one of the new mums, Janine. She's not bonding with her baby at all and she's showing no interest in him, even when we encourage her.'

'Postnatal depression?' Stephanie asked.

'I think she's a bit shell-shocked, the poor love.' Iris grimaced. 'The poor kid's only just turned sixteen.'

The same age as Stephanie's mother had been at Stephanie's birth. Stephanie felt a flood of sympathy. 'Do you want me to see if I can get her to talk to me when I check the baby?'

'If you can, that'd be good,' Iris said. 'Thanks, Stephanie.'

'I'll come with you and introduce you to the first of our mums,' Daniel said.

'Thanks.' Stephanie returned his smile and thought again how easy it was to work with him.

She left Janine until last so she'd time to spend with the girl; it wouldn't matter if the consultation ran over into her break. She introduced herself to Janine. 'Hello, I'm Dr Stephanie Scott, and I'm here to do the newborn check on your baby.' A quick glance showed her that the girl didn't have any congratulations cards or flowers; she seemed totally alone. 'Is that OK, or would you like someone to be here with you while I'm checking your baby?'

The girl simply shrugged and looked away.

Was she shy? Was she shocked by what was happening to her? Or did it go deeper than that? 'OK. Well, I'll talk you through what I'm doing and why.' She looked at baby, and noticed that the blue label on his cot said Baby Rivers; clearly Janine hadn't decided on a name yet. 'He's a beautiful boy,' she said. 'What are you going to call him?'

Another shrug. 'Don't know.'

Was this what it had been like for her own mother, Stephanie wondered, feeling that everyone who walked into the room would judge her and find her wanting? Thirty-two years ago, it would've been even tougher; not just the fact she wasn't married to the baby's father, but her age at the birth as well. Society had learned to be more accepting, but Stephanie knew that Janine was still going to face a tough time.

'It's hard to choose,' she said lightly. 'I'm going to start by looking at the baby's head.' She unwrapped him from the swaddling. 'It looks as if you needed a little bit of help to deliver him.'

Janine simply shrugged again.

'The forceps have left a little bit of a bruise on him, but it's nothing to worry about because it will clear up in a couple of days.' She checked the baby's fontanelles. 'His head looks absolutely fine to me. I'm going to check his eyes now—that means shining a light in his eyes to look for the reflex I expect to see, but it won't hurt him.'

Janine remained silent.

Stephanie performed the procedure. 'I'm glad to say that's fine, too, and there's no sign of cataracts. I'm going to check his mouth now. Are you feeding him yourself?'

Janine shook her head.

Stephanie smiled at her. 'Don't worry, I'm not going to pressure you to try to breastfeed him, though if you do want to try then any of the midwives would be happy to sit down with you and help you with the technique. It can be tricky at first.'

'I'm probably not going to keep him, so there's no point trying.'

But there was a wobble in the girl's voice. Did that mean she wanted to keep the baby and someone was pressuring her to give him up? Again, Stephanie thought of her own mother, the coldness of her parents and the pressure she'd been under.

She sat on the bed. 'Janine, I know you're very young and it's an awful lot to take in, but if you want to keep your baby then we can help you.'

Janine looked away. 'They won't let me.'

They? Stephanie assumed the girl meant her parents. She could understand them being shocked that their daughter was pregnant so young, and underage, but at the same time surely they had to realise that their daughter really needed their support?

'We have people here who can talk to your mum and

dad and reassure them that you'll get the support you need,' she said gently.

There was a glitter of tears in Janine's eyes. 'It's not my mum. If it was just her, we'd probably sort it out between us. It's *him*.'

'Your dad?'

Janine's chin came up and she looked stubborn and hurt. '*Not* my dad. Her husband.'

Now Stephanie began to understand. Janine's stepfather. There had probably already been tension between them before Janine had become pregnant. But, whatever his personal feelings, he was the adult and she was still a child. And it saddened Stephanie that someone would put so much pressure on a young, vulnerable girl at such a difficult time.

Cuddling the baby with one arm, she reached out to squeeze Janine's hand with her free hand. 'I know people who've been in your situation,' she said softly. 'And what you want is important, too. We can support you in the hospital. I can talk to the social services team if you want me to.'

Janine shook her head. 'He says he doesn't want do-gooders round our house, poking their nose in where it's not wanted.'

Poor kid, Stephanie thought. Her stepfather clearly had strong views, and no doubt had given the girl a hard time about falling pregnant. Even though it took two to make a baby.

She put her finger in the baby's mouth to check that there were no gaps in the roof of his mouth and his sucking reflex was working. When he sucked hard on her finger, she smiled. 'I think he's getting hungry.' She checked in his mouth to make sure that his tongue wasn't more anchored than it should be. 'Good, there are no signs of tongue-tie.'

She took her stethoscope out to listen to his breathing. 'Excellent—there's equal air entry into both lungs.' Then she listened to his heart. 'That's fine, too; there's no sign of a heart murmur or an irregular beat.'

Janine didn't reply.

Stephanie remembered the first time she'd heard her unborn baby's heartbeat. It had been magical and had made her want to bond with the baby, even though in the circumstances she knew she couldn't do that and had to stay detached. In the end, it had made no difference, and she'd wept for the baby when she'd lost it as much as any mother would've done.

Maybe this would help Janine, give her the strength to fight for the baby she clearly wanted and was too scared to keep.

'Do you want to listen?' she asked.

For a moment, she thought the girl would refuse. Then Janine's face brightened. 'Can I?'

'Sure you can.' She put the stethoscope on the girl's ears, then the other end over the baby's heart so Janine could hear it beating.

The girl smiled, and Stephanie was relieved to see that she was finally seeming interested in the baby.

Then a man walked into the room and stopped short as he saw them. 'What the hell are you doing?'

Hello to you, too, Stephanie thought, but put her most professional face on.

'I'm Dr Scott and I'm doing the newborn checks on Janine's baby.'

'Not you, I mean *her*.' He looked at Janine in disgust. 'There's no point in getting attached to the baby. You know full well we're not going to let you keep him.'

Janine looked cowed and shrank back into the bed.

So this must be the stepfather. No wonder the poor kid disliked him, Stephanie thought. He was a real martinet. He looked like an army sergeant major, with a very pristine appearance and shiny shoes and cropped hair. But Janine wasn't a soldier he could bark orders at. She was a vulnerable young girl who'd just given birth and needed a bit of sensitivity.

Stephanie wrapped the baby carefully to keep him warm, and put him back safely in the crib. She could finish the newborn checks in a minute. 'I'm afraid I'm going to have to ask you to leave.'

The man turned to her, his stance aggressive. 'Ask me to leave? Who the hell do you think you are?'

'I'm a paediatrician. And your behaviour is upsetting Janine and the baby.'

He bridled. 'That's none of your business.'

She kept her voice neutral. Just. 'Actually, it is my business while they're under my care.'

His lip curled, and she could tell that he was about to unleash a stream of venom at her. His mistake. She could more than look after herself; but this wasn't the place. A maternity unit was meant to be calm, not a battleground.

'I should perhaps remind you,' she said quietly, 'that we have a zero tolerance policy here at the London Victoria. Any abusive or intimidating behaviour towards staff or a patient is unacceptable. So you have two choices. You can leave now, or I can call Security.'

He leaned towards her, staring her down.

She stood her ground, refusing to let him intimidate

her the way he'd cowed his stepdaughter. 'So you're happy for me to call Security to escort you out, then?'

A woman walked in, and looked wide-eyed as she saw the man's aggressive stance and Stephanie standing up to him. 'Bernie? What's going on?'

'This woman—' his voice was full of all the scorn he could muster '—is trying to throw me out.'

'We have a zero tolerance policy at the hospital,' Stephanie repeated.

Daniel came into the room. Clearly he'd overheard the last bit, because he added, 'Which means anyone who abuses or intimidates staff or patients will be asked to leave, and if they won't leave we'll call Security and have them removed.'

'What the hell is it to do with you?' the man snarled.

'I'm the consultant on this ward.' Daniel's voice was very cool, very calm and very authoritative. 'I could hear you shouting across the other side of the ward. And I don't appreciate my mums or my colleagues being bullied. So it's your choice. You can lose the attitude, or you can leave the ward.'

Bernie curled his lip and grabbed the woman's hand. 'Come on, Gail. We're going.'

The woman looked at Janine and the baby, clearly torn between following her husband and wanting to see her daughter.

'Mum,' Janine whispered with an anguished expression, tears trickling down her face. *'Mum.'*

'Come on, Gail,' Bernie repeated, and jerked her hand to make her follow him.

They left, and Janine scrubbed at her eyes with the back of her hand.

'Are you OK, Janine?' Stephanie asked gently.

Janine bit her lip and said nothing. Clearly she was worried that there would be repercussions from what had just happened and her stepfather would give her an even harder time, the next time he saw her.

'OK. I'm going to finish checking over the baby now,' Stephanie said softly, and did so. 'Can you tell me if he's had a wet and dirty nappy since he was born?'

'Both,' Janine whispered.

'Thank you.' Stephanie continued with her checks, leaving the Moro reflex until last; the baby flung out both arms, spreading his fingers and stretching his legs, and started to cry.

Janine looked panicky. 'Is he all right?'

'Absolutely,' Stephanie reassured her. 'I've just checked his reflexes and the way he flung his arms out like that and cried shows that all's well.' She wrapped the baby up warm again and sat on the bed. 'I've pretty much finished checking him over now. He's a beautiful little boy, and you can be very proud of him.' She squeezed Janine's hand. 'Is there anyone I can call for you?'

'No. Thanks,' the girl added belatedly. 'I'll be all right.'

'OK. But the midwives are here to help. So are the doctors. If you want to talk to any of them, they'll listen. They've met plenty of people in your situation, so they know how to help.'

Janine nodded, but didn't look convinced.

'Take care,' Stephanie said, feeling helpless, and left the room.

Before she left the department, she caught up with Iris and Daniel. 'Three perfectly healthy babies, and nothing worrying to report, you'll be pleased to know.'

'Good,' Daniel said. 'We'll look forward to the paperwork.'

'About Janine,' she said. 'Her stepfather's clearly putting pressure on her to give the baby up. That's why she dare not let herself bond with the baby.'

Daniel grimaced. 'We can't interfere, Stephanie.'

'I know, but I'm not going to stand by and let him bully her. Yes, the baby wasn't planned, but it doesn't give him the right to treat her like that.'

'Be careful,' he said. 'You know we have to keep a professional distance from our patients.'

Oh, for pity's sake. Where was his compassion? Sometimes you had to do what your heart told you was the right thing. Clearly Daniel was as much of a stickler for the rules as Joe had been.

Which in turn meant that getting involved with him would be a bad idea. She'd already had one partner who'd wanted total control over her life. It wasn't a mistake she'd make again. Even though she'd enjoyed her date with Daniel, it was time to back off. 'I'll be in touch with the paperwork,' she said coolly, and left the department.

CHAPTER SIX

THE NEXT DAY, before her shift, Stephanie called in to see Janine with flowers and a card and a soft toy for the baby. Janine stared at them in seeming disbelief and a tear slid down her cheek.

'I didn't mean to upset you,' Stephanie said.

Janine gulped. 'You're the only one who's brought me a card and flowers. Even my best friend hasn't come to see me. We fell out, a few weeks ago, and she…' She bit her lip.

'Does she know you've had the baby?' Stephanie asked gently.

Janine shook her head.

'Call her and tell her,' Stephanie said. 'She'd want to know. It doesn't matter that you fell out.'

'And Mum didn't bring anything for the baby. Her first grandchild, and she doesn't want to know.' The tears really started to flow, and Stephanie sat on the edge of the bed and put her arms round the girl.

Once the tears had stopped, Janine said brokenly, 'My mum thinks I had a one-night stand and I don't know who the baby's dad is.' She dragged in a breath. 'It's not true. I'm not like that. She thinks I'm a cheap little tramp and a disappointment, the same as *he* thinks, but I'm not.'

'Of course you're not,' Stephanie soothed.

Janine cried into her shoulder again. 'He won't let me keep the baby.'

Stephanie knew the question she was about to ask was a difficult one, but if her suspicions were correct she couldn't possibly let Janine and the baby go back to that situation. 'Has your stepfather hit you?' Stephanie asked gently.

Janine shuddered. 'No. I thought he was going to when he found out about the baby, but Mum stopped him. He just shouted a lot and called me all kinds of names.'

'What about the baby's father?' Maybe he'd be able to support Janine.

She shook her head, looking terrified.

'You know who he is?' Stephanie checked.

Janine nodded and looked miserable.

'But he doesn't want to know?'

'He—' Janine choked '—he says there's no proof the baby's his.'

'A paternity test would prove it,' Stephanie pointed out quietly. 'And then he'd have to give you some support.' Financially, if not emotionally.

Janine shook her head. 'I don't want my baby anywhere near him.'

Stephanie frowned. 'Why not?'

'Because he—he—' Janine collapsed in tears again.

Stephanie rocked her until the weeping stopped. And then Janine whispered, 'He *made* me.'

Oh, the poor child. Stephanie's heart bled for her. 'Why didn't you tell your mum?' she asked gently.

Janine swallowed hard. 'I wasn't supposed to be at

the party. Bernie had grounded me and I sneaked out to go.'

'OK, she probably would've been angry with you for that,' Stephanie said, 'but if you'd told her what happened she would've helped.'

Janine bit her lip. 'Ryan said nobody would believe me if I told anyone. Everyone at school knew I fancied him, and he said he'd tell everyone I threw myself at him. I felt so dirty, so unclean.'

Stephanie really felt for the girl; she was so alone and had nowhere to turn. She couldn't help wondering, had it been like that for her own mother? 'Couldn't you have told a friend what happened? A teacher?'

Janine shook her head. 'And then my period was late. I knew what that meant but I didn't dare tell anyone. I kept hoping I'd wake up and it'd all be all right, but it just went on and on and I knew I was pregnant. I didn't need to do the test to know. I fainted at school and the school nurse worked it out.' She dragged in a breath. 'Mum was so angry with me. Bernie was even angrier. He said I'd let them both down and dragged their good name through the mud. I knew they wouldn't believe me if I told them about Ryan.'

'You need to tell them the truth,' Stephanie said gently. 'Then they'll understand and start supporting you.'

'What if they don't? What if they throw me out?' Janine looked panicky. 'I'm meant to go home tomorrow. If they throw me out I've got nowhere to go.'

That's exactly what happened to my mum, Stephanie thought. She couldn't lie to Janine and say that it definitely wouldn't happen—but there was one thing that had changed since her mother's pregnancy. 'I hope that won't happen, but if the worst *does* happen then you'll get proper support from social services. And I promise you I'll help with that.' She paused. 'What if I talk to your parents for you and tell them what really happened? If they shout at me, it won't matter.'

Janine shivered. 'You were going to have Bernie thrown out. He won't listen to you—he'll still be angry with you about that.'

'I'll make them listen,' Stephanie said.

'They still won't let me keep the baby,' Janine said.

'Is that what you want?'

The girl nodded. 'I know it's stupid, but my baby's the only one who'll love me for who I am. Ryan didn't love me; he was just using me for sex—and it was horrible.' She dragged in a breath. 'My mum doesn't really love me any more, now she's got Bernie. And he doesn't love me because I'm not the quiet, well-behaved girl he wants, the sort who only speaks when she's spoken to. He hates me because I've dyed my hair different colours and gone to parties. My skirts are too short and my heels are too high. I break all his rules and he just *hates* me for it.'

Stephanie thought again, Is this what my mum went through? 'I'll talk to them,' she promised.

Almost on cue, Janine's parents walked in. They stopped dead as they saw Janine crying.

'*You* again,' Bernie said with a curl to his lip.

'Yes, me,' Stephanie said calmly. She squeezed Janine's hand, and mouthed, '*Don't worry, everything's going to be fine.*' She turned back to her parents. 'I'm glad you're here. I was wondering if we could have a word.'

'Is something wrong with the baby?' Janine's mother said, looking worried.

'Perhaps if we could talk in a private room?' Stephanie said.

For a moment she thought that Janine's stepfather was going to refuse, but then he nodded. 'All right.'

She was relieved to spot Iris on their way out of Janine's room, and went over to her. 'I know it's a bit of a cheek, but can I borrow a room for a moment?'

'Sure.' She glanced at Janine's parents and back at her. 'Do you want me to get Daniel as back-up?'

Absolutely not—after their conversation, the previous day, she knew he wouldn't support her.

'No, that's fine. I can handle it. But thanks for the offer.'

'Use the relatives' room,' Iris said with a smile.

'Thanks.'

She took Janine's parents to the relatives' room. 'Can I get you both a cup of tea or coffee?'

Bernie's eyes narrowed. 'No. Don't waste our time. What's all this about?'

'I'm sorry, I don't know your names—I assume they're not the same as Janine's as she says you're her stepfather, Mr...?'

He glowered at her. 'Seeley.'

'Thank you.' She paused. 'I know you want her to give the baby up for adoption, Mr Seeley, but Janine wants to keep him.'

'It's completely out of the question,' he said firmly. 'She's already made one mistake. I'm not going to let her make it worse by keeping the brat.'

Stephanie sighed inwardly. Clearly he wasn't going to give Janine's mum the chance to get a word in edgeways. She was going to have to appeal to his better nature and hope that, beneath the bluster, he had one.

'Would I be right in thinking you were in the police, or maybe the military?'

He bridled. 'What's that got to do with anything?'

'Because your training teaches you to act when you have all the facts, yes?'

'Yes.' His eyes narrowed again.

'Right now, Mr Seeley, I don't think you have all the facts.'

He scoffed. 'She had a one-night stand with a boy at a party she wasn't supposed to go to. And she didn't tell us she was pregnant until it was too late to get rid of the brat. They're the facts.'

'Not quite all,' she said quietly. 'It wasn't a one-night stand.'

'You mean, she's still seeing the boy?' He looked outraged.

'No. I'm afraid there isn't an easy way to say this, so I apologise for being blunt and not preparing you properly—but you both need to know the truth.' She took a deep breath. 'He forced her.'

Mrs Seeley's hands covered her face, and she gave a distressed moan. 'No! He—no. He couldn't have done that to my baby!'

Stephanie nodded grimly. 'I'm sorry.'

'Why didn't she tell us?' Mrs Seeley asked, looking distressed.

'She didn't think you'd believe her. She knew she'd be in trouble for going to the party when she was grounded. And the boy said he'd deny it. Everyone knew she liked him, so they'd assume she'd made a play for him.'

'I'll kill him,' Mr Seeley said, gritting his teeth.

'I understand you're angry, and I would be too in your shoes. I'd want to kill him, too. But that's not going to help Janine,' Stephanie said quietly. 'And there's something else you should know. She thinks you both despise her as a cheap little tramp. She thinks you don't love her. That's why she didn't tell you. She was too scared about how you'd react. She's worried you're going to throw her out because she's broken all your rules.'

'Oh, God, Bernie, we've let her down,' Mrs Seeley said.

He was utterly still. 'Scared? Is she saying I'd hit her?'

'No. But remember, she's still young. Just sixteen. And frightened.'

He frowned. 'And far too young to be a mum. Far too young.'

'Maybe.' Stephanie spread her hands. 'Or maybe, if she gets the right support, it'll be the making of her.'

'Why are you doing this?' Mr Seeley asked, shaking his head. 'Why are you—well, speaking up for her?'

'Because I know someone who went through something similar. They didn't let her keep the baby. And it broke her.' She took a deep breath. 'I wouldn't want to see that happen to someone else.'

The strength of her feelings must have shown in her face, because Mrs Seeley nodded. 'She really wants to keep the baby, even after what the father did to her?'

'That's not the baby's fault,' Stephanie said gently. 'You might not want to hear this, but I think you need to know how Janine feels. She thinks the baby is the only one who's going to love her for herself.'

'But—that's not true. She's my daughter. Of course I love her,' Mrs Seeley said, looking distraught.

'Maybe she needs to hear you say that.' Words that *she* would so have longed to hear from her own mother. But neither of them had had the chance.

'I— She's my daughter, too,' Mr Seeley said. 'I know it's difficult. I'm used to soldiers, not teenage girls.'

So she'd been right in her guess about the military background.

'Janine and I never really got on since Gail and I first got together.' He shrugged. 'I put it down to jealousy.'

'There probably was an element of that,' Stephanie agreed. 'But at the end of the day she's still only sixteen. She's at a really vulnerable age. She needs to know she's loved. She's made a mistake and paid a really heavy price for it, but she needs to know you'll still support her because you're her family.'

'You're right,' Mrs Seeley said. 'And I feel terrible that it's taken a stranger to tell me what I should've known for myself.'

'Sometimes,' Stephanie said, 'it's a lot easier to talk to a stranger. Someone who doesn't know you, and who doesn't have an emotional stake in the situation.' She thought wryly, how true it had been of her own situation when her marriage to Joe had imploded.

'We've got a spare room,' Mr Seeley said. 'A baby doesn't need a lot of space.'

'It'll mean broken nights. You might wake up when the baby cries.' Mrs Seeley looked anxious.

'They learn to sleep through, soon enough.' He shrugged. 'A grandchild. Grand*son*,' he corrected himself.

So he'd noticed that much. Stephanie smiled to herself. There would be arguments. Bernie Seeley would still lay down the law. But it looked as if he was going to be on Janine's side—and the teenager would get the love and support she wanted so desperately. From a really unexpected quarter.

'Would you like to go and see her now?' Stephanie asked.

'Yes. Yes, we would. Very much,' Mrs Seeley said. 'And—and our grandson.'

She took the Seeleys through to see Janine and lingered just long enough to see Gail hug her and Bernie scoop the baby out of the crib. She smiled and left them to it. They were going to need to do a lot of talking, but she really thought they had a chance of making it now.

'Dan, Harmony's waters have just broken and I need you to check something for me,' Iris said.

Daniel had worked with the senior midwife for long enough to realise that something serious had just happened. 'Sure,' he said, keeping his voice calm for the mum's sake.

A quick examination showed him that the umbilical cord had slipped through before the baby, and the baby's head was pressing against it, cutting off the blood and oxygen supply.

'Harmony, I don't want you to worry,' he said, 'but I need you to turn round on the bed right now, so you're facing the bed, your knees are tucked under, and your bottom is right up in the air.'

'What's happened?'

As he helped her to move round, he explained, 'The umbilical cord has slipped forward before the baby, so we're going to need to give you a Caesarean section. And this isn't going to be too comfortable for you, but until we get you into Theatre Iris is going to push her hand against the baby's head and keep him back there, so the baby can still get the right blood and oxygen supply.'

'Is my baby all right?' Harmony's voice was almost a squeak of panic.

'That's why we're going to deliver him now, to give him the best chance,' Daniel said. 'I know this is scary for you, but I've seen this before and the baby has been just fine. So try not to worry, OK?' He squeezed her hand, and went to the door to call the nearest midwife. 'Can you bleep the anaesthetist for me? I need an emergency section in Theatre One, right now. And I need someone from Paediatrics there when I deliver the baby.'

Knowing his luck, it would be Stephanie; but they were going to have to ignore the slight awkwardness that had sprung up between them since he'd talked to her about keeping a professional distance from Janine.

'I'm on it,' Paula said, and went straight to the phone.

Stephanie picked up the phone. 'Paediatrics, Stephanie Scott.'

'Stephanie, it's Paula in Maternity. We need you in Theatre One, right now, please,' Paula said. 'We have a mum with a prolapsed cord.'

Stephanie knew what that meant: a compromised blood and oxygen supply, so the baby was going to need resuscitating.

Hopefully the surgeon would be Theo Petrakis. Or anyone rather than Daniel. But if it was Daniel, she'd just have to put her personal feelings aside. The mum and baby were the important ones here. 'I'm on my way,' she said.

As soon as she'd scrubbed up and walked into the theatre, she recognised the surgeon—even gowned and masked, his blue eyes were unmistakeable.

She gave him a wary nod, which he returned.

Once the baby had been delivered, he was handed straight to her. 'Can someone take paired cord blood samples for me while I check him over, please?' she asked.

Just as she'd expected, the baby's Apgar score wasn't brilliant. His airways weren't clear, so she suctioned his mouth and then his nose, to make sure he didn't swallow anything. Then she dried him and tapped his feet to stimulate his breathing, but an assessment of his colour and the way he gasped definitely meant that he needed oxygen. She gave him warmed oxygen and checked his heart rate.

'I'm not happy,' she said to Iris. Especially when she checked his breathing rate; even on one hundred per cent oxygen, his breathing rate was too fast. 'I'm going to start chest compressions. Can you bag him for me?'

She wasn't going to lose this baby. No way was she going to let a mother come round after an emergency section only to discover that she'd lost her baby.

'Come on, little one, you can do this,' she crooned.

Between them, she and Iris continued to resuscitate him. She could see his skin starting to change colour. Please, please let this work. 'He's starting to pink up,' she said.

And then, to her relief, the baby finally began to cry.

'We're there,' Iris said softly.

His Apgar score still wasn't brilliant, but he was getting there.

Three minutes later, they had a crying baby who was breathing for himself.

'Thanks, Iris,' she said.

'Hey. It wasn't just me,' the midwife said.

Daniel came over to join them. 'Well done.'

She gave him a cool nod. 'It's my job.'

'I know, but I'm just glad you're so good at it.'

Considering he'd lectured her on getting too involved with a patient, she wasn't so sure he believed she was good at her job.

'We're on the same page, you know,' he said softly, and let the baby's fist curl round his finger.

She wasn't sure what disarmed her more: the expression on his face as he looked at the baby, or the words he'd just said.

Maybe he'd had a point when he'd warned her not to get too involved. Maybe she'd overreacted because she'd still remembered the way Joe had told her what to do all the time, and she'd tarred Daniel with the same brush. Which was unfair. 'I guess,' she said, and let the baby's other fist curl round her finger.

When Harmony came round from the anaesthetic, Stephanie and Daniel were both there to tell her the good news. 'I do want to keep the baby in the neonatal department for a couple of hours, just to help with his breathing,' Stephanie warned.

'So the cord thing—it didn't… He's all right?'

She knew what Harmony was trying not to put into words. 'He's doing fine. We did have to resuscitate him, but I have to do that with a lot of babies—it just means he had a bit of a tricky start. But he's up on the neonatal ward now and you can visit him any time you like to see him and give him a cuddle.'

A tear trickled down Harmony's cheek. 'Thank you. Both of you.' She looked at Daniel and Stephanie. 'If it hadn't been for you…'

'Try not to think about it,' Daniel said gently. 'Everything's fine now.'

'I'd um, better get back to Paediatrics,' Stephanie said, and made a swift exit.

The next day, at the start of her lunch break, Stephanie called in to see Janine, who seemed a lot happier. 'I'm going home today.'

So the Seeleys hadn't thrown her out.

'Mum and Bernie changed their minds. They're going to let me keep the baby. Bernie says he can talk to school and work out how I can do my exams.'

'That's great,' Stephanie said, meaning it.

'Thank you for helping. Without you, I don't know what I would've done.'

'That's what I'm here for. I'm so pleased it's working out for you.' She gave Janine a hug.

'I'm going to call him Peter Bernard. I think Bernie's pleased. Mum's thrilled.' She gave Stephanie a shy smile. 'I know she would've wanted things to be different for me, but we're going to make the best of it. I think she's OK about being a gran.'

'That's great.' Stephanie squeezed her hand. 'I've got a meeting now, and I probably won't get a chance to see you again before you go to say goodbye, but I'm so glad it's working out.'

'You've been brilliant. Thank you so much.'

'My pleasure.'

And now it was time for her to build a bridge. She dropped by Daniel's office, and knocked on the door. 'Hi.' She could see that he was knee-deep in paperwork. 'I was going to suggest lunch, but...' She gestured at the paperwork on his desk.

'I'm surprised you'd ask.'

She took a deep breath. 'That was the other thing. I owe you an apology. I thought it might be easier to make it over a sandwich.'

'You don't have to apologise. I probably owe you an apology, actually. I'm not your boss. I don't have the right to call you on something.'

'As a colleague,' she said, 'then, yes, you do have the right to call me on something if you think my judgement's wrong.'

'OK. So we're both in the wrong,' he said lightly. 'Is that offer of a sandwich still open?'

Could it really be that easy? 'Sure.'

He glanced out of the window. 'It's pouring, so I guess this means the canteen.'

They managed to get a quiet table in the canteen and sat down.

'OK. My apology. You got Janine talking when none of us could,' Daniel said, 'and you sorted things out so she can keep the baby. What did you say to Janine's parents to talk them round?'

Stephanie brought him up to speed with what Janine had told her. 'I just put them in the picture so they knew what really happened.'

'That poor kid.' He looked shocked, then angry. 'If anyone ever laid a hand on my daughter...'

'You'd take him apart, I know,' she said. 'I think Bernie Seeley would like to do that to the boy concerned, but violence really isn't the way to solve things.'

'No, I guess not.' He paused. 'You're good with words. You've made a real difference to their lives.'

'I hope so. I think they've got a better chance of

being able to build a real family relationship, now they're talking and being open with each other.'

He smiled at her. 'Days when you get a chance to make a difference like that are really good, aren't they?'

'Absolutely. They make all the paperwork and the tough days worthwhile.' She didn't have to elaborate on that, because she knew he'd know exactly what she meant: days when you lost a patient or couldn't make a difference. 'And I'm sorry, too. You did have a point about needing to keep a professional distance.'

'Any reason why you found it hard in Janine's case?' he asked lightly.

Yes. Her own mother. Not that she wanted to tell him about that. 'Empathy,' she hedged.

'Fair enough.' He paused. 'I enjoyed our date.'

'Me, too.'

'I know we got off on the wrong foot again, just now, but I wondered if you'd like to come out with me again?'

She ought to be sensible and refuse; she knew that she was hopeless at relationships. But something about Daniel drew her. He was the first man since Joe that she'd actually wanted to get to know better. Maybe, she thought, she should give this another try. 'OK.' She paused. 'How about one of the medical museums? The one with the operating theatre?'

He smiled. 'I've always wanted to go there. When?'

'I'm on a late, next Monday morning.'

He checked his diary. 'That works for me. We can have lunch afterwards. Shall I meet you there straight after the school run?'

'Sure.' And she tried not to think about how much she was looking forward to it.

CHAPTER SEVEN

STEPHANIE WAS GLAD she was working over the weekend, because she knew she would've been antsy if she'd been stuck at home, thinking about her date with Daniel. On the Monday morning she changed her outfit three times before telling herself how ridiculous she was, especially as they were both going to work afterwards and no way could she turn up at work for a late shift on the children's ward looking glitzy. She changed back into the sensible black trousers and three-quarter-sleeved jersey top she normally wore at work.

Although it was the end of September, it was still warm enough outside for her not to need a coat. And she couldn't wait to see Daniel.

They'd agreed to meet outside the museum. She was there first. And it was weird how her stomach felt as if it was filled with butterflies. They were supposed to be taking this slowly, seeing where it took them. So she really shouldn't make such a big deal out of it.

And, actually, she felt vaguely foolish waiting outside for him. Like a teenager on a blind date, wondering if he'd be there or if he'd stand her up.

She was even crosser with herself when her heart felt as if it had just done a backflip when she caught sight of Daniel walking down the road towards her and he raised his hand in greeting.

'Sorry I'm late,' he said. 'Mia's teacher wanted a quick word and then there was a delay on the Tube. Have you been waiting long?'

It had felt like for ever. 'No, it's fine.'

He kissed her cheek. 'You look lovely.'

She laughed. 'Daniel, we're both on a late shift. I'm wearing exactly what I normally wear for work.'

'Exactly.'

She frowned, not following. 'What?'

'You look lovely,' he said again. 'Just as you do at work.'

'Oh.' The compliment warmed her from the inside out. 'Thank you.'

'I'm not trying to soft-soap you, either.'

'I know.' She placed her hand on his arm for a second, just so he'd know she appreciated it.

'Shall we go up?' he asked, gesturing for her to go first.

She made her way up the narrow spiral steps into the old museum. She enjoyed walking with Daniel through the herb garret where the apothecaries used to store their supplies, and looking in the display cases at some of the medical instruments doctors in their positions would've had to use years ago.

'Scary stuff. Imagine trying to talk a child into this now,' she said, gesturing to the leeches.

'I don't think you could talk me into it, either,' Daniel said with a grimace.

They made their way to the theatre itself.

'I didn't expect it to be like this,' Stephanie said. 'It's like an actual theatre, with that narrow wooden operating table as a stage and that horseshoe-shaped stand for onlookers.'

'And of course they didn't have electricity, so they had to rely on the skylight to help them see what they were doing,' Daniel said.

'I'm really glad we didn't have to learn like this as students.' She glanced up at the sign on the wall. 'Look, only the apprentices and dressers of the surgeon could stand around the table and really see what he was doing. The front row was reserved for the dressers of other surgeons, and the last three rows were for pupils.'

'And visitors were allowed by the surgeon's permission. I suppose you were bound to get rich patrons wanting to see what the surgeon did with their money,' he said.

'Probably. And I take it the dressers were the assistants?'

'The ones who sorted out the dressings and tourniquets,' Daniel said. 'And sometimes they had to hold the patients down.'

'I'm so glad we've moved beyond that.' She grimaced. 'Anaesthetic and antiseptic—what would we do without them?'

'A lot less than we do now,' he said. 'It would've been too dangerous to do internal operations.'

'And they had no idea about antiseptic, back when this theatre was first used. They might not even have wiped the surgical tools between patients,' she said.

'No wonder so many women died of puerperal fever.' He shivered. 'It doesn't bear thinking about. I'm so glad we don't have to work in those conditions now.'

She glanced through the brochure. 'They were fast, though. It says they could do amputations and sew up the stump in less than a minute, though they had to give patients alcohol or opiates to numb them first.' She bit her lip. 'Oh, those poor patients.'

'It makes me appreciate the tools of my trade a lot more,' Daniel said.

Afterwards, they had just enough time to grab lunch before their shift.

'I really enjoyed today,' Daniel said. 'Maybe we can go somewhere else next week?'

'I'd like that. We can sort out a date later.'

'Sure.' He smiled at her. 'We'd better get to the hospital or we'll be late for our shift.'

They walked in easy silence towards the hospital. When they were two roads away, he stopped.

'Everything OK?' she asked.

'Yes and no.' He wrinkled his nose. 'I want to kiss you goodbye, but if I do that any nearer to the hospital than now, someone's bound to see us and we'll be the hottest topic on the grapevine. I assume you'd rather avoid that.'

It sounded as if he would, too. Was he having second thoughts about their relationship?

The question must have shown in her expression because he said softly, 'Which doesn't mean that I've changed my mind about us, just that I want to keep it strictly between us for now. It's still early days. I don't want Mia hearing gossip and worrying that her life is going to change dramatically.'

Which was fair enough. She relaxed. 'I've been the hottest topic on the grapevine before now and it wasn't pleasant. I'm not sure whether the whispering was the worst, or the pity.'

'Definitely the pity,' he said, sounding heartfelt.

Of course—he must've had to deal with a lot of that after his wife had been killed in the accident. 'Sorry. I didn't mean to be tactless.'

'I know.' He leaned forward and kissed her very lightly on the mouth. Her lips tingled and warmth seemed to spread through her entire body. He pulled back just far enough so they could look into each other's eyes; in answer to the question she saw in his, she gave the tiniest, tiniest nod and leaned towards him.

This time, he slid one arm round her waist, holding her close, and slid one hand behind her neck, cradling her head. Her mouth still tingled, but this time with anticipation as his lips brushed lightly against hers, and then again, and then a third time, when she found her mouth opening beneath his, letting him deepen the kiss.

By the time he broke the kiss, her pulse was racing; she was pretty sure he was just as affected by it, because his pupils were huge and there was a slight flush across his cheekbones.

She traced the slash of colour with the tip of her finger. 'I don't think either of us was quite expecting that,' she said, her voice husky.

'No. And I dare not kiss you again—much as I want to—or we'll end up being arrested.'

His voice was gratifyingly rough, too. And his words made her smile. 'I feel like a teenager.'

'Me, too,' he admitted. 'If we weren't on duty, I'd suggest finding the nearest funfair. Though kissing you gets my heart beating faster than a roller-coaster would.'

'Better than a roller-coaster. Now that's different.' But the compliment pleased her, because she knew it was genuine. 'Dan, we can't bunk off. They're expecting us. We'd be letting the team down.'

'I know. So we're going to walk to the hospital together like professionals,' he said. 'Two colleagues who've just bumped into each other on the street and are chatting on the way to work. And neither of us is going to think about kissing—right?'

'Right.' Though she had a feeling that that might be easier said than done. That kiss had just about fried her brain.

Over the next couple of weeks, Daniel found himself getting closer to Stephanie. He really hadn't expected it to be so good between them. He liked her sharp mind when it came to work; and she was really good with patients, explaining things clearly yet without patronising them. Working with her was a pleasure.

Outside work, it was even better. He really looked forward to their dates out, and he hadn't expected that, either. For the last four years he'd been protecting his heart from any potential damage by simply not dating and concentrating on bringing up his daughter, but something about Stephanie had drawn him right from the first.

He liked her. He enjoyed spending time with her. She made his heart skip a beat.

Was now the right time for him to move on?

Stephanie was the first woman who'd challenged him out of his comfort zone since Meg's death. The first woman he'd kissed since then. But he had a feeling that she was still holding a lot back from him. Was he expecting too much from her, hoping that she'd fit easily into his life because she'd treated his daughter and Mia had seemed to like her?

And how would the other people in his life react to

him moving on? Mia had said she wanted a mum; Lucy had as good as told him that he had her blessing and that of their parents. But what about Meg's parents?

If he wanted to move forward with this—and he was pretty sure that he did—then he needed to talk to them.

On the Friday night, Daniel called in to see the Parkers.

'Is Mia not with you?' Meg's mum, Hestia, asked. 'Is something wrong?'

'No, she's fine. I just wanted to see you on my own,' Daniel said.

She still looked slightly concerned, but asked, 'Would you like some coffee?'

'That would be lovely, thanks, Hestia.' He followed her into the kitchen.

'So what did you want to see us about?' Ben, Meg's father, asked.

The big question. And the only way Daniel could think of to face it was head on. With a little bit of softening; he didn't want to hurt them. 'Um. There isn't really a tactful way to say this. But you know that Meg was the love of my life, don't you?'

Hestia looked at him and raised an eyebrow. 'You've met someone else, haven't you?'

'Ye-es.' Daniel blew out a breath. 'I haven't introduced her to anyone in the family, yet, because it's still early days.'

Ben frowned. 'But she's obviously special enough for you to start thinking about it.'

'Yes, she is.' He sighed. 'You know I'll always think of you as my other parents, and Mia will always be your granddaughter—that won't ever change.'

'But you want our blessing to see someone else,' Ben said.

He'd wanted to talk to them about it. Not to ask for their permission, exactly, but having their blessing would mean a lot to him. 'I'd feel happier if I knew you understood and won't hold it against me, yes,' Daniel admitted.

Hestia came over to him and hugged him. 'Love, you're still young. Thirty-five's no age at all. You've got most of your life ahead of you. Yes, it hurts to think that you're going to replace our Meg, but we always knew this was going to happen someday.'

'I'm not replacing her,' Daniel reassured her swiftly. 'Meg will always be Mia's mum and she'll always have a place in my heart.'

'But you can't spend the rest of your life on your own, being lonely. I know Mia has us, and your parents, and Lucy, but that's not the same as having a mother figure around. Having someone there for her would be good, too.' Hestia paused. 'Does she like children?'

'She's a doctor on the children's ward, so I guess you could say that.' He smiled at them. 'Actually, Mia's already met her once—but only in her professional capacity. She doesn't know we've been seeing each other.'

'Right. Is she the one we made cakes for?' Hestia asked.

Daniel nodded. 'But I wasn't seeing her then. She was simply a colleague. But I admit, I do feel a bit guilty about seeing her.'

'Because of Meg? She wouldn't have wanted you to be lonely. She would've wanted you to have someone to love. Someone who'd love you back,' Hestia said, and

Daniel could see the film of tears in her eyes. 'If she makes you happy, then you go ahead, love.'

'You've got our blessing,' Ben added.

Daniel could feel the moisture in his own eyes, and had to blink hard. 'Thank you,' he said, his voice rough with emotion.

'No, thank *you*,' Hestia said. 'You don't have to take our feelings into consideration when it comes to your life.' She patted his arm. 'But Meg was right about you. You're a good man. You care, and you don't just ride roughshod over people.' She paused. 'Actually, I'd already guessed.'

Daniel stared at her, surprised. 'How?'

'Mia drew a picture of you while she was here last. You had the biggest smile ever. I asked her about it, and she said you were really smiley nowadays.'

'I hope I wasn't ever a grumpy dad,' he said lightly. He'd tried so hard not to damage his daughter with his own grief after Meg's death.

'No, I think it was her way of saying that you don't have that sadness in your eyes all the time any more. I know how much you've missed Meg—we all have— and if only that woman…' Hestia sighed and shook her head. 'Well, wishing isn't going to bring Meg back. But seeing you happy again is the next best thing.'

That was the last hurdle for Daniel. He knew his parents and Lucy would accept Stephanie immediately, and he was pretty sure that Mia would get on well with her. Now all he had to do was talk Stephanie into meeting them. He had a feeling that she was antsy about families, and he was pretty sure that it was something to do with her divorce. He hadn't asked because it had felt too much like prying. But maybe now he could persuade her to open up to him.

It was a busy week and time seemed to fly past. Stephanie had two lunch meetings with Daniel, both of them discreet; she found herself relaxing more with him, and she looked forward to his company.

When she confessed that to him, he smiled. 'Me, too. It's been a long time since I've…well, had fun like this. Which doesn't mean I resent Mia—I love my daughter and I don't regret a single second I spend with her.'

'No, I know what you mean—just having a little time you can spend doing something for you and not having to worry about someone else.'

On Wednesday, the following week, they went to the Whispering Gallery at St Paul's cathedral. Daniel smiled at Stephanie. 'Stay there. I'm going to the opposite side of the gallery.'

To her delight, he whispered into the wall—and she heard very clearly what he said. 'I want to kiss you.'

'Dan!' she said, and heard him laugh.

'Listen again, and tell me how many echoes you hear,' he said—and then clapped his hands once.

'Four,' she whispered back. 'Did you read up about it or are you a nerd?'

He came back to join her. 'Guilty on both counts,' he said. 'Let's go up to the next gallery.'

They climbed up to the stone gallery, then finally to the Golden Gallery at the stop, where they had a stunning view over London.

'Look, there's the Globe,' he said, pointing it out to her. 'And the Tate Modern.'

'I don't think I ever realised how wide the river Thames is,' she said. 'What a fantastic view.'

He put his arms protectively round her. 'Know what I'm thinking?' he asked.

She glanced round, noticing that nobody had come up to the Golden Gallery. 'Right now it's just you and me, and we're so far above London that nobody's going to notice us, even if they look up—so you can do what you suggested in the Whispering Gallery.'

'I love it that you're so in tune with me,' he said, and kissed her.

Time seemed to stop. All she was aware of was the warmth of Daniel's body, his arms wrapped round her; the softness of his mouth on hers, teasing and promising; and the way his kiss made her temperature spike.

When he broke the kiss, she felt incredibly hot and bothered.

'OK?' he asked softly.

She nodded, not quite trusting herself to speak.

He stroked her face. 'Do you have any idea how pretty you look when you blush?'

And she felt the colour sweep even more strongly into her face. 'Flatterer,' she muttered.

'No. You're lovely.' He stole another kiss. 'And I guess we ought to go down, before someone else comes up here and finds us behaving like teenagers.'

'I guess.'

'So was it what you expected?' Daniel asked when they left the cathedral and walked back out into the street.

'It was beautiful,' she said. 'Thanks for bringing me.'

'My pleasure.'

They walked hand in hand through the streets, Stephanie couldn't remember when she'd last felt so in tune with someone—even Joe.

But there was the sticking point.

She was going to have to tell Daniel about her past, if they were to have a chance at making a go of things. And it was probably better to do it now—because if it made a difference, the way it had with Joe, at least her heart wouldn't be so involved. If she left it until she'd really fallen in love with Daniel Connor, she'd risk getting seriously hurt.

'Dan, there's something you need to know about me if things are going to go any further between us,' she said.

He looked wary. 'What?'

This was it. The thing that could change everything. She took a deep breath. 'I wasn't brought up in a family. I was brought up in a children's home because my mum wasn't allowed to keep me.'

Instead of backing away, like she'd expected, he kept his fingers laced through hers. 'So is this why you stood up for Janine like that?'

She nodded. 'I guess it hit a raw spot with me. My mum was about the same age as Janine when she was pregnant with me. Her parents threw her out when they found out she was expecting.'

'What about your dad?'

'I've no idea—he's not named on my birth certificate.' She swallowed hard. 'I hope he loved her and it just went wrong between them because they were both too young to cope with what was happening. I'd really hate to think that what happened to Janine happened to her, too.'

'That's pretty tough on you. I understand now why

you wanted to talk Janine's parents round.' He paused. 'What happened to your mum? Did you manage to get back in touch with her when you were older?'

She closed her eyes for a moment. 'My mum didn't cope very well on her own. There wasn't the kind of support back then that you get nowadays. I was taken away from her when I was about two. I can just about remember her being allowed to come and see me at the children's home, some weekends. I remember a lady with a pretty flowery dress and she smelled of roses— and then she stopped coming to see me.' She looked away. 'I learned years later that she'd taken an overdose. She couldn't cope with me being taken away from her.'

Daniel wrapped his arms round her. 'That's so sad. Poor woman. She never got the chance to be with you and see you grow up.'

Just like his wife hadn't had the chance to see Mia grow up.

Of course Daniel would understand. He'd sort of been there himself. She should've thought of that before. 'Sorry. I didn't mean to rip the top off your scars.'

'You haven't.' He held her closer.

'I wish I'd known my mum. Or that her parents had looked after her properly.' She had to blink the tears away. 'Sorry, I didn't mean to spoil our date.'

'Not at all. I can't imagine what it would be like to grow up without my family. Dad and I only ever talk about football—typical bloke stuff—but I know if I was in trouble I could talk to him about anything. The same with my mum and my sister.' He paused. 'So you weren't adopted?'

'I guess I slipped through the cracks—and then I was too old.' Not that Joe's family had ever understood that.

They'd made her feel as if she was unlovable, as if there had been something lacking in her. 'The thing is, most people want a baby; they don't want to foster or adopt a stroppy teen. Though I was lucky. My best friend at school was great and her family let me live with them in the sixth form so I could do my A levels. They're pretty much the nearest I have to a family, though obviously I'm not actually related to them. Well, not unless you count me being godmother to Trish's son.'

'I'm glad you had someone.' He held her tighter. 'What about your grandparents? Did you ever try to find them?'

'Yes. I found them when I was eighteen. After I'd done my A levels and I knew I had a place at university to study medicine.' She sighed. 'I had this stupid idea they might be proud of me. But they just didn't want to know me. They didn't even invite me indoors. The just said they weren't interested and shut the front door in my face.'

'More fool them,' he said.

'I'm not upset about it, Dan. I'm glad. I didn't want to be a family with people who were so bigoted and unkind.' She thought, I married into one that was nearly as bad—but at least I'm out of it now.

She shook herself. 'Anyway, it's all in the past now. They're both dead. I don't have anyone related to me in the world—at least, nobody I know of—but I don't actually need a family. I have good friends and a job I love.' And that was enough. It had to be. 'Now, I'll stop being maudlin. Let's go for an ice cream.'

'You're not being maudlin. You're brave and you're strong, and I love that instead of being bitter about life you've focused on the good stuff. I'm proud to know you,' he said.

It made her feel warm inside. And scared, at the same time. Taking things further between them meant taking a risk. She'd shared this much with Daniel; she wasn't ready yet to tell him about what had happened with Joe, but so far he'd seemed to understand. It was a good start.

CHAPTER EIGHT

DANIEL RAISED HIS eyebrows when he met Stephanie outside the canteen for their weekly project liaison meeting. 'You look terrible,' he said.

She grimaced. 'Let's say it's been a bit of a rough morning in the PAU.'

'Want to talk about it?'

She sighed. 'It's something I have to deal with. I shouldn't burden you with my casework.'

He spread his hands. 'Hey, you're a doctor, not a superhero—and we've all had days where we've needed to offload to someone. Tell me.'

She bit her lip. 'I had a case this morning where a baby came in with a broken leg—a spiral fracture, after he rolled off a changing mat.'

'It happens,' he said dryly. 'You think the baby can't roll yet and you turn away for a matter of seconds to get a nappy or a baby wipe or something you've forgotten, and in that tiny, tiny space of time the baby rolls over for the first time and goes straight off the changing mat to the floor.'

'That sounds like experience talking.'

'And how.' He rolled his eyes. 'Luckily, the changing mat was on the floor at the time rather than the changing station,' he said, 'or I would've been there beating myself up about not looking after the baby properly. I imagine the parents were pretty upset about it.'

'The mum was, yes—the dad didn't come in with her. But the social worker thinks it wasn't an accident, especially as it wasn't the only fracture.'

He looked surprised. 'The baby had more than one fracture?'

'No, there's an older brother—he came in with them—and he had a cast on. It seems he ended up with a broken arm last month.'

He winced. 'Nasty. So the social worker thinks it's abuse?'

She nodded.

'But you don't?'

'Dan, you know as well as I do that abuse isn't the only reason for fractures. Yes, it's a possibility, but my gut instinct tells me there's more to this case than that. The family lives in a high-rise flat and the lift is always broken, so it's hard for the mum to get out with pram and a toddler.'

'Which means it can be frustrating, being cooped up all day.'

She could see exactly where he was going with that. 'And then the mother took out the frustration on the baby, shook the children maybe and caused the fractures?' She spread her hands. 'Maybe. But it's not the only possibility, Dan. Being stuck indoors means not getting enough sunlight, and that mean not enough vitamin D is being produced in the body.'

'Rickets?' he said.

'It's a possibility. Soft bones means more likelihood of fractures.'

'There any a few other possible genetic problems,' he said. 'Are there any signs of anything in the mum?'

'I was more focused on treating the baby,' she admitted. 'Actually, you might even know the mum, as she had the baby here at the London Victoria. Her name's Della Goldblum.'

Daniel looked thoughtful. 'Yes, I remember her—if I'm right, I think her mum was looking after her toddler while she was in hospital having the baby and a friend was her birth partner. Isn't her partner in prison?'

She nodded. 'The social worker says it's for GBH. He hasn't seen the baby yet, so he wasn't the cause of either of the fractures, though the social worker was pretty quick to suggest it.'

'Do you think he hits Della when he's out of prison?'

'I don't know.' She bit her lip. 'But the social worker suspects it and she wants both children taken into care. We're keeping the baby in on the ward while we run some tests. Della's only allowed in to see the baby if someone's there to supervise her.' She grimaced. 'It's a horrible situation.'

'It keeps the children safe, though, while the tests are being run,' he pointed out gently.

'I know, and I know there are way too many cases when children slip through the net and the abuse is missed. We don't want that to happen to the Goldblum children.' She shivered. 'I know we're taking the cautious route and it's the right thing to do, but at the same time my gut instinct is telling me that Della Goldblum isn't a baby-batterer. Dan, would the ultrasound pictures of the baby still be on file?'

'Yes.'

'Maybe I need to review them. They might show symptoms we're missing at the moment. Maybe there's some bowing of the long bones, or the skull might not be so clear on the ultrasound, because decreased echogenicity of the bones means that the sound waves won't bounce properly off the surface.'

'You're thinking osteogenesis imperfecta?' he asked.

'It's another possibility. Obviously we're not going to rule out abuse just yet, but I think we need to check any possible medical conditions that affect the bones as well. I'm going to start with vitamin D deficiency and take it from there.'

'I don't want to burst your bubble, but if there were any signs of OI on the prenatal scans,' he said, 'then I'm pretty sure the sonographer would've picked it up and flagged it with the midwife or the consultant.'

She sighed. 'Yes, you're right. Sorry, I'm not thinking straight—and I shouldn't let myself get this involved. I need to keep a professional distance.'

'Good idea,' he said. 'But if there's anything you think I can do to help, let me know. Remember the departmental liaison thing works both ways.'

'Thanks. I appreciate that.' And she appreciated that he'd listened to her rather than dismissing her concerns. Joe had never wanted to hear about her job, saying that she ought to leave her cases at work and not think about them when she was home. But what doctor could cut herself off completely like that?

When the test results came back, the next day, Stephanie reviewed them and her heart sank. No sign of vitamin D deficiency. She'd reviewed the prenatal scans, too; and, just as Daniel had warned, they were clear.

Her patients kept her too busy to brood about it during her shift, but she couldn't stop thinking about the case on the way home and wondering what she was missing. She texted Daniel when she got in.

Seems I was wrong about rickets. Nothing on the pre-natal scans, either.

Five minutes later, his name flashed up on the screen of her phone. 'Are you OK?' he asked when she answered.

'Yes,' she lied.

'You don't sound it.'

'I'll live.'

'Do you want me to come over?' he asked softly.

Yes. Right now, she could really do with a hug. But she also knew she was being totally selfish. 'I can't ask you to do that. You have Mia to think about.'

'You could come here,' he suggested.

'No—that's not fair to her. What if she wakes up, comes downstairs and sees me in the house? She's going to ask questions, and neither of us is ready to give those answers yet.'

'You're right,' he said, and sighed. 'Stephanie, try not to brood about it. You've done what you can.'

'I know, I know—and professional detachment is important.' Though it was easier said than done. Some cases just stayed with you and you couldn't ignore them. 'Thanks for listening, Dan.'

'Any time.'

An hour later, Stephanie's doorbell rang. She frowned. Who would call at this time of night? She picked up the entryphone. 'Hello?'

'Stephanie? It's Dan. Can I come up?'

Dan? What was he doing here? 'What about Mia?'

'Don't worry. My sister's babysitting. That's why I was so long; I needed to wait for Lucy to come over, first.'

She pressed the buzzer to let him in, and met him at her front door.

He handed her a tub of premium ice cream. 'I think you might need this.'

'Thank you.' She gave him a rueful smile. 'I didn't mean for you to come rushing over.'

'Think nothing of it. You're concerned about your patient. It always help to talk it out.' He gave her a hug.

And how much better that made her feel.

'I hope you were intending to share this with me,' she said.

He grinned. 'That was the plan.'

She fetched two spoons, and enjoyed sharing the entire tub with him.

Afterwards, they lay together on her sofa, their arms wrapped round each other. She looked up at him. Was he going to kiss her? And, given that this time they weren't in a public place, would the kiss turn hotter? Would he touch her?

The tips of her fingers tingled; right now, she really wanted to touch him.

On every date they'd been on, he'd been dressed for work in a suit and tie. She'd seen him in scrubs in Theatre, but tonight was the first time she'd seen him in jeans and a T-shirt. And he was utterly gorgeous.

She looked at his mouth. There was the tiniest smear of ice cream against his lips, and couldn't resist reaching up and touching it with the tip of her tongue.

He shivered. 'Stephanie.'

'Ice cream,' she said.

He ran the tip of his forefinger along her mouth. 'I can't see any ice cream here.'

'Oh, there is,' she said with a grin. 'You're using the wrong sense.'

'Am I, now?' he asked, his pupils growing larger.

'Yes,' she whispered.

Then he bent his head to kiss her. Tiny, teasing kisses that brushed against her mouth and made every nerve end sing into life. Her control splintered and she opened her mouth, letting him deepen the kiss.

He slid his hands under her T-shirt, splaying his palms against her back, and it gave her the courage to do the same. His skin was so soft, so smooth. And suddenly none of this was enough; she needed more. She moved her fingertips against his skin in tiny circles, urging him on.

In response, he let one hand glide round to her midriff, stroking her skin, and gradually moved his hand upwards. She arched against him as his other hand released the catch of her bra, and then at last she felt his fingers where she needed them, caressing the undersides of her breasts and teasing her nipples.

She could feel his erection pressing against her, and knew he wanted this as much as she did. The need to be closer to him spiralled, and she broke the kiss. 'Dan. Take me to bed,' she invited.

He groaned and kissed her lightly. 'Stephanie, I wasn't expecting this to happen between us tonight. I haven't got any condoms.' His voice was husky with frustration and need.

'You don't need them,' she said. 'I'm on the Pill—not for contraception, but because my periods are horrible without it.' She dragged in a breath. 'Just so you know, I haven't slept with anyone except my ex for the last few years.'

'And I haven't slept with anyone at all since Meg died, four years ago,' he said. He kissed her lightly. 'It's your call. Are you OK with this?'

She knew he meant more than just worries about pregnancy and disease: was she ready to make love with him, after all this time of being on her own? And Dan was facing the same kind of pressure, if not more—because he at least had loved his wife until Meg had been taken from him, whereas she and Joe had fallen out of love with each other and the end of their marriage had been miserable for both of them.

'I am if you are,' she said.

He smiled. 'I'm very OK.' He kissed her again.

She wasn't quite sure which of them moved first, but then they were on their feet, and he'd scooped her into his arms. Panic skittered through her. Was she doing the right thing? Was this too soon? Would she even remember how to do this?

'Forgive me. I'm having a bit of a caveman moment,' he said, his eyes crinkling at the corners.

And suddenly all her worries dissolved. This was Dan. Everything was going to be all right. She laughed. 'Troglodyte is good.'

'Where's your room?' he asked.

'Next door.'

He carried her out of the living room. He managed to open her bedroom door without dropping her, then slowly lowered her to her feet so her body was pressed against his.

'Are you quite sure about this?' he asked.

'Oh, I'm sure.' She reached up to kiss him.

'Good. Because if we don't do something about this right now, I think I'm going to spontaneously combust.'

'The troglodyte discovers fire?' she teased.

'Oh, and just for that, Stephanie Scott...' He tugged at the hem of her T-shirt and she lifted her arms to let him peel the soft cotton over her head. He'd already undone her lacy bra earlier and it fell to the floor, exposing her to his view.

He sucked in a breath. 'You're beautiful, Stephanie.'

She could feel her skin heating and her body responding to his.

He kissed the curve of her neck, and traced a path of kisses along her collarbones. Then he dropped to his knees and kissed a path down her sternum, over her abdomen.

She shivered and he undid the button of her jeans, slowly lowered the zip and stroked the material down over her hips until her jeans fell to the floor.

She stepped out of them, not wanting to fall over and make an idiot of herself, breaking the mood. She stood with her hands on her hips; eyes narrowed, she surveyed him. 'You're a bit overdressed now,' she said.

'What do you suggest?' he asked.

She pursed her lips. 'You could always take your clothes off for me.'

He stilled momentarily before speedily peeling off his T-shirt.

Stephanie stifled a gasp. Dan was gorgeous. A perfect six-pack. Even though she doubted he had the time to work out at a gym, he hadn't just let himself go to seed.

'You're beautiful, Dan,' she said softly.

'So are you.' He dropped his T-shirt. 'How about you finish this, Stephanie? Because right now I really need to feel your hands on me.'

Her thoughts exactly. Her hands were shaking as she lowered the zip of his jeans. She stroked his abdomen, enjoying the feel of his musculature, then peeled the denim down.

He stepped out of his jeans, then drew her close and kissed her hard. 'You're absolutely, absolutely sure about this?'

No. She was terrified that she was going to make an idiot of herself. 'Yes,' she lied.

'OK.' He pulled her duvet back, lifted her up and laid her gently against the pillows. He knelt between her thighs and stayed there for a moment, just looking at her. 'You're so beautiful, Stephanie.' He stroked her midriff. 'Your skin's so soft.' He let his hands slide up to cup her breasts. 'And you're so responsive.'

She shivered. 'You're beautiful, too—and I want you, Dan. I really want you. Right here, right now.'

He leaned forward to kiss her lightly, then kissed his way down her abdomen. She shivered again as he slid one finger under the lacy trim of her knickers. He gently pushed one finger inside her and moved his thumb to tease her clitoris.

She shuddered and he stopped. 'OK?' he checked.

'Very OK.' Her voice had practically dropped an octave, she was so turned on.

But he didn't tease her about it, to her relief; he simply kissed her lightly. 'Good.' He kept stroking her, and the pleasure coiled tighter and tighter.

Then Stephanie stopped thinking at all as her body convulsed round him.

He held her until the aftershocks had died down.

'Thank you— I…' She grimaced. 'Sorry, I'm a bit incoherent.'

He chuckled and stole a kiss. 'You don't know what that does to my ego, knowing that I've reduced such a clever woman to mush like this.'

'Um.' She didn't know what to say. 'Thank you.'

'My pleasure.' He stroked her hair back from her face. 'I wanted the first time to be for you.'

When had someone last been so considerate of her feelings? Certainly not Joe. It brought her close to tears; to hide her emotion, she kissed him and explored his body until his breathing went shallow and he was shaking.

'Now?' she asked.

'Yes.' The word came out as a hiss of need.

He shifted to kneel between her thighs. The tip of his penis nudged against her.

And then slowly, sweetly, he slid deep inside her. He stayed still, letting her adjust to the weight of his body; then, finally, he began to move, holding her close as he pushed deeper.

His lovemaking was warm and sweet and slow, and Stephanie really hadn't expected it to be like this— sweet and sharp at the same time. She was shockingly aware of another climax building; was it simply that her body had been so starved for pleasure, it was making up for lost time? Or was it because it was Dan making love with her?

Her body tightened around his, tipping him into his own climax, and as her heart rate slowed to normal she was aware of the tears spilling down her cheeks.

'Stephanie? Are you OK?' he asked, looking worried

'More than OK,' she whispered. 'It's been a long time. I wasn't expecting this to be so good. To—well…' She blushed, and was cross with herself. How could she be shy with him after what they'd just done?

'Me, too.' He kissed her gently. 'Stephanie. I feel horrible about this, as if I've just got what I wanted and now I'm deserting you, but I—' He dragged in a breath. 'Much as I'd like to, I'm sorry, I can't stay with you tonight.'

'Of course you can't,' she said. Did he really think she didn't know that? 'You have Mia to think about, and you can't expect your sister to stay babysit all night. You've probably already been longer than you said you'd be.' And that was all her fault, for being needy.

'Thank you for understanding.' He kissed her again. 'Next time—oh, hell, that makes it sound as if I'm taking you for granted, and I don't mean that. Just that you and I, we're good together, and I'd like to do this again.'

'Me, too,' she admitted. And hearing him sound all flustered made her feel so much better.

'Next time,' he said, 'my timing's going to be better. And I won't have to rush off.'

'It's OK. Really it is,' she said.

He smiled and stole another kiss. 'Stay there—you look comfortable. I'll see myself out.'

'OK.' She watched him dressing. Daniel was beautiful, and she was still amazed by how he'd given her so much pleasure. Whatever happened between them in the future, they'd had this. And he'd made her feel wonderful. Special. *Cherished.*

He kissed her goodbye. 'See you tomorrow, honey. Sweet dreams.'

'You, too.' And they would be sweet, she knew, thanks to him.

CHAPTER NINE

'I CAN'T BELIEVE they've got Christmas cards for sale in the hospital shop,' Daniel said. 'It's still only October!'

'There's wrapping, tinsel and tree decorations in the supermarket, too,' Stephanie told him dryly. 'There's no escape.'

He sighed. 'I shouldn't be so bah humbug about it all. It's lovely having babies on the ward at Christmas.'

'But?' she asked, seeing the doubts in his expression.

'Christmas is always bitter-sweet for me,' he said. 'If I didn't have Mia, I'd probably go abroad somewhere to avoid it.'

She waited, knowing there was more.

Eventually, he raked his hand through his hair and told her. 'Meg's accident was at the beginning of December,' he said. 'That year, Mia was the only thing that kept me going. I had to face it for her sake and make the day special for her.'

But inside his heart had been breaking. She'd just bet he'd had as many sympathy cards as Christmas cards that year. And how hard it must've been to celebrate Christmas when he'd had a funeral to plan.

Christmas, birthdays and anniversaries were always tough when you'd lost someone, she knew. Or when you didn't have a family to make the days special for you; even if you had good friends to celebrate the good times with you, there was still something missing. A family-shaped hole.

He'd shared something tough with her. Maybe it was her turn to let him know he wasn't alone. 'Actually, I know what you mean,' she said. 'I, um—my marriage finally broke up just before Christmas.' And it was the anniversary of the miscarriage next month: a day she always found hard, even though the baby had never been hers. 'It's a tough time of year.'

'Break-ups are never easy,' he agreed, 'but Christmas always makes things harder.'

She shrugged. 'There was one plus point. I didn't have to spend Christmas with Joe's family that year.'

Given what Stephanie had told him about growing up in care, Daniel was pretty sure that Christmas had always been hard for her. And it sounded as if she hadn't found the family she'd been hoping for when she'd got married.

Something in her expression warned him not to ask any more. So, instead, he said lightly, 'Not all in-laws are difficult, you know.'

'I guess not.' Though she didn't look convinced.

'Mine are nice.'

'Your in-laws or your family?'

'Both,' he said. 'Actually, my in-laws are very much part of my family.'

She looked surprised. 'Even though...?'

'Meg's dead? Yes. Mia's still their granddaughter. And I'm still their son-in-law. That's not going to change, even if I see someone else. Even if...' He paused. No. It was too early to talk about a future. She hadn't even met his family, yet. And it sounded as if she had real issues about families. As if she found them painful. This could end up being a sticking point in their relationship.

Right now, he needed to lighten their moods. 'Well. I hope you're prepared for Christmas on the children's ward.'

'If it's anything like it was in Manchester,' she said, 'we'll have a huge tree, the Friends of the Hospital will have bought and wrapped a little gift for every child and every sibling, and someone's going to be Father Christmas to deliver them—my guess is that it'll be Rhys.'

'Don't forget the sausage rolls and mince pies,' he said. 'Parents bring them in by the plateful. And tins of chocolate biscuits.'

'Good. I love chocolate biscuits.'

He smiled. 'I'll remember that.'

She smiled back. 'I'd better get back. I have clinic in ten minutes.'

'Yeah. I'll call you later,' he said. On days when they weren't going to get the chance to see each other, they'd fallen into the habit of chatting on the phone. At the same time that he enjoyed it, it also made him feel antsy; was getting close to Stephanie the right thing to do? Could they overcome each other's doubts and really make a go of this?

'See you,' she said, and took her tray and dirty plate back to the rack.

Stephanie had been called in to the maternity floor while Daniel was in the middle of performing a Caesarean section for a mum who'd spent the last day and

a half in a back-to-back labour. Although she'd really
wanted to have a normal delivery, the baby was starting to get distressed and Iris had explained to her that
her labour simply wasn't progressing and it wasn't fair
on her or the baby. The patient had discussed it with her
husband, then agreed, in tears, to a C-section.

After the delivery, Stephanie was doing the newborn checks. She said quietly to Iris, 'The baby's grunting a bit and the Apgar score's a bit low for my liking.
I'd like to take her through to Special Care to help her
breathing.'

'Agreed,' Iris said.

Stephanie wrapped the baby up and took her over to
the parents, noting that the mum was still in tears. 'You
have a gorgeous baby girl here.'

'I can't cuddle her until I've been sewn up, can I?'
she asked, looking miserable.

'No, but she can hold your finger while her dad gives
her a cuddle,' Stephanie reassured her.

'Is she all right?' the dad asked, looking anxious.

'She'll be fine,' Stephanie said. 'But at the moment
she's breathing a little bit fast—it's what we call tran-
sient tachypnoea of the newborn or TTN. It only lasts
for two or three days and we can make her better, but
we do need to take her through to the special care unit,
once you've had a cuddle.'

'Why has she got this TTN thing? It is a virus or
something?' the mum asked.

'No. While the baby's still inside the womb, her lungs
are filled with fluid. If you have a vaginal birth, the
fluid is squeezed out as the baby passes through the
birth canal. With a C-section, that doesn't happen, so
there's still some fluid in the lungs. That makes it harder

for the baby to take in oxygen, and she breathes faster to make up for it.'

The mum's eyes widened. 'So it's my fault?'

'No, not at all. And it's quite common, so try not to worry. What we're going to do is put her under an oxygen hood for a couple of hours. It will help her breathe normally, and she won't have any problems afterwards. I promise, there's nothing to worry about.'

'Can we see her?' the dad asked.

'You can see her whenever you like in the unit and you'll be able to cuddle her and feed her,' Stephanie reassured them.

'Though for your comfort I'd prefer you to wait until the spinal block has worn off and you can move your legs again,' Daniel said.

'How long will that take?' the mum asked.

'A couple of hours, so she might even come back to you before you get a chance to go to the ward,' Daniel explained.

'You might notice some little grunting sounds when she breathes and her nostrils might flare a bit. She might look a little bit blue round her mouth, and the skin will suck in between her ribs when she breathes, but these are all symptoms of TTN and they'll go away in a couple of days,' Stephanie said. 'If you've got any worries, the midwives will be around, and I happen to know I'm on the roster for doing the first-day checks on the babies tomorrow, so you can ask me anything you like. Even if you think it's little or a silly question—I'd much rather you asked so I can reassure you that everything's fine, rather than sat there worrying.'

'Thank you.' The mum's lower lip wobbled slightly. 'I wanted to feed her myself.'

'And you can,' Stephanie reassured her. 'You've got a beautiful little girl there, so well done.' She rested her hand on the mum's shoulder. 'You take care, and I'll see you in a little bit.'

She sorted out the baby's admission to the special care unit, and took the baby up after the mum had had a brief cuddle; then she came back down to report that the baby had settled in nicely and they could visit whenever they liked.

Daniel caught up with her in the corridor. 'That was a really nice explanation you gave of TTN. I like the way you reassured the mum.'

She shrugged. 'It's my job.'

'I guess.' He leaned forward and stole a kiss right there in the corridor.

'Dan!' she exclaimed, scandalised.

'Nobody was looking.' He winked at her. 'See you later.'

Stephanie felt herself flushing, but was smiling all the way back to ward. Especially when she checked her phone after her shift to find a message from Dan.

It seems I have a babysitter for tonight. Fancy going to the movies?

She typed back.

Love to. Tell me where and when. Don't mind what we see.

Great. Leicester Square at 7.30.

Daniel was already waiting outside the cinema when he saw Stephanie walk round the corner into Leicester Square. His heart skipped a beat when he saw her. He'd never expected to feel like this again, but Stephanie drew him.

And then there was the fact that their relationship had moved to the next stage. He'd forgotten how much he liked the closeness of lovemaking—not just the sex side, but holding his lover afterwards, feeling warm and sated and just a little bit blissed out, talking about anything and everything. He'd really missed that. He'd missed going for a walk, just holding hands. He'd missed the sweetness of a shared glance. With Stephanie, he'd rediscovered all of it.

She saw him and lifted her hand in acknowledgement, smiling at him.

He met her with a hug, lifted her off her feet and whirled her round, then kissed her.

'Anyone would think you hadn't seen me for ages,' she teased.

'It feels like it.' Weirdly, that was true. He'd missed her. Something else he hadn't expected.

'Poor baby.' She batted her eyelashes at him, and laughed.

'Did you have time to eat anything before you came out?'

'I grabbed a sandwich. How about you?'

'I ate with Mia,' he said. 'Sorry, I should've said.'

'It's fine. It's totally what I expected you to do, so stop worrying.'

She was so in tune with him. And he didn't feel pressured by her; she'd accepted that Mia was a huge part of his life and didn't expect to come first. 'Is a rom-com OK with you?'

'Very OK. I like most sorts of films—well, as long as they're not super-gory,' she said.

He smiled. 'Noted.'

They held hands all the way through the film and fed each other popcorn, making Daniel feel like a teenager again. He'd forgotten what it felt like just to have fun like this.

'Do you want to come back to my place?' Stephanie asked, half shyly, as they left the cinema.

He stole a kiss. 'Would you mind if I didn't? This babysitting was a last-minute thing, and although Lucy brought a pile of marking with her—'

'—it's not fair to take her for granted,' Stephanie finished, surprising him by how much in tune she was with him. She kissed him lightly. 'It's OK. I'm happy just being with you, and tonight was an unexpected bonus.'

'I'm happy, too,' he said softly. 'I never thought I would be again, after I lost Meg.'

She gave him a rueful smile. 'Me neither, after my divorce.'

They shared a glance.

Should he tell her he was falling in love with her? Would she work it out for herself that he'd pretty much just told her that?

And was she telling him the same, or was he over-reading this?

He wasn't quite ready to take that risk. He didn't want to scare her off by telling her straight. Instead, he kissed her again. 'I'm glad you're happy.'

She stroked his face. 'Right now, life's good,' she said softly.

In other words, he thought, don't jinx it by saying it out loud. Well, he could live with that. For now.

* * *

'Obviously you missed it last time,' the social worker said.

'It's a new break,' Stephanie countered.

'Oh, come on. How likely is it that he's broken his arm again, the day after the cast came off? Unless the foster-parents let his mother see him without telling us.'

Stephanie didn't usually have a problem dealing with people from other departments and institutions, but this particular woman drove her crazy. Once she'd decided something, she wouldn't allow for any alternatives, and Stephanie hated that. 'That's speculation,' Stephanie said, 'and unfair. And surely Oscar Goldblum's health and comfort come first?'

The social worker just glowered at her.

'If you'll excuse me, I have children to treat,' Stephanie said, icily polite and resisting the temptation to yell at the woman and tell her to do her job fairly. Oscar Goldblum had broken his arm for a second time, and he'd been living with foster-parents rather than with his mother; surely that had to cast doubt on the theory that Della was the cause of the fractures?

But at least she was able to talk to Daniel about it after work.

'Stephanie, don't get me wrong, but maybe you're getting a bit too involved?' he said.

'How do you mean?'

'Don't go defensive on me,' he said gently. 'I'm not making a judgement. But you grew up in care and your childhood was maybe not as happy as it could've been, so my guess is that you don't like to see families broken and children put in care. Look at the way you were about Janine.'

'I know, but I was right about her, wasn't I?'

'Yes, but are you sure you're right about this one? I mean *really* right, not just seeing what you want to see?'

She lifted her chin. It stung that he'd actually raised the question. Just like Joe had always questioned her decisions. 'Daniel, I'm a good doctor.'

'I know you are. All I'm saying is that sometimes we get cases where our judgement isn't quite as good as it could be—look at the way I panicked over Mia.'

'You were absolutely right to panic. She has reactive airways and she needed treatment.'

He spread his hands. 'And I should've been able to work that out for myself instead of thinking of all the serious conditions she could have.'

He really was being unfair to himself, she thought. 'She's your daughter.'

'Exactly. And I'm both parents to her, so I feel doubly bound to get everything right, all the time. It's the same sort of thing with you and your patients.'

She looked at him, hurt. 'Dan, that's not fair.'

He squeezed her hand. 'I'm not saying you're wrong about this, just that maybe you need to keep your mind a bit more open.'

What? She wasn't the narrow-minded one here. That was the social worker.

'Is it possible that everyone missed a break last time round?' he asked.

'No. I've reviewed the X-rays from last time. It was a Colles' fracture. According to the notes, Della said he tripped over and put his hands out to stop himself falling, and you know as well as I do that's exactly how Colles' fractures happen. This new one's further up his forearm, but it would've shown up.'

'So you think the foster-parents might've caused the fracture?' he asked.

She wrinkled her nose. 'It's possible, but how likely is it that firstly a parent and then a foster-parent would batter a child? Oscar would have to be incredibly unlucky. Screening of foster-parents is pretty thorough nowadays so, although it's technically possible, I don't think it's the explanation. I think it's much more likely he has a medical condition.'

'And you've got one in mind?'

She nodded. 'Type one osteogenesis imperfecta would explain why Oscar has a history of breaks. I wouldn't be surprised if baby Charlie comes in with another break in the next four months. If one of their parents has OI, then the children have a fifty per cent chance of inheriting it.'

'Brittle bone? Which parent?'

She grimaced. 'That I don't know yet. Della's a little shorter than average, but that's not enough to prove my theory. We'd need to check her properly—see if she has the blue tints to the whites of her eyes, a history of fractures and poor muscle tone. I want to take another look at Oscar, too. I can check if his birth weight was a little lower than average and see how his teeth are.'

'Talk to Della about her medical history. And you can send her for a DEXA scan to see about the bone density,' he suggested.

'A DEXA scan will show up any problems with Della, but maybe not in the children because they're so young—a tiny baby and a three-year-old.' She frowned. 'We need a skin-punch biopsy to check collagen synthesis, which can take weeks; and DNA testing on a blood sample can take months.'

He nodded. 'And you're worrying about this.'

'Yes,' she admitted. 'It's not that I think all care places are bad, but if there isn't a good reason to split them up then surely it's better for the family to stay together? I said from the start that I don't think it's abuse, and this new fracture makes me more convinced that I'm right and we need to treat the family for OI. I'm really not bringing my own background into this, Dan.'

'OK, I'll get off your case.' He squeezed her hand. 'If there's anything I can do to help, let me know.'

'Thank you. I appreciate it.'

He kissed her. 'There was something else I wanted to talk to you about.'

'Oh?'

'I was thinking…' He paused. 'Maybe we could take Mia out on Saturday.'

What? He wanted her to go out with him on a *family* basis?

That was where it had all gone wrong with Joe.

'Stephanie?' he prompted when she remained silent.

She took a deep breath. 'Are you sure about… well…?'

'Introducing you to my daughter?' He nodded. 'Don't forget, she's already met you and liked you.'

'As her doctor. This is different.'

'You think I'm rushing it?' he asked. 'We've been seeing each other for a few weeks now. I like you, and I think you like me.'

She did. And it scared her. 'How's Mia going to feel about this? I mean, you bringing someone in to…' There was no point in beating about the bush. 'Her mother's place?' Especially as she herself had no real experience of what it was like to *have* a mother, let alone *be* a mother. Mia was six years old. Vulnerable. Stephanie knew she couldn't afford to make a mess of this.

Daniel cupped her face and kissed her lightly on the lips. 'The accident was four years ago. Mia only remembers Meg from photos and videos. She's not going to give you a hard time over this.'

'Isn't she going to need some time to get used to the idea?' Right at that moment, Stephanie thought she could do with some time, too.

'Maybe. But I think she's ready to meet you.' He paused. 'Or would you rather meet the rest of my family first?'

Now he was getting into *really* scary territory. She couldn't get a single word out in reply.

'I know you haven't told me what happened with your ex and his family. I'm not going to press you,' Daniel said. 'But I'll listen whenever you're ready to talk about it.'

Help. What did she say now?

'What I did pick up,' he continued, 'is that you had a hard time with them. You won't get that with mine.' He kissed her lightly. 'I can tell you that until I'm blue in the face, but the only way you'll believe me is if you see if for yourself. Meet them.'

She swallowed hard. Meet them? No, no and no. 'I'm sorry.' The doubts were there and she couldn't get past them. She bit her lip. 'I wish I could be different.'

'Actually, I quite like you as you are.' He stole another kiss. 'Just think about it, OK?'

'OK.'

There was a glint in his eye. 'We've got forty minutes until I need to go back.'

'Indeed.'

'And I have some great ideas on how to use those forty minutes.' He grinned and scooped her up in his arms. 'Me caveman.'

And she pushed her fears aside and laughed back as he carried her through to her bedroom.

CHAPTER TEN

STEPHANIE THOUGHT ABOUT what Daniel had said all that evening, after he'd left.

And all the way to work.

And every second of her shift, in between seeing patients.

He was asking her to take a huge leap of faith. To trust him. And by asking her to go out with him and Mia, he was showing that same trust in her.

Could she do this?

Could she take the risk of being part of a family?

As if he understood that she needed some space, Daniel didn't suggest meeting for lunch, and he didn't call or text her. Or was he feeling the same way that she was—confused, scared, and wanting to back out?

There was only one way to find out. She called him, that evening.

'Hi. How are you doing?' he asked.

'OK,' she fibbed. 'Um, what you said about taking Mia out.'

That got his interest. 'Yes?'

'If you're sure about it, then yes. I'd like to go with you.'

'How about the Natural History Museum?' he suggested. 'It's her favourite place, and she'll enjoy showing you around.'

Neutral territory. Lots of other people around. No pressure. And she could always do a fake call on her mobile phone and say that she'd been called in, if need be. Which meant that if it all went wrong, she wasn't trapped and nobody would get hurt. 'I'd like that.'

'That's great. We'll meet you outside the entrance at ten on Saturday morning.'

She took a deep breath. 'OK.'

'Don't be scared,' he said softly. 'It's all going to be fine.'

She really hoped he was right.

On Saturday morning, Stephanie caught the train through to South Kensington and came out of the Tube entrance to see the beautiful Victorian building. Daniel and Mia were already there, waiting for her. He raised a hand to greet her and she hurried over to them. He looked gorgeous in a mulberry-coloured sweater and jeans, and Stephanie was glad that she'd dressed casually, too.

She crouched down so she was at a level height with Mia. 'Hello, Mia. Do you remember me?'

The little girl nodded, her brown eyes wide. 'Hello, Dr Scott.'

'You can call me Stephanie, if you like.' She smiled at the little girl. 'Thank you for letting me come to see the dinosaurs with you and your dad. I've never seen them before.'

'There's a big, really scary one,' Mia said, 'but it's all right. I'll hold your hand so you don't have to be afraid.'

Stephanie had to swallow the lump in her throat. Mia

clearly had the same warm, generous nature as her father; then again, she already knew that from when the little girl had brought in the cakes for the nursing staff after her night on the ward. 'I'd like that. Very much.'

She was amazed by how big the diplodocus was in the main hall.

'Don't worry,' Mia said, 'it didn't eat people, just leaves, so it wouldn't have eaten you.'

She chatted to the little girl about dinosaurs, surprised at how much Mia knew about them.

'Daddy likes dinosaurs,' Mia confided. 'He reads me stories about dinosaurs, too.'

'That sounds like fun.' She shared a glance with Daniel. He was clearly a brilliant father and Mia seemed incredibly well adjusted, confident and cheerful.

She thoroughly enjoyed going round the museum with Daniel and Mia, exclaiming over the dinosaurs, the skeleton of the big blue whale, and her favourite bit, the fossilised lightning.

So this was what being part of a family could feel like.

Being right where you belonged.

And it was like a sunny spring day with all the daffodils coming out, after months of grey days full of ice and snow.

Daniel was taking a huge risk, opening his life up to her like this. If it went wrong, the two of them wouldn't be the only ones hurt. She really had to make sure she got it right this time.

They went out for a late lunch after the museum. 'This is my treat, to say thank you for taking me to the museum—no arguments, Dan,' she added, with a warning look.

They found a small family restaurant, a chain that Daniel told her Mia liked. The little girl ordered popcorn chicken, fries and a smoothie; Dan ordered Moroccan chicken and couscous; and Stephanie ordered salad with chicken, mango and prawns.

When their food arrived, Mia glanced at Stephanie's plate. 'That looks really nice.'

'Do you want to try it?' Stephanie asked. Then she realised what she'd done. 'If that's OK with your dad, that is,' she added swiftly. Oh, help. She should've checked with Dan first. She'd put him in an awkward position, and that wasn't fair.

He smiled. 'It's fine—provided I get to try it as well.'

She smiled back. She hadn't done any damage yet, then.

He fed her a taste of his chicken from his fork. It felt incredibly intimate; yet, at the same time, it felt as if this was simply part of a normal family meal out—something she'd never quite felt with Joe.

They went for a walk in the park afterwards, and Mia insisted that Stephanie join her on the slide and the swings. It had been years and years since Stephanie had been to a children's playground; she'd forgotten what fun it could be. And sharing this day with Mia and Daniel felt really, really special.

Finally, Daniel said, 'OK, sweetheart—time to head for home. It's starting to get dark.'

'Are you coming, too, Stephanie?' Mia asked

Stephanie didn't want to overstay her welcome; at the same time, she didn't want to push the little girl away. This was clearly an overture. Should he accept it? She looked at Daniel for guidance, and he gave her a tiny nod.

'I'd like that. Thank you for inviting me, Mia.'

It was the first time she'd been to Daniel's house, but it was pretty much what she'd expected: a small, pretty terraced house. The living room was full of books, as well as a state-of-the-art computer and a box of toys for Mia.

'That's my mummy,' Mia said, taking Stephanie's hand and leading her over to the photographs on the mantelpiece.

The house was obviously filled with memories of the past. Meg Connor had been beautiful, and she'd clearly been very much loved. And, even though Stephanie knew it was selfish and inappropriate, she couldn't help a flood of doubt. How was she going to fit into Daniel and Mia's lives? They were already a very tight unit. So this would be exactly the same as it had been with Joe; she'd be the outsider again, never quite sure of her place in their family and knowing that she wasn't really a part of it.

'And that's my favourite picture of us,' Mia said, pointing to the picture of a dark-haired woman holding a toddler in her arms, with a background of a spectacular blue-flowered bush. 'It's in our garden.'

How could she possibly knock the little girl back?

'She's very pretty,' Stephanie said. 'She looks a lot like you.' Though she could see Daniel in the little girl, too; they both had the same warmth in their smiles.

'Do you look like your mummy?' Mia asked.

The question was totally out of left field, and it was a hard one to answer as Stephanie didn't even have a photograph of her mother. In the end, she fudged it with a smile and said, 'Yes, but sadly I don't have a mummy any more either.'

'Did your mummy die?' Mia asked.

'Yes.' Though she'd lie about how, if she had to. No way would Stephanie let that misery hurt Mia, too.

'So we're the same,' Mia said, 'even though your eyes are green and mine are brown.'

'I guess so.' There was a lump in Stephanie's throat.

'Do you want to play a game?' Mia asked.

Safer ground. Something she'd do with her patients, especially the ones who didn't get visitors. 'I'd love to.'

Daniel brought through two mugs of coffee, plus a mug of hot chocolate for Mia, in time to overhear the last bit. 'Games, hmm?'

'You can play, too, Daddy,' Mia said.

They played Snap until Mia had won for the fifth time.

'Enough for now, I think, sweetheart,' Daniel said gently.

Mia looked at Stephanie. 'Will you stay for tea tonight?' she asked.

It was tempting, but Stephanie didn't push it. 'I can't, sweetheart. I have things I need to do back at my flat.'

'That means laundry. Daddy always does laundry on Saturday nights,' Mia said, rolling her eyes. 'And he says ironing is slavery.'

Stephanie had to hide her smile at the thought of Daniel being enslaved to the ironing board. 'He's right.'

'But we have to look smart at work,' Daniel said. 'It gives the patients more confidence in us.'

Mia shook her head. 'It's your face that does that, Daddy, not your suit. You look kind and clever, so people know they can trust you to make them better.' She looked at Stephanie. 'You, too. I was scared when I went to hospital, even though I was with Daddy and

Fred Bear, but you stopped me being scared and I knew you'd make me better.'

Stephanie felt the tears filming her eyes. 'I'm glad.'

'Out of the mouths of babes,' Daniel said when he saw Stephanie to the door. 'She's right. You're kind and you're clever.' He paused. 'And you make the world feel a better place.'

She felt the same way about him. And the hope in her heart burned just that little bit brighter.

Daniel called Stephanie later that night. 'You were a huge hit with Mia.'

'I'm glad.'

'Not that I want to put you under any pressure, you understand, but before she went to sleep she gave me strict instructions to call you and ask if you'll come to the aquarium with us next weekend.'

'She really wants me to come?' He wasn't just saying that?

'She really wants you to come,' he confirmed. 'And so do I.' He paused. 'That is…if you want to see us again. I worried that maybe it put you off when you saw the photos of Meg. You wouldn't stay for tea.'

'I didn't want to overstay my welcome,' she said lightly. 'Dan, of course you're going to have pictures of Mia's mum around. I wouldn't expect anything else.'

'Just as long as you know it doesn't mean…' He sighed. 'We should be having this conversation face to face.'

'It's OK.' But his words intrigued her, at the same time as they worried her. 'What were you going to say?'

'It's been four years. Of course I still miss Meg. And she'll always be part of my life. But I'm at the point now where I'm ready to move on.' He sighed again. 'Which isn't meant to put pressure on you.'

'Do you really think I'm that fragile?'

'No.' But he didn't sound too sure.

'Dan?'

'Not fragile, no. But I think you had a hard time growing up, and you're clearly not used to a family situation. Whatever happened with your ex, I think it's made you wary. And it's a lot to ask, expecting someone to take me on as a package.'

'I met Mia at the same time as I met you, remember,' she said softly. 'And she's a lovely little girl. You're doing a fantastic job of bringing her up to be as warm and kind as you are.'

'I wasn't fishing for compliments,' he said.

'I know. And I didn't say it because I thought you were,' she said.

'Are you ready to move on?' he asked softly. 'To think about taking this forward?'

'Do you mean, meet the rest of your family?'

He laughed. 'Not yet. I know that's a big ask.' He paused. 'But, yes, I'd like you to meet them in the future. Just take this day by day for now, hmm?'

Day by day. Give her time to get used to the idea. 'That works for me.'

The following weekend, Stephanie and Daniel took Mia to the aquarium. The little girl held Stephanie's hand and pointed out her favourite fish. And on the Sunday, Stephanie cooked them a roast dinner at her flat, with strawberries and ice cream for pudding.

'You're a better cook than Daddy,' Mia said with a

smile. 'Daddy tries. But he's better at breaded chicken and oven chips.'

Stephanie smiled. 'Well, I like cooking.' She'd taught herself and made plenty of mistakes, but now she was happy to try new recipes and even tinker with them before she tried cooking them.

'Is that your sister?' Mia asked, looking at the photographs on the fridge.

'No, my best friend, Trish. And that's her little boy, Calum—he's my godson.'

'So you're sort of a mummy, then,' Mia said thoughtfully.

'Sort of. I like children.' In her experience they didn't judge you the way adults did. They took you for who you were rather than who they wanted you to be.

'I like you,' Mia said solemnly.

Stephanie hugged her. 'Good. Because I like you, too.'

Though when Mia gave her a small parcel wrapped in tissue paper, the next weekend, there was a real lump in her throat when she opened it. It was a home-made picture frame, with pasta shapes glued onto a cardboard frame and then spray-painted silver, and in the middle of the frame was a photograph someone had taken for them at the aquarium: the three of them together, with Mia in the middle.

'I made it with Aunty Lucy, after school,' Mia said solemnly. 'She helped me a bit with the paint, but I did the rest of it.'

'It's beautiful,' Stephanie said. 'Thank you very, very much. And I'm going to put it right here on the mantelpiece, where everyone can see it.'

Mia beamed, looking pleased. 'You really like it?'

'I really, *really* like it,' Stephanie said, hugging her.

So maybe this was going to work out. Mia had seemed to accept her, and she was growing closer to Daniel. The only sticking point now would be if his family didn't like her—and if Meg's parents couldn't cope with the idea of someone else in their daughter's place. She knew she'd have to face it eventually, but for now she was happy in their little bubble—just the three of them.

CHAPTER ELEVEN

STEPHANIE CHECKED HER diary for the sixth time. And she reached the same horrible conclusion for the sixth time too: her period was late.

And, thanks to the Pill, her period was *never* late. She was regular down to the hour of the day. Maybe the stress of the Goldblum case was making her period go haywire, she thought. Then again, she was on the Pill to regulate her periods, so stress shouldn't make a difference. She shouldn't miss a period, ever.

Then she went cold.

Could she actually be pregnant?

She and Daniel had had that takeaway meal a couple of weeks ago, and they'd both had an upset stomach the following day. So, technically, it was possible that she could be pregnant. The upset stomach could mean that the Pill hadn't worked, and she remembered that they'd made love that night, after the meal. Before she'd been ill. Sperm could live for five days inside her body. So if she'd been ovulating that day...

No, no and *no*.

The risks of actually conceiving were tiny.

She couldn't be pregnant.

It would be a total disaster. Just as it had been when

she'd last fallen pregnant—when she'd tried to be a surrogate mother and carry a baby for Joe's sister.

And why did this have to happen the same week as the anniversary of her miscarriage?

She'd have to take a pregnancy test. But her period was only *just* late. It might be too soon for the HGC hormone to show up, so the test could give a false negative. She'd give it a few days—a week—and see if her period started.

In the meantime, she avoided Daniel, not wanting to burden him with her worries. Maybe she was being a coward; but on the other hand there was Trish's favourite saying about not troubling trouble. Until she knew for definite that there was a problem, what was the point of telling him and worrying him, too?

But she didn't tell Trish, either. She knew her best friend would worry about her and rush straight down to London to see her, and she also knew that Trish had enough worries of her own; Trish's husband's job was under threat of redundancy. So it was better to keep this to herself until she knew what was going on.

At least it was half term, so Daniel was taking time off to be with Mia and she didn't have to see him at work. She was guiltily aware that they'd made plans for her to take leave, too—but she couldn't do that, not when all this was up in the air.

The fib was easy, especially as she did it by text:

Sorry, short of staff, bug going round, they need me in at work.

But she felt even guiltier when Daniel called her and was nice about it. 'You must be up to your eyes if people are off sick. Come over to ours for dinner after work—then you won't have to cook.'

'Sorry, Dan. I'm doing split shifts.' Another lie.

'OK. Though Mia says to tell you she misses you.'

Oh, help. She missed Mia, too. And Dan. This wasn't fair. 'Tell her I'm sorry. And I'll make it up to her.' If she had the chance.

'I will, but the offer's open. You don't have to give us notice—just turn up.'

She really, *really* didn't deserve this. And her voice cracked when she whispered, 'Thank you.'

Somehow she managed to get through the next couple of days, keeping her distance and lying through her teeth. But then Daniel sent her a text.

Being a guy, I can bit a bit slow on the uptake sometimes. Have I done something to upset you?

Guilt flooded through her as she read the words.

If I have, then I apologise—and please let me know what I've done so I can make sure I don't do it again.

Oh, help. How mean was she, just staying out of his way and not telling him what was wrong, especially as none of this was his fault? She wasn't being fair.

But she also couldn't tell him what was wrong. Not until she knew for certain.

In the meantime, what did she say to him?

This really wasn't his fault. Daniel hadn't done anything to upset her. But she wasn't ready to have a conversation about babies and families. It would change everything. How would he feel about the idea of having more children? Even if he wanted more children, surely Mia would need time to get used to the idea too. Yes, she was bonding with the little girl, but all of this was happening way too fast. They needed time.

And Stephanie definitely wasn't ready to move on to the next stage. To go public. Be an item with him. It scared her rigid; that was when everything had started to go wrong between herself and Joe. Both of them had been too stubborn to heed the warnings when his family hadn't taken to her. She wouldn't make that mistake again.

What a mess. She typed back.

It's not you

But that sounded like the beginning of a Dear John letter, as if she was planning to dump him. Which she wasn't. She was just waiting until she knew what was happening.

She deleted the words, and instead typed in:

Just got a lot on my plate right now.

That was true enough, though she was guiltily aware that she was skirting the issue. But she couldn't see him yet. Not until she knew whether she was pregnant or not. She just couldn't. It wouldn't be fair to either of them. Not that the current situation was fair, either; but right now she felt as if she was caught between a rock and a hard place.

On the Tuesday evening, Stephanie caught the Tube to the West End on the way home from work, called into a pharmacy where she knew she'd be totally anonymous, and bought a pregnancy test from a shelf festooned with tinsel and Christmas decorations. Ha. This could turn out to be her very worst Christmas yet, and she'd already had quite a few tough ones in her thirty years.

She felt sick, but hopefully that was owing to adrenalin and worry rather than pregnancy hormones. This wasn't like the last time she'd taken a pregnancy test. Unless she was totally in denial. God, if only Daniel was here. But that was selfish. She couldn't burden him with her miseries. He had enough to deal with.

Her steps dragged as she walked back from the Tube station to her flat. Once she'd closed the front door behind her, she closed her eyes and leaned back against it. 'Get a grip,' she told herself fiercely. 'You need to know the truth so you can work out what to do next.' If the test was negative, maybe she could pretend that the last few days hadn't happened and try to rescue her relationship with Daniel. And if it was positive...

Well, she'd cross that bridge when she came to it.

She took a deep breath and headed for the bathroom. Even though she knew that the digital pregnancy tests gave reasonably quick results, it still felt as though it took for ever for the two minutes to tick round. Two minutes in which she restored order to her clothes, washed her hands and tidied the bathroom—even though it didn't actually need tidying.

And then the two minutes were up.

Crunch time.

Pregnant, or not pregnant?

Her hand was shaking and her mouth was dry as she lifted the stick to look at the test window. This one tiny little result could change her entire life.

Not pregnant.

Relief made her knees buckle and she had to hold on to the sink.

She wasn't pregnant. Life wasn't going to change. She and Daniel could still carry on exactly as they were. Everything was fine.

Though, at the same time, it wasn't fine at all. Because all the memories slammed into her. Memories of doing a pregnancy test before, of her hand shaking and her mouth being dry, because it was so, so important that the test should be positive. Memories of the relief in Joe's face when she told him that the procedure had worked. Memories of the joy in Kitty's face when they'd told her the news—that the implantation had been successful and Kitty was finally going to have the baby she'd wanted to desperately.

And memories of the choking disappointment, only a few weeks later, when she'd lost the baby. Seeing Kitty's dreams shatter. Seeing the joy in her face turn to hatred.

It took Stephanie a while to realise that her face was wet.

And a while longer to realise that her doorbell was buzzing.

Hopefully whoever it was would just go away.

Except they didn't. They just kept ringing her doorbell, as if they knew she was there and they weren't going to give up until she answered.

She gave in and made her way to the hallway. She picked up the entryphone with a shaking hand and just hoped that her emotion didn't show in her voice. 'Yes?'

'Stephanie?'

Oh, no. Of all the people she didn't want to face right now. 'Daniel.'

'Can I come up?'

Her brain had temporarily gone into frozen mode and she couldn't think of an excuse. 'I...'

'Stephanie?'

If she said no, she knew he'd push her for an explanation. 'OK.'

She didn't have time to splash her face with water; she could only hope that her eyes weren't too red and puffy.

Though the first thing he did when he walked in—after handing her some gorgeous flowers that she didn't deserve—was to put his hands on her shoulders and look at her. 'You look as if you've been crying.'

She could hardly deny it. 'I, um... Yeah.'

'What's wrong?'

'That's a bit of a difficult question, and there isn't a short answer,' she said. 'I need to put these beautiful flowers in water. Can I make you a mug of tea?'

It was obvious from the expression on his face that he knew she was trying to sidestep the issue and buy herself some time, but to her relief he let her get away with it. 'That'd be nice.'

He waited until she'd put both mugs of tea on the kitchen table before wrapping his arms round her. 'Talk to me.'

She owed it to him. She knew that. So why couldn't she get the words out? She simply stared at him, wide-eyed, wishing she knew what to say.

'OK. Let's try it another way. Why have you been avoiding me?'

'Because...' She had to be honest. 'I was scared it was all going to go wrong between us.'

'Why would it go wrong between us?'

That was the big question. And she didn't have a clue how he was going to react when she told him.

'Stephanie?'

She blew out a breath. 'There isn't an easy way to say this.'

'Then tell me straight.'

'Because I thought I might be pregnant.'

He went very, very still. 'And are you?'

She couldn't tell a thing from his voice. It was totally inscrutable. Was he shocked, angry, hurt? She didn't have a clue. 'No-o.' And her voice *would* have to waver.

'Is that why you were crying?'

She gulped. Another tough question, but she owed him the truth. 'Yes.'

'Because you were relieved?' He paused. 'Or because you were disappointed?'

A messed-up mixture of the two. 'It's complicated.' She pulled away. 'Let's sit down.' Hopefully it would be easier to talk to him with the table between them. A little bit of distance.

He waited. Patiently. And she cracked.

'I've been here before,' she whispered.

'Is that why your marriage broke up? Because you were pregnant?'

She shook her head. 'Because I lost the baby. And, I guess, worrying that maybe I was pregnant because we'd both been ill after that prawn thing and maybe that meant the Pill hadn't worked…it brought everything back to me. Everything that happened. And that probably makes me the wettest person in the world, to cry over something that happened a long time ago.'

'I'm not judging you,' Daniel said.

'No, but you were honest with me about your past. I

haven't told you much at all about mine.' She should've told him about this weeks ago. She sighed. 'Joe and I met at a party, in my third year as a student. I was twenty-one; he was five years older than me, worked in banking. I fell in love with him, and when he asked me to marry him I said yes. I thought we'd be fine together, both of us professionals looking for a good career. I thought I'd be part of a family.' The family she'd wanted so very much.

Daniel said nothing; he simply waited while she stared into her mug of tea.

In the end, she broke the silence. 'But his family never really took to me. I think it was from my being brought up in care—they were always just that little bit suspicious of me. They never asked, but I knew they were thinking it. What was so wrong with me, that my parents had obviously given me up and nobody wanted to adopt me? Why was I so unlovable?'

He still said nothing, but he reached across the table to squeeze her hand, and kept his hand folded round hers.

'I never really felt part of Joe's family. I never knew what to say to them. Maybe they thought I was being snotty with them because I was a bit quiet around them.' She shrugged. 'I wasn't being snotty. I'm just not used to families and I'm not very good with them.'

'You're good with Mia,' he said.

'That's different.'

'How?'

'It just is.'

'And you're good with people,' he said softly. 'I've seen you with patients and staff.'

'Because it's my job. And I work in an institution.

I can do institutions. I understand how they work. But families? They're so much more complicated. I don't get the dynamics.' She'd never really explained that to anyone before, not even Trish. 'I don't get how siblings feel about each other, because I've never had one. I don't understand the rivalry, or the blood-is-thicker-than-water stuff, or anything like that.' She blew out a breath. 'I did make an effort, really I did. Joe's older sister, Kitty—she was desperate for a baby. She tried and tried and tried to conceive, but she couldn't. She had PCOS.'

'That's tough.'

Being an obstetrician, Daniel would know all about polycystic ovary syndrome, Stephanie knew. 'She was thirty-five. Time was running out for her. She tried fertility drugs, she tried laparascopic ovarian drilling to stop her ovaries producing testosterone, she tried insulin-sensitising drugs in the hope they'd kick-start the fertility drugs into working, but nothing worked. Nothing at all. And every month she was getting more and more desperate for a baby, more and more depressed.' She closed her eyes.

'And then Kitty said they were thinking about asking a surrogate mum to carry a baby for her. An IVF baby, so it would be her egg and Robin's sperm—meaning it would still be their biological baby, even though she couldn't carry it herself. And I thought…I thought maybe this was something I could do for her. That maybe it would bring us closer. That maybe it would help her—and the rest of the family—accept me as Joe's partner.'

'You already had a child?' Daniel asked.

She shook her head. 'I know that's usually one of the

criteria, but in special circumstances that's relaxed. Joe and I talked about it. Really talked. We went through all the implications—well, nearly all. I didn't admit that I was doing it because I wanted his family to like me, probably because I knew it was completely the wrong reason and I was being selfish. I said I could see what not being able to have a baby was doing to Kitty and I wanted to do something to help.

'And that was true, Dan. I *did* want to help. Joe and I weren't quite ready to have our own family—I was twenty-five, just qualified, so I wanted to wait for a bit—but we could do this for Kitty and Robin without our lives being radically changed. Joe was happy for me to do it—he'd seen how being childless was destroying his sister. And so we went ahead with the surrogacy.'

She swallowed hard. 'Kitty was so grateful. She was there when I went to book in with the midwife, and she came to the dating scan. She cried when she saw the baby on the screen. And what I'd hoped for? It happened, Dan. Joe's family finally started to accept me. Kitty and I even started to be friends. I know maybe it was the wrong reason to do it, that I was thinking of myself more than her, but I wanted so much to be part of their family.'

'No, I can understand that,' he said softly.

She sighed. 'And then I broke their hearts. I lost the baby.'

'You had a miscarriage?'

She nodded. 'At twelve weeks. The day before Kitty was going to tell everyone that she and Robin were going to be parents. And it was my fault.'

Daniel frowned. 'How do you work that out?'

She grimaced. 'If I hadn't been on duty…'

He shook his head. 'That's not fair. Plenty of pregnant women work and manage to carry a baby to term. It wasn't your fault, Stephanie, and it wasn't because you were working.'

'Once the pregnancy was confirmed, Kitty and Robin wanted me to take a sabbatical until after the baby was born. I said no. I didn't want to give up my job. I love being a paediatrician. Maybe if I hadn't been so selfish about it, the pregnancy would've gone to full term.'

'And maybe it wouldn't. Babies and pregnancy are *my* specialty, remember,' he said gently. 'There are plenty of reasons why women miscarry. One in five pregnancies end up with a miscarriage, and most of them happen before thirteen weeks. Did your obstetrician say why you lost the baby—if there were any issues with hormone levels or if you had any blood clotting disorder?'

'No.'

'Most miscarriages happen because of chance abnormalities in the foetus,' he said. 'It wasn't your fault. It wasn't anything you did or didn't do.'

'No? I'd had some spotting the previous day. I should've taken notice of that and called in sick, instead of ignoring it and working my shift.'

'Plenty of women experience spotting in the first trimester. Was the bleeding heavy or painful?'

'Well—no,' she admitted.

'Then it wasn't anything to worry about.'

'I miscarried at work, the next day,' she said softly. 'So, actually, I think it *was* something to worry about.'

'The miscarriage still wasn't something you could have prevented, honey.' He moved round to her side of the table, scooped her up and settled her on his lap so he could hold her close. 'That's with my professional hat on. I'm being honest with you, not trying to make you feel better. Surely your obstetrician told you that?'

She swallowed hard. 'It wasn't my baby. It wasn't my place to grieve.'

He stroked her hair. 'Yes, it was, just as much as if the egg had been yours and you weren't the surrogate. You were the one carrying the baby. Of course you were going to grieve when you miscarried. It'd be upsetting for anyone.'

'Kitty was in bits. I destroyed her dreams, Dan. She couldn't forgive me for that. Ever.'

'Maybe at first she blamed you because she was grieving, Stephanie, and it was easier to lash out at you than accept that you'd lost the baby. But she must've realised that you couldn't have done anything to prevent it.'

Stephanie shook her head. 'She couldn't forgive me, and neither could Joe.'

He stared at her, looking shocked. 'Your husband blamed you, too?'

She gave him a sad smile. 'That's what I was saying about blood being thicker than water. And wouldn't you support your sister?'

'If she was in the right, of course I would. And, if she wasn't, then I'd try to talk her round to a more reasonable point of view. Because I love Lucy and I wouldn't want her to get things so badly wrong and end up in a needless mess when it could all be sorted out.' He blew out a breath. 'I'm sorry you had to go through something as painful as that.'

She shrugged. 'I did tell you I wasn't any good at families.'

'Honey, believe me, that really isn't what a family's about. Families pull together. They support each other.'

'Only if you're really one of them,' she said. And she hadn't been. At all.

'It sounds as if they were all upset and you were the easy scapegoat. It wasn't fair of them to blame you—and it's definitely not fair of you to blame yourself. Especially as you're a qualified doctor and you already know all the stuff I just quoted at you.' He stroked her hair and gave her the sweetest, sweetest smile that made her want to bawl all over him. 'I guess it's my turn to teach you to suck eggs.'

'I guess.'

'You do know it wasn't your fault, don't you?'

She grimaced. 'There's a bit of a difference between knowing something with your head and knowing it with your heart, Dan. I went over and over everything I'd done for the previous few weeks, trying to work out if there was anything I'd done to cause the miscarriage.'

'And you found nothing.'

'Maybe if I'd taken it easier…'

'It would still have happened.' He held her close. 'When did it happen?'

'Four years ago this week,' she admitted.

He stroked her hair. 'Oh, Stephanie. So this has brought back all the bad memories for you.' He looked sad. 'I wish you'd told me.'

She shook her head. 'You already have enough on your plate. I wasn't going to dump that on you.'

He kissed her lightly. 'I still have space for you.'

She felt the tears prick her eyelids again. Why did

he have to be so nice about everything? Why couldn't he be a control freak like Joe—the control freak she'd thought he was at work? Then it would be so much easier to walk away.

She didn't trust herself to speak and she didn't know what to say anyway, so she stayed silent.

'So that's why you split up with Joe?' Daniel asked.

She nodded. 'I could see it in his face every time he looked at me. The blame. The guilt. It got to the point where I hated going home at night.' The little terraced house she'd done up with Joe, where they'd loved and laughed and been so happy at first, hadn't felt like home to her from the minute she'd driven herself home from the hospital after the miscarriage. She'd felt like an interloper. Unwanted. Despised.

'In the end, I gave up and left, the week before Christmas. I didn't take anything with me except my clothes. My best friend put me up for a couple of nights until I managed to find myself a flat.'

'I can't believe he'd just let you go like that. Surely he realised how upset you were?'

'But I wasn't the one who'd lost her dreams. He couldn't forgive me for making a promise to his sister and not keeping it.'

'Through no fault of your own.'

'I still didn't keep my promise. I didn't have the baby for her.'

'What about his promises to you? You were married.'

'Between the guilt and the blame and the resentment, there wasn't anything left of our marriage worth fighting for. I think we both knew that. The divorce went through on the grounds of irreconcilable differences.' She gave him a sad little smile.

'He hasn't been in touch with you since?'

'Only through his lawyer. And neither of us went to court for the hearing. We both knew it was the end of the road for us. There was no point in heaping up bitterness on top of bitterness. I didn't want anything from him.' Only what he hadn't been able to give her. A stable family, one that loved her for herself.

'I'm sorry you had to go through all that. No wonder you were wary of relationships afterwards—anyone would be, in your shoes.'

'You went through a tougher time. You lost your wife and you had to deal with your daughter's grief as well as your own,' she pointed out.

'Yes, but I had people to support me. It sounds as if you were totally alone.'

'Not totally. I had Trish. My best friend. She's the family I'd choose to have.'

'I'm glad she was there for you.' He stroked her face. 'Why didn't you talk to me before? When you first thought you might be pregnant?'

'Because I panicked.'

'Did you think I'd walk away from you?'

'No. But I worried that you'd feel trapped. And this is all too soon. What about Mia? She's just getting to know me. It's…it's a mess.' She sighed. 'Like I said, I'm not good at family stuff. I had no idea how you'd react.' She didn't dare look at him, too scared to see the answers in his face; but she needed to know the truth. She had to ask the question. 'What if I had been pregnant?'

CHAPTER TWELVE

'THEN WE WOULD'VE worked something out. Talked about what we both wanted.'

This was getting seriously scary, Stephanie thought. As if they were talking about more than just a fling. As if they were talking about having a real relationship. As if they were talking about a *future*.

'What do you want, Stephanie?' he asked.

You. Mia. A family.

And no way could she admit that. Especially as she didn't know exactly how Daniel felt. He might have given her signals, but she knew she was rubbish at interpreting them. Work was fine; friendship, she could do; but relationships were like walking through a room with a blindfold and headphones on, so she couldn't help tripping over every obstacle instead of avoiding them. 'I don't know,' she mumbled.

Gently, he cupped her face in his hands and moved her so she had to look at him. 'Are you going to ask me what I want?'

And now he was moving her really outside her comfort zone. She didn't want to ask. She was too scared about what the answer might be.

'Ask me,' he said softly.

What choice did she have? Her pulse rate spiking, she asked, 'What do you want?'

'You,' he said softly. 'I want *you*, Stephanie. And I don't mean just having sex with you, much as I like that. I mean I want to be with you.'

She felt her eyes widen. He wanted her. Which meant taking things more seriously. 'You mean you want to move our relationship on to the next stage?'

He nodded.

Exactly what he'd suggested a few weeks ago. 'You want me to meet—' her mouth felt as if it was full of sand '—your family.'

'Yes. They're not like Joe's family. They won't judge you and find you wanting.'

'How do you know? I'm rubbish at families. I don't fit in.' She dragged in a breath. 'And how am I ever going to measure up to Meg? She was perfect.'

'No, Meg wasn't perfect,' he corrected. 'She was human. We had our fights, just like every other couple. I loved her deeply, and there will always be a part of my heart that belongs to her,' he said. 'But love isn't like a pie, Stephanie. You don't slice it up and suddenly there isn't anything left. It grows and changes with you.'

That wasn't her experience. At all. So how could she believe him?

'Stephanie, I'm not asking you to step into Meg's place,' he said gently. 'I don't want you as a substitute. I want you for *you*. I'm asking you to step into your own place in my family.'

Her own place. As part of his family. Was it really going to be that easy?

And did he really know his family that well? Joe had thought that his family would accept her, and they hadn't. What was to say that Daniel's family would be any different? Mia seemed to like her, but what if Stephanie was misreading the signals?

'I need to be honest with you.' It was the least he deserved. 'This absolutely terrifies me,' she said.

'Don't overthink it,' he said softly, and stole a kiss. 'I know what I'm asking scares you. Now you've told me what happened with your ex, I understand why. But this is different, and I'll be beside you every step of the way.'

Joe had made a similar promise. And he'd broken it. Even if Daniel meant well—and Stephanie was sure he did—how could he be so sure that he could keep his promise? How could he know that circumstances wouldn't change? And what if his family really didn't like her? She couldn't ask him to choose between them. She'd just have to back off. She'd lose, just as she'd lost last time.

'Mia likes you,' he said. 'Just in case you were worrying about that.'

She swallowed hard. 'But what you're talking about is different. It means being a mum to her.'

'She told me she wanted a mum,' he said softly.

Was that why he was dating her? Because he was looking for a mother for his daughter, not because he really wanted her? The questions must have shown on her face, because he said, 'That isn't why I asked you out.'

'So why *did* you ask me out?' She needed this spelled out. Preferably in words of one syllable.

'Because you drew me,' he said simply. 'You're the first woman I've actually noticed as a woman in four years. The first woman I've wanted to be with.'

And she wanted to be with him, too. But she couldn't get past the fear.

'I need to think about it,' she said again.

And it would be a lot easier to think straight if he wasn't holding her.

As if he guessed what she was thinking, he stroked her face. 'OK. I'll give you some space. As long as you promise to talk to me when you've worked out what you want. I mean *really* talk.'

She nodded. 'I promise.'

'So we'll talk about this again in, say, a week? Next Thursday night?'

She knew she couldn't make him wait indefinitely. And he was being more than patient with her. Given that this couldn't be easy for him either—he had Mia to worry about, too—the least she could do was agree. 'That's fair. A week.' Surely she'd manage to get her head together by then? 'We'll talk then.'

'OK.'

She slid off his lap, not trusting herself not to give in to the urge to ask him to stay with her, and he clearly took it as a sign that she wanted him to leave right now, because he pushed his chair back.

'I'll stay out of your way for now,' he said.

'I'm sorry, Dan. I wish I could be different,' she said. She wished she could stop herself being scared and let herself trust him. But she'd been there before and she'd had a hard time picking up the pieces when it had all gone wrong. She wasn't sure she could do it a second time.

'Don't apologise.' He brushed his mouth against hers in the sweetest, sweetest kiss, and she had a job to hold the tears back.

'Until next week,' he said. 'I'll see myself out.'

Just as he'd promised, he kept his distance over the next couple of days. It was what she'd asked for, so why did it feel so bad? Why was she missing him like crazy and worrying that, now he was giving her space, he'd change his mind about her?

'Daddy, when are we going out with Stephanie again?' Mia asked.

'Soon, darling.' He hoped. And it was so hard, giving Stephanie the space she'd asked for when all he wanted to do was to hold her close and make her realise how he felt about her.

'Aren't you friends any more?'

Out of the mouths of babes. Help. He'd tried to keep his worries away from Mia, but she'd clearly picked up that something was wrong. 'She's really busy at work right now,' he prevaricated. 'Like when I have to go in to make someone better and Nanna Parker or Nanna Connor comes to look after you.'

'Sometimes,' Mia said, her little face serious, 'I fall out with Ashley at school.' Her best friend, Daniel knew. 'And then we make up and we're friends again.'

Was his daughter giving him relationship advice?

He was torn between amusement and being deeply touched that she cared so much. And they were very wise words from all of her six years. He hugged her. 'I love you, Mia,' he said.

'I love you too, Daddy.' She hugged him back. 'If you fell out with Stephanie, say sorry. She'll say sorry, too, just like me and Ashley do. And then you can be friends again and we can go to Nanna Connor's firework party together.'

The party his parents held every year. So Stephanie would be meeting his whole family at once; he knew that would be a huge ask. 'We'll see, darling. She might have to work,' he said.

But when Mia was in bed that evening, the guilt kicked in. He had no idea whether Stephanie would give his family a chance, or if it would be too much for her—if her experience with Joe's family had damaged her too much to allow her to trust again. And, if she walked away, Mia would be so hurt. He sighed. He'd been an idiot. Rushed everything. He'd pushed Stephanie into meeting Mia before she was really ready, and now—thanks to his selfishness—his daughter could end up badly hurt.

Had he expected too much, thinking that Stephanie could fit into their lives? Thinking that she could put her past behind her and reach out to a future with him and Mia?

Maybe he should let her off the hook and call the whole thing off. Maybe that would be the fairest thing for all of them.

On Monday morning, Stephanie was on duty in the paediatric assessment unit. She was walking into the reception of the emergency department to call the next patient on her list when paramedics rushed past her with a trolley. She recognised the woman on the trolley as Della Goldblum.

What on earth had happened?

Marina Fenton came to meet the paramedics for the handover, and Stephanie heard the words 'beaten up' as they went down the corridor. Someone had punched Della? She thought of Della's partner, who was in prison for GBH. Had he been let out and discovered that the children were in care, blamed Della for it and then started using his fists to ask the questions?

Not that now was the right time to ask. Della wasn't

her patient; the children were. Even so, Stephanie was concerned. At the end of her shift, she went into the emergency department reception and asked quietly about Della.

'Are you treating her, Dr Scott?' the receptionist asked.

It was a reminder that this definitely wasn't her place, but she bluffed it out. 'I'm treating her children, and I wanted a quick word with her about it. Has she been discharged, do you know?'

The receptionist looked up the record on the computer. 'She's been admitted to the general surgical ward.'

'Right. I'll go and see if they'd mind me having a quick chat. Thanks for your help,' Stephanie said.

She knew the surgical ward had a strict no-flowers policy, or she could've taken Della something to cheer her up. As it was, she had to go empty-handed.

'Dr Scott.' Della looked bruised and tired; she was on a drip.

'What happened to you?' Stephanie asked softly.

'I ran into some of the neighbours.'

Stephanie felt her eyes widen. 'Your neighbours did this to you?'

'They heard the kids had been taken into care, about the fractures.' Della swallowed hard. 'They decided I was obviously a child-batterer and needed to be taught a lesson.'

Stephanie stared at her, shocked. Without any proof, the neighbours had delivered some rough justice. Mob justice. 'Della, that's so...' She shook her head. 'I really don't know what to say.'

'The doctor says I'm going to be in here for a while.

I've got broken ribs. She said something about flail chest.'

Work, not emotional stuff. Stephanie could deal with that. 'It means there's more than one break in at least two of your ribs, so the bone can move freely,' she explained. 'It affects the way your lungs expand when you breathe.'

'It hurts to breathe,' Della said. 'They've given me an epidural—like when I had the kids.' A tear trickled down her cheek. 'I miss them so much.'

'What did the doctor say?'

Della grimaced. 'I can't talk to him. They gave me an X-ray and he says I've got healed rib fractures. He decided it's because someone must've hit me hard enough to break my ribs at some time in the past, and because I've been battered that makes me more likely to hit my kids.'

Someone who'd been abused often turned into an abuser. Stephanie knew the theory.

Della dragged in a breath. 'But I've never hit them, never. And nobody's ever hit me until the neighbours jumped me in the corridor, and I've never had broken ribs. I'd know if I had broken bones, wouldn't I?'

Unless she had osteogenesis imperfecta. Brittle bones. In which case her tolerance for pain was much higher than the average person's. And in which case she must be in major pain right now, to need an epidural.

'I know my bloke's doing time for GBH, but he's never violent with me. He just lost it with the other guy. He knows he shouldn't have done it, and he's having anger management therapy while he's in prison.'

Stephanie felt guilty about the fact she'd jumped to a similar conclusion about Della's partner without knowing the facts. It made her almost as bad as the people who'd beaten Della up. 'Mmm,' she said noncommittally.

'I'll never, ever get my children back now, and I love them so much. I hate it that they're going to grow up without me. It's so wrong.'

She sat holding Della's hand while the woman sobbed, feeling helpless.

My mother must've been through something like this, she thought, lonely and desperate when I was taken away from her instead of being given the support she needed. Would Della end up making the same mistake and take her own life?

'Della, try not to cry like this. It's going to make your ribs hurt even more,' she said gently.

'I don't care,' Della sobbed. 'I don't care about anything any more. Not without my kids.'

How could she just stand aside and let that happen? 'I'll go and see if I can have a word with your doctor. Try not to worry. We'll sort something out.'

She went to find the doctor on duty, and glanced at his hospital identity badge.

'Can I have a quick word about one of your patients, please, Dr Hamilton?' she asked.

He frowned. 'Are you a relative?'

'No. I'm Stephanie Scott from the children's ward. I'm treating the children of one of your patients, and I think their cases might be relevant to her injuries. Della Goldblum.'

Dr Hamilton looked thoughtful. 'The woman who was beaten up.'

'And who *isn't* a baby-batterer,' Stephanie said firmly. 'Though her children have both been in with fractures.'

'So they're clumsy, hmm?' Dr Hamilton asked, sounding unconvinced.

'Can we go somewhere a bit more private to talk?' she asked.

For a moment, she thought he was going to refuse. Then he nodded and led her into an office. 'OK. So what's this about?'

'I know Della was beaten up, but the fact she's got so many fractures—it's not necessarily because of the force they used. And there are a few old fractures on her X-rays.'

'From past beatings,' Dr Hamilton said.

'She says not. And she can't remember ever breaking any bones. I don't think she's in denial—I think she's got a high tolerance for pain.'

Dr Hamilton frowned. 'This sounds as if you have a theory.'

Stephanie nodded. 'I think she has osteogenesis imperfecta. Daniel Connor in Maternity thinks it's a possibility, too. I did book a skin biopsy for the children to test the collagen, but as you know it takes at least six weeks to culture the cells. The results aren't back yet.'

'Did you order DNA tests?' Dr Hamilton asked.

Stephanie shook her head. 'They take at least three months, and I didn't think it would be that helpful. What I'm thinking is a DEXA scan—though obviously I couldn't order that on her because she's not my patient.' But Dr Hamilton could order it.

'OI. Hmm.' He glanced at his watch. 'It's too late to send her down to X-Ray now. But what you've just said makes a lot of sense to me. We'll get a DEXA scan done on Della tomorrow to check her bone density. If it *is* suspected OI, then we need to start physio and get her mobile as quickly as possible, because prolonged immobilisation can weaken the bones further and cause muscle loss.' He frowned. 'It worries me now that she's got an epidural so she can't move. I'll have to talk to her about different forms of pain relief. Obviously I can't leave her in pain, but if she has OI then we need to keep her mobile.'

Stephanie had geared herself up for a fight, and the fact that she didn't actually need to argue her case—that Dr Hamilton could make those same connections—made her feel suddenly weak at the knees. 'Thank you.'

'No, thank *you*. I didn't know about her kids having fractures, or it would've raised warning flags with me. The doctor who saw her this morning assumed the old breaks on the X-ray were because of...' He looked awkward. 'Well, domestic violence. We can't rule that out just yet, but we also need to confirm or rule out OI, so she gets the right treatment.'

'Absolutely.' Stephanie took a deep breath. 'Look, the children's ward has a liaison project running with the maternity unit, and it's really helping both of our departments. Maybe it's worth getting a few of the heads of department together and seeing if we can roll out the project between other departments, too.'

'To make sure we all have the information we need for our patients, you mean? Good idea.' Dr Hamilton smiled. 'I'll bring that one up at the departmental meeting next week and ask my head of department to talk to Rhys Morgan and Theo Petrakis.'

'Thanks. I, um, did say to Della that I'd see if I could have a word and get someone to bat for her.'

He nodded. 'I'll go and tell her what we're doing now.'

Insisting on being there wouldn't be fair; it would be interfering in another department, and Stephanie had no reason to doubt that Dr Hamilton would do his job properly. He certainly had a more open mind than the colleague who'd pigeonholed Della earlier. 'I haven't talked to her about a DEXA scan.'

'Don't worry. I'll explain what we're doing and re-assure her,' Dr Hamilton promised.

'Thank you.'

Stephanie walked home, thinking about how ripped apart Della Goldblum was without her children. It was painfully close to how Stephanie herself felt about not having a family. She'd tried not to let it bother her, but deep down she knew it always had. Was there some-thing unlovable about her? Why had she never managed to be part of a family?

And that made her question her feelings for Daniel. Did she want him because she wanted to be part of a family—exactly what he was offering her—or because she wanted him?

She had to be honest with herself and admit that it was both. But primarily she wanted Daniel. She wanted to be with him.

'Daddy, have you made it up with Stephanie yet?' Mia asked.

'We haven't fallen out,' Daniel replied, feeling guilty because he knew he was being economical with the truth. But it was complicated, and it was too much to expect a six-year-old to deal with.

'I miss her,' Mia said.

So did he. 'I'll see her soon, darling.'

'You could text her,' Mia persisted.

He smiled. 'Maybe later.' And not when his daughter was around. Because she'd want to know what Stepha-nie said, and he wanted to have enough time to work out how to deal with things.

He was halfway through cooking dinner when his phone beeped to signal an incoming text message.

Do you want to bring Thursday night forward?

She was ready to talk? Hope leaped in his veins.

Where and when?

Tonight. Mine. Dinner?

Oh, hell. He didn't want to knock Stephanie back, especially if she was going to tell him that she'd give his family a chance, but he couldn't just drop everything, either. He texted back.

Cooking dinner for Mia right now.

There was a long pause, and he thought maybe she'd backed off again, when his phone beeped.
Tomorrow night, if you can get a babysitter?

I'll be there. Half seven?

There was another long pause, and then another message:

Perfect.

Daniel was antsy all the next day. Dinner, she'd said. If she was going to call a halt to everything, she wouldn't suggest dinner, would she? Then again, how well did he know her?

His stomach was in knots by the time he rang her doorbell.

'Hi. Come up.' She buzzed him in and met him at her front door.

He handed her a bottle of wine. 'I wasn't sure whether to bring red or white, so I played it safe.'

She looked at the bottle. 'I love Chablis. Thank you—and it goes well with what I'm cooking. Actually, I should've asked—do you like fish?'

He smiled. 'Even if I didn't normally, I would tonight.'

She frowned at him. 'Dan, if you don't like fish, I can cook something else. There are other things in my fridge.'

'No, fish is fine.'

'And I'm being a bit lazy. It'll be literally five minutes until dinner.'

He raised an eyebrow. 'You're telling me you bought it from the supermarket?'

'No. I'm cooking. But fast food doesn't have to mean junk.'

'Says the foodie,' he teased.

For a moment, she thought he was going to kiss her. But he didn't. Had he changed his mind about her? No. She was being paranoid. He wouldn't be here if he didn't want to be. He was giving her space, not trying to bulldoze her.

And she loved him for it.

Her knees went weak as the thought registered. *She loved him.*

She busied herself with the food, just to stop herself thinking. Scallops in lime and chilli butter served with quinoa, steamed tenderstem broccoli and asparagus. She'd made pudding earlier: white chocolate mousse with raspberries. And although they chatted easily over dinner, both of them avoided the real issue.

Until she'd made coffee. Then Daniel asked, 'So are we going to talk about the elephant in the room?'

She took a deep breath. 'That's why I texted you yesterday. I was talking to a patient yesterday and it made me think about what I really want.'

He gave her a very intense look. 'What do you want, Stephanie?'

This was where she should come straight out with it. But fear made her check. 'Honestly?'

'Honestly.'

OK. She could do this. She could tell him. 'I want *you*. You, and Mia.' She dragged in a breath. 'But I'm so scared it's going to go wrong, Dan. I messed it up before. I can't afford to do the same again—there's not just you and me to think about. There's Mia. I don't want to hurt her.'

'I know. I want you, too,' he said. 'And it scares me just as much. I lost someone I loved very much and it was a random accident. There was nothing I could have done to stop that. But if I spend the rest of my life trying to wrap everyone I love in cotton wool, it'll drive me crazy and them even crazier. I just have to trust that lightning doesn't strike twice.' He paused. 'Actually, I might as well tell you the truth.'

'Truth?' Oh, help. Was he going to say now that he'd changed his mind?

'I love you, Stephanie.'

She stared at him, hope brimming over. 'You love me?'

'You make my world a better place,' he said simply. 'And I haven't been this happy in years.'

'Neither have I. And that scares me, too. How can I be sure that this is real—that it will last?'

'You can't. You just have to trust.'

'Which is a lot easier said than done,' she said dryly.

'I know. If it makes you feel any better, it scares me, too. Especially as I don't know how you feel about me.'

She hadn't told him? She stared at him in surprise. 'I love you, too, Dan.'

He came round to her side of the table then, and drew her into his arms. Kissed her. Yet it wasn't demanding; it was full of sweetness and tenderness. Giving, rather than taking.

She was shaking when he broke the kiss.

'What's wrong?' he asked softly.

'Too many mixed-up emotions in my head.' She swallowed hard. 'The biggest one being fear.'

'Of what?'

'Letting you down.' Just like she'd let Joe down.

'You're not going to let me down.'

'How do you know?'

'Because I trust you.' He stroked her face. 'I think you need to trust yourself, Stephanie. I know your ex's family pretty much trampled your confidence in yourself—but they were totally wrong about you. You trust yourself at work, don't you?'

'Of course I do. It's my job.'

'And you can bring exactly the same qualities to a family as you do to work,' he said softly. 'Kindness. Caring. Listening.'

She felt the tears well up. 'What if your family doesn't like me?'

'That's highly unlikely,' he said. 'Mia adores you. She's missed you.'

'I missed her, too.' She held his gaze. 'And you.'

'Good.'

'But what if the rest of your family doesn't feel the same way?' she persisted.

'Then we'll cross that bridge when we come to it. And there's really only one way to find out.'

Meet them. The thing she'd been holding back on. It didn't look as if she had a choice any more.

'What's going to be easier for you?' he asked. 'Meeting them all together, or keeping it small—say, meeting Lucy first, and then my parents?'

'Right at the moment, it's all one big, scary blur,' she admitted.

'OK. We'll tackle Lucy first. The next time we're both on a late, we'll meet her for coffee in her lunch break.' He kissed her lightly. 'It's all going to be fine. I promise you, my family's nice. And I don't break my promises.'

All she had to do was believe. Or at least *try.*

She took a deep breath. 'OK. Next time we're on a late. Friday morning?'

'That works for me.' He held her close. 'Thank you. I promise you won't regret it.'

She just hoped he was right.

CHAPTER THIRTEEN

THE NEXT MORNING, at work, Dr Hamilton called Stephanie about Della Goldblum's DEXA test.

'You were right. There are more X-rays and slight bowing of the long bones, some vertebral compressions, and her bone density is definitely not as good as it should be—her T-score is minus two.'

Stephanie had researched it and knew that meant Della's bone density was much lower than that of a normal, healthy person whose bone mass was at its peak; anything above minus one was fine, but anything below minus two was heading towards osteoporosis.

'I think you're right about the OI and we need to be really careful how we manage this,' he said. 'I don't want Della to be in pain, but I also don't want her immobilised with an epidural, so we'll need to look at a different form of pain management.'

'Thanks for letting me know,' Stephanie said. 'I'll set up a meeting with the social worker, because that's also going to affect the way the children are cared for. Obviously we still have to wait for the collagen results to prove that the children have it, too, but this is a pretty good indication of the way things will go.'

She'd stuck her neck out over this one, and she was

so glad she had. Della's family stood a real chance of being able to stick together and be happy.

Just before she was due in clinic, her phone shrilled again.

'Sorry, me again,' Dr Hamilton said. 'I know it's not your department, so strictly speaking I shouldn't even ask you this, but Della's asking if you'll be here while we talk about her condition. You're the only one she seems to trust.'

'Probably because I'm the only one who's listened to her, until you,' she said. 'Look, I have clinic now, but I'll come down on my break. Is it OK if I see you in a couple of hours?'

'That's great. Thanks.'

'Are you on duty tomorrow?' she asked.

'Yes.'

'It's my turn to be a bit cheeky,' she said. 'I have a meeting set up with the social worker tomorrow afternoon to discuss the children. Given that you're treating Della, it might help if you were there.'

'OK. I'll be there,' Dr Hamilton promised.

After clinic, Stephanie went over to the general surgical ward.

'Thanks for coming, Dr Scott,' Dr Hamilton said.

'We're colleagues, so I think we ought to be on first-name terms by now. I'm Stephanie.' She smiled at him.

'Ross.' He smiled back. 'Let's go and see Della.'

Della was lying in bed, clearly not feeling up to anything, but her face brightened when she saw Stephanie. 'You came.'

'Of course. Dr Hamilton here can explain a bit more

about your condition than I can, but if you have any questions just ask,' Stephanie reassured her.

Ross Hamilton quickly explained about osteogenesis imperfecta. 'Basically it's a type of brittle bone disease and it's genetic, so your children have a fifty per cent chance of inheriting it from you.'

'Is it definite?'

'Not until we get the test results back,' Stephanie said. 'But, given they've both had fractures, my guess is that they have it, too.'

'If I'd known…' Della swallowed hard. 'I don't wish my kids away—of course I don't. I love them so much. But I hate myself for giving this to them.'

'You weren't to know,' Dr Hamilton said. 'It's only if you come to hospital to have a fracture treated and we do tests that you find out about the condition.'

Della bit her lip. 'So what does this mean for the kids? Can you cure it?'

'No, but we can manage it,' Dr Hamilton explained. 'As Stephanie said, at the moment we don't know for sure that they have it, but given that they've both had fractures it's a very strong possibility. We have to wait for the test results.'

'How long will that take?' Della asked.

'A few weeks, I'm afraid,' Stephanie said.

'Physiotherapy and exercise can help, and swimming's very good,' Dr Hamilton said. 'They might need surgery later; if they end up with a lot of fractures in their legs and arms, we can put a metal rod into the long bones to help manage that.'

'It's not going to affect their ability to think or to learn, and they can lead a pretty normal life with friends and a family,' Stephanie reassured her. 'We just need to try to minimise the risk of fractures.'

'And we can put you in touch with a support group,' Dr Hamilton added.

'It's pretty much business as usual, though you need to be careful how you hold the baby and change him—I mean his clothes as well as his nappy,' Stephanie said.

Della looked anxious. 'The foster-parents need to know about this. I don't want him getting hurt.'

'We'll talk to them,' Stephanie promised. 'I have a meeting with social worker tomorrow so we can make sure they understand more about the condition, and Dr Hamilton is going to be there to back me up.'

Hope flared in Della's face. 'Does this mean they'll let me have the children back?'

The big question. Stephanie took a deep breath. 'Your diagnosis is proof that they were wrong about you. And I'll certainly bat for you.'

'Me, too,' Dr Hamilton said. 'We'll do our best for you, Della.'

'Thank you—both of you,' Della said. A tear trickled down her cheek. 'I thought I'd never get to see the kids again.'

'We're still not quite out of the woods,' Stephanie said. 'But we'll fight this to the top, if we have to.'

If only she had the same confidence about her personal life as she did about her private life, she thought wryly. Though that wasn't Della's problem, it was her own. And she needed to deal with it.

On Friday morning, on the way to meet Daniel's sister at the café, Stephanie felt physically sick. This was where it could all go wrong. Badly wrong.

Daniel laced his fingers through Stephanie's and squeezed gently. 'Stop worrying. This is going to be fine.'

'Uh-huh.' She knew he meant well, but she still couldn't stop the panic. Kitty hadn't liked her. What if Lucy didn't like her, either? She was pretty sure that Daniel was as close to Lucy as Joe had been to Kitty.

'Lucy knows you're worried about this and that you had a hard time with your ex's family,' Daniel said gently. 'Obviously I haven't told her any details—what you told me was in strict confidence and I won't break that—but I thought it only fair to let her know that there was something worrying you.'

'I guess so.' She took a deep breath.

He frowned. 'You're shaking.'

'I know I'm being a coward. This is way outside my comfort zone.'

'If you didn't know she was my sister—if you met her at a party or something—I think you'd become friends.'

Joe had been so sure that she'd be great friends with Kitty, and he'd been wrong. Was Dan just as blinkered where his sister was concerned? Or was she worrying over nothing?

'Let's go and sit down,' he said when they reached the café. 'I'll bring you a coffee.'

'Flat white, please.' If nothing else, it would give her something to do. Something to distract her from this horrible, horrible waiting. Something to distract her from the feeling of impending disaster.

Every time the door opened, Stephanie looked up, wondering if it was Lucy. But she was almost halfway through her coffee when a woman with the same dark hair and stunning blue eyes as Daniel walked in.

Daniel raised a hand in greeting, and Stephanie felt the adrenalin seep through to her fingertips. This was it.

The woman walked over to them, greeted Daniel with a hug, then held her hand out to Stephanie. 'Hi. I'm Lucy. Nice to meet you.'

Stephanie shook her hand. 'Nice to meet you, too.' It wasn't a total fib; she just didn't say that the whole thing terrified her. 'Can I get you a coffee?'

'Dan can do that.' She shooed her brother in the direction of the café's counter, then sat down at the table next to Stephanie. 'Thanks for agreeing to meet me. I know this must be pretty intimidating for you.'

'Dan told you about me.'

'Not much—but I'm in a similar situation. I've been seeing Jeff for a few weeks and we're getting to the point where we ought to introduce each other to the family, except I know his family really liked his ex, and it worries me they'll think I'm the only reason why Jeff and his ex aren't getting back together,' Lucy confided.

'Ouch, that's a tough one.'

'Mmm, particularly as he didn't tell them the real reason they broke up. He didn't want them to say anything about it accidentally in front of his son. You'd think that they'd work it out for themselves, given that Jeff has custody, but...' She grimaced. 'They blame him. Even though she was the one who had the affair and walked out.'

'That's hard on him—and on you.'

'Yeah.' Lucy took a deep breath. 'So hopefully, by me telling you that, you'll realise that I'm not going to judge you, because I'm secretly terrified of Jeff's family judging me too and deciding I'm not good enough.' She smiled at Stephanie. 'No doubt you're worrying about Meg, too. For what it's worth, yes, we all adored Meg, but it's not good for Dan to be alone. And I for one am glad he met you. It's nice to see him smile a bit more and look less lonely. Plus Mia told me all about you. As a primary school teacher, I know that kids tend to be good judges of character.'

The same, Stephanie knew, as being a paediatrician.

And then suddenly it was easy.

By the time Daniel came back with the coffees, Stephanie had relaxed enough to chat to Lucy, discovering they had shared tastes in books and music.

Finally, Lucy glanced at her watch. 'I have to be back at school. Stephanie, if we'd met for the first time at a book club or an exercise class, we would've become friends. I hope you can ignore the fact I'm Dan's sister and we can be friends.'

'Yes. I'd like that,' Stephanie said.

'Good.' Lucy hugged her. 'We'll do something girly together. Without Dan. I've got to rush back now, but get Dan to give you my number and call me. I mean it, Stephanie. Call me.'

'I will,' Stephanie promised, and meant it.

She and Daniel had time to linger for a bit longer until their shift was due to start.

'So was it as bad as you were expecting?' Daniel asked.

'No. She's nice,' Stephanie said. 'And you were right. If we'd met somewhere else and I didn't know she was your sister, we would've made friends.'

'She's not like your ex's sister?' he checked.

'No. I never had that kind of easiness with Kitty, not

even in the few weeks when she did seem to soften a bit towards me.' She bit her lip. 'Actually, Dan, this does feel a bit too good to be true.'

'It isn't,' he said softly. 'Just believe. In yourself as well as in us.'

Could she take the risk? Could it really happen for her, this time, and she'd fit in?

On Friday afternoon, Ross Hamilton joined Stephanie for the meeting with the social worker. This time, to her relief, the social worker listened to their concerns and promised to talk to the foster-parents.

On her break, she visited Della. 'So has Dr Hamilton told you the good news?'

'They'll let me keep my kids?'

'The children will stay in care while you're in hospital,' Stephanie said. 'And if the tests show that the children have OI, then your case is proven and the children will be back with you.'

'Will the tests show it?' Della asked.

Stephanie smiled. 'I'm pretty sure they will.'

Daniel arranged to meet his parents for lunch in a nearby café, the following Tuesday.

'I know you're going to worry about this,' he said to Stephanie, 'but please give them a chance and don't assume they're going to be like your ex's family. Give it half an hour, and if you're still totally uncomfortable, I'll get you out of there. I'll do a fake call to you from the hospital so you can say you have to rush back, and I'll go with you, OK?'

'Thank you.' She gave him a rueful smile. 'I feel a bit pathetic. And mean, expecting you to give me a let-out like that.'

'It's understandable, given your past experience—but, remember, you got on fine with Lucy. You'll get on with my parents too.'

'Do they know?'

'That your in-laws have made you wary?' He nodded. 'I didn't go into detail. But I thought they needed to know why you're a bit antsy about meeting them.'

'Fair enough.' She squeezed his hand. 'I will try, Dan.'

'I know. And that's all I ask.'

Daniel's parents were already waiting for them in the café. Stephanie wasn't sure if she was relieved because it meant she wouldn't have to wait and worry or panicky because she still felt unprepared for this.

Daniel introduced them swiftly. 'Mum, Dad, this is Stephanie. Stephanie, these are my parents, Hayley and Neville.'

'Pleased to meet you,' Stephanie said politely, and held her hand out to shake theirs in turn. Both had warm, firm handshakes. Please, please, let them be like their son, she thought.

Trying to ignore the rush of fear, she sat down.

'Dan, Nev, do you want to go and sort out the drinks?' Hayley asked with a smile.

Oh, help. This meant she was going to be on her own with Dan's mother. Then again, it had been fine when she'd been on her own with Lucy. She just had to trust Dan on this.

'Thanks for coming to meet us,' Hayley said.

Stephanie bit her lip. 'I'm sorry. You must think I'm really odd.'

'No. Dan obviously wouldn't break any confidences, but he did say that your in-laws were nightmares. Anyone would be wary after an experience like that.' Hayley smiled at her. 'I'm lucky. My mother-in-law was great. But my best friend's mother-in-law was a monster— she always made quite sure that she was the centre of attention. She would've tried the patience of a saint.'

'Ouch.' Stephanie looked at her. 'May I be honest with you?'

'Yes, of course.' Hayley looked slightly worried. 'What is it?'

'If you're uncomfortable with what I'm about to tell you, then tell me when I've finished and I'll back away from Dan.'

Hayley nodded. 'OK.'

Stephanie took a deep breath. 'Just to be clear, I'm not asking for sympathy. I'm just telling you the facts. I grew up in care. My mum was very young when she had me, and she found it hard to cope. The authorities took me away, but being without me was too much for her. Shortly after that she took her own life, leaving me parentless. And I guess I slipped through the net when it came to adoption. So I'm—well, not used to being in a family. I'm not very good at it.'

'Is that why your in-laws gave you a hard time?' Hayley asked.

'It wasn't all their fault. I can understand why. Of course they'd wonder what it was about me that had put people off.'

'More like you had a difficult start in life, and you've done remarkably well to get past that and train in such a caring profession. If I can be just as honest,' Hayley said, 'I think your in-laws needed a kick up the back-side. They sound narrow-minded and petty, and you're well rid of them.'

Stephanie stared at her, not sure what to say. She really hadn't expected Hayley to come down so firmly on her side. Especially when they'd barely met.

Hayley reached over to squeeze her hand. 'You're the first woman Dan's dated since Meg was killed, and it's the first time I've seen the smile reach his eyes without being damped down by worry in a very, very long time. Mia never stops chatting about you. So, as far as I'm concerned, I'm more than happy to welcome you into his life. And I know Meg's parents feel the same way.'

That was even more shocking. Surely Meg's parents wouldn't want anyone taking their daughter's place? 'You've talked about it?' Stephanie asked, her voice scratchy with nerves.

'We're friends—and, yes, we've talked about it. We were worried about Dan because he'd pretty much shut himself away from the world. But we knew something was going on because he'd started to smile again and he's more relaxed with Mia. He's not so panicky that he's doing something wrong or that something's going to happen to Mia and he'll lose her, the same way he lost Meg.' Hayley squeezed Stephanie's hand again. 'And that's thanks to you. We owe you.'

'Of course you don't. I'm nothing special,' Stephanie said.

Hayley smiled. 'And the fact you can't see it for yourself…that makes you even more special, love.'

Unquestioning acceptance. Stephanie was almost too stunned to believe this was happening. She'd wanted it so badly from Joe's family, tried so hard, and got nowhere. Now it was being offered by Dan's family. Unconditionally.

Maybe she could have the family she'd always wanted. All she had to do was accept it.

Over lunch, Stephanie discovered that Neville was as warm and accepting as Hayley. He had a dry sense of humour and a nerdy streak that she really appreciated.

And when it was time to leave for the hospital, Daniel's parents hugged her warmly. 'I hope we'll see you again very soon,' Hayley said.

'I'd like that,' Stephanie said, hugging them back.

Daniel didn't say a word when they walked to the hospital. And she knew he was waiting for her to tell him what she thought.

In the end, she gave in. 'OK. You were right. They're lovely.'

He lifted both hands in a gesture of surrender. 'I'm not saying a word.'

'You're dying to say "I told you so", aren't you?' she teased.

'Well just a little bit.' His eyes crinkled at the corners. 'I'm glad you liked them. And they liked you.'

'I'm glad.'

He stood outside the hospital entrance. 'So does that mean we're officially an item now, Dr Scott?'

In answer, she reached up and kissed him. 'I don't care if the hospital grapevine talks about us. They'll soon find something else to talk about.'

Her reward was the brightest, brightest smile, and another kiss.

Katrina Morgan smiled at Stephanie as soon as she walked onto the ward. 'Hi, there. Are you OK to do the handover?'

'Sure,' Stephanie said, smiling back.

It didn't take long to go through the cases.

And then Katrina leaned back and folded her arms. 'I hear that a certain blue-eyed obstetrician has been seen with you.'

'Lunchtimes? That's to do with Rhys's pet project,' Stephanie said.

'I'm not sure Rhys gave you instructions to kiss the man silly outside the hospital entrance this afternoon.'

Stephanie felt her face flame. 'Um.'

Katrina just grinned and patted her hand. 'I'm teasing. Seriously, it's good that you and Dan are an item. He's a nice guy—and he's more than overdue a bit of sunshine in his life. As,' she added perceptively, 'I think you might be, too.'

'Maybe. It's early days.' Stephanie tried to play it down.

'Even so. You've looked happier lately. Now I know why. And I'm glad for both of you.'

CHAPTER FOURTEEN

OVER THE NEXT couple of weeks, Stephanie found herself growing closer to Daniel's family. Lucy talked her into going to a Pilates class with her, and Hayley met them both for a coffee afterwards.

'You should come with us, Mum,' Lucy said with a smile. 'It'd be really good for you.'

'I'll stick to walking the dog,' Hayley said. 'Right—bonfire night. Stephanie, we always have a bit of a party for Mia, with fireworks in the back garden and then food after. She's probably already badgered you about it, but will you come this year?'

'I, um—well, if you're sure.'

Hayley rolled her eyes. 'Love, I wouldn't ask you if I didn't want you there. Are you on duty, or can you swap?'

'Is that Bonfire Night itself, or the nearest Saturday?' Stephanie asked.

'Bonfire Night. I'm doing pulled pork this year, with Boston beans and jacket potatoes.'

'Can I bring something?' Stephanie asked. 'I have this great recipe for toffee-apple cookies. I've promised Mia for ages that we'll make them together.'

'Perfect,' Hayley said with a smile. 'Dan will pick you up.'

'And you'll get to meet Jeff,' Lucy said. 'He's bringing Mikey.'

Hayley looked slightly awkward. 'I normally invite Meg's parents, too. Will you be all right with that?'

'That's fine,' Stephanie fibbed.

'They're looking forward to meeting you,' Hayley said, and squeezed her hand. 'They know we like you, and I promise it's not going to be difficult for anyone.'

To Stephanie's surprise, she discovered that the Parkers were just as welcoming as the Connors. And she enjoyed herself hugely at the party, holding Mia's hand while the men took turns in lighting the fireworks, and joining Hayley, Lucy and Hestia in the kitchen to help serve the food.

'Those cookies are awesome,' Lucy said after the first mouthful. 'Next school fundraiser, I'm *so* going to be begging you to make these for us.'

'Any time,' Stephanie said, meaning it.

'So was it OK?' Daniel asked afterwards, when Mia was tucked up in bed and Stephanie was sharing a glass of wine with him.

'More than OK. Obviously I've been to bonfire parties before, but they've always been work things. I've never done the fireworks in the back garden thing. And I loved it.' She smiled at him. 'Meg's parents were nice. I can't believe they were so sweet to me.'

'The Parkers are lovely,' he said. 'Actually, Hestia had a quiet word with me when I was helping with the dishes. She said she approves of you, and thinks Meg would've liked you a lot.'

Stephanie had to blink tears away. 'I still wonder if

I'm going to pinch myself and wake up. This is almost too good to be true.'

He leaned over and kissed her. 'Believe me, it's real all right.'

By the middle of November, Christmas preparations were everywhere; the lights in Oxford Street had been turned on and the shops were full of tinsel and presents. Every ward in the hospital had made arrangements for bran-tub Christmas presents, and the children's ward had organised Rhys to come in on Christmas morning as Santa, to deliver presents from the Friends of the London Victoria for the in-patient children and their brothers and sisters.

Was this Christmas going to be her first truly happy Christmas? Stephanie wondered.

'What are you doing for Christmas?' Daniel asked.

'I'm on duty,' she said. She'd slipped into the habit fairly soon after marrying Joe, as a way out of spending the day with his family. 'What about you?'

'I'm going over to Mum and Dad's with Mia,' he said. 'If you'd like to join us, that'd be lovely.'

'Thanks, but, um...'

He sighed. 'I was hoping you felt more comfortable around my family now.'

'I know—and I honestly am.' And she knew it was ridiculous to fear that Christmas would be when everything changed—when she found out that she didn't really fit in after all, and it really was too good to be true.

'OK. I won't nag,' he said, and she was relieved to change the subject.

Until she had lunch with Lucy and Hayley.

'So are you coming to us for Christmas?' Hayley asked.

Oh, help. 'Dan said something, didn't he?' she asked.

'Well—yes,' Hayley admitted. 'I have to admit, I just assumed that you'd be coming. We'd love you to be with us at Christmas.'

'But, just in case you think we're just being nice,' Lucy said, 'we do have an ulterior motive.'

'Which is?'

Lucy gave her a hug. 'Don't look so worried. I'm teasing.'

As usual, Stephanie had misread the cues. Why couldn't she get it right?

'Well, ish,' Lucy continued. 'We've heard that you're the departmental quiz queen, and we really want you on our Trivial Pursuit side so Dan and Dad have to eat humble pie for the first year ever. So you have to come for Christmas. We need you. Desperately.'

'You're really sure about this?' Stephanie asked.

'Really,' Hayley assured her.

'Jeff and Mikey are coming,' Lucy added, 'so you won't be the only one there for the first time.'

'It's really kind of you to invite me, but I'm working on Christmas Day,' Stephanie said. 'I thought it was only fair to let the people with children spend the day with them.'

'That's not a problem,' Hayley said. 'We can have Christmas dinner in the evening instead of at lunchtime.'

Stephanie looked at her, horrified. 'You don't have to change things for me.'

Lucy punched her arm. 'Steffie, have you ever considered that we might want to?'

'Oh—well, no,' Stephanie admitted.

'Are we railroading you?' Lucy asked.

Stephanie wrinkled her nose. 'I'm not very good with families.'

'You are with ours,' Hayley reminded her. 'What's really worrying you?'

She sighed. 'There were strict traditions at Joe's parents' house.'

'Such as?' Hayley asked.

'When you were allowed to open presents, what you had to eat and when—and they always ended up in a kind of huddle round the sofa, talking about Christmases past.'

'Excluding you?' Lucy asked perceptively.

'I don't think they meant to, exactly,' Stephanie said, trying hard to be fair. 'It was just how it was.'

'Well, it's not like that in our house,' Hayley said. 'Yes, there are some things we do traditionally but traditions are supposed to grow and change with you.'

Stephanie gave a noncommittal murmur.

'Your ex-in-laws have a lot to answer for,' Hayley said dryly. 'Well, you're part of us now, and we want you there for Christmas. It won't be the same without you.'

Stephanie knew when she was beaten. 'Is there anything I can do to help?'

'No, just be there,' Hayley said.

'Though, if you want to make cookies, we won't say no,' Lucy added.

'Cookies it is,' Stephanie said. 'And Mia can help. She loves baking.'

'Daddy's sad,' Mia confided to Stephanie. 'He's always sad today.'

'Why?' Stephanie asked carefully.

'Because it's Mummy's anniversary. He always takes

her flowers today. And that's why Auntie Lucy was supposed to bring me home from school. 'Cept she had a
'mergency meeting, and Nanna Parker's sad today, and
Nanna Connor's visiting her sister in Scotland…'

'And that's why Lucy rang me to see if I could pick
you up?' Stephanie said.

Mia nodded. 'Will you help me make Daddy smile?'

Stephanie sat down and scooped the little girl onto
her lap. 'I'll try. But sometimes you can't help being
sad when you miss someone, and today's the day he'll
miss your mum.'

'I don't really remember her now,' Mia said. 'But
I know what she looks like, because we have photos.
Lots of photos.'

'That's good,' Stephanie said, a lump forming in
her throat.

'Do you have a day when you miss your mum?' Mia
asked.

'I do,' Stephanie said. 'I take her flowers, just like
your dad takes your mum flowers. It's in April, when
the daffodils are out.'

'I like daffodils,' Mia said. 'Yellow flowers are happy
flowers.' She frowned. 'But they won't make Daddy
happy.'

'We could make him something special for tea,'
Stephanie said. 'A pizza with a smiley face on it.'

'Brilliant,' Mia said. 'And you make him happy. He
smiles a lot more.' She hugged Stephanie. 'You make
me happy, too.'

Stephanie had to blink back the tears.

'Are you crying?' Mia asked, looking shocked.

'Happy tears,' Stephanie said. 'Because you and your
dad make me happy, too.'

She spent a while making a pizza from scratch with Mia and letting the little girl decorate it. And she quietly texted Daniel to let him know that she was looking after Mia and he wasn't to worry about anything; she'd stay as long as he was needed.

Daniel turned up half an hour later, when Mia had had a bath and talked Stephanie into reading three stories to her.

He hugged her. 'Thanks for being here.'

'Any time.' And she meant it. She'd loved every second of looking after Mia. And today had shown her that she really could connect with the little girl, be there for her when she was sad and explain things to her so she felt better. That maybe, just maybe, she could be the mother Mia clearly wanted.

Daniel made the effort to be excited about Mia's smiley-face pizza, and when Mia was in bed—after three more stories read by Stephanie—he poured them both a glass of wine.

'Are you sure you don't want me to go?' she asked. 'I know what today is.'

'I'm sure.' He held her close. 'Knowing I was coming home to you and Mia—that made a real difference to me. It's made today less bleak. It still hurts, but I'm finally healing. And that's all thanks to you.'

She stroked his face. 'Hardly. I come with just as much baggage.'

'I hate this time of year,' he said. 'And I guess it's the same for you.'

'When you have to be all smiley-smiley because it's Christmas, and everyone's getting excited about parties, and all my patients are getting excited about Father

Christmas…' She nodded. 'But it's not quite as hard this year. Thanks to you and Mia.'

'I can never face decorating the house until after today,' Daniel said. 'It doesn't feel right doing it before then. But this weekend Mia and I always go to choose a tree. Come with us?'

Choose a tree. Something she'd never, ever done—because Joe had always insisted on having an artificial tree rather than a real one. A tree that wouldn't shed needles or look scruffy at any point. And he'd insisted on keeping the tree he'd bought the year before he'd met her, so she'd had no part in choosing a tree or any kind of decorations.

'I'd like that,' she said. 'Very much.'

On the Saturday morning, Stephanie went with Mia and Daniel to choose a Christmas tree, then spent the afternoon at their house, helping to decorate it.

'Have you already decorated your tree? 'Mia asked.

'Um, no—I don't have one,' Stephanie admitted.

Mia frowned. 'Why not?'

Oh, help. She didn't want to upset the little girl with the real reason: she hadn't bothered with one since the divorce because it had seemed pointless having a Christmas tree just for one. 'I haven't had time to buy one,' she hedged.

'We could help you buy one,' Mia said, looking hopeful.

'I…' She gave in. 'OK.'

'Tomorrow?'

'If your dad doesn't already have plans.'

Daniel came back in to overhear the last bit. 'Plans for what?'

'Finding a Christmas tree for Stephanie,' Mia said.

He smiled. 'That's fair enough. You helped us with ours.'

Mia hugged her. 'That's settled, then.'

Stephanie couldn't help smiling; she could hear Lucy and Hayley so clearly in Mia's voice. 'It's settled,' she agreed.

Mia was thrilled to help choose not only the tree but the decorations, too. They spent half the afternoon putting the decorations on the tree, and Stephanie lifted her up so she could put the angel on the very top.

'You've done a fantastic job. Thank you so much,' Stephanie said, and kissed the tip of Mia's nose.

Mia stared at her, then put her arms round Stephanie's neck. 'You kissed me.'

'Is that OK?' Had she gone too far?

Mia nodded. 'But you only kiss people you love.'

'Ye-es.'

'I love you,' Mia said, and kissed the end of Stephanie's nose.

And Stephanie had a huge lump in her throat as she whispered, 'I love you, too.'

The little girl fell asleep on the sofa not long afterwards, clearly tired out. Stephanie gently put a blanket over her.

'I ought to get her home,' Daniel said.

Stephanie shook her head. 'Don't wake her just yet, Dan.' She paused. 'Well, now I have a tree, I really ought to have a Christmas party.'

'The three of us?' he asked.

'I was thinking, is it too late to ask your family over for Christmas Eve?'

'That's a great idea,' Dan said. 'Call them.'

'What, now?'

He smiled. 'Yes, now.'

By the time she'd ended the call, he was smiling. 'I think half of London must've heard the shrieks of glee from Mum and Lucy.'

'It's only a party,' Stephanie said lightly. 'A simple buffet. Lucy's bringing a pudding, and your mum's bringing chocolates to go with the coffee.'

He looked slightly worried. 'Are they taking over?'

'No,' she said softly. 'They want to feel part of it. And they want me to feel that I'm—well, part of the family.'

'You *are* part of the family.' He kissed her lightly. 'And I'm proud of you. That must've been hard.'

'Baby steps,' Stephanie said. And, with Daniel and Mia by her side, they were easier than she could ever have imagined.

CHAPTER FIFTEEN

A FEW DAYS later, Daniel and Stephanie took Mia to see Father Christmas.

'Now, young lady, what do you want Father Christmas to bring you this year?' he asked.

The little girl beckoned him closer. 'I want a mummy for Christmas,' she whispered.

'But isn't that your mummy and daddy there?' he whispered back.

'No, just my daddy. My mummy's in heaven.'

'But you'd like someone to be your mummy?'

'I want Stephanie,' she said simply. 'Daddy loves her and so do I. I know she loves me. I just want her to love Daddy, too, and get married.'

'I'll see what I can do,' Father Christmas said. 'For now, my elves made this especially for you.' He handed her a parcel. 'Merry Christmas. Ho, ho, ho.'

'Merry Christmas, Santa,' Mia said.

But when Mia joined Daniel and Stephanie, Father Christmas beckoned Stephanie to him. 'Can I have a quick word?' he asked.

She stared at him, surprised. 'Sure. Daniel, I'll catch you and Mia up in a second, OK?' She turned to Father Christmas. 'Is something the matter?'

'Not exactly.' He sighed. 'I'm not supposed to do

this—but it's Christmas and I've got a daughter a couple of years younger than your little one. And if this is my chance to do a real Santa thing and give someone the present they most want in the world, I'm taking it.'

Stephanie blinked. 'What did she ask you for?'

'A mummy for Christmas,' he said.

'Oh.' Her breath caught. 'That's what she said?'

'She says her dad loves you and so does she. She just wants you to love her dad and get married.'

Stephanie blew out a breath. 'For Christmas. Right.'

'Sorry if I've spoken out of turn. I didn't mean to offend. But—well, what she said touched my heart.'

Stephanie smiled at him. 'You haven't offended me at all. And thank you. Now I know what she's thinking. And her dad and I definitely need to talk about this when she's asleep.'

'Good luck,' he said. 'And Merry Christmas.'

'You, too,' she said.

'So what did you want to talk to me about?' Daniel asked, once Mia was asleep.

'Father Christmas,' she said.

He frowned. 'I'm not with you.'

'Mia told him what she wanted.' She paused. 'She wants a mummy for Christmas.'

He grimaced. 'One of her friends just got a new stepmum. Don't feel pressured. It's probably a phase.'

'No. She, um, wants me,' Stephanie said softly, and told him what Father Christmas had told her. 'I think she's accepted me, Dan.'

'More than accepted, I'd say. She loves you. My whole family loves you,' he said.

And the fact that she'd told him all this instead of keeping it to herself gave him hope. Maybe now she

was ready to put the past behind her. 'And she's right. I
love you.' He stroked her face, 'I probably should wait
and do this in a much more romantic place than my living room, but…' He dropped to one knee. 'Stephanie,
you make me happy and you make my daughter happy,
too—will you marry us?'

Her eyes filled with tears, and he knew she wasn't
going to say yes.

'I need to think about it, Dan,' she said quietly.

Because she was still worried it would all go wrong?

He wondered if he was ever going to be able to help
her over that last hurdle. He could believe in them and
trust that they would stay together and she wouldn't
be taken from him like Meg was. So why couldn't she
trust that he wouldn't put her last, the way her ex had?

'OK. Think about it,' he said. 'But know that I love
you, Mia loves you, and we're not giving up on you
any time soon.'

Stephanie thought about it.

And thought some more.

And thought about it even more on the train back
to Manchester, where she'd arranged to visit Trish to
swap Christmas presents.

Trish met her at the station with a warm hug, and
drove them back to her house. But it wasn't until Calum
had an afternoon nap that Stephanie finally spilled the
beans.

'Dan asked me to marry him.'

'What? That's fantastic!' Trish whooped. 'I get to
be maid of honour, right?'

'I haven't said yes.'

'Why? Are you insane?' Trish asked. 'All right. Let's

take this slowly. Dan loves you and wants you to marry him. Mia wants you to be her mum. Yes?'

'Yes.'

'Is that what you want?'

Stephanie bit her lip and nodded.

Trish hugged her. 'Steffie, you have to let the past go. From what you've told me about Dan's family, they're lovely. They're nothing like Joe's lot.'

'I know,' Stephanie said in a small voice. 'But there's just something inside me that panics.'

'You think that because your mum had to give you up and you were never adopted, there's something wrong with you—that you're not lovable?' Trish asked softly.

'It's crossed my mind a couple of times,' Stephanie admitted.

'More like, you've been brooding about it. You idiot.' Trish hugged her again. 'You really need to talk more and worry less. Your mum loved you, but she was too young to cope. Her parents—well, they weren't real parents, were they? All they thought about was their social standing, and they would've made you unhappy.'

'I know that.'

'And as for Joe—nobody would've been good enough for him, in his parents' eyes. And Joe himself didn't have the backbone to stand up for you when he should've done.' She paused. 'What would Dan have done, in his shoes?'

'Stood up for me,' Stephanie said. 'But he wouldn't have been in that situation, because his family like me.'

'Like you?' Trish pushed.

'Love me.' Stephanie sighed. 'And I love them. I love Mia. I love Dan.'

'All you have to do is say yes. That's what you want isn't it?'

Stephanie nodded. 'But I've given Dan such a hard time. He's opened himself up despite losing his first wife in such tragic circumstances. And I've pushed him away. I've let the past get in the way.'

'So make it up to him,' Trish said with a grin. 'Are you seeing him tonight, when you get back to London?'

'No. It'll be late when I get back.'

'Doesn't matter. Surprise him,' Trish said.

Stephanie thought about it all the way home on the train.

Surprise him.

Yes, she could do that. Prove to him that she believed in him and she believed in their future. But she'd need a teensy little bit of help.

She grabbed her mobile phone and called Lucy. 'I need to meet you and your mum for a drink,' she said.

'Why?'

'Because I need to talk to you about something—oh, and please don't breathe a word to Dan.'

'This,' Lucy said, 'sounds like a plot. I'm intrigued. OK. The wine bar round the corner from my flat, tomorrow at seven. We'll be there waiting for you.'

'Thanks, Lucy. I really appreciate it.'

Just as Lucy had promised, she and Hayley were at the wine bar. They waved to Stephanie as soon as she walked in.

'Don't keep us in suspense any longer,' Lucy begged.

'OK.' Stephanie told them about Father Christmas. 'And Dan asked me to marry him,' she finished.

Lucy hugged her. 'Fantastic—I get a sister!'

Hayley hugged her, too. 'And I get another daughter. I'm so pleased for you both, sweetheart.'

Stephanie bit her lip. 'I feel like the meanest woman on the planet. I, um, haven't said yes.'

Lucy looked shocked. 'Why not?'

Stephanie took a deep breath. 'Because I'm stupid and stubborn and scared.'

'Do you love him?' Hayley asked.

'I do. I asked him to give me some time to think about it. But I really think I need to show some faith in him. I need to show him what he means to me. And I was thinking about it all the way home from Manchester yesterday.' She outlined her plan. 'Do you think that would work?'

'That's just lovely,' Lucy said. 'And I think Mia could keep a secret this big. You're going to tell her, right?'

'She's going to be my wing woman on this—well, wing girl,' Stephanie said. 'And you're both sworn to secrecy.'

'More secrets,' Hayley grumbled, but she was smiling. 'This is going to be the best Christmas ever.'

'Why can't I come in?' Daniel asked plaintively in the kitchen doorway on Christmas Eve.

'Because this is woman's work,' Mia said, with her hands on her hips. 'And you're not a girl.'

Stephanie just about managed to stop herself laughing. 'I'll bring you a cup of tea and a sandwich,' she promised. 'But Mia's right. You have to stay out of the kitchen.'

Mia gave her a high five. 'He won't be cross any more when he sees them,' she said in a stage whisper, indicating the cupcakes that they'd been decorating together.

They finished decorating the cakes and arranged

them carefully on a platter. Then Stephanie covered them, just in case Daniel decided to sneak into the kitchen. She didn't want him seeing them until she was ready.

'You,' she said to Mia, 'are the best helper ever.'

'And you,' Mia said, 'are a brilliant cook. We're a good team.'

They were, Stephanie thought. And that included Dan.

She helped Mia get ready in a pretty party dress, and painted her nails the same colour as Mia's.

'That's perfect,' Mia said with a broad smile.

Daniel was kept busy answering the door and letting everyone up to the flat. And when everyone was there, Mia said, 'It's time.'

'Time for what?' Daniel asked.

'Stephanie's got something to ask you,' Mia said importantly.

He frowned. 'What?'

Together, Stephanie and Mia lifted the cover from the cakes. 'Dan, you need to read this,' Stephanie said softly. 'And this is why we wouldn't let you in the kitchen this afternoon.'

He read the message iced onto the cupcakes—a different letter on each one.

Will you marry me?

The lump in his throat was so big that he couldn't speak at first. He could hardly believe that she'd done this. It was a public declaration of love, in front of all the people closest to him. He'd been so sure that she'd be too scared to accept his proposal; since she'd asked him for time to think about it, he'd backed off.

And now she was asking him.

'I asked you first,' he said shakily. 'You're not supposed to answer a question with another question.'

She smiled. 'That's my answer. I love you, Daniel Connor.'

And all the shadows, all the fear in her eyes, had gone. 'I love you, too.' He wrapped her in his arms. 'Yes. I'll be proud to marry you, Stephanie Scott.'

'And I'll be your flower girl,' Mia piped up, 'with Aunty Lucy and Stephanie's best friend Trish as your bridesmaids.'

Clearly, Dan thought, Mia and Stephanie had been discussing this. They'd probably even started planning colours and dresses and flowers.

His girls.

His family.

Lucy said, 'I think this calls for champagne.'

'Funnily enough,' Hayley said, 'we brought some.'

The smiles on their faces told him that they'd known all about this, too. Stephanie had been confident enough to let them in on her plans. Accepted them as her family. Taken her place, right in the middle of everyone.

'Santa's given me what I really wanted,' said Mia. 'A mummy for Christmas.'

Stephanie smiled. 'And I get what I really want, too. All I've ever wanted. A family of my own. The best family in the world...'

* * * * *

CHRISTMAS EVE DELIVERY

BY
CONNIE COX

MILLS & BOON

First published in Great Britain 2013
by Mills & Boon, an imprint of Harlequin (UK) Limited.
Harlequin (UK) Limited, Eton House, 18-24 Paradise Road,
Richmond, Surrey TW9 1SR

© Connie Cox 2013

ISBN: 978 0 263 89925 2

Harlequin (UK) policy is to use papers that are natural, renewable and recyclable products and made from wood grown in sustainable forests. The logging and manufacturing process conform to the legal environmental regulations of the country of origin.

Printed and bound in Spain
by Blackprint CPI, Barcelona

Dear Reader

Best wishes for a great Christmas holiday season!

Do you ever wish for your very own cowboy? Nurse Practitioner Deseré Novak left New Orleans for East Texas wishing for a job, not the jingle of spurs. Dr Jordan Hart, in his jeans and boots and hat, could give her both if she was only brave enough to open her healing heart as well as her healing hands.

But she has her hands full, carrying the *in vitro* child within her to full term and avoiding the man who would take that child from her, without adding the further complication of a strong, silent cowboy into her life. Especially a cowboy who refuses to open up to her about the guilt he has carried for too many years—the guilt that keeps him from living and loving to the fullest.

Jordan wants what is best for his patients. That's why he hires Deseré Novak—so she can give the people of Piney Woods what he can't: compassion and care. While he can competently treat their physical illnesses, he avoids the emotional aspect of their cases. How can he help them when he can't even help himself?

But Dr Jordan Hart can't avoid the joy Deseré adds into his days, or the dreams she adds to his nights. And when he starts to care for her, to love her, he can't avoid wanting to be a better man, a whole and healed man—both for her and for her unborn child.

All the characters in this novel are fictional and are not reflective of anyone living or dead.

Connie

DEDICATION

This one's for you, Deseré Steenberg!
Here's to strong men and the brave women who love them!

Recent titles by Connie Cox:

WHEN THE CAMERAS STOP ROLLING...
HIS HIDDEN AMERICAN BEAUTY
THE BABY WHO SAVED DR CYNICAL
RETURN OF THE REBEL SURGEON

CHAPTER ONE

DESERÉ WEDGED HER car into a parking place between a dual-axel diesel truck and a huge silver horse trailer as red dust swirled around her. East Texas dust.

So different from New Orleans pavement.

She put her hand over her stomach. New town. New life. "Here's to us, baby James. To our future." She hefted the bottle of milk she'd purchased at her last gas and restroom stop, toasted her sister's unborn baby and chugged.

Reinforced by lukewarm milk, she gathered her purse along with her courage and opened the door.

The sultriness of the heavy, humid air hit her hard. One step behind was the scent of pine trees and the odor of horse manure.

The pine trees had towered over her as she'd travelled down the unpaved road leading to the rodeo arena. In the dusk, those tall skinny evergreens appeared imposing, like sentinels warning her that she wasn't in the big city anymore.

For the baby's sake, she wouldn't let this alien landscape intimidate her.

"Everything will be just fine." She said it out loud to force conviction.

A gaunt, stooped cowboy with a weathered straw

hat shadowing his leathered face stopped on the way to his truck.

She knew he drove a truck even though she didn't know which one. She knew it had to be a truck because she had the only car in the parking lot.

He put two fingers to the brim of his hat and nodded before asking, "You okay, ma'am?"

"I'm fine. Thank you."

The old man gave her a strong look, half-wary that she might be crazy talking to herself and the other half suspicious of the overdressed stranger in their midst.

She tried to reassure him with the brightest smile she could muster after eight hours of driving with all her worldly goods crammed into her little compact car.

"I'm fine, really."

He glanced at her stomach as if he knew. How could he? She was only four and a half months and had barely begun to show.

She was being fanciful. A fleeting look of no consequence was all it had been.

Working hard to shrug off her supposition, she blamed it on her sensitivity to the situation. On hormones. On paranoia from lack of sleep.

He couldn't know her secret.

Because if he did, the man she had driven all these hundreds of miles to find would know, too. And then where would she be?

She couldn't even think about a near future that bleak.

He had to say yes. There was no other option.

She'd called in the only favor she had and it had been a weak one. A doctor she'd once dated. A relationship that hadn't worked out. What were the odds of that wildcard making the difference?

The odds were already stacked against her and her chances plummeted if the cowboy she was looking for realized she was pregnant.

In her open-toed sandals, she picked her way across the ruts cut into the dried mud and scarce grass sprigs that made up the entrance in front of the arena. Dusky shadows made the short distance seem treacherous.

Ringed by a tall wooden fence, the arena was hidden from her. Looking up, she could see only the glare of the tall lights and the wash of bodies in the stands. Cowboy hats on everyone's heads made each person's features indistinguishable from each other.

How would she ever find him?

With only nineteen dollars and twenty-nine cents in her wallet, she had to find him. She could sleep in her car again, but she needed a few gallons in her gas tank to keep her car rolling and a decent meal to keep the baby healthy.

Her stomach chose that moment to growl. Except for her daily dose of midmorning nausea, her pregnancy kept her continually hungry.

She circled the arena, looking for an opening into this world of rodeo that personified testosterone, muscle and mastery of will.

Carefully, she skirted the hitching posts where horses were tethered with only thin strips of rope or single leather reins. Didn't these monsters know they could pull away with only a shake of their heads?

How far could they kick? A protective hand over her stomach, she gave them wide berth.

Pulling out her thin wallet, she prepared to pay admission, whatever it cost. She had no other choice.

"Excuse me?" She stopped a young girl in perfect make-up, painted-on jeans, embossed boots, long blonde curls and rhinestones in the band of her white cowgirl hat.

"Yes, ma'am?"

Another "ma'am." This time it made her feel more old than honored.

Giving the girl the last smile she had in her, Deseré asked, "Where's the entrance and how much is the entry fee?"

The girl gave a kind, sympathetic glance at her inappropriate tailored slacks, silk blouse and strappy sandals before she waved toward the end of the wooden fence. "All the events are free to watch. Just go right on in. But watch your step, okay?"

Deseré looked down to where the girl pointed. She'd missed a huge pile of horse droppings by scant millimeters.

"Thanks."

As she minced her way toward the stands, she had to get a bit too close for comfort to the massive horses that were either tied to the backs of the stands or were being ridden in various directions from the barns to the arena.

No one else seemed concerned as the tons of muscle on delicate hoofs pranced by so close.

So this was Friday night in Piney Woods, Texas.

"We're definitely not in New Orleans anymore," she whispered to the baby nestled in her womb.

As she approached the full stands, several rows of observers started scooting over, packing themselves in tighter as they made room for her.

One of the cowboys on the end stood. He gave her an appreciative, if curious once-over as he touched the brim of his hat. "Please, ma'am, have my seat. I'll stand."

"Thank you." Instead of sliding onto the hard wooden

bench, Deseré took a deep breath. No turning back from here. "I'm looking for Dr. Hart."

"Jordan will be first one out of the gate as soon as we get started again." He drew his brows together in concern. "You're not needing him, are you? Do I need to go and fetch him for you?"

It was more the other way around. She was hoping—counting on—Dr. Hart needing her. If he didn't, she didn't know what she would do.

Almost on instinct, her hand moved to cover her abdomen. At the last moment she diverted it to the strap of the purse slung across her body.

"No emergency."

"After his ride, I'll tell him you're waiting for him." He waved her toward his vacated seat on the bench. "Best seat in the house."

"Thanks."

"Rusty." He touched his hat again. "Folks call me Rusty."

He left the introduction hanging with his expectant look. What would it hurt to introduce herself?

"Deseré."

"Nice to meet you, Miss Deseré."

Miss Deseré. She knew, even if she'd been wearing a wedding ring that was bigger than Dallas, Rusty would have called her "Miss" as a sign of respect. Among the gentlemen she knew in New Orleans, it was a sign of respect there, too.

The familiar custom eased the tension across her shoulders by the slightest of muscle twitches.

Before she could return the nicety a loudspeaker boomed, "Up next is Jordan Hart, points leader for this event."

Distantly, she heard a deep voice call out, "Cowboy up."

She looked in that direction, to see a calf burst from a narrow chute into the arena. Hot on its heels was a cowboy on a very large red horse.

With only the slightest flick of his wrist, Dr. Jordan Hart unfurled his rope. The stiff loop shot out and fell neatly over the neck of the running calf.

His horse stopped short, jerking the calf to a standstill.

Quicker than she could comprehend, Jordan slid out of his saddle and began taking big strides toward the snared calf as his horse backed away without direction to keep the rope taut, with its end looped around the saddle horn.

He grabbed the calf, tipped it onto its side and wrapped three of its four legs using the short ropes he'd carried in his mouth.

Once done, he threw his hands in the air. Another man looking official with his stopwatch and mounted on a horse that stood as still as a statue called, "Time," as he nodded to someone in the speaker's booth next to the complex structure Rusty had called "*the gate*."

A smattering of applause broke out from the stands. Deseré couldn't help but notice that most of the cheering came from the women and girls, all dressed similarly to the first girl Deseré had met.

If those were his type of women, then she definitely didn't fit his mold.

Not that she needed to be Jordan Hart's type.

She just needed his money.

As Jordan loosened the cinch on his mare, he saw his cousin and ranch foreman, Rusty, approach him.

"Nice run, cuz." Rusty gave Jordan's mare a rub on her neck. She leaned into it, clearly enjoying his touch.

"Thanks."

"Jordan…" Rusty hesitated. "Are you expecting to meet a woman here tonight?"

He quirked his eyebrow at his cousin's cautious question. "No, I'm not."

"Well, there's one waiting for you on the bleachers."

She wouldn't be the first buckle bunny to approach him. Under the brim of his hat, he checked her out.

In her city clothes, she certainly wasn't dressed for a rodeo pickup. He couldn't be sure as she was slumped on the bench, arms tightly wrapped around her huge purse, but he thought she might be five feet seven or so to his six one. Tall enough to kiss without getting a crick in his neck.

Where had that thought come from?

And the accompanying spark in his veins?

At first he was jolted by it. But by his second heartbeat he welcomed it. It had been so long since he'd felt even a flicker of interest.

Gently blowing on that internal ember, he continued to examine her.

Her mink-brown hair shimmered in the bright overhead lights as it fell to her shoulder blades. It was the perfect length. A man could tangle his hands in that silky softness as they lay together, but the length wouldn't get caught underneath her when they tangled arms and legs.

Jordan let that image grow, reveling in the way his nerve endings seemed to be waking up.

Hope. He'd despaired of ever feeling that emotion again.

She moved her purse, revealing the way she filled out her blouse.

No model-skinny skeleton here.

Ample.

Just the way he liked them.

A flame of interest burned through the apathy he'd been living in these last months.

It felt good, and not just in his groin.

Want. Desire. The burning sensation in the pit of his solar plexus was a very good thing.

Need.

Not so good. He didn't need anyone.

"She said she was looking for Dr. Hart. When I pointed you out, she didn't seem to recognize you. Do you know her?"

Jordan shook his head. "Nope."

"Got any suspicions?"

Jordan ignored his cousin's curiosity, giving a strong stare at Rusty's bronc-riding vest instead. "You sure you want to do this?"

Not that Jordan didn't want to climb on a bucking bronc himself. Only, as the older cousin, he felt duty-bound to make a token protest after Rusty's last unsuccessful ride and consequent fall.

He refrained from rubbing his hand over his face.

He felt so old lately. And so numb.

"It's what we do, right?" Rusty shifted under Jordan's gaze. "Get thrown. Get right back on."

Jordan shook his head. "Until you get smart enough to realize you don't have to prove anything to anybody."

Unwanted sympathy showed in Rusty's eyes. "I guess you've had enough adrenaline rush to last a lifetime, huh?"

Jordan tightened his lips, neither confirming nor denying it.

He was supposed to be recovering from too much living on the edge. How could he admit to anyone that without that infusion of fight-or-flight-induced chemical his life was gray and deadly dull, bordering on meaningless?

His mare nudged him, clearly jealous when he should be paying attention to her. She didn't need words to make herself clear.

Absently, he reached up to scratch behind her ears. "No need to worry, Valkyrie. You're my best girl."

Rusty punched Jordan in his shoulder.

Jordan welcomed the pain to bring him back to himself.

"That's your problem, cuz. You've got women driving all the way out from who knows where to find you and you'd rather keep company with your horse." Rusty gave him a serious stare. "Get thrown. Get back on. That's what we do."

"Or wise up and learn I don't have to prove anything to anybody." With conviction, Jordan repeated his earlier statement, knowing neither he nor Rusty were talking about anything close to bull riding.

Rusty jostled him. "I'll say this about that city girl you brought us a few years ago. She tried. She really tried. You must have been doing something right for her to stay so long."

"What I was doing right was being a doctor. She was really impressed with that."

He ignored the worried look in Rusty's eyes and forced a grin to lighten the moment as he answered, "When she found out the only store within a fifty-mile radius was a combination feed store/hardware store/

boot shop with a smattering of jeans, hats and pearl button shirts to choose from, she quickly become disillusioned with small-town living."

Forcing those smiles was getting harder and harder.

"That was it? The lack of fancy department stores?" Rusty wasn't the first to try to pry out more information.

But a gentleman didn't kiss and tell. Jordan might not have a lot left going for him, but he was determined to keep his dignity.

He gave a self-deprecating shrug. "She loved boutiques more than me. I've learned to live with it."

"And you've had plenty of offers of companionship from the buckle bunnies to sooth any man's ego."

Jordan had to admit he'd taken advantage of enough of those offers that his ego should be well soothed.

But afterglow didn't last much past sunrise, did it?

He stole a quick glance at the woman in the stands. Should he recognize her?

"Old history." He leaned into Valkyrie, taking comfort in how the mare supported his weight. "I've grown up a bit since then."

As his shoulder throbbed where Rusty had punched him, he felt much older than his years.

Between the physical exertion he'd been doing to try to exhaust himself enough to sleep and the tossing and turning he'd done once he finally forced himself into bed, his bones hurt to the marrow.

Add that to his clinic schedule that had him working over sixty hours a week and he was starting to feel trapped in a dark tunnel as the light of the freight train bore toward him faster and faster.

What were the odds of finding a nurse practitioner who could take some of his load from him?

Over the loud speaker, the announcer called Rusty to the gate.

Jordan squared his shoulders. "Good luck."

"I don't need luck. Just a bull that wants to buck. Skill will take care of the rest." Rusty gave him a cocky grin then strutted toward the gates.

He watched his younger cousin with envy. What would it be like to feel alive again? To feel the blood rush through his veins? To feel his heart beat fast and his mind flash with lightning-quick thoughts? To feel a connection with another human being?

Although he tried to stop himself, he couldn't stop from glancing over at the woman staring intensely at him as if she were looking inside his head.

What did she see?

He pulled the brim of his hat lower and turned away, determined to ignore the feeling of being evaluated.

CHAPTER TWO

DESERÉ TOOK HER time studying Dr. Jordan Hart. Under cover of this crowd, there was no way he would notice a single pair of eyes trained on him. That she kept thinking he was glancing in her direction was purely her imagination as she never caught his eye, even though she tried.

He stood at least six feet one or two. His cowboy hat and boots made him look even taller. With his hat pulled low, she couldn't make out the color of his eyes or hair, but thought they might both be dark brown.

He was rangy with a stringy kind of muscle that would make his movements graceful.

As he shifted his weight, the chaps he wore emphasized his package. Modestly, she tried to look away, but her raging hormones wouldn't let her.

Something about being pregnant had kicked her libido into high gear. Whether it was because she no longer needed to worry about an accidental pregnancy or a release of hormones gone wild, or something else entirely, she couldn't tell for sure. She just knew that she was noticing men even more than she had during her intensely boy-crazy teenage years.

And she didn't want just sex. She wanted to be touched, petted, protected.

How many nights had she gone to sleep lately, pretending that her fantasy lover lay next to her, that he wrapped his arm around her and pulled her close, his big hand over her slightly softening belly?

Keeping this baby she carried hadn't been the original plan. But, then, the plan hadn't been for her sister to die, either.

Deseré pushed down her grief and straightened her spine. She was a survivor. Always had been. And always would be—especially now with her son to care for.

Her son.

Get a grip, Deseré. That's what her sister would have told her if she were here. *We do what we have to do to survive.*

That's what her sister had told her ten years ago as Deseré, acting as maid of honor, had arranged her sister's wedding veil so Celeste could walk down the aisle into the arms of the rich and powerful neurosurgeon who would provide for them both.

Deseré had thought that being a surrogate for Celeste would make up for some of the sacrifices her older sister had made for her. And it had, until Celeste had run a red light while talking on the phone and had crashed into an oncoming eighteen-wheeler.

Even though Deseré knew it was too early, she imagined baby James moving deep inside her.

She would do more than survive. She would build a happy, healthy life for her son and for herself.

In the indigo sky, the first star appeared opposite the fading sunset. Feeling foolish, she made a wish. *A miracle. Just a little one. Just a chance to prove myself, okay?*

A feeling of *be careful what you ask for* washed through her.

She shook it off. Fanciful and unrealistic things had no place in her practical world.

The reality was that everyone would say the politically correct thing. They would say her pregnancy didn't matter in her job hunt.

But the truth was no one wanted to hire a woman who would need time off to have a baby, not to mention time out of her workday for the morning sickness that struck like clockwork at ten a.m. each and every morning.

In less than a month her pregnancy would be evident. But by then she'd have had the job long enough to show her competence, long enough to make herself indispensable.

Her stomach lurched as she thought of how badly she needed this job.

With great willpower she stopped herself from staring at the man who could give her a safe, secure future.

Surely, her sister's husband, the great Dr. Santone, didn't have influence over every sleepy little town in Texas, did he?

What would a small-town country doctor care that a big-time surgeon who sat on the board of the largest hospital in Louisiana would be heartily upset if his sister-in-law found a job in the medical field?

Gathering her purse and slinging it over her shoulder, she pushed off the bench, remembering at the last moment to watch where she stepped as she walked toward Dr. Jordan Hart.

Feeling self-conscious, she looked up in time to see he was watching her every step of the way.

A challenge? Why?

Under the wide brim of his hat his eyes were too shaded by the darkening night skies to read. But his lips, so full and rich only a moment ago, were now set tight and grim.

"Dr. Hart?" Deseré called out.

"Just Jordan, ma'am." Automatically, Jordan touched the brim of his hat, not even thinking about it until he saw her eyes follow the movement of his hand.

She held out her hand. "Deseré Novak. Your new nurse practitioner."

Not a rodeo groupie at all. But she *was* an assertive little thing, wasn't she?

Dr. Wong's recommendation had seemed to contain a lot more between the lines than in black-and-white.

Dr. Wong hadn't exactly said she'd worked for him. The letter had been carefully worded. What Dr. Wong had said was that Deseré Novak deserved a chance.

So Jordan would give her one. But he'd only promised an interview.

Or did she think Dr. Wong's recommendations carried that much weight with him? Jordan was a man who made up his own mind about things.

"You're early for your interview. We didn't expect you until Monday."

She gave him a smile. "I thought I'd check out the place first."

"Makes sense." He put his hand in hers. "Thanks for coming to Piney Woods. I know we're a long way from New Orleans."

Her grip was firm. No-nonsense. Assertive. With just enough give to suggest hidden softness.

Ms. Novak's eyes flicked in worry before bravado had her lifting her chin. "I've already researched your practice. I'm sure it's perfect for me. You won't be sorry to hire me."

If Jordan hadn't noticed the slight quiver he would

have been fooled into thinking she was totally confident that she had the job.

It wasn't that he'd had any better-qualified applicants. How many experienced nurse practitioners wanted to move out to the edge of nowhere, taking room and board as a significant portion of their pay, when they could be pulling in the big bucks in any major city?

"We'll talk about it in the morning." He gestured to the open arena, still and quiet between events. "I've got other things going on tonight."

She stood still waiting for—for what?

Something about her stillness made him notice the dark circles under her eyes.

"The closest hotel is back toward Longview about two hours away. You may want to head in that direction before it gets much later."

She shook her head, shaking off his suggestion. "I understood room and board would be part of the deal. If you could point me toward this boarding house, maybe I could stay the night?"

"Boarding house." Jordan's smile was so tight it made his mouth hurt, way too tight to be reassuring, he was sure. "I guess, in a way, it is."

His office administrator had drawn up the job description.

It would be just like Nancy to gloss over the details to get what she wanted.

And what she wanted was a local medical facility for the folks of Piney Woods, solving two problems at once. The town and surrounding ranches would have good medical attention.

The loudspeaker blasted over the explanation he was about to give to clear up his office administrator's oversight.

Like everyone else in the stands, he turned to the gate to see his cousin poised over the back of a snorting and twisting bull.

Bull riding was a young man's sport. Rusty was getting too old for this.

But, then, his bullheaded cousin would probably realize that in the morning when he was too stiff to roll out of bed.

Jordan had been there, done that, got the belt buckle—and the scars—to prove it.

The woman next to him winced as she saw Rusty drop down onto the wide back of the bull.

Rusty settled in—as well as a man could settle onto the back of an angry bull—and gave a sharp nod.

The gate opened, the bull rushed out, and Jordan silently counted in his head, *one second, two seconds, three—*

And Rusty was off the bull and on the ground.

The rodeo clowns rushed in to distract the twenty-five-hundred-pound, four-legged kicking fury so Rusty could roll away from the dangerous hoofs.

Jordan squinted through the falling light, looking for that first twitch that said Rusty was going to catch his breath, jump up and walk out of the arena any second now.

"Come on, Rusty, shake it off," he murmured, as if saying it would send his cousin into action.

Dust hung in the air, as time stood still.

Rusty didn't move.

But the woman next to Jordan did.

She rushed toward the arena, looking like she intended to climb through the iron-pipe fence separating her from the bull.

Without thought, Jordan reached out and pulled her close to him.

"No." It came out harsh and uncompromising. It had been meant to. He'd been trained to give orders that were followed without question. He'd had too much practice to break the habit now.

There were a lot of habits he needed to work on breaking—like waking up in a cold sweat every night from his murky, twisted memory dreams. And jumping every time the barn door slammed closed, sounding too much like metal exploding.

And getting an adrenaline rush when he pulled a woman close to him to protect her from a non-existent danger.

Of course, she wasn't intending to go over the rail into an arena with an enraged bull running loose. Who in their right mind would?

His stomach sank as he had a surge of doubt in his ability to judge a situation. His instincts, which had always served him so well, might be a tad on the twisted side now.

A tad?

Still, he held her tightly pressed against his body as she struggled to get free, something deep inside him telling him to hold on tight and not let go.

Under other circumstances Jordan would have tried to defuse the situation by making a joke at his own expense, along with an apology as he sheepishly laughed off his rash and inappropriate behavior.

But his cousin lay facedown in the dirt, too still for too long, and Jordan had no words, much less a laugh.

"Let me go." She struggled against him. "Can't you see he needs help?"

Maybe his instincts weren't as far off as he'd thought they were.

Jordan gave a quick glance at the clowns as they herded the bull through the gate. One more second to make sure they latched it tight.

Then he let her loose, moved around her to put one boot on the top rung and vaulted over the fence racing toward Rusty with too many dire diagnoses running through his head for him to think straight.

As he knelt by his cousin's side, Deseré knelt on the other side. Had she gone over the top, too? Or squeezed between the rails? Did it matter? All that mattered was Rusty, lying so still. He was never still. But now...

Jordan felt frozen, inside and out.

Deseré was on her hands and knees, her silk shirt and slacks getting filthy as she tried to assess Rusty's state of consciousness.

Oh, God. Jordan thought it as a prayer, as cold dread started in the pit of his stomach, making its icy way to his heart. He hadn't even considered that Rusty might be...

"Unconscious," she said, her voice clipped.

She put her hand on Rusty's back, noting its rise and fall.

"Breathing," she reported.

Jordan nodded, realizing he'd been holding his own breath. Vacantly, he gazed down at his cousin's body, trying to get his own breathing regulated.

Worn, dusty boots stopped next to Jordan's knees. Jordan didn't know and didn't care who they belonged to.

With creaking knees Plato squatted down and touched Jordan's elbow. "Emergency Dispatch says the ambulances and paramedic crews are tied up. A truckload of teenagers tried to beat a train across the tracks. They don't know how long it will be. Do we need a chopper?" His calm voice, steady rheumy eyes and familiar wrinkled face piercing Jordan's fog.

Jordan tried to make the words make sense. The only thing getting through to him was that Rusty lay still, too still.

He put his hand on Rusty's back, willing him to take another breath.

"Dr. Hart?" Deseré prompted. "Authorize air transport?"

She nodded her head in the affirmative, giving him an obvious hint as to what his answer should be.

Jordan squeezed out a reply. "Yes."

How long had it been between the time Rusty had hit the ground and now? It seemed like hours. Or years. But it could have only been minutes. They would have called emergency services immediately, right?

His brain seemed to be thawing—finally. He was applying logic and making assumptions. Now he needed to apply that brain to Rus—to his patient. Thinking of his cousin as his patient would help him put some distance between his panic and his personal pain.

Vacantly, he noted that Deseré was positioning herself flat on her stomach, almost nose to nose with Rusty, something he should have already done.

"I'll stabilize his head while you check for spinal injuries," she said, stirring the churned-up dirt of the arena with her breath.

Jordan noted her technique. Thumbs on collarbone, fingers behind shoulders, Rusty's head firmly supported on her forearms. She definitely knew what she was doing.

She would be stuck like that until the emergency

crew arrived with their cervical collar and backboard and trained crew to whisk Rusty to the hospital in Longview, the closest trauma center but still twenty-five minutes away by air.

If the last ten minutes had seemed to be a decade, the next twenty-five would pass like centuries.

The way Deseré lay flat on her belly with her arms extended, holding Rusty tight to keep him immobile, breathing in the thick red dust, each minute must be torture.

Running his hands over Rusty's head then down, he started to check his cousin's spine carefully.

No weird angles. But that didn't mean much after the unnatural contortions Rusty's body had gone through while airborne.

As he got to mid-back, Rusty stirred.

"Tickles," he complained, as he tried to lift his face from the dirt.

But Jordan put one hand firmly on his lower hips and the other high on his back to hold him firmly in place.

"Be still," he growled, not caring about his lack of bedside manner.

"Can't. Back muscles are cramping."

"You can and you will. Be still while I finish checking to see if anything's broken."

Rusty lay still, as ordered.

Distantly Jordan noticed that his voice sounded fierce and uncompromising. Distantly, he also noticed his hands were following the correct path, searching for injuries.

Distantly. As if he was watching himself from a place not here, not now. As if his heart and soul weren't even connected to his mind or body. As if this wasn't his one and only cousin who he'd grown up with, shared camping trips with, shared double dates with and had left behind when he'd enlisted so the army would pay for his education all those years ago.

"Can you feel my hand on yours?" Jordan steeled himself to hear the wrong answer, going into total thinking mode and leaving no room for mind-clouding emotions like fear.

"Yeah, I can."

Holding his relief at bay, Jordan touched Rusty's other hand then both his calves above his boots. As Rusty gave an affirmative to each touch, Jordan felt his emotions continue to detach themselves.

Stoicism and survival—at least mental survival—went hand in hand. It was a lesson he'd apparently missed during his time in medical school but had discovered quickly enough for himself while in the field. Combat conditions had made him a fast learner.

In a meek, scared voice, Rusty asked, "Jordan, am I okay?"

"Just checking you out, Rust Bucket." From that place far remote from him where he'd left his emotions, Jordan knew calling his cousin by his detested nickname would be reassuring. Until the hospital's helicopter arrived, soothing the patient was all he could do.

The patient. Jordan lumped Rusty in with the thousands of patients he'd treated. He wouldn't allow himself to connect, wouldn't allow himself to care. Not here. Not now.

Maybe that other Jordan, the one who seemed so far away from him right now, was caring. But all this Jordan felt was numb. And efficient.

Being efficient was critical.

Maybe later he could feel.

Or maybe later would never come.

CONNIE COX 29

But none of that mattered right now.

Finally, after he'd lost count of the breaths he'd begun to count in and out, he heard the helicopter land in the dark clearing where someone had set out flares.

As the paramedic crew got into place with their backboard and cervical collar and their professionalism, he heard himself give them a succinct account of the accident, of Rusty's state of consciousness, of his initial findings of a possible broken arm and of Rusty's pain level.

And the pain of Rusty, lying facedown in the dirt, hit him in the heart.

Too late, he remembered that numbness was better.

Still on his knees, he moved back, getting out of a paramedic's way so he could do his job.

Desperately, he grasped for that numbness before it could slip away.

Instead, he could only kneel there in the dirt as he fought back the moisture that blurred his vision.

How many times had he knelt at the side of young men and women while he'd served his time in Afghanistan as they'd waited to be airlifted to safety? As if any place over there had felt safe.

Now was not the time to think of that.

Not now. Not ever, if he could keep pushing all those memories back.

Any second now he would find the strength, the motivation to stand.

He just needed to shore up his personal dam and everything would be fine.

Deseré stood next to him. When had she relinquished her position to the paramedic? When the paramedic had slipped the collar on and loaded Rusty onto the backboard, of course.

She put her hand on his shoulder, a firm touch followed by a squeeze.

And just like that he didn't feel so alone, so isolated, so *solely* responsible.

As if Deseré's voice had breached the invisible wall around him, he heard her tell the paramedics, "We'll notify his family."

That's when he realized they had been speaking to him, asking him questions about next of kin, giving him information about where they were taking Rusty and how to contact the hospital for updates.

How many times had he spoken with families, giving them the same kind of information? Only he'd had to talk via phone to loved ones who had been continents away, speaking into an unsympathetic piece of plastic in his hand as he'd explained that their soldier had lost hands or eyes or legs.

He'd heard everything from silence to deep soulful keening over those invisible airwaves. Each response had burned itself into his mind.

How long would he fight the memories?

A paramedic knelt next to him, gently jostling him. "We've got the patient, Dr. Hart."

How long had he knelt there, in the way?

Too long, even if it had only been for a few seconds.

He stood and backed away. From somewhere outside himself, he said, "I'll follow in my truck."

One of the rodeo clowns, who had been standing behind him and whom he'd been vaguely aware of, though he didn't seem to belong in this scene with his brightly painted face, baggy clothes and suspenders, said quietly, "Jordan, you're our medical professional on duty. We'll have to shut down the event if you leave. I understand about Rusty and all, but there are some big purses and points on the line here."

Jordan looked over at the woman with the ruined pants and blouse, filthy, too-delicate shoes and streaks of dirt on her cheek.

As if he were standing beside himself, watching, he saw himself lift his hand and wipe at a streak near her mouth with his thumb.

Her eyes deepened into a dark navy as she froze. She didn't even blink. Just looked at him like a deer in the headlights, too stunned to run away.

Embarrassment dropped him back into himself as he realized what he'd done.

He clenched his fist as he focused on the problem at hand and made his decision. "My nurse practitioner will take over my duties here."

He looked up, spotting Plato and Sissy, and motioned them over.

"Deseré Novak, meet Plato, my ranch help, and Sissy Hart, my sister and resident veterinarian. Ms. Novak will be taking over in my absence. Plato will introduce you around and show you the medical supplies. Sissy will make sure you have a place to stay tonight." He paused, looking into each of their faces. "Any questions?"

Plato swiped his hand over his face. "You can take the officer out of the military, but you can't…" He let the rest of his statement trail off under Jordan's glare.

Beside him, Deseré was nodding her acceptance as if nothing could ruffle her composure.

Sissy frowned. "Jordan, where—?"

Jordan looked at the lights of the helicopter growing dimmer in the sky. "Call Nancy. This is her mess."

"We've got this, Doctor." Deseré gave him a calm, if tight smile. "Go do what you need to do."

As if two massive boulders had fallen from his shoulders, Jordan felt energy course through him, the energy he needed to make it through tonight.

"Thanks." Emotion had him sounding gruffer than he had intended.

Deseré didn't seem to mind. "You're welcome. Now go."

Ignoring the shocked expressions on Sissy's and Plato's faces, Jordan took long, quick strides toward his truck as the helicopter lifted off, strobing bright light into the darkening sky.

As he climbed into his truck, he thought he should have nagging guilt about deserting his post. Instead, he felt comfort, deep down from the place where his instincts were born.

He was no longer alone.

For the first time in a very long time he could feel the tight, invisible bands around his chest loosen enough to let him draw in a deep breath.

The feeling of relief was seductive and he wanted to breathe in more.

But he couldn't forget—wouldn't forget—that letting down his guard created a sure-fire path to disappointment and bone-crushing pain.

CHAPTER THREE

WATCHING DR. HART stride away, stretching out his steps, going over the pipe-rail fence in one fluid motion, making the most of those incredibly long, lean legs of his while seeming to be unhurried and in control, left Deseré feeling lost and alone.

But wasn't that her status quo with men?

Not that Dr. Hart was a— Of course he was a man, but he wasn't a relationship or a potential relationship, except purely in the professional sense.

And that's the only sense she needed. Except for her common sense, which she seemed to have misplaced.

My nurse practitioner, Dr. Jordan had said. That meant she was hired, right?

She hadn't been able to acknowledge her worries and doubt before, not even to herself, but now she could admit to herself that she'd had no other options if this one hadn't worked out.

Going back the way she had come hadn't been an option. She'd never been afraid of any man. Cautious, sure. Wary, always. But not out-and-out afraid.

Not until her brother-in-law had sidled up to her at her sister's funeral and said he'd made arrangements out of state for an off-the-books abortion. They could call it a miscarriage, blaming it on grief.

When she'd refused, she'd seen pure evil in his eyes.

As time had passed, he'd changed his tune, deciding Deseré would take her sister's place as mother to the child that wasn't biologically his—and in his bed. He'd had it all figured out in that twisted mind of his, even down to the admiration of his friends when he'd magnanimously taken on the responsibility of his dead wife's sister.

An icy chill ran down her spine as she remembered his threats, the least of which had been unemployment as he'd tried to wreck her financially so she would have to comply with his plans.

Her brother-in-law had made it very clear she would never work in New Orleans again. And the interviews she'd had at all the major hospitals in Louisiana, Mississippi and most of Texas had emphasized the reach of his power.

Thankfully, he had forgotten this tiny fly speck on the map. Hopefully, he'd never find it.

"Ma'am? I'm Plato." The old cowboy she'd first seen in the parking lot was at her side. He tipped his hat as he officially introduced himself.

Deseré figured that meant something, some kind of acceptance into this world of boots and spurs.

"Deseré Novak." She held out her dirty hand then tried to pull it back. "Sorry."

He took her hand in his. His gnarled knuckles stood out as he gave her a light but firm pressure. "No, ma'am. The way I see it, that's angel dust coating your hand, not dirt. What you did for Rusty, well…" He rubbed his eyes with the back of his hand before he cleared his throat. "I'm sure one of the girls could come up with something for you to wear, if you wanted to change."

Deseré looked down at her blouse and slacks, covered in red-tinged dust. "It's a good thing I'm not a dry cleaning-only kind of woman."

She brushed at her pants leg and her hand became as dirt-coated as her pants. Not that her hands or arms were especially clean after she'd lain on her belly in the dirt, stabilizing Rusty's head and neck. She probably had red dirt all over her face, too.

Plato gave her a rueful look. "We've got iron ore in our soil around here." He pointed to her pants. "That might not come out."

Deseré categorized her limited wardrobe. Three pairs of slacks, two blouses, a set of very washed and worn scrubs, one little black dress inherited from her sister's closet, a pair of jeans with the waistband already too snug, a pair of sweats and three oversize T-shirts she slept in.

"I've got it covered." She turned to head toward her car in the parking lot but all she saw was a solid ring of pipe fencing.

And bleachers full of people watching her every move as she stood under the bright arena lights.

As she moved, the crowd erupted into cheers.

For her? She'd only done what any medical professional would have done.

Her heart beat as if pure energy surged through it instead of blood as she soaked in the approval. It had been so long since she'd felt like anyone was on her side. And now bleachers full of strangers were cheering her on.

It felt good, but overwhelming at the same time.

"This way, ma'am." Plato put his hand on her elbow, making her feel like rodeo royalty.

Cowgirl princess had always been a fantasy of hers. But her cowboy prince had already left the arena.

Her cowboy prince? It must be the adrenaline swing,

the sleepless nights—her stomach growled—and the hunger getting to her.

She didn't believe in princes on white horses rescuing damsels in distress. She didn't believe in damsels in distress, either. All she believed in was herself—and some days that was hard enough, without trying to add fairy-tales to the mix.

As they reached a part of the fence that looked as solid as every other part, Plato swung a gate open. It creaked and squealed on its hinges, proving it didn't get much use.

A woman in her forties, or well-preserved fifties, with big white-blonde hair and huge diamonds at her ears, neck and fingers, met her at the gate. She could have been the mother of any of the blonde cowgirls now crowding the rail.

"I'm Gayle-Anne." Her smile was orthodontia perfect. "Honey, you can use my trailer to change in. It's not very big but it's private."

Deseré bet it was a lot bigger than the bathroom stall at the discount department store where she'd last changed.

"Thanks. I'll just get clean clothes from my car."

If the woman wondered why Deseré had a wardrobe change in her car, she was polite enough not to ask about it.

How long did rodeos last? Hours?

Squeezing into her tight jeans had no appeal, especially if she was going to be stuck on one of those wooden benches for any length of time.

Too tired to give fashion decisions any more thought, she unzipped her bag and grabbed the first thing that came to hand, her sweats and a T-shirt.

The promise of comfort more than made up for her lack of ability to make a better decision.

Digging into the bottom of the bag, she snagged her tennis shoes and exchanged them for her useless sandals. The beat-up shoes had seen better days but, then, so had she.

And so had Jordan Hart.

She might have been the one lying in the dirt, but he was the one walking through hell. She'd seen it in his eyes as he'd gazed down at his cousin. Being a stoic medical professional worked just fine until it was someone close to you who needed your care.

She'd felt so helpless. So useless. The only thing she'd been able to do for her sister had been to promise to take care of her baby, a promise she'd given without reservation, then had had to fight dirty to keep.

She didn't regret the loss of her home or her career even a fraction as much as she grieved the loss of her sister.

Inside, baby James moved. Everyone would tell her that he was too small to feel, but they would all be wrong. She might not feel his tiny body, but she felt his great soul inside her.

She would keep her promise. She'd given her word.

And right now her word was the only significant thing she had to call her own.

Jordan paced the hallway, waiting, waiting. X-ray. CT scan. Radiologist report.

Rusty.

And the woman he'd left behind. What had he done, hiring her like that? Being impulsive wasn't like him. Had never been like him.

While it was true that he hadn't been himself in a while now, had he completely lost his mind?

He stopped pacing. Maybe.

Pain arced through him, starting in his heart and spreading through his veins. The pain of fear.

Not now. Now was not the time to have a panic attack.

Through sheer force of will he made himself start walking again. Walk. Breathe. Don't think.

Don't think about the woman waiting at his house, confused. Needing a job. Desperate.

He'd seen it in her eyes.

What had she seen in his?

Deseré's back screamed in pain from sitting on that hard wooden bench so long and her stomach burned with indigestion that had to rival the pits of hell.

The old cowboy had brought her a hot dog and a Frito pie, both covered in spicy chili, apologizing that this was all the little makeshift food stand had to offer.

She'd eaten them, of course. Even if she hadn't been starving, turning down free food would have been foolish in her financial situation.

But now, if she could go back in time, she probably would have done the same thing. Heartburn would eventually fade away and she needed the calories and scant nutrients the food provided.

As for going back in time—if she had that ability, she'd certainly take herself back a lot further than a few hours ago.

But how far back? Back before their father had died in Hurricane Katrina's flooding and Celeste had taken on the responsibility of raising her younger sister? Would that be far enough back?

What part of her history would she be willing to accept as her starting point for life?

Here and now. That's all she had. That's all she'd ever had.

But Dr. Hart had given her a future. *My nurse practitioner*, he'd said, giving her his stamp of approval, his acceptance and his protection all in one hasty pronouncement.

In a small community like this, everything he'd said and done was significant. Even now, she'd bet plenty of folks were dissecting and discussing every nuance.

Even after she was invited to the announcers' booth, their flimsy metal chairs weren't an improvement over the hard wooden benches and the staleness of the booth, the odor of burnt coffee mixed with dust and sweat that had built up over the years made her stomach roil.

She swatted at a gnat on her neck, one of millions in league with the mosquitoes that flocked to taste any sliver of exposed skin.

She'd opted to sit outside as the night air brought the heat and humidity down a few degrees. The perspiration soaking her shirt chilled her, making her shiver.

And she was so tired she was having difficulty deciding if she was awake or asleep. She wrapped her arms around herself, surprised to find a blue jean jacket awkwardly draped around her chair and over her shoulders.

That answered it. She'd been asleep—asleep enough that she was startled when the older cowboy, the one she recognized from the parking lot, cleared his throat.

"Ma'am?" Plato's volume, a touch above a normal speaking voice, firm but still calm and gentle, clued her in that this wasn't the first time he'd tried to awaken her.

She blinked, trying to bring his leathered face into focus.

Pasting on the best smile she could, even though it felt extremely weak to her, she answered in kind, "Sir?"

Relief showed in his rheumy blue eyes.

Cataracts? Glaucoma? The medical professional started to evaluate diagnoses.

But the exhausted woman overruled them, appreciating the concern and sympathy she found in those bloodshot, yellow-tinged eyes.

"Ready to go home now?" His words made his rough voice sound sweeter than any angel's song.

Home. Had she finally found home?

"Yes." Awkwardly, she gathered her purse, trying to hold the jacket around her shoulders while she wiggled functionality into her swollen feet.

He reached out for her.

As an independent woman, she usually waved away the courtesy.

But tonight, his hand on her elbow, guiding her, steadying her, gave her more comfort than she would ever have imagined.

Gratefully and graciously, she accepted the other hand he held out for her as she made the step from the second-row bleacher to the ground.

"You can follow Sissy, or I can drive your car for you and catch a ride back here for my truck."

Her car. All that she owned was in that car. The stark reality was enough to push away the blanket of sleep that weakened her.

Her brain jump-started and she remembered who Sissy was—Jordan's sister.

Jordan. When had he become Jordan in her head instead of Dr. Hart?

"I'll follow Sissy."

* * *

Deseré should have let the old man drive her.

Bleary-eyed, she slammed on her brakes and slowed enough to just miss the bumper of Sissy's truck as the vet turned off the two-lane road onto a crumbling black-topped street that had deteriorated on the edges so that it was only the width of a car and a half.

Carefully, she put distance between her car and the truck in front of her, on alert for sudden brake lights.

And her caution was validated when Sissy slowed her truck to a crawl and turned into a dirt and gravel drive without bothering to use her blinkers first.

Trees crowded the driveway—and Deseré used the description of driveway very loosely. How far away from the street was the house?

And then they turned a steep curve and there it was, a farmhouse that could have come from a movie set, or her dreams.

Headlights showed a huge, two-storied, white-painted wooden house with gray shingles and a darker gray double door centered under a deep covered wrap-around porch. Rocking chairs promised the good life once the grimy cushions were replaced and they were swept clear of cobwebs.

If Deseré had to pick out the perfect picture of a po-tential home, this would be it.

Which meant she immediately put herself on guard.

Nothing was this easy. This neat. This perfect.

Where was the catch?

Ahead of her, Sissy had her arm stuck out her truck's window as she wildly gestured to an empty carport that branched off from the drive.

Deseré interpreted that to mean, "Park here." She could always move it later if she was wrong.

She pulled into the expansive parking place, taking up most of the room by sloppily not squaring her car with the open space. The lack of order felt off, but not as off as her head, which chose that moment to swim in that dizzy, depleted way that meant she'd gone as far as she could today.

Sissy inspected her parking job and clearly found it lacking. With a frown, she shrugged and said, "Jordan will just have to deal with it."

Deseré knew she should ask for clarification but right now she didn't really want to know. Knowing might mean exerting more energy than she had to give.

Grabbing her backpack and wriggling her arms through the straps, she breathed deeply to gather her strength for wrestling her rolling suitcase from the back seat.

"Since Jordan has hired you *sans* interview, Nancy said to bring you here and she would get everything sorted out later." Sissy swept her hand to indicate the house before her. "Home, sweet home."

Deseré felt like Sissy was waiting for a reply.

"It's large," she answered politely, reserving judgment until she saw the inside of the house.

Sissy nudged her aside and pulled the suitcase out for her, handling it like it was full of popcorn. "I'll carry this one for you."

Normally, Deseré would have protested, but she didn't have it in her. Instead, she muttered a tired "Thanks" and pulled her purse and smaller duffel bag from the front seat of the car.

On autopilot, she followed Sissy up the three steps to the front porch then through the wooden and etched-glass front door.

Sissy paused as she looked down the short wing to

the left then up to the second floor. She bit her lower lip and her brow creased as she seemed to be puzzling out a dilemma. "I'm not sure where to put you."

"Anywhere is fine." Deseré mustered up a polite smile, wondering how many other tenants shared the boarding house.

Sissy quit deliberating and nodded her head. "Okay, then. This way." She headed up a staircase lit with just enough wall sconces to cast shadows on the floral patterned carpet runner covering each oak-plank step, dragging Deseré's large suitcase over each one.

Deseré didn't need to respond. She would only have been talking to Sissy's back. Instead, she meekly followed the diminutive woman hefting the large suitcase to the end of the hallway to the left.

Sissy swung open the last door to reveal a bedroom. The room was enormous, bigger than the whole living room and den combination in Deseré's old apartment.

The sight of that luxurious bed put the rest of the room into the background. A huge queen-size bed held a half-dozen big pillows propped against the headboard and the promise of sweet dreams.

A calming lavender color scheme and trophies and blue ribbons displayed on every inch of shelf space gave the room a mixed attitude of super-girly but highly competitive.

"This was my room before I moved out. I should probably pack up some of this stuff, huh? But the closet's cleared out so at least you can unpack." She pointed to a closed door next to a substantial desk. "The bathroom's through that door."

Sissy dumped the suitcase outside the bifold louvered doors of a closet then shoved aside a group of trophies on a wide chest of drawers, took Deserés duffel bag from her and plopped it onto the cleared space.

An unexpected expression of doubt crossed Sissy's eyes. "I hope this will do."

"It's great." Deseré didn't need to dredge up a fake smile. It came quite naturally as she emphasized her answer. "Really. It's wonderful."

"Well, okay, then." Sissy looked out into the hallway, obviously ready to make her exit. "I'm sure Jordan will straighten out any questions you might have in the morning."

Absently, Deseré nodded, wishing Sissy would leave. Falling into that lovely bed and stretching out her back was the only thing she wanted to straighten out right now.

"Good night, then." Sissy didn't wait for a reply. Her duty done, she started out the bedroom door.

"Good night," Deseré said to Sissy's retreating backside, then closed the door as soon as she thought it polite to do so.

Her first inclination was to fall into that bed and sleep for a week. But her mouth had a sour taste that couldn't be ignored and grit coated her face and hands.

Cleanliness warred with exhaustion. A quick washup would be worth the extra time and energy.

Opening the solid door next to the desk, Deseré was sure she'd opened the door to bathroom heaven.

The modernized bathroom was the size of a normal bedroom, with two basins and a huge vanity. The size of each of the basins put the discount store's basins she'd been spot-bathing in to shame. A wall-to-wall mirror hung over the vanity, reflecting the light from nickel-plated fixtures that caught the atmosphere of farmhouse yet produced enough light for professional make-up application.

An alcove held the toilet separately from the frosted glass doors, which must hide the shower enclosure.

Immediately, every inch of skin on Deseré's body wanted scrubbing. She couldn't stop herself from wondering where Jordan would be showering tonight. Would anyone be washing his back?

How could her libido be so wide-awake when the rest of her was practically sleepwalking?

Because she couldn't help herself, she opened the frosted door to inspect the shower.

Oh, my. She had no doubt she had entered an entirely different world than the one she had come from.

With three shower heads embedded in each wall of the hexagon-shaped shower and a marble bench wide and deep enough to lie down on, the shower was big enough to hold an orgy in.

Hedonistic didn't begin to cover it.

With no further thought needed, Deseré stripped off her filthy clothes, grabbed a towel and washcloth from the cabinets under the vanity and jumped in to adjust the temperature and spray.

Five minutes later, she stood in the middle of the multiple streams of steaming water. Each spray felt like firm fingers massaging her skin, pulsating against her sore muscles, sending slick, soapy water sluicing from head to toe.

Better than sleep.

Better than sex.

The phrases kept going through her head like a seductive song as she stretched and soaped and rinsed and soaped again, washing away all the demoralizing spot baths she'd taken with paper towels and harsh pink antibacterial soap while hiding in public toilet stalls.

The soap smelled of cedar and sage. The shampoo held a hint of musk. The masculine tinge only underscored the sensual feel of the spray tingling against her skin.

What would it be like to make love in this shower?

That was a very improper thought for an expectant mother.

Determined to shrug off her fantasies, she squirted another handful of shampoo into her palm to work it through her hair and into her scalp.

Ah. Heaven.

Through her sudsing and soaping and spraying, she had the vague notion she might have heard the bathroom door swing open.

No, she was not going to let a little paranoia invade this moment of bliss.

Instead, she let the fancy shower heads push pulsating fingers of hot water into her spine as she stretched, reaching far, far over her head, reaching for the stars.

Her moan of sheer pleasure echoed in the cavernous shower.

She grabbed her wet hair, intending to flop over at the waist and wash away the shampoo while she stretched in the opposite direction, when she heard him.

"What the hell?"

Despite the rich, thick shampoo bubbles filling her ears, Jordan Hart's voice came through loud and clear.

CHAPTER FOUR

As JORDAN PUSHED the bathroom door open, worry for Rusty gave way to reality and the sound of the shower running.

"Um— Hello? Is someone out there?" Her voice was breathy, reminding Jordan too much of mornings-after he hadn't experienced in too long.

"I— Uh." Now was not the time to have his brain go blank as his world unfolded in slow motion.

For the first time in a very, very long time Jordan felt like a teenager caught in the back seat of his girlfriend's car. Two parts shocked, one part guilty and another part as excited as a lightning bolt.

She turned away from him, giving him a foggy view of her backside.

Hell, make that a whole lightning storm raging through him. He clenched and unclenched his fists.

"Uh, would you get out now, please?" Her whispery voice breached his confusion. It broke, sounding scared, making him feel big and hulking and embarrassed.

Making him feel.

His numbness washed away like soap scum down the drain.

"Sorry," he said, and headed for the door that connected to his bedroom, firmly closing it behind him.

Sleeping was difficult at the best of times.

No way would he get any rest with every nerve ending in his body popping.

Kicking off his jeans and boots, he pulled on shorts and running shoes instead. As he slammed out the door and hit the road, a full range of emotions hit him.

After being safely numb for so long, reaction after delayed reaction now threatened to bring him to his knees.

Lust for the woman who was now his employee and, therefore, hands off. Relief that Rusty was going to be fine. Pressure of caring for his heavy patient load when he couldn't even care for himself.

And fear that all the emotion he had under such tight control, all the guilt and angst and anger would finally burst free, consuming him and everyone around him.

If only he could run far enough, fast enough...

If only he could outrun the agony of feeling again that dogged his every step.

Nothing like being walked in on by your boss, a man you'd only met a few short hours ago, to jumpstart your heart.

Deseré used her newfound energy to grab her towel, lock the door she hadn't noticed opposite the one that led into her bedroom and, for good measure, lock her door, too, all in under three seconds.

Keeping one towel tightly around her and tucked under her armpits, she grabbed a second one, toweled off her legs and arms and then squeezed the water from her hair, letting her mind settle from flight mode into thinking mode.

A second door meant a second bedroom, right?

Shampoo and soap... She opened the drawer under

both basins—used toothbrush and a squeezed tube of toothpaste, deodorant and a man's electric razor. A full bottle of cologne covered with dust. And an opened box of condoms.

She would not peek inside to see how many were left. It was none of her business.

Did she really think a man who looked like him, a man who walked like him, who talked like him, each word so slow and deep it rumbled with masculinity, would be celibate?

Again, what did it matter to her?

So they shared a bathroom.

She took another look at the luxurious shower.

She could deal with it.

She'd shared living quarters, including a bathroom, with a man before. But that man hadn't been the slightest bit interested in her—not when her sister had been sharing his bed.

If only Celeste had stuck with that particular boyfriend instead of dumping him for money...

But who could have predicted this future?

Once again she pushed down her grief for her sister. She'd done her crying when she'd heard the news. All it had done was make her sick at her stomach.

Crying solved nothing. Thinking, planning then taking action was the way to move forward.

Whatever you do, don't stand still, Deseré. Moving targets are harder to hit. Celeste had always felt safer on the move, dragging them both from boyfriend to homeless shelter to a room over the garage in exchange for babysitting services.

But she wanted more for Celeste's son—her son—than a life on the run.

And, like her sister before her, she would never lose hope.

A chill shook her as the overhead vents blew centralized air conditioning onto her damp skin.

Still wet under the tightly wrapped towel, she cringed at the thought of putting on the filthy clothes she'd shed when she'd made the spontaneous decision to explore the wonders of that magnificent shower.

Scrubs it would be.

And tomorrow she would avail herself of the washer and dryer.

With the beginning of the weekend, she would have a chance to wash and dry out the wrinkles before donning them for work on Monday and she would also have a chance to scope out her surroundings, both the town and the office, and begin working on fitting in.

Most importantly, she would have a chance to get that awkward encounter with her boss behind her.

The sooner, the better.

Because she wasn't going anywhere.

Anywhere but bed.

After pulling on her scrubs and unlocking the connecting doors, she allowed herself to pull back the duvet on the huge, beautiful bed that dominated the room.

Sure that she would lie awake spending hours thinking about today and tomorrow and yesterday, at least she would do it in comfort.

But the moment she lay down among the half-dozen pillows and stretched out to her full length, exhaustion overtook her.

As her world went sleepily hazy, she reached out for a pillow, wondering what it would be like to encounter a warm male body instead. A body like Jordan Hart's.

* * *

Jordan cranked up the volume as music blasted through his earbuds. The vintage rock classic about running down the road, trying to loosen his load, fit the situation perfectly except for the part about seven women on his mind. He only had one woman on his mind.

And no matter how hard he pushed his pace, he couldn't outrun her steamy, naked body in his shower.

His imagination wanted to take off where his memory ended.

And he let it.

Would he feel electricity in her touch?

Or would he feel nothing.

Nothing. Nothing. Nothing.

It became his mantra superimposed over the music in his ears as he made his way back home.

Home became interspersed in his internal chant.

Nothing.

Home.

Nothing.

Home.

Nothing.

The trance he'd set out to find finally wrapped itself around him as his stride became a part of his breath, a part of his world, a world that only encompassed his next step.

He gasped for breath, realizing he'd been sprinting full out instead of at his long-distance endurance pace.

The pounding of his heart competed with the throbbing in his chest.

Physical pain.

Bringing him back to here and now, reminding him that, no matter how fast or how far he ran, he could never outrun reality.

He climbed the front steps of his porch, unlocking his front door as silently as he could manage, creeping up the stairs, stepping over the fifth step that had creaked since his youth and headed for a shower—a cold one where he would fight his memories, fight the imaginary world of what-if, fight his inclination to keep on running.

And remember why he was there. Why the clinic was so important. Why he couldn't just check out, no matter how seductive that thought was.

As he had a hundred thousand times before, to too many unanswered questions, he raised his face to the stream of water pouring down on him and silently pleaded, Why?

Deseré woke up slowly, drowsily, until she was awake enough to be confused.

Spread across the huge, soft bed, she began to remember.

The rodeo.

Jordan.

The bull-riding accident.

Jordan.

This house.

And Jordan.

Walking in on her in the shower. Seeing her naked. Turning away.

Which had been the right thing to do.

Anything else would have been creepy. Scary. Dangerous.

Those words didn't go with Jordan Hart.

At least the creepy, scary words didn't.

Dangerous?

Something about him hinted that he could be. But he would never harm her.

How could she know that about him? He was a stranger, a man she'd just met only briefly under trying circumstances.

She knew nothing about him.

But she knew, deep down, that he would never hurt her.

She had that sense, too well developed over too many years, that told her which man was dangerous and which was safe.

Jordan. A dangerous thrill shivered down her spine.

No, he wouldn't hurt her. At least, not physically. What that man could do to a woman's psyche was another matter entirely.

And her heart?

Deseré pushed that thought away. No man would ever get close to her heart unless she allowed it. And she definitely hadn't been in a permissive mood lately.

The urge that had woken her hit her with an intensity that had her sitting up in bed.

Bathroom.

Oh, the luxury of having one right outside her bedroom door.

Using moon shadows to navigate, she padded across the room—to find the connecting door locked from the bathroom side.

The sound of water running at full blast made her instinctively twitch.

Knowing Jordan was showering on the other side of this door made her twitch even more.

He's a stranger, she reminded herself.

But she'd seen beyond his socially acceptable stranger's mask.

She'd seen his eyes as he'd looked down at his cousin.

She'd seen his eyes as he'd stared at her in the foggy mirror.

She'd seen his eyes as he'd turned away.

She'd seen that glimpse of emotion that could only be his soul.

Deseré shook herself, shaking off her high-drama fantasy.

It was not like her to wax poetic over a man's eyes.

She had never been one of those girls who fell in love with the idea of love the second she laid eyes on an attractive guy.

Practical. Realistic. Survivor.

That's what she was.

Pregnancy hormones. What other reason could it be?

Finally, just when she thought she would have to go in search of a second bathroom in an unfamiliar house, she heard the shower shut off, heard the bathroom door open—

And jiggled her own doorhandle, only to find it still locked.

What?

Had he forgotten to unlock the connecting door?

So, her choices were limited, both in option and in the time factor. She could pound on his bedroom door or she could find another bathroom.

Remembering their last encounter in this very bathroom, Deseré choose option two.

Barefoot, she sprinted toward the stairs, using memory more than vision. No windows? Not enough moon to cast a glow?

Not an issue to ponder now. Maybe she should have gone with option one.

No, she still had time.

As she hopped from foot to foot, her hand swept the wall near the first step.

Light switch? Light switch?

No light switch.

Holding onto the stair rail, Deseré took each step as cautiously as she could while making maximum haste.

She really should have just knocked on his door.

But with only two steps left, turning around now would take too much time.

Really, I love you, baby James. But sometimes you make Momma's thinking process short-circuit.

Momma.

She'd never called herself that before. As dire as her need was, she had to stop for a moment.

"Momma," she said aloud, making it real. She was going to me a mother. Responsible for this fragile life inside her until he reached manhood.

She couldn't imagine letting go even then.

The wonder of it all was so big it momentarily distracted her from her mission.

But then cool air swirled around her as the air-conditioner kicked in and the importance of finding a bathroom became very important.

Opening the door under the staircase, she found a closet full of winter coats. The closet smelled of mustiness and—and Jordan.

Jordan, who she was going to great pains to avoid. Jordan, who she would see in the morning anyway.

Jordan, on whose bedroom door she should have knocked instead of putting herself through this wild-goose chase.

Jordan, who she had just dreamed about in a way that would make seeing him in the light of day awkward.

Seeing him tonight in his bedroom, feeling sleepy and vulnerable, would have been much worse.

She had made the right decision.

Her bladder twinged.

Maybe.

Another door yielded a bedroom in disrepair, spooky in the shadows coming through the curtainless windows. Drop cloths draped the floor and furniture, turning everything into ghosts. But a small open doorway gave her a glimpse of white tile.

Yes!

Quickly, she picked her way through the paintbrushes and wallpaper rolls to come face-to-face with a toilet that lay on its side, awaiting installation.

That. Hurt.

She turned on her heel, stepping on a roller and almost going to her knees.

Steadying herself on the corner of a dresser-shaped ghost, she regained her balance.

Enough of this. What was the big deal, knocking on Jordan Hart's door?

Seeing him fresh from his bed.

Would his hair be mussed, as if a lover's fingers had just run through it?

Would his mouth be full, relaxed from a deep sleep?

Would his eyes—those wonderful eyes—be slightly unfocused as he blinked the sleep away?

Option one. It's all she had left.

She raced up the stairs as fast as she could manage.

Outside his door, she raised her hand and knocked.

CHAPTER FIVE

AS SHE WAITED for Jordan to answer her knock, Deseré felt like one of those too-stupid-to-live teenage girls in a cheesy horror flick who goes into the dark basement defenseless and too dumb to be scared.

Not that she had any reason to fear Jordan Hart if her instincts were right. And they had never failed her before.

But, then, she'd never been suffused with pregnancy hormones before, either.

Realistically, she didn't know the man. And she was all alone with him.

Her desperate search for a bathroom had confirmed that there were no other residents. This wasn't a boarding house but a private home. A home that only she and Jordan presently occupied.

But plenty of people knew where she was, right?

No. Wrong. Only his sister and the old cowboy Plato and a woman named Nancy, whom she had never met.

She shifted from foot to foot and pounded again, impatiently waiting for him to open that door. The sooner the better. Right?

Or not so right?

What a great time to get scared—or get smart.

She had an absurd vision of Plato leaning on a shovel, peering down into a freshly dug—

Jordan answered the door, a look of total blankness on his face. "You need something?"

His lack of emotion unsettled her more than a frown or a scowl would have. That and the way his gym shorts showed off his muscular legs. His worn T-shirt draped across his wide shoulders. His uncombed hair fell onto his forehead, creating the illusion of vulnerability.

Deseré swallowed. Her dry throat made it painful. She was staring at him, staring at his face, staring into his eyes and seeing nothing but flat black pupils surrounded by whiskey-brown with specks of black.

"Well?" His voice was firm and solid and impatient. That vulnerability thing was definitely an illusion.

He blinked.

Was that a touch of wariness he blinked away?

"Bathroom." She pointed, unable to put any other thoughts into words.

His body shifted, giving her the impression he was moving back from the door to let her in.

She couldn't wait anymore.

Brushing against him, she headed for that little slice of heaven she needed so desperately.

Anyone would think that her single-minded mission would block everything else from her world. How did the heat of his arm against hers stand out from all the other things she was feeling?

Slamming the bathroom door a little harder than she'd intended, Deseré fumbled with the lock, hoping it caught, then found blessed relief.

As she washed her hands, she debated her next move, even while shaking her head at the silliness of letting something as simple as using the bathroom get so out blown out of proportion in her mind.

But she couldn't help it.

Jordan Hart was larger than life. Wait—she meant he was crucial to her life, not larger than life.

He was an ordinary man. Nothing special. Nothing scary.

But he did scare her. Not in the axe-murderer kind of way but in the change-her-life kind of way.

Rolling her eyes at herself in the mirror, she dried her hands on the hand towel more roughly than was warranted.

This wasn't a big deal. She'd had male roommates before, although none of them had affected her like Jordan did.

She unlocked the door leading to her room and threw it open so she could make a fast exit.

Then she unlocked Jordan's door, pushed it open a few inches and called through it, "All done. Sorry to bother you," before sprinting for the safety of her bedroom.

Where she would normally have stared at the ceiling the rest of the night, the exhaustion of pregnancy had her dropping off to sleep. She also blamed pregnancy hormones for her vivid dreams of Jordan's touch warming her skin, his mouth making her lips ache, his eyes peering into her soul.

As she awoke the next morning feeling as if she'd crammed four months of catch-up sleep into one night, she attributed that heart-thudding bit of loneliness to pregnancy, too.

She did her best to shrug it all off. All the literature had said to expect exhaustion, mood swings and strange dreams.

A pitter-patter on her door had her trying to push the sleep from her befuddled brain.

A hesitant feminine voice called through the thick wood. "Miss Novak? Are you all right in there?"

"Fine." Her voice came out sleep-roughened and cracked. She cleared her throat. "Just fine."

She didn't sound any finer the second time around.

"Oh. Okay." Youth and uncertainty carried through the door. "Well, if you want me to give you a lift into work…"

Work?

Deseré opened the door about four inches, hanging onto the edge for security. Trying to make sense of this morning, she stuck her head out to see the girl face-to-face, too aware that she hadn't even given her herself a glance yet. "It's Saturday, right?"

The girl's gaze took in Deseré's hair and rumpled scrubs before politely going back to her face. "Yes, ma'am."

Deseré could feel the drying drool in the corner of her mouth as her reasoning skills kicked in. "Um, we have Saturday hours, don't we?"

Sympathy and understanding showed in the girl's tone of voice. "Yes, ma'am."

Deep-breath time. "Give me a few seconds."

In record time Deseré ran a toothbrush across her teeth and a hairbrush across her bride-of-Frankenstein hair.

With only a half second of deliberation, she threw on horribly wrinkled dress pants, leaving the top button undone, a blouse that should be tucked in and looked tacky hanging loose, her sturdy nursing tennis shoes with the laces loosened because her swelling feet couldn't take those filthy, flimsy sandals, and a dusting of face powder and blush with a dash of lipstick because she couldn't stop herself.

Fighting to keep panic from her voice, she threw open her bedroom door and called into the hallway, "Ready."

"Yes, ma'am." The girl waiting in the hallway across from her bedroom door inspected her. "We've got spare scrubs at work if you'd rather."

"That would be nice."

And that was the last opportunity she had to speak before they arrived at the clinic just a few minutes away as she'd had no inclination to shout over the radio playing country music cranked up loud enough to buzz the car's speakers.

The clinic was a sixties-style square box with pink brick and white plastic shutters. Skeletons of dead chrysanthemums spiked up in the untended front flowerbed. Stenciled on the glass of the door were the office hours, including eight till noon Saturdays.

And it was now nine-fifteen. She would start her daily bout of morning sickness in approximately forty-five minutes.

Jordan Hart plastered on his best doctor face as he listened to Mrs. Mabel tell him all about her pie-baking incident while he bandaged her cut thumb.

It was a nick. A butterfly bandage would do.

His mind wandered as he pulled out one drawer and then another, looking for supplies.

He'd once been organized, obsessively. But now he couldn't seem to stay focused long enough to put anything in order, including his own mind.

Everyone he'd talked to, all the counselors they'd set him up with before his discharge, had assured him that re-entry into the calm, sedate civilian world would take a bit of adjustment after being on the front lines for eighteen months.

Okay. He got that. But in the meantime his patients were suffering for his weakness.

Where was that nurse practitioner he'd hired last night?

Jordan drew in a big breath. He knew exactly what had happened. No one had mentioned to her that they kept Saturday hours.

His fault. He was in charge of this clinic and therefore responsible.

Jordan froze. Something felt off. What was it?

The exam room was quiet. Mrs. Mabel had stopped talking.

She was staring at him, expecting—expecting what?

He replayed the last few seconds in his mind.

"I'm sure your pie is worth the effort. A store-bought pie wouldn't be the same." It came out flat and mechanical. But apparently Mabel didn't need enthusiasm as she gave him a wrinkled smile.

"That's what my husband always used to say."

Jordan knew that. Somewhere in his subconscious he'd remembered Mrs. Mabel saying that exact thing about her dearly departed husband of forty-five years, which was why he'd parroted it back to her.

A knock sounded on the exam-room door, a no-nonsense, staccato rap.

He pushed the door open and saw his newest employee standing there. Deseré.

He had an instant collage of images in his brain of her body against his as he held her back from climbing into the arena too soon, of her holding Rusty's head, of her in his shower.

The emotions associated with those memories over-shadowed his powers of speech. He'd been putting his feelings in a box for a long time—for years, way before Afghanistan. Way before medical school. Way before adulthood.

After he'd successfully exerted control over them for so many years, why now? Why now did that control elude him so that his emotions could play havoc with his logic?

As memories of seeing her naked kept flashing in his mind, Jordan didn't dare look at her too closely right now.

Last night had almost been his undoing.

And today he was too close to losing his control to risk an in-depth analysis of why the V seemed deeper on her boxy top than on his other employees' tops.

"Are you the new girl I heard about? The one who showed up at the rodeo last night?" Mrs. Mabel asked, looking from him to Deseré and back again.

Deseré as in desire. Yeah, it fit her.

A wedge of reality crowded past the image of her foggy image in the mirror.

Making a half-turn back to Mrs. Mabel, he told her, "This is my new nurse practitioner, Deseré Novak. She'll take good care of you."

He dragged his attention to a point around her right earlobe as he said, "Take over here, Deseré." He sounded gruff, even to his own ears.

He'd never considered scrubs sexy before. But now—now he thought of them as a clever disguise to hide what was underneath.

With a nod of his head he gestured to Mrs. Mabel, who was staring at Deseré.

"Simple cut. A butterfly bandage will do," he said,

to have something to say. A nurse practitioner would know that as well as he did.

She wouldn't know where anything was, but she could do no worse job of this than he was doing. At least Mrs. Mabel's chart was in plain sight on the counter.

Without a glance in Deseré's direction, he walked past her and out the door. Even though he had been overly cautious to not brush against her, he still felt the heat of her body as he walked past.

In fact, he felt that heat all the way down the hallway, even after he'd shut the door to his private office.

Too many thoughts rushed his brain—what little brain he still had functioning. Lust was at the top of the list. Then there was the relief he'd felt last night when he'd been able to walk away from responsibility, dumping it all on Deseré. And guilt for both the dumping of responsibility and for the relief he'd felt about it. Yeah, he was screwed up.

Worry for Rusty, worry about money, worry about the gossip his living arrangements with Deseré would cause—not that he wasn't used to it, but she didn't deserve it—all crowded and swirled around, giving him a headache.

He didn't know what he would do about most of those chaotic thoughts, other than try to ignore them.

Ha! That would be like ignoring a stampede of longhorns barreling down on him.

But ignore them he would. It was the only way to make it through patient rounds.

He clenched his jaw, ignoring the shooting pain arcing through his whole head. No—welcoming the pain because it would help to seal in his intention to ignore anything and everything having to do with Deseré Novak.

Real practical, Hart. She works for you. She sleeps in the bedroom next to yours. How are you going to ignore that?

He could no more ignore Deseré than he could ignore the light but persistent knock on his door.

"Doc Hart?" a small female voice called.

Not Deseré, he was relieved to hear, but Katey, who only spoke in a shy voice barely above a whisper.

He rubbed his hand over his face, trying to erase any signs of turmoil as he moved toward his office door.

"Do you need something, Katey?"

Katey blushed under his direct questioning, even though he'd been sure to keep his tone quiet and calm.

She was as skittish as a wild colt. Not the best quality for a part-time receptionist, but she needed the job and was willing to work a short week in return for work/study credit and a pittance of a paycheck, which was pretty much all he could afford to pay.

Katey looked down at the pink handwritten note in her hand. "Rusty called from the hospital. They set his arm this morning. His concussion is out of the danger range. He's being released later this afternoon and could use a ride home. Could you send Plato?"

"Good news." Very good news. Not only was Rusty doing well, but now he had a reason to stay away from his own house until Deseré had had time to do her bathroom stuff and climb into bed.

Ignoring the image his brain had supplied of her in *his* bed, he deliberately blinked. "Thanks, Katey. Call him back and tell him I'll pick him up."

He stepped back to close his door but Katey took a step forward, stopping him. No small feat for her.

Good for her. Maybe this job was helping her in some small way, just like his sister had hoped it would.

Sissy was good at nudging people into the right places so everyone ended up better for it.

Only with him her nudge had always been more like a shove. He guessed he was just stubborn that way. When he'd been ready to cut the clinic's hours, she'd nagged him ceaselessly until she'd talked him into hiring help instead, even doing all the applicant searches herself.

Jordan was fairly sure Sissy had screwed up this time, though, by pushing Deseré into his path. Deseré didn't deserve to be tarnished by his shortcomings and sins.

Katey gave a nervous squeak and Jordan realized his expression might have turned less than placid.

He kept his voice low and soft, like he was gentling a new foal. "Okay. Anything else?"

Katey dug one toe of her shoe into the worn tile flooring. "You said we could order pizzas on Saturdays if we get the two-for-ones?"

"Sure."

"Pepperoni for me and Nurse Harper. Sausage and onion for you, right, Dr. Hart?"

"Yes, please." He should let it go. It was a little thing and he should let it work itself out but… "Wait. Find out what Ms. Novak likes. I'll eat whatever she chooses."

As long as she didn't choose mushroom. But, then, that would put an end to the fantasy, wouldn't it? What man could fall for a woman who liked mushrooms on her pizza?

Deseré rolled the taste of hot pizza around her mouth, savoring every burst on her tastebuds. Who would have guessed that a town this size would have such great pizza?

The sausage was homemade, Katey had told her. And the mushrooms were fresh and sautéed instead of raw to bring out a more intense flavor.

Utterly delicious. Especially since last night's dinner of chili-covered everything had been too many hours ago to satisfy baby James and he clearly hadn't appreciated the super-sugary cinnamon rolls Katey had fetched when she'd found out Deseré hadn't had breakfast.

Deseré's standard ten o'clock stomach flip had confirmed baby James's opinion of her food choice—not that she'd really had a choice.

Free food, baby. We don't turn down food. Then she promised, *It won't always be this way,* determined to sound confident even in her private thoughts. Who knew what babies picked up?

A shifting movement from her dining partner reminded her that reticent doctors could pick up plenty, so she quickly smoothed out any expression she might have inadvertently been showing.

Just as the man across from her was doing.

Apparently, Dr. Hart was also a picky eater.

He sat across from her in the minuscule staff break room, and carefully used his fork to remove the offending fungi, making sure the little gray bits didn't touch his fingers.

Dr. Hart. After he'd done the arrogant doctor stereotype thing and abandoned her to muddle through the rest of the morning exams on her own, she'd been able to think of him as Dr. Hart all morning long, instead of the Jordan of her dreams.

But now, with his hair falling into his eyes as he picked his way through another piece of pizza, he was fast becoming Jordan again.

"I'm sure Nancy and Katey would have saved you

some of their pizza if you'd asked them to." Although the way those two had almost inhaled their lunch earlier made her statement more doubtful supposition than solid reality.

He shrugged, not bothering to answer her.

The silence made eating uncomfortable as he totally ignored her. It also challenged her.

"Mrs. Mabel promised to bring by a pie. I guess you're saving room for it, huh?" Inane conversation was better than no conversation.

He looked up from under his lashes, giving her a look as if she was interrupting an intricate surgical procedure. "Hmm."

Okay, so much for polite small talk.

"I owe a great deal of thanks to Nancy for helping me get acquainted with the clinic's normal operating procedures today. I learned by doing."

He swallowed, as if he'd just forced down one of the innocent mushrooms he found so offensive.

"You did fine." That he'd had to force the compliment out was evident in his brusque delivery.

He looked away toward the corner of the room then back at her again. "Because you were here, we're getting out of the office on time. Usually, I'd still have patients in the waiting room and I'd be here until after six."

As if stringing all those words together at once made him restless, he pushed back from the table and stood. "You can leave whenever you're done here. I'll lock up."

"Wait."

"Oh, Katey picked you up. You need a ride back to the house?"

"No, I can walk it."

"There's not enough shoulder on the road for that

and the ditches are steep. Even though it's close, I'd rather drive you."

Not only did his words sound protective, so did his tone—and his eyes.

A comforting warmth crept up from deep inside her, but it suddenly became uncomfortable. She could take care of herself.

This sensation felt—what did it feel like? She searched through words like suffocating and overbearing. No. None of those.

It felt—nice. "Thanks."

But then he frowned at her, erasing all the good will he'd gained. "About last night…"

Again he looked toward the corner of the room for his words. Very deliberately, he looked back at her, meeting her eyes.

His intensity had her looking away. She ended up focusing on his mouth, instead of those deep, dark eyes of his. His lips revealed a lot more emotion than his eyes did anyway.

"Yes?" she prompted.

"I'm…" He glanced down, breaking contact momentarily before he looked back up and pinned her again. "I'm sorry for walking in on you. I didn't realize… And for forgetting to unlock the door, too. My sister hasn't lived there in a while and I'm not used to sharing…."

His voice sounded like he was being sliced with razorblades, so raw she had to put an end to his pain.

"It's okay. Just a simple mistake." She drew attention to her own mistake to try to ease things. "Like me missing Saturday office hours."

She bit her bottom lip, thinking he had no sense of humor, but she was going for it anyway. "No Sunday hours, right?"

His lips loosened up the slightest bit at the corners, knocking a good half-decade off his age and making the whole room feel easier. "No Sunday hours. My mistake on the weekend mix-up, too."

His mouth, that subtly expressive mouth, relinquished the slightest of quirks at the corners. But Deseré sensed self-deprecating irony more than good humor. Still, it was an improvement of sorts.

"Forgiven." It was one of those words she always wanted to hear but could rarely say herself. But with this man across from her, this stranger who seemed so hard-shelled except for the smallest of tell-tale slips that she was probably imagining, it was easy to say.

"All forgiven," she said, as much for herself as for him, to see how it felt the second time around.

Did she imagine his jaw loosening or was that a trick of the dust dancing on the sunlight as the rays shone through the ancient metal venetian blinds?

Baby James kicked, reminding her of her priorities.

What did it matter, really, how Jordan Hart reacted to her? Except in a professional sense, of course. She had to make herself so valuable he'd keep her, even when he found out about baby James.

"I'll help you close up. I need to know how. Show me what you do."

Jordan hesitated, then nodded. "Okay. We'll start with double-checking the locks on the drug safes."

As he led her through the building, he instructed her to throw all the locks, especially the double bolts on the rear door, to turn on the answering-machine and forward the emergency number to the fire department as the more rural areas didn't have the 911 facility yet and to turn down the thermostat.

As he held the front door open for her—his gentleman gene wouldn't have let him do otherwise—he cleared his throat. "Let's drive you home."

She walked toward where he pointed at his truck in the far corner of the parking lot.

He opened the unlocked passenger door of his truck and held out his hand to help her make the big step from ground to truck cab.

Bracing herself for that moment of contact that should be so impersonal but wouldn't be after the dreams she'd had last night, she put her hand in his.

His strength practically lifted her up and into the truck.

His touch practically burned from her palm into her core.

"Thanks." Hoping he would attribute her breathlessness to the way she had to twist to fasten her seat belt, she covertly rubbed her arm to stop the tingling. The rubbing didn't help.

Maybe scrubbing would.

Which brought her thoughts back to the shower they hadn't shared last night.

Dear heavens, what was happening to her? Why couldn't she keep her wayward thoughts under control?

Before Jordan put the truck into gear, he looked over at her, his expression blank.

"Deseré."

Her name sounded so sexy coming from his mouth. He'd said it soft and low, as if he was afraid of startling her. With just the smallest amount of imagination, she could imagine him whispering like that in her ear.

Pregnant, Deseré, she reminded herself. *You're pregnant. Which means unavailable. So curb the S-E-X contemplations.*

She couldn't look at him. Not right now. Not until she got her hormone-fueled libido under control.

Instead, she turned to look out the side window. The lighting and angle were perfect for catching his reflection there. She'd run out of willpower to look away.

Clearing her throat, she answered, "Yes?"

Motionless, accept for the muscles in his jaw that stood out, clenching and clenching, he stared at her. The air became heavier and heavier with tension.

Deseré would have broken the silence if she could have, but she had no words. And there were times when guttural moans just wouldn't do.

Finally he blew out a breath and his muscles twitched into resignation. "We have to talk."

CHAPTER SIX

WE HAVE TO TALK.

There went all thoughts of sex. Well, most of them anyway.

"Okay." She turned to face him, needing to read more of his body language than the window reflection allowed.

This didn't mean Jordan was firing her, did it? After her first day?

She had worked hard. Had thought quickly on her feet. Had been competent under less than ideal conditions.

Or was it something else? A hundred possible conversations floated through her head, none of them bringing a smile to her face.

But she plastered on a smile anyway, hoping she could defuse whatever situation was about to unfold. "We need to talk? That's usually my line."

He didn't crack the slightest of grins. Didn't loosen the tightness of his shoulders or jaw. Didn't even glance in her direction. Just stared straight ahead through the windshield, his hands loosely crossed and resting on the steering wheel.

The pose was deceptively relaxed. But Deseré had had to read too many men in her life to fall for it.

"You know—" she forced a strained laugh "—it's usually the woman who wants to talk."

No softening on his face, not even a token to be polite. If anything, he seemed to tense more.

She wouldn't go down without a fight. "I'm really sorry about being late today. I didn't know. But it will never happen again, I promise. And I learned a lot about how your office runs. I really like the laid-back family atmosphere and your processes are simple but thorough. Nancy and Katey and I worked really well together, I think."

"You did fine." His fingers were white-knuckled on the steering-wheel. "You did better than fine."

Relief had her sagging back against the seat. "Good. I'm glad you were pleased."

To her own ears, she sounded so polite. So stiff and formal. So puzzled.

Surely he couldn't miss her confusion. Did he like playing games? He hadn't seemed that type. But, then, she wasn't the type most people thought she was, either.

Another reminder that she really didn't know this man.

Suddenly, the truck seemed way too small. And she was sleeping in the same house with him.

Without realizing until she'd done it, she touched the doorhandle, reassuring herself.

He flexed his fingers, leaving them propped loosely once again.

"People will talk." He turned to look at her, leaning back himself, but not in a smooth, relaxed kind of way. More like he was putting space between them.

Then he turned and pinned her, his focus so intense she wanted to look away.

Why had this just become a contest of wills?

Words, she wanted to say. *Use words.*

But obviously he was one of those stoic types.

She made herself hold her ground. It was a pride thing, without reason but so very important to her.

"These *people*. What will they say?"

"They'll say things about you living with me. Not only is this an old-fashioned kind of town, but I'm not their favorite native son." He broke his stare by rubbing a hand across his face. "I had intended to cover all this in the interview and give you a chance to back out gracefully. Sissy, the woman who dropped you off at the house last night, says she didn't bother to mention to you that we would be living there—uh—unchaperoned."

No, he was not going to fire her because of what people might say. No way. No how. "Unchaperoned? That's a rather odd word for two people who are well into adulthood."

Again, he stared out the window. "I don't have the money to pay you more. And, if there is a place that comes open for rent in town, they'll want more than you can afford."

She nodded her understanding. "Nancy told me you've only been back from Afghanistan five weeks."

"Eight." A muscle in his jaw jumped. "I've been back eight weeks. But I've only recently reopened the clinic. It never made much before, but…"

"But?" she encouraged.

But he'd borrowed as much as he could to get it going again. He'd put up the house and the ranch as collateral. And the banker, an old friend of his father's, had given him more than either of the deflated properties were worth.

"You did fine today. Better than fine." He repeated what he'd said earlier. "But I can't ask you to stay."

She realized she'd been clenching her own fingers as she untangled them. Blood rushed to her fingertips, making them tingle with pain. The pain was good. It helped keep the panic at bay.

"We can make this work."

He shook his head. "I can't ask you to—"

"I need this job," she interrupted. "I need this job," she said again, as if repeating herself would make him understand.

He gave her his attention. This time, though, a glimmer of something soft showed in his eyes. Was he giving her a chance? Was she reading hope there as a reflection of her own attitude?

Lifting her chin, she put strength into her voice. "I've got a really thick skin and I've never cared much what people said about me."

Jordan studied the woman who sat as far from him as the truck seat would permit. Her eyes said it all. Determination. Bravado. Desperation.

And a glint that warned anyone and everyone who stood in her way that they wouldn't have an easy time of it.

"Neither have I." He put behind him all the gossip they would have to endure. All the censure. The possible loss of business because Jordan Hart was up to his wild ways again.

No, he didn't put it behind him. He welcomed it. *Judge me? Bring it on.*

He was at his best when he was fighting the status quo. That's how he had survived his childhood and teenage years. That's how he would survive now.

And for the second time in two days this woman had brought life to the soul he'd thought had died within his body.

* * *

That was all the talking Jordan did voluntarily as they drove toward his house—now her home, too. But his silence wasn't awkward at all. In fact, it was rather comforting. The radio played in the background, softening the air.

Deseré felt her shoulders start to relax, not realizing until now that she'd had them hunched so defensively.

This might be the first time since she'd shoved all her belongings into her car that she felt she could let down her guard.

Santone might come after her, as he'd threatened to, but the man sitting next to her would never let Santone harm her. She knew that as well as she knew the sun would set in the west this evening.

Jordon broke into her contemplations. "I've got to run by the post office and pick up the mail."

"Okay." No mail delivery meant one step farther away from her sister's husband being able to track her down.

A quick stop, a handful of envelopes and circulars, most of which got dumped in the trash can outside the post office, and they were on their way again.

As they wove in and out of the narrow asphalt streets, Deseré paid better attention to landmarks and street names than she had when Katey had driven her to the clinic. Judging by the architecture, the small town seemed to have had two growth spurts, once in the nineteen-twenties and again in the nineteen-sixties.

"The town's been around awhile, huh?"

"Uh-huh."

"Nancy said your dad live in Dallas now."

"Uh-huh."

Nancy hadn't said why his dad no longer lived there,

but there was an air of taboo about Jordan's brief answers.

Jordan was definitely the strong, silent type.

Nancy had said he'd always been quiet. She'd hinted at some teenage tragedy that had made him remote. Or made the town remote from him.

Whatever the town was holding against him—and didn't they all have teenage moments they'd rather forget—? Deseré was certain they were wrong. Her ability to read people had never been so far off that she had totally misjudged someone.

Since the conversation had been in whispered snatches, Deseré wasn't quite sure about the whole story. But she'd rather hear it from Jordan than from gossip. If she needed to hear it at all.

"Have you always lived in Piney Woods?"

He let out a breath at her question. For a moment she thought he wouldn't answer. "Until high school graduation when I joined the army. Then there was college while I was in the reserves."

Turning onto the street that led to Jordan's home, she saw huge front yards mostly landscaped with mature oak and pecan trees and drought-tolerant evergreen bushes.

"Nancy said you were in Afghanistan. How long?"

"Three tours of duty."

"I hear things got pretty rough over there."

He shrugged, the casual gesture marred by the tenseness in his jaw. "I had a job to do. I did it."

Obviously, not a place he wanted to go. Deseré wasn't sure why she'd tried to lead him there.

She'd just as soon not tell Jordan her own life story. She understood privacy. Exposure led to vulnerability. And vulnerability led to pain.

Trying to get back to a neutral, impersonal place, she said, "I bet you're glad to be home, huh?"

Jordan slowed to a crawl to turn into the driveway. "It needs work."

From what Deseré had seen, the Hart house was one of the largest in town but not the best cared for. The deep covered porch needed a good sweeping to clear the dust and cobwebs. It could use a couple of lawn chairs or, better yet, a couple of rockers to make it look inviting. Maybe a few flowering plants, too.

But, then, it wasn't really her home, was it? Just a place to stay for however long she could manage it.

Jordan stopped short of the garage where she had parked so haphazardly last night, quickly climbed out of the truck and opened her door as she was still unbuckling her seat belt and gathering her purse.

He held out his hand and she took it—and barely kept herself from jerking back when their palms touched, creating a tingle that reached from her fingertips to her heart.

Which must be the pregnancy hormones talking, of course. The same hormones that were insisting she needed a nap as soon as possible.

But sleeping in the house with the man who made her tingle didn't give her a warm, cozy feeling. In fact, it gave her the exact opposite, where beds were desired but sleeping was optional.

She was an idiot. If she had any sense at all, she would be wary, afraid even. But her good sense failed her.

And now, seconds too late, she realized she was still holding Jordan's hand.

"You okay?" His drawl made his deep voice sound richer than cane syrup.

"Fine." She rubbed her hand on her pants leg. "Just tired."

She hadn't meant to admit that. Hadn't meant to show any weakness. Hadn't meant to hold onto his hand, either.

But she was too tired to do anything but tell the truth.

He nodded, accepting her explanation without question.

"I'm going to run in for a few minutes and pack enough to keep me overnight. I'll spend it out at the ranch and give you the house to yourself. The pantry and refrigerator are stocked fairly well. Help yourself."

Nancy had told her about the family ranch, the one Jordan had refused to take over from his father, choosing the army instead. It existed as a scaled-back version of its former self, as they bred cutting horses instead of the hundreds of head of cattle they had once raised. It produced only enough income for his foreman, his cousin Rusty, with the help of one aging cowboy, the one she'd met last night that everyone called Plato.

She wanted to ask how he could trust her to turn over his house to her without even knowing her. She would have never trusted a stranger like this.

Instead, she said, "I thought we talked about not worrying about town gossip. You really don't have to be so noble."

He shook his head. "Don't paint me as something I'm not. Being noble isn't what this is about."

Then what is this about? She wanted to ask what she should do if she heard things go bump in the middle of the night—not that she'd ever needed a man around for that. In fact, it was usually a man wanting to go bump that she did her best to avoid. But Jordan made her feel—protected? Respected? Safe?

How could that be? She'd only met him yesterday. Pregnancy hormones, right? But even to herself that explanation was running thin.

"I don't want to push you out of your own home."

"You're not pushing me anywhere." He tightened his lips as if he was trying to keep the words in. Finally, he said, "With Rusty out of commission, I need to pick up his slack at the ranch. There's no sense in driving out there, getting in a few hours then driving back, when I can stay the night and use those extra hours to get some work in."

That made sense. But...

She wanted to ask him to stay, and she had no idea why.

So all she said was, "Okay."

He paused as if waiting for more. But when no more was forthcoming, he nodded and said, "Okay," too.

And five minutes later, while she sequestered herself in her room, listening for him to leave, she heard the front door close and his truck drive off.

And she was so overcome with—well, with everything that exhaustion struck her and she fell into bed and slept a solid ten hours.

Jordan drove away, resisting looking in the rear-view mirror. *Don't look back.* It's something he'd tried to learn, but so far hadn't been very successful.

No, she wasn't standing on the porch, watching him drive away. Why did that disappoint him?

Why did he feel lonely and alone when all these weeks he'd felt nothing but numb?

Why did he think it had something to do with Deseré Novak?

And what was he going to do about it?

Nothing. Absolutely nothing.

He spent all his next waking hours mending fences, hauling hay and throwing himself into whatever hard labor he could find to make himself think about nothing. Absolutely nothing but the work in front of him.

If he could only control his sleeping hours as well.

After waking up and fixing a middle-of-the-night snack of scrambled eggs, Deseré went back to bed and slept until midmorning.

And that's how her weekend went. Eat, sleep, do a load of laundry and take another nap.

By Monday morning she felt better rested than she had felt in years.

And she made it to the office early, ready to begin her new life, realizing she felt happier than she'd felt in years, too.

If only she could see further into the future than today, her life would be perfect.

But for now one day at a time was enough.

Jordan Hart was one unhappy man.

Sleeping on a cot in the tack room of the barn might have been fun when he was in his pre-teens, but that flimsy twenty-year-old rack of metal and saggy canvas didn't offer much comfort to his used and abused adult body.

Used. His thoughts went back to the dreams that had kept him on edge as much as the rickety cot had.

The sound of a truck pulling up outside the barn made Jordan push himself off the cot, stretching and moaning as he tried to loosen up the tight muscles making his back and ribs scream.

He'd just shaken out the boots he'd taken off the night

before and was stamping onto his feet when he heard Rusty call out, "Hey, Jordan, is that you in there?"

"Yes, Rusty, it's me."

Rusty leaned against the door frame. The thick linen canvas of his sling draped across his chest kept his arm immobile. "Plato said you were out here early. I didn't realize that meant you slept out here, too."

"Easier to get an early start this way."

"So you just left that little nurse to herself in your house?"

"Nurse practitioner. And, yes, she's a grown woman. She can take care of herself."

"That's not really what I was talking about. What if she strips your house and drives off with all your stuff?"

"Then I'll have less stuff I have to clean and dust, won't I?" But Jordan couldn't leave it there. For some reason he had to go one step further and defend her. "Deseré's not like that."

"Deseré. Pretty sexy name, huh?" Rusty grinned. "Just what is she like?"

Jordan glared at Rusty with enough fierceness to wipe the grin off Rusty's face. "She's a good enough nurse practitioner to take care of you when you're unconscious, facedown in the dirt."

Rusty backed off. "If you trust her, I trust her."

Trust. That word made him uncomfortable. "It's not a matter of trust. Letting her live in the house is a matter of necessity."

"Necessity is getting Madonna groomed for the possible buyer coming in this afternoon."

Jordan nodded in agreement. He deeply regretted needing to sell the brood mare, but she wasn't in foal and he couldn't afford to keep feeding her over the winter if she wasn't going to produce offspring that he could sell in the spring.

While Rusty awkwardly reached for the curry brush and other grooming equipment single-handedly, Jordan turned away from his cousin to fold up the blanket and cot he'd used.

Rusty knew the financial difficulties Jordan was going through. They had talked about it when Jordan had reopened the clinic. Rusty and Plato had both agreed to work only part-time at the ranch and to make the difference up helping out on neighboring ranches. Which meant that Jordan had needed to spend more hours at the ranch even before Rusty had injured himself.

But those hours wouldn't include sleeping in the tack room again. He'd tortured his body to put some mind-clearing distance between himself and Deseré Novak, only to have her inside his head the moment he'd fallen asleep.

Deseré. Yes, it was a sexy name. And she had a sexy body to go with it.

He'd dreamed of her all night long.

Anyone would think that the hard, sweaty, muscle-wrecking job of making hay from sunup to past sundown all day yesterday would have meant he had a dreamless sleep last night.

Not so.

But he hadn't had nightmares. Far from it. The only thing disturbing about the dreams he'd had was the frustration of waking up alone.

Rusty stopped on his way out of the tack room. "You know, Jordan, it's been a long time since I've seen you smile."

He groaned and wiped his hand over his face, too

aware of his wry grin as he thought about those wonderfully provocative nocturnal fantasies he'd enjoyed.

How long had it been since he'd actually woken up happy?

Before he could come up with an explanation, Rusty punched him in the shoulder. "If Deseré Novak is responsible, I might just be in love with the woman."

Irrational jealousy forced a growl from Jordan's throat. Deseré was his—at least, in his dreams.

Thankfully, Rusty left the tack room before Jordan had to explain his caveman growl.

But the futility of turning that fantasy into reality had made his attitude plummet.

As he drove back into town to catch a shower before going into the clinic, he attempted to rationalize his thoughts about the drastic mood swings he owed to a woman he'd only met a few days ago, a woman he employed.

A woman who shared his responsibilities, lightening his load, providing him with a safety net for when his head wasn't in the game.

A woman he hardly knew.

A woman who had already vacated his house and left for her day at the clinic by the time he pulled up in his driveway.

His head was throbbing by the time he climbed from his truck. He needed aspirin and a shower, in that order.

With Deseré gone, he could catch a private moment of peace. Well, as much peace as his overactive imagination would allow him anyway. Although the bathroom they shared was spotless, Deseré's scent lingered in the air.

During his icy shower Jordan deliberately concentrated on the work that needed to be done on the ranch.

With Rusty's arm broken, a lot of the physical labor would fall on Plato, but the man was in his seventies. Jordan would make a point of going out there more often.

If Deseré settled in the way he thought she would, he would have more free time away from the office, which would be good for everyone.

But what was he going to do about his fascination with her?

He'd always been a man who preferred to face problems straight on. But how prudent was telling the woman who now lived in his house that he dreamed of her?

Deseré had got in to the clinic an hour early. If anyone asked, she would truthfully tell them she wanted to review charts for the patients coming in today. Her nature was to be thorough. Working in this small clinic would let her indulge in that thoroughness, unlike the walk-in clinic she'd worked at in New Orleans.

But the real reason was that the house was filled with Jordan, even though he hadn't been there all weekend. She saw him in the jeans and shirts hanging in the laundry room. She smelled him in the scent of his detergent. She heard him in the songs on the radio, tuned to the same channel as in his truck.

And she felt him in her dreams, as if he were right beside her, running his hand down her spine, breathing in her ear. Whispering words of love and assurance.

While love at first sight might be a myth, lust at first sight certainly wasn't.

Playing it safe, ignoring her fascination with him, pretending it didn't exist was the prudent thing to do. But Deseré had always taken problems on straight on.

Letting them build until they were too big to handle
wasn't her way.

She needed this job. Would being forthright about
her attraction to Jordan put it in jeopardy?

And how would they live together amicably and pla-
tonically afterward?

It wasn't like her enthrallment with Jordan was going
to go anywhere. It was all fantasy in her own head with
not a shred of reality about it.

She bit her lip, agonizing over her indecision.

Play it safe, Deseré. That's what her sister would
tell her.

But she wasn't Celeste. And Jordan definitely wasn't
Santone.

For which Deseré was very grateful.

"Good morning, Dr. Hart," said Deseré as Jordan
twisted his key and pushed the self-locking door open.

From over the top of the computer monitor she shot
him a bright smile.

He had remembered that she was on the high end of
the pretty scale, but that smile turned her into a radi-
ant beauty.

He swallowed down his reaction and answered
evenly, "Good morning. Busy schedule today?"

"Looks like it. No open time slots but they aren't
all doubles, so we will have a few minutes every now
and then."

"I wouldn't count on that. We have more walk-ins
than appointments." He should be glad about the heavy
schedule and the revenue it would bring in. Instead, he
was worried about the focus he would need to keep his
head in the game, patient after patient.

But, then, he no longer carried the full load himself, did he? All because of her.

He took a step toward Deseré, to look over her shoulder, to surreptitiously smell her hair. To find a reason to brush against her. To see if that blood-rushing excitement when they touched had only been in his imagination.

A knock on the glass office door interrupted that little trip down fantasy lane. Taking his attention away from this woman who would be on her way to something bigger and better as soon as she exorcised whatever demons she was running from, if she had any smarts at all.

And Jordan had seen evidence that she was very, very smart.

"Dr. Hart? Dr. Hart?" Mrs. Mabel had her face pressed against the glass, the better to look in and see what was happening beyond that locked door.

Jordan didn't know if he was more exasperated or relieved that Mrs. Mabel was interrupting these moments alone with Deseré. He wasn't sure about most things when it came to his new nurse practitioner.

Mrs. Mabel came in with a pie carrier in one hand and a clear plastic freezer bag in the other.

"Fresh, just out of the oven," she said by way of greeting. The odor of burnt pie crust filled the air as she lifted the cover.

"Lovely," Deseré murmured as she reached for the pie.

But Mabel held tight. Giving Jordan a once-over, she turned her full attention to Deseré.

"How did you find Dr. Hart's home, dear? It was quite the showplace back when it was built. Such a shame, though, that Dr. Hart had to be displaced. I'm sure those old bunks at your father's ranch aren't nearly as comfortable. And such a long drive back and forth every day.

"But, then, it wouldn't do at all for the two of you to stay in the same house, now, would it? Your momma would roll over in her grave if she thought the two of you were staying in the same house all by yourselves. So, of course, when someone from my Sunday School class, and I won't say who because we don't tell tales, now, do we, said she thought you both slept there Friday night, I told her I'd met you and you were a nice girl and she must be mistaken. Right, dear?"

Jordan hoped he would never be the recipient of the cold smile Deseré gave Mabel. Tightly, she asked, "Would you like me to take that pie to our break room?"

Jordan admired her restraint. He also wasn't sure what to do or say next. If it were only him, he'd let Mrs. Mabel know she had overstepped the mark. But that would be confirming the rumors, wouldn't it? And that didn't seem to be the gentlemanly thing to do. But neither did it sit well with him to let Mabel's nosey comments go unrebuked.

"Of course, dear. I have something a bit delicate to ask Dr. Hart and this will give us a chance to chat."

Jordan narrowed his eyes. "Do we need to step into an examination room? If so, I can check the schedule and work you in, but it may be a while."

At the mention of being alone with Jordan in an exam room Mabel's eyes lit up. But when he said she'd have to wait her turn, that light died a quick death.

"No need for that," she said. She held up the plastic bag. "I need to know what this is."

Inside was a used pregnancy test. Mabel was at least two decades past her childbearing years.

"And why do you need to know that?" His tone was low and quiet. Anyone who knew him well knew to back off immediately.

But Mrs. Mabel didn't know him well at all.

Instead, she pressed on. "I found it in my niece's bathroom trashcan. She's staying with me, you know? Such a handful."

Her niece, *the handful*, had recently returned to Piney Woods after her cheating husband had left her. She was working at a church daycare during the day and the local diner at night, trying to get back on her feet. Jordan knew all this because she'd come in to request an STD test just to be sure she was okay.

"I suggest you stop dealing in trash." Jordan drew himself up to his full height and glared down at Mabel, making his meaning crystal clear. He took the plastic bag from her and walked to the door, holding it open. "Next time, make an appointment."

From behind him, Deseré cleared her throat. "Oh, and, Mrs. Mabel, not only are Jordan and I sharing a house, we also shared a shower."

The second the door closed behind Mrs. Mabel, Deseré clasped her hand over her mouth. "I am *so* sorry," filtered through her fingers loud and clear.

And Jordan laughed—a real, honest-to-goodness, joyous laugh.

"I'm not," he answered her, laughing again just because he could. When had he last felt this light? This unrestricted? Ever?

With that laugh, it felt like he released a lifetime of anxiety.

Still mortified, Deseré uncovered her mouth but bit her bottom lip.

"Don't." He had the strongest desire to kiss that lip free.

What was it about this woman that entranced him?

This was so unlike him. What was wrong with him?

And why did it feel so right?

It had been so long since he'd felt anything for anyone but this wasn't just anyone.

The urge was so strong to touch her that he reached out and brushed a strand of hair from her cheek.

His fingertips tingled, wanting more.

Her indrawn breath told him she'd been affected, too.

But how had he affected her?

He struggled to think rationally, to read her downcast eyes, to interpret the brace of her shoulders. To determine if she had really leaned into him or if it was purely his wishful thinking.

He shifted on his feet, subtly putting distance between them. What had he just done?

This was the woman he worked with. The woman he employed. The woman who lived in his house and *whom he had seen naked in his shower.*

Now was not the time to be thinking of that.

Shreds of professionalism as well as practicality wrapped around him, reining him in.

Deseré wasn't a one-night stand.

She could not be trifled with.

Not that he would do that. He had too much respect for her.

Immediately he lowered his hand to his side and took a step back. "Now it's my turn to say I'm sorry."

Catching her lip again, but this time with a sparkle in her eye, she looked at him. "I'm not."

Her admission changed everything, turning their relationship from purely professional into the possibility of more.

Under his intense study she glowed a beautiful shade of pink.

"I've never known a woman who blushed before."

With color still high in her cheeks, she took a deep breath. "This isn't normal for me. I don't usually—"

Trying to smooth over the awkwardness, he interrupted with, "We're both adults—" until she held up her hand.

"I'd like to clear the air here, please."

"Okay." He crossed his arms to keep from reaching for her again.

"This is—what I'm feeling is—" She took a breath, her eyes begging him to understand. "Not real."

He raised one eyebrow. "Not real? It feels pretty real to me."

Deseré took another deep breath. "Maybe you had better tell me what you're feeling, then." Because she knew he couldn't be feeling what she was feeling.

His jaw worked, like he was mulling over a particularly difficult problem. Blowing out a breath, he nodded, apparently coming to a decision.

"Attraction?" Looking away from her, not meeting her eyes. "Insanity?" He answered as questions, giving her room to confirm or deny them.

"Attraction," she confirmed, relieved to have it out in the open. Her practical nature couldn't let her leave it at that. "But we don't really know each other. And we are living in the same house. So maybe we'd better not act on it, okay?"

Watching him closely, Deseré identified regret, loss

and relief among all the myriad emotions that crossed through his eyes.

And then there was that gut-wrenching blankness as his eyes lost their luster and turned flat and unreadable.

With his face as still and solemn as the night he'd opened his bedroom door to her, he said, "Okay. Yeah. That was a mistake."

His eyes left her feeling cold and lonely. What could she do? What could she say to warm those eyes again?

She cleared her throat, swallowing past the caution Celeste would have advised. "How about growing friendship? We could do that, couldn't we?"

A faint spark flickered in his eyes. "Maybe."

She couldn't resist. She reached toward him to—

She would never know what she would have done because Nancy rapped on the door, calling loud enough for them to hear her. "Hey, can you unlock this? I gave Deseré my key and haven't made a new one yet."

How long had she been out there? What had she heard? What did it matter, with the story Mrs. Mabel was surely spreading far and wide?

As if Jordan had exactly the same thought, he turned a searching gaze on her, capturing her total focus. "About Mrs. Mabel. Chin high has always worked the best for me."

"Chin high—" she lifted hers a few millimeters "—has always worked for me, too."

As if that moment of shared pasts knocked down a few of the bricks between them, Jordan's eyes deepened so that a glimmer of his former laughing self showed through.

And with that he turned and unlocked the door and they began their day.

* * *

Jordan found enough to do to keep himself busy as Deseré finished her charting duties. A stickler for precise charting, he'd been relieved to find that Deseré was as thorough as he could have asked for.

In fact, she was thorough and competent all round. Saturday's office hours hadn't been a fluke.

For the first time since he'd returned, Jordan didn't feel drained at the end of the workday.

Plastering on his best meet-the-patient face hadn't taken as much out of him as usual, especially when he'd given the more trying patients to Deseré.

And she carried her load, seeing almost as many patients as he had. She had the knack of being able to engage in conversation enough to make the patient comfortable yet not spend too long with one patient at another patient's expense.

And she hadn't seemed to mind the chatty ones at all. She was a good listener, able to pick out enough clues from the prattle of Mr. Grayson to figure out he hadn't been taking his insulin consistently. Figuring out Tina's stomachache was due to a math test she hadn't studied for, instead of some rare and mysterious ailment that made her roll her eyes dramatically while pressing her fist into her belly.

Listening compassionately to Mrs. Mabel's niece talk about options for her pregnancy, even though they didn't handle obstetrics in their office and Deseré had already given the girl the names of several obstetricians to see in Longview.

His day had been unstressed, with a few football physicals, a sinus infection, two head colds and a case of colic that had made the whole office wince in sympathy.

He realized he was staring at her when she looked

up from filing the last chart and asked, "You're waiting on me, aren't you? I think I've got the closing procedure down, but you might want to check me on it."

He gave her a shrug, not really knowing why he was waiting for her but willing to use her explanation instead of telling her the truth, that he felt good in her company and it was a feeling he wanted to hang onto as long as it lasted.

As with everything else she'd done that day, she closed up thoroughly and efficiently, ignoring him as she went through the checklist.

As she turned the last key in the last lock, he touched her arm to claim her attention.

Worry crinkled the corners of her eyes. "Did I forget something?"

"No, you didn't forget anything."

"I told you I was good at what I did." She gave him one of those life-affirming smiles with a side order of self-confidence. The combination made him want to do more than touch her. He wanted to put his lips on that smile and draw it in to become a part of him.

He wanted to be a part of her, too.

For a man who had always wanted to live his life alone, the sensation made him feel too hemmed in.

Plato had said he'd known, the moment he'd laid eyes on his wife, that she was the one. Now, fifty-three years later, she still made his heart race.

Jordan's heart was racing. Did that mean—?

No, those things only happened in movies and romance novels. Lust at first sight? Sure. But the other thing? No. No way.

He took a step away, noting the swing of her hair as she shifted her purse onto her shoulder. That oversize bag was an excellent barrier, intended or not. He took another step back, putting more space between them.

That's it. Keep the attraction at arm's length.

"We're out of milk. I need to stop by the grocery store. Since your compensation comes with room and board, you could come with me and pick up whatever you want to stock the refrigerator and pantry with. We can swing by here afterward and pick up your car."

Darkness crossed Deseré's bright eyes, but she blinked it away.

"That sounds wonderful." Her voice was far more enthusiastic than a simple trip to the grocery store warranted.

They were just groceries. What gave him the suspicion she'd gone hungry before?

Never again. Not under his watch.

"I'll add you to my account while we're there so you can buy whatever you need whenever you need it."

She nodded, acknowledging without replying except for the hope and gratitude her eyes reflected, making him feel like some kind of superhero.

He held the clinic door open for her then gave it a good jerk behind him to make sure it had locked when it closed. She was a couple of paces in front of him and as Jordan followed Deseré out to his truck, he tried to look anywhere but at her sassy bottom.

But he failed.

Don't think about her. Don't think about that almost-kiss. Don't think about wanting to take it all the way. Don't think.

Yeah, not thinking would not be a good thing. That would mean he'd let his body take over, do its own thing, and frankly, after her big statement about not wanting to do anything about their attraction, that would be a mistake.

Because his body wanted her. And hers wanted his. But there were too many reasons why that would be a bad thing, not least that his head wasn't in the right place for a relationship.

Taking two big steps forward, he reached the passenger door, unlocked it and opened it. Not thinking, he reached for her elbow to help her in. A thrill went through him so strongly it made him shake in his boots.

Not thinking.

Not thinking, he dropped her elbow and she had to grab the doorhandle to keep her balance.

"Sorry," he muttered, his voice raw from the strain of keeping his hands to himself.

"No biggie," she murmured back, sounding raspy. What would she sound like after a hard night in his bed, screaming his name?

How could one innocent touch make him come so alive?

And why was he so reluctant to sink back into that safe numb state he'd been in before she'd shown up at the rodeo arena?

Once he was securely belted into his own seat, he forced himself to think.

This was about sex. Pure and simple. It had been a while—a long while.

He should look up old friends. Make a few calls. Plan to go out of town for the weekend.

The ragged-edged psychologist's card he'd carried in his wallet ever since he'd been discharged felt heavy. Urgent, even.

As if Deseré could overhear his thoughts—as if it would make a difference if she could—he fiddled with the volume on the radio, turning it loud enough to make talking inconvenient.

Raising his voice, he asked, "Is this okay?"

She nodded her head, not bothering to answer.

Maybe that was for the best. Right now, her voice was beginning to cause as much reaction in him as her touch did.

He took a deep breath, and realized her scent did the same.

The cab of his truck had never seemed so small and his need for a woman had never seemed so large.

As he put the truck in gear, he admitted to himself that not just any woman would do.

Deseré. She was the only one he wanted.

And she had said it wasn't real.

CHAPTER SEVEN

As THE NEXT few days turned into weeks, Deseré and Jordan fell into an easy working relationship.

So Deseré's world was half-good. If only their personal relationship was as easy.

But personal experience had taught her that half-good was better than no good.

The gossip going around in town seemed to increase business instead of diminish it. Everyone was grateful to have medical facilities operating in Piney Woods so they only whispered behind her back. And some of the town's people had even gone out of their way to be friendly. Deseré suspected she had Nancy with her strong community ties to thank for that. And maybe the town wasn't as strongly against Jordan as they once had been, or as he'd thought they were.

She rubbed her belly, feeling the weight of baby James as she felt the weight on her mind. How hard was it to say, "Jordan, I'm pregnant."?

How hard was it to talk about her sister? To say aloud how alone she felt? To give voice to all her uncertainties and fears?

No. Easier to swallow all that down.

Time would make the telling unavoidable. But until then she would continue to do her job, make herself indispensable and save as much as possible for a future too murky to plan for beyond the next few weeks or months at most.

Once Deseré had gotten used to the way the office ran, they had split up the workload.

Jordan worked Mondays and Fridays with half-days the rest of the week. Deseré wasn't quite sure what he did with his time off. He seemed to spend quite a bit of it at his ranch. But whatever he did, the lines around his mouth and the dark circles under his eyes seemed to be fading a bit.

Deseré worked Tuesday through Saturday with Mondays off. On the days when Jordan wasn't working Nancy would regale Deseré with stories of his youth. Wild was a description Nancy often used.

But to Deseré's ears the stories had an edge to them, as if there was more behind Jordan's reckless behavior than a wild nature. Or maybe that's just what she wanted to hear.

She was all too aware that she had a bit of hero-worship for Jordan. What woman wouldn't when the man she lived with cooked supper? And on many nights when he could tell she'd had a particularly trying day, he did the dishes, too.

While their arrangement sounded cozy, they were fraught with underlying tension. Tension that would often awaken Deseré from her sleep. Tension that would make her yearn to feel Jordan's lips on her mouth. His hands on her thickening waist. His heart pounding beneath her ear as she laid her head on his chest. Dreams that would never come true.

Because that gentle, almost-there kiss had been a fluke. A moment out of time. And now, all these weeks later, he'd probably forgotten all about it.

Which was a good thing, right?

Not able to ignore the urge any longer, Deseré stumbled out of bed for the second time in so many hours, feeling as if her bladder was the size of an English pea.

"Well, baby James, I'll certainly be used to broken sleep when you need your night-time feedings."

After she received her first paycheck, she used her Monday off to visit an ob/gyn in Longview, who said baby James was doing just fine. The office visit and the prescription for prenatal vitamins she had refilled took a significant chunk of her paycheck, which prompted her to drop in and take a look at the hospital for low-to-no-income patients.

The facilities were clean and functional. Everyone appeared to be confident, bustling here and there with smiles on their faces. Who needed a luxurious birthing suite with decorator décor? Baby James wouldn't know the difference if he was born in a barn!

Soon. She would have to tell Jordan about James soon. But how to start that conversation?

She should have told Jordan way before now about the baby. Should have trusted that her employment status was safe. That her living arrangements were safe. That their friendship was safe.

But safe wasn't a word Deseré embraced easily. In fact, she had been getting a little paranoid lately.

She'd had two mysterious hang-up calls on her cellphone, even though Santone shouldn't have the number and a man in an expensive suit had been hanging around outside the post office last Wednesday, looking as out of place as a mardi gras ballgown at a cattle round-up. All innocent enough, except they gave her a creepy feeling down her spine each time.

And her instincts were almost always right.

Except when it came to Jordan.

There, her emotions were all over the place.

No matter how Deseré tried to stop them, both her feelings of friendship and attraction were growing. One was deep, warm and comforting. The other was frustrating beyond measure. Both were dangerously seductive.

And when the two collided...

Had it only been last week when Jordan had come in from ranch work with his back obviously hurting? As they'd sat reading, she'd offered to rub the soreness away. When her hands had slipped under his T-shirt, he'd moaned so low and deep that she hadn't been able to help moaning back.

They'd both pretended not to hear, but she'd finished that backrub right then and there and fled to her room.

By the next morning everything had been normal.

Normal, as if her palms didn't tingle from thinking about the feel of his muscles and skin under her palms.

As if she didn't bury her moans in her pillow then spend all night dreaming of him.

Frustrating. If only they didn't live together as easily as they worked together, maybe she could put some distance between them.

From kitchen duty to downtime, they were in sync with each other.

Jordan cooked; Deseré did dishes. They both liked their food hot and spicy. Neither were big on desserts. And, except for a few favorite television shows they both enjoyed, they would rather read than anything else. Hours would pass with each of them sitting in the den, engrossed in their books.

Apart from the sexual tension, it was the most comforting, relaxing, safe environment Deseré had ever lived in, and she owed it all to Jordan.

What would he think to learn she still thought about that kiss all those weeks ago?

What would he think to learn she dreamed of him at night in ways that made her ache all the way through when she woke up alone?

While washing her hands, Deseré studied her full face in the bathroom mirror. She loosened the waistband tie of her sweatpants and renewed her determination to making herself so indispensable that when Jordan found out about baby James, he would have no choice but to take her pregnancy and resulting rest days in his stride.

Because she not only needed this job, she loved this job.

As she was drying her hands, she heard it.

From Jordan's side of the bathroom door she heard him talking, although his words were indistinguishable, then heard him groaning as if he was in pain. No, that was more the sound of emotional agony than physical pain.

It was a pattern that had repeated itself too often.

She quickly slipped out of the bathroom, knowing he'd be coming in soon. Then she would hear footsteps on the stairs and, if she listened closely, she would hear the front door close behind him as he tried to outrun whatever had woken him from sleep.

Tonight she couldn't blithely go back to sleep, ignoring that the man who was fast becoming her friend was hurting.

Against the central air-conditioner's chill, she layered on her sweatshirt over the extra-large T-shirt she'd gotten free from the drug salesman last week, tugging it down across her full breasts and growing belly and trying to ignore the claustrophobic binding feeling. A little over five months.

Soon baby James would no longer be her secret and her secret alone.

She just wasn't ready yet. Wasn't ready for so much…

As she took her seat on the top step of the stair so Jordan couldn't possibly get by her without her notice, she pushed back the cringing thoughts she had about how incredibly unattractive she must look. This wasn't about abstract attraction. It was about friendship. The kind of deep friendship she'd never known before.

But how could it be? They had known each other such a short time. Surely it was too soon to call it anything more.

She had tried to cover it up by calling it lust. But unrequited lust didn't last week after week. And while lust for Jordan swirled low in her belly, love for Jordan filled her heart.

When had she begun to feel this way about Jordan? The moment she'd first seen him at the rodeo? The first time he'd cooked breakfast? The day he'd told all his patients she was an extraordinarily good nurse practitioner and they should thank their lucky stars she had agreed to serve their little backwoods community?

What was she to Jordan?

Friend? Definitely.

More?

Except for that almost-kiss she couldn't forget, he'd never indicated he felt anything for her other than…

Other than what?

And she was lying to herself. She'd caught him staring, running his eyes over her when he'd thought she wouldn't notice. But she was wise enough to know that admiration had been egged on by the extra-large bra size she now needed.

Wasn't that why he was staring?

What about the times she was sure he'd "accidentally" brushed against her? And the resulting tingle that he must have felt, too. Otherwise why would he act so startled when she "accidentally" brushed against him, too?

She knew why she did it. She craved the warmth as well as the electricity his touch built in her. Why did he reach out his hand at the same time as hers, his fingertips brushing the back of her hand or her forearm?

And then there were the times he stood close to her, as if looking over her shoulder at a chart or reaching past her for some inane object. But he would breathe in, as if he were breathing her in. And she would do the same. That melting would happen, starting around her shoulders and spreading through the rest of her body, and she would feel soft and open and vulnerable—and safe.

She'd never felt that with anyone before. Hadn't even imagined it would be possible.

So what did Jordan feel? What did he want? What did *she* want?

Knights on white horses didn't happen in real life. Jordan wasn't a knight, he was a cowboy. And his horse was a dark mahogany. Roan, he called the color. He'd named her Valkyrie.

Okay. She could live with Jordan being a Norse god instead of a white knight.

Her silliness made her grin. But her smile faded as she realized she didn't know where her fantasies stopped and reality started.

Jordan ran for all he was worth, knowing he couldn't outrun all the thoughts bombarding his mind but trying to anyway.

Yes, there was the dream that had woken him, but it had started to fade back into the shadows from which it had sprung before he could get a good hold on it to figure out what it had been about.

But he could guess.

Tomorrow—or was it today already?—was the anniversary of the day he'd killed his best friend.

Pumping his arms and legs until his heart pumped in his ears, he took a big hill with every ounce of energy he could pour into it. Running wouldn't help with these thoughts and vague, faulty memories, but it would help with the restlessness, the vibrations inside him that threatened to shake him apart.

How could no one else see the frantic unrhythmic explosion of nerve endings, the random popping of synapses inside him as one memory piled onto another and another until finally every soldier he'd ever failed to return home hale and whole stared at him, mocking his failure.

Think about the successes. Think about something else. Think about something that makes you feel good about yourself. That's what his therapist was telling him.

Deseré. He thought about Deseré, thought about the admiring way she looked at him when he'd charmed a child out of being afraid of his tongue depressor, about the way she smelled with her hair still damp, about the warmth that built in him whenever she stood near him. About the fire she started in him whenever she touched him.

Now he could draw in a deep breath, loosen his shoulders, lengthen his stride and bear to turn around and head back home, back to the bed he dreaded crawling into.

How would he feel if he knew Deseré awaited him in his bed?

But she'd already had experience with a man who couldn't make a stable home for her. Her growing belly was proof of that.

He couldn't even begin to ask her to take him on with all the problems he was working out.

But he *was* working them out.

His concentration was better. He could feel again without being overwhelmed with a heaviness that had made feeling anything impossible only a few months before. He could even laugh on occasion.

Deseré, with her quiet acceptance, her easy calmness and her exquisite sexiness, which had first brought him out of his apathy, was the reason why he now had hope that someday he would be okay in his own skin again.

Maybe someday he could even be okay enough for her.

He headed toward his own driveway with hope giving extra energy to each step.

Bang!

The noise had his heart racing as he hit the ditch, feeling the coldness of the night seep through his shorts and T-shirt as a nervous sweat covered him. He reached for a sidearm that wasn't there, ready to defend himself against—

Against a metal trash-can lid that had blown loose into the side of a car.

As he fought to get his breathing under control, to slow his heart rate, to make his mind work in an orderly fashion, instead of sending disjointed clips of memory racing behind his eyes.

He wasn't okay. He was far from it.

He wasn't fit to be Deseré's anything.

On trembling legs he walked the last few yards to his front door, ignoring the nausea and the tunnel vision that had come with his abrupt adrenaline surge.

A shower and a book would take care of the rest of the night.

And he would have to let tomorrow take care of itself. There was only so much he could handle at a time.

Deseré must have dozed. As she heard the opening of the front door she found herself leaning against the wall. Her neck and shoulders ached because her head had fallen against that same wall at an awkward angle.

Hoping her smile was more welcome than a grimace, she waited for Jordan to look up and notice her.

His face was grim, his movements ungraceful.

He must have sensed her because he jerked his attention in her direction with alarm. That alarm quickly turned into a glare. But she'd seen a glimpse of sadness, loss and despair before the flatness had come down to hide it.

"I woke you." His voice was as flat as his eyes.

She brushed it off. "No biggie."

"You need your rest."

"And you don't?" She softened her response. "Tomorrow's Sunday. We can both sleep in."

She swallowed, realizing he could have interpreted what she'd said as if she was implying they would be sleeping together. He stood still in the shadows, giving no indication what he thought.

She didn't know how to fix it without making it worse.

Then he moved into the light she'd turned on. His shorts and T-shirt were stained with grass and mud. His shin had a scrape than ran the long length of it. And he was shivering.

Catching the stair rail, she pulled herself up. "You're hurt?"

"No."

Before she could stop herself, she winced at his sharpness.

And he grimaced at her reaction.

"Why are you here, Deseré?"

Did he mean on his staircase or in Piney Woods? Or was it a great existential question, like why was she there in his life?

She chose the easy answer. "I heard you get up and leave."

"And you chose to sit here in the cold in the middle of the night and wait for me to get back home." He narrowed his eyes at her. "Why?"

"Because I…" She hesitated, searching for a word big enough, all-encompassing enough, but couldn't find the right one. "I care."

"Well, don't."

"Don't care?"

He nodded his confirmation. "Don't care."

All her emotional conflict resolved itself in anger. "You don't get to tell me who I can and can't care for. I'll choose my own friends, thank you very much. And you're it." She realized she was yelling so she said more softly, "You're my friend."

To make her point, she crossed her arms, very aware they no longer folded easily across her expanding chest. "And there's nothing you can do to change that."

He gave her a twisted grin. The flatness in his eyes changed to unmistakable sadness. "I wish that were true."

He took three steps up, then stopped and looked at her, where she was determined not to move out of his way. "Good night, Deseré."

Still she stood there. He would have to pass by her, have to brush against her, have to touch her to get to his room.

And she needed that touch, needed it to know he was okay. Needed it to know she was okay.

When he continued to stand there, waiting for her to move away, she took three steps down, meeting him halfway.

The difference in steps put their chins on an equal level.

She had intended to reach out and put her hand on his shoulder in a gesture of comfort. Instead, she found herself leaning forward. She placed her lips on his.

Although his mouth had looked hard, his lips were warm and soft.

And they moved against hers as his arm came up around her, pulling her into him.

Before she could stop herself, she moaned as she swayed into him. His arms steadied her.

She pushed her tongue between his lips and he let her. Then he lifted his head, turning away enough so that their lips were no longer lined up. With a gentle hand he turned her round, putting his hand in the small of her back to get her moving up the stairs.

She followed his direction, although vaguely she realized if she hadn't been so dazed by that kiss, she would have protested.

He walked her to her door, with his hand guiding her and warming her, and even opened her bedroom door for her.

If she reached back and caught his hand, would

he follow her in to her room? Into her bed? Was that really what she wanted?

Ever so gently, his big, solid hand put pressure on her back, encouraging her to step forward.

As soon as she crossed the threshold, he dropped his hand and she felt chilled and alone.

But then he leaned in close to her ear and breathed deeply.

His voice husky and deep, he whispered, "Good night, friend."

And closed the door between them.

CHAPTER EIGHT

CLOSING THAT DOOR between them had been both the easiest and the hardest thing he'd ever done.

Jordan sat on the edge of his bed, knowing sleep would be nearly impossible.

Instead, he made his way downstairs, to the unfinished room that should have been hers.

He studied the new rolls of wallpaper. A nondescript beige with no personality. So wrong in every way.

Friends. The word bounced through Jordan's head as he began to strip the last of the old paper from the walls.

Once that task was completed, it was well past midnight and he willed himself to stop. Maybe he could get in a few hours of rest. He stretched and yawned, making his way upstairs and climbing underneath sheets and a blanket that no longer felt so ominously threatening.

They smelled of the fabric softener Deseré had started buying. They smelled of comfort and refuge.

Friends. The last word on his mind when he went to sleep and the first one on his mind when he woke up.

But in the stark light of morning the word cut as well as comforted.

Why couldn't he be satisfied with just being friends? Why did he have to want, crave, more?

That craving made him edgy as he listened for

sounds from the shared bathroom, heard none and took a quick cold shower.

Hopefully, Deseré *would* sleep in. She'd been up too late for her stage of pregnancy.

Jordan broke and whisked enough eggs for breakfast for the two of them. He would scramble them on the stove when Deseré came downstairs. Deseré would make the toast, like she always did.

She was the perfect roommate. Not only did they both enjoy the same televisions shows but they both liked their quiet time to read, too. Before he'd met Deseré, he'd thought it was a calm he could only find by himself.

But with Deseré the silence between them was comfortable, pleasant and anything but lonely. Sitting in the den together, with the flipping of pages being the only sounds, fed his soul in a way he hadn't known was possible.

He never wanted it to end. Jordan pulled himself up short at that thought.

If he had told her about Brad, if he told her what he'd done, would he lose her?

He squeezed his eyes shut and ground his jaw. *He didn't know what he would do without her.*

And that thought made panic rise up in him. He took a deep breath, deliberately turning his thoughts away from the reasons for his near panic attack. He took deep breaths, concentrating on the here and now, on the eggs he stirred, on the birds outside, on the sounds of Deseré coming down the stairs.

He wanted better for Deseré than he could give her. But, then, she didn't want him except as a friend, did she?

He was damned fortunate she wanted a friendship between them. So why couldn't it be enough?

It wasn't like he had an overabundance of friends.

Rusty and Plato were about the extent of them. One of them was related to him and they were both employed by him, so should that even count?

Then again, Deseré was employed by him, too. But he was certain that had no bearing on their friendship, just as with Rusty and Plato.

Jordan had never been friends with a woman before.

But Deseré and he talked. They talked about their patients and about the little things that went on in town and about the televisions shows they watched together and about the ranch he had yet to take her to and anything else that came up—except her past and his military experiences.

By unspoken mutual agreement, they both steered clear of those topics.

And then there was the baby growing in her belly. She was obviously showing. And the morning sickness that had been fairly hard to ignore hadn't abated until a few weeks ago.

Jordan struggled with whether to mention the elephant in the room or allowing Deseré her privacy.

At the sound of her footsteps he turned round from scooping up the eggs. Her eyes looked tired today. He should take more of her shifts and start giving her more days off.

"Morning," he said.

"I'm pregnant." Her voice broke.

He ignored the break.

"I know." He put her plate on the table, too aware that his conflicting thoughts had come through in his short response. But there was no such things as a do-over, was there?

She stopped, frozen. Her mouth worked but nothing came out.

He poured two glasses of milk and set them on the table. "Could you put grape jelly on my toast this morning instead of that orange marmalade stuff you like?"

"You know?"

"I'm trained to notice that kind of thing, remember?" He glanced at the toaster as an excuse to look away. Highly charged emotions weren't his thing.

"How long?"

"I would guess five months."

"Yes, five and a little more." Her hand touched her belly. "No, I mean how long have you known?"

He shrugged. "A while, I guess."

"Why didn't you say anything?"

Now he turned round, leaving behind all pretense of keeping this conversation casual.

"Say what, Deseré? Trust me? Like that would work. Have you ever trusted someone because they told you to? Or maybe I should have said something like, 'I can help you through this.' But, then, that goes back to that trust thing, doesn't it?"

His voice was getting stronger, firmer, maybe even agitated. But something deep inside him had decided to come out and he couldn't seem to stop it. "I thought we had something here, some kind of a connection. But, no, every day is the same. We co-exist. That's it. Just two bodies sharing the same space."

Bodies. Hers set him on fire. To rein himself in he mentioned the baby. "Make that three bodies, one of which you failed to mention because…" He scrubbed his hand through his hair. "Why, Deseré? What did you think I'd do? What did you think I'd say? Did you think I would judge you? Me? Who has lived through the censure of everyone I know?"

Looking at the raw anguish in Jordan's face almost broke her heart. But self-preservation won through.

"Trust, Jordan? What do you know of trust?" She propped her hands on her hips. "Do you know how many nights I've heard you cry out in your sleep? Do you know how many times I've stood on the opposite side of your locked door, wanting to go to you, to comfort you, to chase away your nightmares? But have you trusted me with anything that really means anything to you?"

Baby James chose that moment to kick her hard in the kidneys. Apparently, he didn't approve of her raised voice, of her agitated state. She took a deep breath, trying to calm herself.

She reached for courage to ask, "So where does that leave us?" and found her world stop as she waited for his answer.

He looked away from her, his shoulders sagging, then turned back and looked her square in the eyes with his chin held high.

"Friends." He nodded and said it again. "We're friends."

He turned back to put butter into the skillet on the stove. "I haven't had a lot of practice, though, so I may screw up from time to time."

The muscles in his neck stood out, exposing the strain he was trying to hide.

She opened the refrigerator to hunt for the marmalade and jelly. From inside the cold depths, she answered him. "Neither have I, on the practice thing. But I'd like to get better at it."

When she turned round with the jars in her hands, he was holding the skillet away from the flames and looking at her.

"Me, too," he said. And his smile was both hopeful and pleading at the same time.

"I'll pick up milk today. Anything else we need?" He threw away the empty milk container and picked up a mug of hot tea.

"Bananas, please. I've been craving them lately."

"Are you having leg cramps? Is your potassium level okay? You're taking your prenatal vitamins, right?"

"No leg cramps. Yes, I'm taking my vitamins. Can't a pregnant lady simply like bananas?"

"You're seeing an ob/gyn regularly, right?"

"Yes, I've been driving to Dallas on my days off."

"The baby is okay?"

"He's perfect."

"Let me know when your next appointment is and I'll drive over with you."

She grinned, warmed all the way through at the protectiveness in his voice. "I'm fine to drive myself."

"But I want to." He raised his eyebrow. "I care for you."

"Okay." She put her hand on his shoulder as she passed behind him. Impulsively, she rose up on tiptoe and planted a kiss at the base of his neck. "Thanks."

Under her palm, Jordan stilled, not even breathing. Deseré held her own breath until Jordan drew in a lungful of air.

"You're welcome. It's what friends do."

"Could I have the butter, please?" Deseré held out her hand, mindful of the way Jordan brushed his fingers along hers as he handed her the butter tray.

Would she ever get used to that tingle when they touched? Did Jordan feel it, too? Friends. More?

She made a decision and took a risk.

"Last night was rough." Deseré spread butter and jelly on his toast and then her own, trying to keep strong emotion from her voice. Nothing made Jordan back off quicker than high emotion.

Deseré knew what came next. Something impersonal. Something distracting. Something that made Jordan feel safely in control.

But Jordan wasn't in control, was he? His nightmares were.

"You shouldn't get up. I'll try to be quieter." He washed out the skillet and put it away. "The downstairs room will be done soon. I won't disturb you when you move down there."

"No hurry. I'm content where I am." More than content. Being so close to Jordan, she felt comfortable and safe.

She took a swallow of tea to wet her throat, determined to see this conversation through.

"The dreams. Nightmares from your time in the army, right?" She continued before he could deny it. She didn't want to put him in a position to lie to her. She was already walking a thin line as it was. "Do you think you might have PTSD? You can get help."

With a fork full of eggs poised halfway to his mouth, he stopped and looked at her, shaking his head.

She could see it in his eyes. He was on the verge of talking. If she was just patient enough…

Very deliberately, he took a bite, chewed and swallowed while she waited, trying not to turn her watchfulness into an awkward stare.

He drew his fork through his leftover eggs. "I got the

paper stripped off the walls last night. I'm thinking we might want to go with different paper and paint. That beige seems too dull."

Exasperated at his deliberate shift in conversation, she plopped her toast onto her plate and crossed her arms. "You want to talk about wallpaper?"

He nodded, taking a sip of his tea and totally ignoring the frustration she was broadcasting as clearly as she could.

"I was thinking you might want to pick it out. We'll need to order it from the feed store. It may take a week or so for it to come in."

"You have nightmares that drive you from your bed—from your house—and you want to talk about wallpaper?"

She broke off to catch her breath while he sat, swirling his mug of cooling tea in his hands, studying the motion as it made circular waves almost as if he was hypnotizing himself, taking himself away from here, away from *her*.

"Fine. Don't talk."

As she began noisily stacking her silverware on her plate, he reached over, putting his hand over her wrist. "Deseré…"

He looked away, up to the ceiling over her head. "I thought, if you're really okay keeping the room you're in, we might fix up the downstairs room for the baby."

All her emotion gathered into a large ball and dropped into her stomach.

As her eyes filled with tears, he looked down from the ceiling and into her face.

"I've been seeing a therapist on my days off. For the baby. He's going to need a stable home life. I'm going to do everything I can to give that to him."

Deseré wanted to say—she wasn't really sure what she wanted to say. But it didn't matter since she couldn't swallow past the lump in her throat to respond.

He twirled his cup again, sloshing tea over the rim. "It's not PTSD, at least not yet. My therapist has labeled it acute stress response for now. It doesn't become full-blown chronic PTSD unless it goes on for more than ninety days. We're close to that place on the timeline, but as I've been showing improvement we're holding off on calling it anything more."

He took a sip and she echoed his movements. Her dry throat appreciated the liquid, although her stomach was still thinking about it.

He held her gaze the whole time and she didn't dare look away. Not when his eyes were pleading for her to stay connected.

The half-smile she gave him as encouragement seemed to do the trick as he returned it and put his mug back on the table.

Jordan felt the floor stop shifting beneath him, allowing him to find a precarious balance.

He could do this. Deseré *was* his friend and he trusted her. Trusted her enough to not think less of him because of his weaknesses. Trusted her enough to not use his weakness against him. Almost trusted her enough to tell her more.

"It's not all about my time away." Time away. It was what he felt most comfortable calling those three tours of duty. "It's about…" He swallowed another sip of tea, feeling the too-tight muscles in his throat work against each other. He had to look down at his plate to get this next part out. "Some other stuff that happened when I was a teenager." Without raising his head, he watched from under his lashes, ready to look away before she could pierce him with a spear-like look.

But this was Deseré. She wouldn't do that—would she?

"You've probably already heard about it. Too many people still talk about it."

"No, I haven't." She dragged her fork through the eggs on her plate without looking at them. Instead, she kept her gaze fixed on him. "I've heard about how wild you were. And there's an undertone I don't understand, but I didn't know anything in particular that happened."

She'd left the conversation wide-open for him to explain. He could tell her. Get it out between them. Test their bonds of friendship. And risk losing the best thing that had ever happened to him.

"There's a storm front coming in tonight. Drastic temperature drops. Sleet. Hail. Possible tornadoes. I'm going out to the ranch to secure everything I can tie down."

"Weather? We're going to talk about the weather now?"

"It's all I can handle right now, okay?"

Silently, she stared at him as if she was trying to see inside his soul. She licked her lips and he was so hot for her he had to shift in his chair to keep himself from coming out of it.

He'd never been into pregnant women before, but he was into her. What would she be like in his bed? *There you go, Hart. Divert this heavy emotional scene by thinking about sex.*

"Okay," she said.

Okay? Had he said something about sex out loud? It took his head a few seconds to catch up as he realized she'd agreed to back off her emotional probing. For now.

She was the kind of woman who wouldn't let something go. Stubborn. He liked that about her. She would never give up on anything she cared about.

She'd told him she cared about him.

Did that mean that *anything* included him?

He hoped so.

"Do you want to drive out with me?" he surprised himself by asking. Of course she didn't. His ex had made it all too clear that hay and horse manure were not the way to woo a woman.

"Sure."

"Okay." He realized he was grinning as if she *had* just agreed to have sex with him.

Have sex. With Deseré it would be making love.

"You'll need your coat," he cautioned her.

"I don't think so. It's barely chilly outside. Besides—" she grinned "—I've got my belly to keep me warm. Pregnancy seems to have turned me warm-natured."

If they had been more than friends, he would have made an insinuating quip about how hot her body was to him. Instead, he said, "It will be cold by the time we get home tonight. The temperature is likely to drop twenty or so degrees by then."

She frowned, skeptical. "In east Texas? How does that work?"

"Warm air from the Gulf Stream meets cold air from the Arctic front. We're in an area that gets it a couple times each fall and sometimes in the spring, too" He picked up both their plates. "As soon as I get the dishes done, we'll leave. You might want to add a hat and gloves to that coat."

As she bit her lip, he realized the problem. "It's okay, Deseré, I've got to stop by the feed store on the way out of town. We'll pick up a coat for you there."

Deseré thought of the small amount of money she'd been stockpiling for medical bills for herself and the baby. "Maybe I should just stay here."

"I want you to come." Jordan turned off the water and dried his hands on the kitchen towel. "Please."

Her pride said no, she couldn't afford to. But deep inside she knew Jordan wasn't a man who said please easily or often. And she couldn't say no to him. Not now. Not ever.

Friends. Maybe it was enough for him. But it was way too little for her.

But that was her problem, wasn't it? Not his problem at all.

She touched her belly. He'd offered to help—sort of.

Her heart sank as she reminded herself it was her problem. Not his at all.

CHAPTER NINE

THE FEED STORE was a place of wonder. It was every discount store Deseré had ever seen all scrunched into one small space.

She thought about checking out the wallpaper sample books, but then decided she'd rather look at them with Jordan by her side. That he wanted to make a home for her son was a concept that kept growing and growing inside her like a bubble of pure joy.

As Jordan drove his truck round past the public entrance to supervise the loading of supplies "out back", Deseré wandered among the scented candles and saddles and jewelry and baby clothes and a display of bananas. From a rack of women's coats she pulled off a soft pink one and tried it on. Swing-coat style, it fit perfectly for her expanding middle. After checking the price tag, she put it back. Instead, she drifted over to a counter with a sale sign, chose a man's thick, thermal-lined hoodie and tucked it under her arm.

Then, to waste time, she wandered toward the women's clothing section with its single rack of maternity clothes squeezed between the junior-size skinny jeans and the more matronly boot-cut ones.

At this time last year, if someone had suggested

that Deseré would be lusting after a pair of pants with a stretchy tummy panel, she would have called them crazy.

But even without tying her scrubs, the band dug into her waist. And it would only get worse before it got better.

With a mixture of reluctance and relief she added a functional pair of pregnancy jeans to the hoodie and set them both on the cash register counter.

The sales clerk gave her an acknowledging nod. "Will that be all?"

"Yes, but first would you point me to the restroom, please?"

"Yes, ma'am. Straight back past the lava lamps and sleeping bags then turn right. The door says 'Employees Only', but just ignore that."

Lava lamps? Deseré didn't have much time to ponder them as she picked up her pace toward the restroom.

When she came out again, Jordan was waiting for her as he checked out the sleeping bags.

"Waiting for me long?"

"Not long," he lied. He'd gotten worried when he hadn't been able to find her in the store. Ever since the pregnancy had come out in the open between them, he'd felt his protective urges go into overtime. "Are you okay?"

"Fine." She pointed to the lava lamp next to the sleeping bag he'd been inspecting. "I like the green one with all the glitter floating in it."

"And here I thought you'd go for the yellow one with the globs of blue swirling around." He gave her a grin. Deseré made him do that—grin—more than anyone he'd ever known before.

She walked past him, brushing against him in the

tight space then almost knocking her favorite lamp off the shelf as she jerked away.

Jordan wasn't sure what to think of that reaction. Should he be flattered or insulted? Either way, he knew she wasn't neutral about him.

"Easy." Deliberately, he caught hold of her arm to steady her.

This time she didn't try to move away. In fact, for the slightest of seconds he could have sworn she leaned into him instead.

"I'm okay." Then she let him hold onto her as she led him toward the counter. "I need to pay."

"Already done." They were close enough to the cash-register counter for him to grab the large sack without breaking stride. "Don't make an issue of it, okay?"

Swallowing down her protests, she came up with a wavering smile. "Okay. Thank you."

He gave her an acknowledging nod. "Ready to get going?"

She eyed the sack. "Did a bit of shopping yourself?"

"Yup. I do most of my shopping here. If Monroe's Feed and Seed ain't got it, I don't need it." He looked closely at her as he said it. The first time he'd said that to his ex she had given him a sick little laugh then turned pale as she'd realized he'd meant it.

But Deseré gave him one of those smiles that lit his world as she said, "Ain't that the truth?", matching both his vernacular and his sincerity.

"Not much of a shopper?" he pushed as he opened the truck door for her.

She took his extended hand as she climbed up into the truck. "Never have been."

As they often did, they fell into a safe, comfortable

silence. Too rarely in his life had Jordan found a friend who knew that words weren't always necessary.

Brad had been one of those friends. Up until the day Jordan had killed him.

Pain squeezed Jordan's heart. Almost twenty years ago, yet some days it still hurt like it had been yesterday.

As if she knew he was in agony, she reached her hand across the truck and laid it, palm up, on the console that separated them.

Lightly, loosely, Jordan rested his hand on hers, palm to palm.

He stole a glance at her, but she was looking out the passenger-side window, giving him what he needed without taking from him what he couldn't give.

Jordan had never been so grateful for the quiet acceptance.

As they listened to the radio, the warmth of her hand in his warmed his heart, making the agonizing clenching ease.

And today, of all days, didn't seem so bad after all.

Grateful for the warmth of the hoodie, Deseré sat on a stump as Rusty leaned against a fence, flexing his fingers from the sling that held his arm still.

"I hate this helpless feeling," he said.

Deseré watched as one of the mares jerked her head, pulling taut the rope Jordan had just thrown over her neck.

The calm, quiet rumble of Jordan's voice carried to her on a cold gust. Although the sun shone brightly in the clear sky, the wind was picking up and the temperature was falling.

She gave Rusty a sympathetic smile. "Compound fractures take a while to heal completely."

"I'll finish up that guest room as soon as I can."

"No hurry. Jordan's working on it, little by little." The thought of Jordan making the room into a nursery filled her with a sense of wholeness and security she would never had imagined before now.

Rusty gave her a long look as if he could see inside her.

Clearing his throat, he said, "I hope you don't mind me saying so, but you've been really good for Jordan."

A burst of joy exploded in her, warming her more than an on-sale hoodie ever could. But she really didn't know what to say to that in reply.

Before she could think of a response Rusty continued, "For this to be such a hard day for Jordan, he's getting through it really well. I think we've all got you to thank for that."

In the pasture Plato shooed away a bigger horse so Jordan could rope the next mare.

"They're kind of wild, with the storm coming in. It doesn't help with that big buck stallion being so protective." Rusty looked out, watching Plato and Jordan do the work he usually did. "That stallion isn't usually much for letting anyone or anything near him. I keep telling Jordan he's more trouble than he's worth, but he's a good breeder and once the mares are pregnant, his whole attitude changes. He barely lets those mares out of his sight."

As if he could feel himself being watched, Jordan looked over, giving her a smile and a nod.

Rusty grinned at her. "Kind of like another stud I know."

A hundred thoughts popped into Deseré's mind, but the one that popped out was, "So what is everyone saying about me being pregnant?"

Rusty gave her a surprised look that failed miserably. "You're pregnant?"

She smirked back at him. "No. I'm only fat in my midsection."

"My momma taught me to never assume a woman's pregnant just because she looks it."

"Wise momma."

He nodded. "Yes, ma'am. She is." He flexed his fingers again. "She'd like you to come for Thanksgiving dinner. It will be the first one in three years that Jordan's been home for."

"He told me he was in Afghanistan for three tours of duty. He's missed a lot of holidays, hasn't he?"

"Yes, he has."

"Is that why today is so bad for him? Something happened over there?"

Rusty's eyes turned bleak. "No."

Then he turned his attention back to the men working the horses in the pasture.

She thought that was all he would say. But then he squared his shoulders and turned back to her. "I'm not sure I should be telling you this."

"Then maybe you shouldn't."

"I feel worse not telling you. I think you'll understand and, heaven knows, he needs someone who understands him." Rusty rubbed his eyes. "When Jordan was eighteen there was an accident. It was a stupid, teenage thing but, well, his best friend, Brad, died. Today is the anniversary of that death."

Sympathy for Jordan's pain made her throat thicken. "That must have been devastating."

"Yeah. It still is." He flexed his fingers. "Jordan trusts you. He needs to talk about it. Maybe you could ask him."

"I don't know if he really trusts me that well."

"He brought you here."

"So?"

Rusty must have read the confusion on her face. "He's never brought anyone here before. Not even his ex when they were at their hottest and heaviest. This ranch is his safe place. Only Plato and I come out here. And his sister when she has vet duties. Otherwise even she steers clear, respecting Jordan's boundaries."

"Safe places and boundaries?" Hearing a cowhand like Rusty spout pop-psychology reminded Deseré to keep away from stereotypes and labeling.

He grinned at her. "My girlfriend's a high-school counselor. She uses words like safe place and boundaries so often I've pretty much picked up the lingo."

Deseré watched Jordan slowly lay the gentlest of hands on a mare's nose, steadying her with his own steadiness.

Feeling like she was indulging in gossip, the kind she didn't want people indulging in where she was concerned, she asked anyway, "So what was Jordan like, growing up? I keep hearing he was wild, but nobody will say exactly what that means."

Rusty stared out at Jordan, too. He stared so long his silence started to feel like he was condemning her for asking.

Almost, she shrugged off the question. But she was learning that these cowboy types required as much patience as the animals they tended and if she bided her time, Rusty would eventually talk.

She counted her breaths, getting to forty-three before Rusty spoke.

"It was like he was two different kids. One was the kid who was always defying authority. Take football, for instance. He'd do things like make his own calls on the football field instead of the ones the coach told him to play. Stay out past midnight when coach set curfew for ten. It was like he dared anyone to kick him off the team. Of course, nobody would. He was Dean Hart's son. And Dean Hart was the most generous Booster Club contributor this town's ever had."

"Do you think he might not have wanted to play?"

Rusty scratched his head. "He really didn't have much of a choice. His dad wanted him to play, so that was it."

"And rodeo? Nancy told me he injured himself bull-riding."

"He was good with riding the junior rodeo circuit." Rusty paused, as if he was deciding to say more.

Deseré waited while she watched Jordan manipulate the controls of his tractor to drop a bale of hay into the back of an old beat-up farm truck and give Plato a thumbs-up to move out to a farther pasture with it.

Finally, Rusty finished his thought. "I think he was into rodeo because it took him away from his parents. He got to be on the road most of his summers that way."

"By himself?"

"Not always." Rusty grinned. "We grow up fast out here in Texas. It's not unusual for us to get our driver's license the day we turn sixteen—fifteen, if we get a farm license—then head out the next day pulling a six-place horse trailer. We've all been driving since we could touch the pedals and see over the steering-wheel while sitting on a phone book. Besides, rodeo folks take care of each other. If he'd needed something, somebody would have been there for him." Rusty added as an afterthought, "More so on the road than at home.

I guess you think that's pretty young to be so independent, huh?"

"My sister and I were practically on our own ever since our mother died."

"How old were you then?"

"I was ten and Celeste was twelve. But we weren't totally on our own until Hurricane Katrina took our dad. Celeste was eighteen by then and kept me from being placed in a foster home or becoming a ward of the state. So I understand growing up fast. I can see that kind of independence and maturity in Jordan. But that doesn't fit with the wild-child stories I keep hearing. Not just the rebellion against authority but the drinking and reckless driving everyone whispers about."

Rusty shrugged his shoulder then stood restlessly. "That's one you need to ask Jordan about." He looked down at her, his eyes going soft and hopeful. "He needs to talk about so much. Maybe you'll be the one."

He reached down his good hand for her. "Looks like they're finishing up here."

She took the offered hand, very aware of the extra weight she was carrying. But the easy way he pulled her up showed her baby weight was no problem for him.

Valkyrie, the horse Deseré remembered from the rodeo, seemed reluctant to be led into the barn. Jordan looped his arm over her neck and whispered in her large triangular ear, making it twitch. Putting his hand on her near withers, he coaxed her to move with him.

"Jordan's always loved animals."

Deseré nodded. That she knew. "So why didn't Jordan become a veterinarian, like his sister?"

"That's another one of those deep-seated Jordan issues. To tell the truth, I'd just be guessing anyway. Add that to your list of things to talk about."

"I can't imagine Jordan voluntarily talking about anything of importance to him."

"Would you try? Please?" Rusty must have heard more in her voice than she'd meant to show because he put his arm around her shoulder and pulled her in for a hug. "And if he won't open up at first, hang in there. He's worth the effort."

"Hey!" Jordan called as he latched the barn door closed. "Everything okay over there?"

When Deseré would have pulled away, Rusty pulled her in tighter instead. "Just keeping Miss Deseré warm."

Jordan narrowed his eyes at both of them. "I left the keys in the truck if you want to turn the heater on," he directed at her.

"I'm fine," she called back, squirming free of Rusty's hold.

"We'll be through here in a few minutes."

"Really, I'm fine."

"Sooner if Rusty would quit flapping his jaws and help out a little." Jordan pointed to a bucket hanging on a nail outside the barn. "The brood mares could use a cup or two of oats, if you can free up your unbroken arm long enough to scoop from the oats bin."

"On it, boss." With a wink Rusty loped toward the bucket before disappearing into the part of the barn sectioned off to hold the various types of feed they portioned out to the horses.

Without Rusty to distract her, Deseré realized how cold those strong gusts were getting.

She climbed into the truck, started it up and turned the heater on. The rumbling underscored the song on the radio, some plaintive cowgirl singing about the man that got away.

That's what men do, honey. That's what Celeste

would have told her. Celeste had certainly had enough experience with men to see that pattern time and time again, including in her marriage where she had suspected that Santone had been unfaithful time and time again for the ego-thrilling power of it.

That's what Deseré believed, too.

But somehow she couldn't make that love-'em-and-leave-'em image fit where Jordan was concerned.

Friends. With benefits?

Deseré rubbed her belly. Not for her.

Her baby deserved stability. And so did she.

Finally, another song started up, this one about going fishing. She liked it much better.

Jordan was in the barn. He'd bought the sleeping bag he'd been inspecting at the feed store earlier and was storing it in the tack room, along with an air mattress and pump.

The thought that he would be spending more time sleeping at the ranch made her feel incredibly sad and relieved at the same time. If the tension at the house didn't let up soon…

She had no idea what would happen.

And their conversation that morning was sure to have some backlash, especially if she followed through on what Rusty wanted and tried to talk to Jordan.

Jordan would try to put distance between them, or maybe she would be the one to back away. It was probably the best way to handle the attraction they kept trying to ignore.

But it was a temporary solution.

If only she could think of a more permanent one, she would go for it.

Images of Jordan and her cuddled together flooded her mind and Deseré pushed them away.

Fantasies had their place, but not when she was trying to figure out what to do in real life.

Her cellphone buzzed, showing a number she didn't recognize. No message—again.

Since she had the cheapest plan with just enough minutes for emergencies, she didn't bother to call back. The last two had resulted in nothing but a voice mail with the name of some firm she'd never heard of.

She tried to push down her paranoia with logic. Why would Santone go to the bother of finding her? He'd only wanted her to step into her sister's place to save face in front of all his friends, right? He'd wanted to show how magnanimous he was to his dead wife's sister.

Her instincts told her she was wrong. He'd wanted more than that. He'd said she owed him for all the money he'd spent on the in vitro pregnancy. He'd even hinted that he owned both her and her son.

A twinge of fear made her shake.

"Still cold?" Jordan slid inside, closed the truck door, and turned the thermostat higher. He caught her hands in his, rubbing them, then turned and pulled the sack from behind the seat. Inside, she saw the pink swing coat she'd admired, along with the maternity jeans, several shirts and a dress she'd been looking at. He pulled gloves from the bottom of the sack.

"You bought all those?" On the heels of Santone wanting to own her, her tone wasn't as gracious as it could have been.

Jordan scowled as he shoved the sack back over the seat. "Part of your room and board."

"Since when has clothing ever come under that heading?"

"Since I obviously don't pay you enough to buy what

you need." He put the truck in gear and headed for the highway.

"You pay me what we agreed on. I'm saving up for medical expenses for the baby." She put the gloves on. The fleece warmed her fingers, but not as much as Jordan's hands had. "You should take the cost of these out of my next paycheck. I'll take the rest of it back."

His jaw jutted out. "No, you won't."

"I won't?" This argument was just what she needed to keep her mind off the worries she had no solution for. "You're my boss, not my keeper."

That muscle worked in Jordan's jaw, even though he kept his eyes on the road. Finally, he swallowed. She could see by the bobbing of his throat that whatever he'd swallowed down must have been a mouthful.

"The clothes are gifts, okay?" He glanced over at her before turning his attention back to the road. His tone was soft and seductive. "Just say okay."

When he asked so sweetly, how could she say anything else? "Okay."

CHAPTER TEN

AFTER A QUICK trip to fill the truck's dual tanks with gas, they headed home to beat the darkening skies and howling wind.

Deseré kept glancing at him, obviously nervous.

"It's okay. Just a storm." He clamped down tight to keep from adding, *I'll keep you safe*.

That would imply too much.

Too much for him or for her?

He cranked up the radio so he wouldn't have to think about it. His therapist would not have been pleased at his choice of coping skill.

Deseré cooked while Jordan took care of the outside work. Grilled cheese sandwiches and canned tomato soup. Compared to Jordan's cooking, hers felt inadequate. *She* felt inadequate.

She wanted to do more. Help in some way. And not just tonight in the house. But every night in Jordan's head.

Which rhymed too neatly with *in Jordan's bed*.

And neither place was where she should be.

Jordan didn't need her, no matter what Rusty had said. The way he'd avoided having a conversation with her as they drove home proved that.

She touched her growing belly.

Soon, very soon, she would have her hands full of someone who needed her. Someone to take care of.

But who would take care of her? As quickly as the question forced itself on her, the answer came. *Jordan would do it.*

In the midst of giving herself a strong sermon on standing on her own two feet, she jumped as the door burst open with a blast of wild, freezing wind along with the scent of warm male. It totally derailed her private discussion on independence.

"Supper smells great." Jordan rubbed his hands together, lathering up under the kitchen faucet.

"Hot tea?"

"That would be perfect."

For a moment, only the slightest of seconds, Deseré had the strongest desire to take two steps forward, go up on her toes, lean in two inches and kiss him as if he were her man, come in from the cold.

She turned to the stove to pour boiling water from a kettle over a tea bag resting in a coffee mug.

It was a good thing she had a reason to turn away before he could see her face. She had no idea what expression she was broadcasting, but it couldn't be the calm, confident, self-contained one she wanted to show him. She wasn't that good an actress.

As Jordan took the plate of sandwiches and the oversize mugs of soup to the table, the lights flickered, dimmed, but then came back strongly.

"I couldn't get the generator to crank. So, just in case..." He pulled out an old-fashioned oil lamp from the hall closet, lit it and set it in the middle of the table.

At the exact moment he set down the lamp the lights

flickered one last time and then the house was plunged into darkness.

The effect was quaint and rustic and too charming for Deseré to ignore the romanticism of it all. Although she counted on the soft lamplight to cover any emotion that might spill out into her body language.

What would it be like to be herself, completely, without restrictions? Why did Jordan make her want to be that vulnerable?

As they sat across from each other, the table they ate at together every morning and every night seemed to have shrunk in size to only the circle of light, a light that dimmed and danced, flickered and shadowed the farther it tried to reach outside the circle.

Jordan's face was cast as all angles and planes and deep-set eyes by the simple lamplight.

She probably looked round and starkly pale.

But it didn't really matter, did it?

She sipped at her soup. "Maybe they'll come back on in a few minutes, huh?"

Jordan shrugged. "Doesn't matter, does it? We're set for the night." He chewed a bite of his sandwich. "This is good."

"It's just grilled cheese." She brushed away the compliment. "How long before the house gets cold? Socks and sweats for bed tonight, I guess." And didn't that present a lovely image?

His sipped at his soup, looking up over the rim of the oversize cup to meet her eyes. His brown eyes seemed to sparkle and dim by turns as the lamplight wavered. "I'll light the wood in the fireplace after we eat. If we stay downstairs in the den, that should keep us warm."

With her mouth full she nodded while the image of

the two of them sharing an intimate fire took full bloom in her imagination. The sandwich was hard to swallow.

Something about the setting made them both linger over their supper, taking breaths between bites, opening their eyes wide to the grays that softened all the harsh edges between them, listening to the silence of whirs and clicks and hums that electricity usually sent into the air.

Reveling in the quiet between them, the quiet that said more than any words could have expressed or explained.

Finally, after minutes? Hours? What did it matter? But finally the last of the crumbs were consumed, the last of the tea drunk and a chill started to invade their small space, because nothing lasted for ever.

Jordan moved first, picking up his dishes and hers, too, and putting them in the sink. "I'll light that fire now."

Using touch more than sight, Jordan knelt in front of the fireplace and struck a match to the logs he had laid earlier. The tinder caught, curling in on itself as the kindling took on the flame, then the bark on one of the larger logs started to burn until the fire swept under the whole triangle of wood, creating flames of blue to yellow at the tips.

He felt her come close then lean over his shoulder, putting her hand on his shoulder for support.

"Pretty." Her voice reflected the wonder of the ever-changing flames.

He only needed a quarter-turn of his head to bury his nose in her sweet-smelling hair. Instead, he stared straight ahead, trying to remember why he shouldn't touch, shouldn't taste.

"Yes." His thick throat produced a low, growling whisper. He should cough to clear it. But that would break the spell, wouldn't it?

Then again, he wasn't any woman's Prince Charming, was he? He could never be one of those men in the books Deseré read. He was just himself. A common man with a few truckloads of extra hang-ups…that he was trying to straighten out. He added that last thought like his therapist had told him to, cancelling out the negative with a positive.

The fire popped, startling Deseré so that she jumped back, lost her balance, tripped over his booted feet and ended up sprawled on her back on the rug, barely missing the coffee table.

He spun round, instinctively placing his hand across her belly as if he could keep her baby safe that way.

Her own hand lay over his, their fingers intermeshing.

The baby moved, sliding a hand or a foot from left to right, proving his existence under Jordan's hand.

And tears gathered in Jordan's eyes, tears he blinked to hide in the shadows of the flickering fire.

Tears that had too much emotion behind them to let them loose.

Tears that Deseré saw anyway.

"The miracle of life," she said softly as she sat up. "You can't help but be filled with emotion over something so mysteriously magnificent, can you?"

"Are you okay?"

"I'm fine." She shifted, gathering herself.

"Let me help you." Jordan reached around her, hugging her and pulling her close as he rose from his knees to his feet.

He'd been right that first day he'd seen her. Deseré's

head fit perfectly on his shoulder. Her body fit perfectly against his. Warmth greater than any fire lit him low in the pit of his solar plexus.

It would be so easy to drop his head mere inches, to touch his lips to hers, to feel that flame leap between them.

It would be so easy.

And so wrong.

Because Deseré deserved more than what he could give her.

She deserved a mentally stable man who could hold her through the night without waking her from his fight with imaginary foes.

She deserved a financially stable man who could buy her fancy clothes from fancy stores instead of last year's leftovers from a feed store.

She deserved an emotionally stable man who didn't need to pay a professional to help him figure out what he felt and how to deal with those feelings.

Deseré deserved more than him.

With all his willpower, he looked down into her eyes, saw the question in them, and silently answered, in the negative.

Putting his hands on her shoulders to steady her, maybe to steady himself as well, he took a step back.

In the vaguely red-tinged light of the fireplace, he saw her face color in embarrassment.

"No," he said. "Don't."

She ducked her head, took her own step back and crossed her arms, tucking her hands in.

"Sorry." Her voice cracked.

"Me, too." He looked at the ceiling, trying to read any divine answers written there. But he only saw moving shadows. Ghosts that followed him wherever he went. "I can't have you."

She freed her hands to rub them up and down her arms. "Can you at least hold me? Just for tonight?"

His willpower broke. "Yes. Just for tonight."

Walking past him, brushing against him, she made her way to the couch. Sitting, she patted a place next to her. "Come sit with me."

He couldn't have told her no for all the gold in heaven.

He sat as far from her as he could, as if distance would create a barrier between them.

Drawing her knees up to her chin, she turned sideways to face him. "Aren't you lonely sometimes?"

He looked past her, trying to avoid the susceptibility in her face, sure it echoed his own. But he couldn't lie to her. Couldn't put her off with a shrug. He had to tell her the truth. "All the time."

Her smile drew his keen focus even though he fought it. It was a sad smile, delicate and fragile. "Me, too," she said.

He had to touch her, had to give her comfort.

He reached for her feet, covered in her oversize socks, and put them on his lap. He put his thumb against the arch of one foot, making slow, methodical circles against the thick wool.

Gracefully, she lay back, away from him, one arm flung over her head as she breathed out to let the rigidity of her body go. Still, the tension pulled and pushed between them, too strong to be so easily put to rest.

Distance. He needed distance.

"Tell me about your baby's father."

And the tension ratcheted up, not just between the two of them but between Deseré and the world.

Jordan wanted to stand guard over her and promise her he wouldn't let anyone hurt her ever again. But he couldn't do that. It wasn't his right.

And deep down, in that part of himself he tried to avoid exploring, he wasn't sure he could keep that promise anyway. Who was he to promise to keep anyone safe?

Instead, he just kept rubbing.

In the shifting shadows she said to the room at large, "I don't know who the father is."

Jordan's rubbing slowed, then picked up the rhythm again.

Deseré realized how that must sound. Should she let the words hang there, knowing he wouldn't ask anymore, or…?

"The baby is my sister's. In vitro. But she…"

Just say it, Deseré. Say it out loud and get it over with. "She died a few months ago in a car accident."

Her heart clenched as if a knife had just been thrust into it.

"She died. She died, she died, she died." Somewhere, in a distant part of her, she knew she kept repeating it over and over again.

She knew she had drawn herself up as tight as she could, arms and legs folded in as she rocked back and forth.

She knew that Jordan had shifted to pull her back against his chest as he sat sideways on the wide couch.

And she knew that it was Jordan's arms wrapped around her, keeping her from shattering into so many fractured pieces that she would have never been whole again.

For the first time since she'd answered the door to the two uniformed policemen who'd broken the news as carefully as they could, she had found a safe place to cry.

"Go ahead and cry, sweetheart. Cry as long as you need to. I've got you."

His deep voice in her ear broke through the last of her reserves.

How did he know? How could he have known that had been the perfect thing to say?

Everyone else, all those people at the hospital and at the funeral home who had hugged her, even though she hadn't wanted it, had tried to shush her, saying, "Don't cry. It will be all right," even though she hadn't even been crying at the time and she had known it would never be all right again.

Deseré let her emotions show, in the raw, with no holding back. She didn't think she could stop herself if she tried. But she knew that, safe in Jordan's arms, she didn't have to try. He had her, tightly. Securely. Safely. For as long as she needed him.

The fire had died down before her sobs turned to whimpers and still he held her.

The realization of what she'd just done, how she'd just let herself go, brought her back to herself and she sat up, pushing away from Jordan's emotionally and physically warm embrace.

Involuntarily, she shivered. She didn't have to do this. She didn't have to be strong alone.

"I need to put more logs on the fire," Jordan whispered in her ear. It was the same tone he'd used to tell her to go ahead and cry, that he would hold her until all her tears were spent.

"Don't go." That pleading tone was hers, left over from her childhood, with all her childhood fears behind it.

"I'll be right back," he promised.

"I believe you."

And when he crawled back in behind her and wrapped his arms around her once again, she leaned her head back and said, "I trust you."

He brushed his lips across her cheek, near her ear. "Thank you."

Though he left unsaid, *I trust you, too*. Why was that so important to her? She already had more than she would have dreamed of as she leaned against him, absorbing his strength.

Jordan thought she had drifted off into that half-sleep state when she shifted against him.

Quietly into the night, barely above the roar of the wind around them, she said, "This baby was never meant to be mine."

She faltered, as if waiting for encouragement from him. He didn't know what to do. What he wanted to do was to touch her face, touch her hair, *touch her soul as she was touching his*.

But he couldn't. This was a miracle moment between them. Deseré was made for a forever lifetime—and he wasn't.

Forevers were made up of responsibilities he couldn't handle.

He gave in to the impulse and pushed her hair from her cheek. His thumb came away damp.

Her tears tore at him.

He tried to speak. The words stuck in his throat.

But this was important to her. She needed to share her burdens and he was all she had.

He had to swallow twice, hard, to get his words out. "Why did you keep him, then?"

"At first, because he's a part of me. A part of my sister. He's all the family I have." She put her hand over her stomach. "And now—because I love him."

She lay so still he could hear her breathing. She gulped in air as if she needed the extra push, and sighed it out again in a rush.

Then she tensed, as if gathering herself together. He felt every muscle tighten, from neck through back to thighs and feet, as she lay on him.

"Relax, sweetheart. I've got you," he said, before he could stop himself. That was twice tonight. He clenched his jaw. What was he saying?

Then he made himself relax, too, to keep Deseré from feeding off his tension.

He must have been successful because she snuggled in deeper against him. "For all the years they were married, my sister Celeste gave up herself to be everything Santone told her to be.

"She helped him fool the world into thinking they were a perfect couple even though their marriage was never what my sister had hoped for. The illusion was important to Santone. He's very much into his public image.

"But it had a major flaw—they couldn't have children. He was sterile."

"Santone. This is Dr. Santone, who gave you a bad reference? The neurosurgeon on the board of the hospital you worked for?"

"That's the one."

"When I agreed to be their surrogate, Santone publicly explained it by blaming their fertility problems on my sister. I had the procedure done out of town so no one would know we used donor sperm instead of his sperm. Apparently, his self-esteem would have

suffered if his inner circle knew of his inability to pro-
create." Bitterness threaded through her tone, making
her voice harsh.

He hadn't known she could get any tenser, but she
did. Now she was so brittle he was afraid to touch her
in case she might break.

As if she'd read his mind, she threaded her fingers
through his.

Jordan squeezed her fingers. Knowing sympathy
would shut her down, he took a different tack and said
as sarcastically as he could, "Nice guy."

"Santone touted his progressiveness by telling everyone how we would all be the perfect family, me included. For a while Celeste was even able to convince
me to believe him." Deseré coughed up a hostile laugh.
"But Celeste helped Santone hide a lot more than fertility problems from the world and from me. I knew
Santone had a temper. Celeste denied that he'd ever
physically hurt her, but I have my doubts. What I don't
doubt is that Santone mentally tortured Celeste for all
the years they were married."

She let go of his hand to wipe a tear from her cheek
then immediately searched out his hand again, holding
on even tighter than before.

"My sister turned from an outgoing, outspoken,
brave woman to a compliant shadow who followed her
husband's orders without question."

Jordan sadly thought of a girl he'd gone to grade
school and high school with. "I've seen it happen."

He refused to think of his own relationship with his
father, an expert in mental abuse and physical abuse
as well. He hadn't turned meek and mild but had gone
the other way.

Wild, the town at large had all said. They'd all had

great sympathy for his parents when——his stomach clenched as he finished his thought——he'd killed Brad.

He'd had to leave town, had to leave behind the reminders everywhere he'd gone of the accident that should have never happened. If only…

But there were no such things as if-onlys.

"My sister always stood up for me."

So had his sister. She'd been the only one on his side. That's why he would do anything for her, including coming back to town to open the clinic.

"I would do anything for her." Deseré echoed his thoughts as she rubbed the baby that should have been her sister's. "I knew I was a point of contention between them, most probably because I urged my sister to stand up for herself." The crack in her voice told Jordan that Deseré might be second-guessing herself.

"You did the right thing."

She pulled the hand that was intertwined with hers over her belly, placing it so he could feel the baby move within her.

"I'm not sure why Santone agreed for me to become a surrogate for them. I have my suspicions it was to keep my sister in line. I don't know what happened——what changed. All I know is that Celeste was on the phone with me while on her way to the airport, crying, telling me she had to get away, when she ran the red light that killed her."

He let the silence fall as he honored her sister's memory with her. As he honored the memory of his best friend. As he grieved losses so deep he had been forever changed by them.

And he grieved that he could do nothing, give her nothing, promise her nothing to make her hurt go away.

She squeezed his hand, offering him comfort instead.

"I will always have a part of my sister in this baby she loved so deeply, even though she never knew him."

He squeezed back, feeling helpless and inadequate.

He untangled his fingers, pulling back and adjusting her off his lap, putting inches of distance between them.

Her eyes looked bruised in the shadows of the flickering fire.

What did his own look like? He turned away from her and shifted.

"It sounds like the wind has died down. I think I'll take a quick look around and then go on up to bed."

"In the dark? What if power lines are down?"

"I'll take a flashlight." He would take any risk to gain much-needed personal space between them.

"I've told you my deepest, darkest secrets, tell me yours. Tell me, Jordan, why everyone in this town talks about you in whispers." She grabbed for his hand but had to settle for covering his fist. "Please, stay."

If he were to open his palm, she might intertwine her fingers in his again and then he would have to stay, wouldn't he?

What to say? How to divert her? How to avoid a confession that would make Deseré want to get as far away from him as she could?

"Deseré, I—"

"Please, Jordan. You've given me comfort. Let me do the same for you." She picked up his hand and rubbed the back of it along her lips. The softness of her mouth emphasized the roughness of his hand. "It's what friends do. Share our burdens."

Was this his second chance? Could he tell her? Would she understand? Offer forgiveness he didn't deserve?

He took a breath, ready to speak, ready to—

In a startling, noisy instant all the lights came back

on, turning their cozy den into an overly bright interrogation room. Motors began to run as the central-heating fan whirred and the refrigerator rumbled. Life as he knew it returned to normal.

Gently, he sat up, raising Deseré with him.

Still, she clung to him. "Tell me."

But her eyes reflected what they both knew.

The moment had been lost.

And for him there was no forgiveness, no second chances, no new, innocent life to fill the hole in his soul.

He untwined their fingers, putting her hands in her lap, and stood. "I'm going to take a look around to see if there's any obvious damage."

As he grabbed his flashlight and stepped outside, he thought he would feel grateful that he had avoided revealing his own damaged self.

Instead, he felt more isolated and alone than he had since that day so long ago when he'd woken up in the hospital and his father had told him that his best friend was dead and it was all his fault.

CHAPTER ELEVEN

DESERÉ FELT LIKE she'd just been pushed out into the cold.

What had happened?

She'd thought they had finally breached that wall between them. In fact, she was sure of it.

But then the lights had come on and she'd found she had been so wrong. Jordan's eyes had been flat, his face drained of all emotion. His movements stiff and unyielding, like he'd had to keep his shoulders braced for an onslaught.

Was that what he'd thought of her questions? Of her concern? That she had been bombarding him through curiosity instead of trying to comfort him with compassion?

Rubbing her hands over the chill bumps on her arms, she stood, refusing to wait for him when he obviously didn't want her to.

Instead, she took herself to bed. Normally, she would have stayed awake, replaying those last few minutes of conversation over and over in her head, assuring herself she hadn't read them wrong. He had felt close to her. He had been about to open up. He had been about to share, sealing the bond between them.

And there was a bond. Of that she had no doubt.

But baby James took care of putting her to sleep as exhaustion dragged her down into a deep and dreamless rest when morning came too soon with the ringing of her alarm clock and soft morning sunshine beaming through her half-open curtains.

Coming face to face with Jordan was a certainty. What would she do? What would she say?

She still didn't know as she walked down the stairs to smell breakfast cooking.

Kitchen noise, which normally comforted her, jangled her nerves.

He had the table set for two. Omelets, her favorite, were on plates kept warm on the stove. A glass of milk and a cup of hot tea sat next to her plate.

Although she'd been greeted with plenty of breakfasts just like this one, this morning seemed very different, as if he was putting special effort into it.

But, then, last night had felt the same.

"Good morning." His voice flat and emotionless, he didn't look at her as he said it, his attention focused on the omelet in the pan instead.

Having shown a smidgeon of vulnerability, now Jordan was pulling more into himself than he'd ever been. She recognized the tendency in herself.

But what they had between them was too much to let it go—as if letting go was even an option for her anymore.

She loved him. It was both that simple and that complex. She had to try. "About last night—"

He turned to her, interrupting. "Are you okay?"

"Yes. Are you?"

He turned away. "Yeah, sure. I'm fine."

He dropped the spatula in the sink. It clattered, jangling her nerves.

"I've got things to do today. Let me know if you need anything before I leave and I'll add it to the list," he said, but his tone didn't encourage her.

"I need to know more about you."

He shook his head. "Let it go."

"Just like that? No more friendship?"

The cords in his neck tightened. "There are better people in town to be friends with."

He turned to her, his face blank. But his eyes showed her a fleeting moment of sadness. "Let's eat."

Her stomach clenched at the thought of food, at the idea of sitting across from him as he pulled back from her further with every bite she took. As she watched him build walls around himself to keep her out.

"I've got to go myself. Don't want to be late. The boss has a thing about that." Her laugh sounded painful, like a broken branch scraping down a tin roof.

She would have to walk past him to get her purse and keys. Being that close to him, breathing in his scent, feeling the heat from his body, feeling that undefinable presence that set her nerve endings tingling and her heart on fire, would be the details that had her throwing herself into his arms, seeking his strength, his protection, his love.

Futility made every breath heavy to draw in and release as if the air held no life-sustaining energy for her.

"You've got to eat." Even as he issued it as an order, his concern came through.

Damn it. Why couldn't he be an overbearing jerk? That would make all this so much easier.

She shook her head. "No appetite."

"I'll wrap your breakfast up for you."

"No. I don't need you to do anything for me. Just like

you don't need me doing anything for you." And those words made her armor drop solidly into place. *Survive, Deseré. Keep yourself safe and survive.*

It had been a while since Celeste had invaded her thoughts, but now her sister was first and foremost in her head. *He's a man, honey. And men can't be trusted.*

She found the fortitude to brush by him to grab her purse and keys.

If he had reached for her, even shifted his weight in her direction, she would have stopped, turned and lost her resolve.

But he didn't. He actually shifted farther away from her. The warmth she always felt around him wasn't there. In its place was a cold pulling in, a severing of that connection that had built so slowly she hadn't even noticed it was there until now.

The void made her knees feel weak. Worse, it made her heart feel empty.

Before he could see the tears gathering in her eyes she pushed her way out the door and down the steps.

By the time she slid into her car, she had forcibly pushed their whole night's conversation into a box she would avoid opening at all costs.

As she unlocked the door to the clinic, she had a plan. Pretend this had never happened.

"I'm glad you're here early," Nancy said in way of greeting. "You've got a full schedule."

"Good. Glad to hear it." Finally, she was catching a break. Keeping herself busy would keep her mind off Jordan and the conversation they weren't going to have.

As she slipped on her lab coat, she also slipped on the professionalism she'd worked so hard to obtain. The professionalism and self-respect and independence no man would take from her.

But he'd never tried to take any of those things from, her wayward subconscious said. In fact, Jordan had done everything in his power to build her reputation—except for the living-together part. And that part was worth a whisper or two behind her back.

Or it had been until last night. This morning's coldness—no, it was worse than coldness, it was nothingness—would make living with Jordan very empty with a hole in her soul that ached to be filled. How long could she withstand that kind of pain?

She didn't make enough money to move out. What would she do?

She had no choice but to keep on doing what she'd been doing, sharing living space with him. She would keep to herself, stay in her room, become a ghost in his house.

Not the best solution, but the only one she had right now.

Nancy handed her the first chart. "Regina Taylor. She's missed her period but has been on the Pill. She says she been consistent but she's only sixteen. How many of us are consistent at sixteen?" Nancy glanced down at Deseré's stomach. "Or at any age?"

Nancy's look held so many questions. What did Nancy think of her? What did the whole town, the town where she would be raising her son, think of her?

As she pushed the door open she decided she couldn't dwell on that now. Instead, she plastered on her professional face and entered the room. "Regina, how are you feeling today?"

This is how she would survive. Burying herself in

her job then in her son. It had been enough before Jordan. It would be enough now, too.

She smiled past the pain in her heart. For her patient's sake. For baby James's sake. For her own sake.

She would survive.

CHAPTER TWELVE

SITTING IN HIS truck with the radio playing soft and low, Jordan waited outside the clinic, watching for Deseré to lock the door behind her and head toward her car. After his therapy session he felt raw and exposed. Vulnerable. He could so easily be hurt.

But he would survive it. His therapist and he had talked about that so many times in the past. He had never had a reason to risk it, though, risk the pain that came with misunderstanding or rejection.

Finally, he saw the overhead lights flick off, with only the safety lights leaving a glow inside the building.

He saw Deseré. His heart jumped then plunged.

This could go wrong, terribly wrong. Then what would happen? They lived together. They had little choice.

But they couldn't keep living together with all he had bottled up inside him.

So he had no choice.

He opened the door to his truck.

She looked up, wariness on her face.

"Hi." His throat felt tight and hot. He worked hard to keep from clenching his jaw but he couldn't manage the conciliatory expression he wanted to offer her.

All he could offer was open and honest desperation and yearning.

She froze and stared at him. Whatever she saw made her thaw, at least enough to give him a half-smile. "Hi."

"Take a drive with me?"

She looked back at her car, as if looking for an escape route before she turned back and said, "Okay."

He held out his keys. After what he had to tell her, she would feel more secure if she drove.

And, he admitted to himself, he didn't trust himself to drive responsibly if the conversation went where he intended it to go.

She took them, careful to touch only the key ring and not his hand. "Okay."

He opened the door for her and held out his hand to help her into the driver's seat.

Heat passed between them, so much heat he felt the need to wipe off her burning touch. But then he would feel cold again, wouldn't he?

He didn't say anything other than to direct her out of town toward the two-lane highway in the opposite direction of the ranch.

She bit her lip as she drove but kept her silence, too.

Yes, they meshed. Just like the natural way their fingers intertwined, their spirits intertwined, too.

Casually, tentatively, he put his hand out, palm open, on the console armrest that separated them.

Without looking at him, he felt her hand slide onto his, bridging the gap. Palm to palm, her fingertips resting on his, her touch gave him the courage he needed.

"Wild and out of control. That's how my teachers described me when I hit my teens. The ones who knew me from middle school didn't know what happened. I'd always been quiet, almost invisible before then. I liked to read. I liked spending time at the ranch with the horses." He laughed, but it sounded more like a bubble of pain bursting than a bubble of happiness.

"My father always had visitors out to the ranch and he expected me to make an impression on them but the ranch was big enough that I could usually escape that. My favorite days were spent mucking out the stalls, working with the foals, then finding a corner in a quiet loft and reading until someone found me. Plato made sure to never find me until it was time to go home."

Softly, she asked, "What changed?"

"Having quiet, shy offspring didn't suit Dean Hart. As his firstborn and only son, I was supposed to make my mark on the town, on the world. My sister was doing it. She was head cheerleader. President of her class. Always hanging with the popular kids. She led volunteer groups and always knew how to brighten up a room. And she was younger than me. If she could do it, why couldn't I?

"So I tried. I dated the popular girls, whether I wanted to or not. Of course, they didn't turn down Dean Hart's son, even if I wasn't their ideal date. I played football and didn't do half-badly, even though I hated it. Made friends with Brad, who was all the things my father wanted me to be, except in a wild way instead of a socially acceptable way. It was the best I could do."

When he fell silent, Deseré nudged him by asking, "How was school?"

"Before high school I had always made good grades. Drinking hard, partying all night and skipping class to sleep off my hangovers made keeping up my school work impossible. The drinking was probably the key to it all. But I couldn't be outgoing without it.

"So, the more I disappointed my father, the harder I

tried to get it right, which meant I drank more. My teen years were not my best."

"What happened?" Deseré had no judgment in her tone. Maybe, Jordan hoped, he even heard understanding and compassion there.

"I flunked my college entrance exams." He blinked, realizing how far they had come. "Turn onto the next road. It's a small single-lane dirt road and not well marked, so you'll have to slow down to not miss it."

She nodded to indicate she'd heard him.

He swallowed to push down the lump that would keep the rest of his confession from coming out. "I was too hungover from celebrating winning the big game the night before to concentrate on the four-hour test."

She tightened her threaded fingers on his fingers, making an anchor there when his memories made him feel as if he might go spinning off the edge of the universe.

"Totally flunked?" she asked, as if she knew he had overstated his failure. Her faith in him made him less empty inside.

"A far as my father went, I flunked. In truth, I had made a high enough score to get into a state college but not good enough to get me into A&M, where my father wanted me to go. There was a fight, of course. All the usual things were said. How I was stupid and a disgrace and he could hardly believe I was a Hart."

"What did you say to him?"

The question surprised him. "Nothing. I never said anything. It wouldn't have done any good and would have only prolonged the lecture." He pointed ahead. "Turn in there."

She slowed, putting on her blinker to turn onto the road that was barely a path cut into the woods.

"This once led to an active oil field. My father had a partnership in the company that drilled. It was shut down about the time I was born, I think."

"Not that you're to blame for the oilfield running dry, right?" She said it lightly but with a touch of seriousness beneath her question.

"Not to hear my father talk about it. According to him, I'm responsible for everything bad that has ever happened to his family."

"His family. Not your family?"

He shook his head, trying to shake off the sense of loss. "Not my family. Not anymore. It's better that way." He blinked, getting his bearings. "You'll come to a hairpin curve in a moment. When you do, stop there, okay?"

"Okay." She let stillness fall between them just long enough for him to start retreating into himself before she asked, "Then what happened?", calling him back to her.

He took a breath and readied himself to finish it.

"When my grades came in and every college my father wanted me to attend had turned me down, he said..." The pain of his father's words struck him silent. He skipped to the part he could say aloud. "So Brad and I raided both our parents' stashes of alcohol then drove my truck as fast as it would go. We ended up on this dirt road leading to nowhere, running from nothing and everything."

Jordan realized they weren't moving. Deseré had stopped at the curve, the one with the big ditch and the scarred, skeletal, dead oak tree on the other side of it. How had she known?

"This is where the truck left the road and ended upside down there." He pointed to the ditch he had visited too many times. "I wound up with a concussion."

Deseré wiped the tears from her cheeks as she stared at the place his best friend had lost his life and he had lost his soul.

And now, after all these years of keeping quiet, he couldn't keep it in anymore. "No one could say for sure who'd been driving and I don't remember.

"I was thrown clear. Brad didn't have as much luck.

"All I remember is that the white walls of the hospital seemed to close in on me and I wondered if Brad had felt as trapped in his coffin as I did in my hospital bed."

Now Deseré wiped the tears from his cheeks. Her soft, strong hand smelled of lotion. He kissed her fingertips as she rubbed them across his lips.

"I wasn't allowed to attend the funeral. His parents didn't want me there. Two weeks later I joined the army and took myself out of their sight so they could try to heal."

Deseré untangled her hand from his. He clenched it into a fist to keep from reaching for her.

But then she opened the door of the truck and slid out. Coming around to his door, she opened it for him and held her hand out. "Come on."

He reached for her, holding on too tightly, but she didn't protest. Instead, she led him to the side of the road, to the ditch where Brad had died.

She cleared her throat and looked up at the sky. "You were a good friend when Jordan needed one. Thank you, Brad. He's sorry and he misses you and he'll never forget you."

She said the words he'd always wanted to say, the words he'd never thought he had a right to say.

Huge gulps of pain rushed through him, making him shake. She pulled his arm over her shoulder, steadying him.

As a breeze swayed the tall grasses she touched his face, making sure he was listening.

"Do you hear that?" she whispered.

The wind was making the grasses swish. It was a fragile, gentle sound, very clean and pure.

"I hear it." The sound felt like the subtle brush against his soul he had lived so long without.

"Brad says he forgives you." She put her hand on his cheek, to comfort and to keep him from turning away. "Now it's time you forgave yourself."

For the first time Jordan thought that someday he might be able to.

CHAPTER THIRTEEN

AND JORDAN DID his typical pulling away from her.

After a week of living with a man who was no more than a warm body—make that a cold spirit—Deseré broke down and talked to Nancy.

"What should I do?"

"Jordan's never had it easy. Not with that father of his." Nancy picked up a file and put it down again. "There were rumors that Dean Hart thought Jordan wasn't his. Maybe that's why he was so hard on his son. But Jordan could do nothing right—while his sister could do nothing wrong."

"Was it always like that?"

Nancy nodded. "My daughter and he were in the same classes. Jordan was a quiet kind of boy. Very bright. He never had to study, just got it the first time, whatever subject he was learning. And he was interested in everything. I used to volunteer in the school library. Jordan read everything he could get his hands on."

"He still does." Those many hours she and Jordan spent reading in easy company were some of the best of her life.

"But being smart wasn't good enough for his father. Dean wanted Jordan to be popular, to be outgoing, to be the life of the party. After all, his sister was."

Nancy clasped her hands together. "Jordan would come to school with bruises. No one had the courage to ask him about them. I'm not sure he would have told anyone anything anyway. What good would it have done? No one stood up to Dean Hart."

"What about his mother?"

"Least of all her. She wouldn't risk the lifestyle she enjoyed. Shopping trips to Dallas kept her in line."

"Did his father beat his sister, too?"

"I don't think so. It seems Dean only treated his son poorly."

"We were making progress. So much progress. But now... It's like we've reached a limit and now we're sliding backward." Helplessness made Deseré's heart sink. "What can I do?"

Nancy shook her head. "I don't know. Have patience. Show compassion. The same things you do here in the office but on a more personal scale."

On a more personal scale. Everything about Jordan was personal to her.

"How do I do that?"

Outside, Jordan's truck rumbled into the parking lot. He got out, stopping to give his leftover lunch to a dog that had recently begun to hang around the clinic. Slowly, cautiously, to keep from spooking the dog, Jordan held out his hand but the dog turned and ran for a few feet before stopping to look over his shoulder.

Jordan stayed still until the dog turned to face him fully.

When the dog showed trust, Jordan rewarded him by putting a bite of hamburger on the ground then backing away so the dog could eat in peace. While Deseré couldn't hear Jordan's words, she was sure he was speaking quietly and encouragingly to the animal. The same way you would gentle an injured wild animal.

So for the next days and weeks Deseré spoke quietly, rewarded with smiles and encouraging words.

And little by little Jordan responded.

When she walked past him she would let her hand casually brush him. He no longer jerked away, and once or twice she was certain he leaned into it. And maybe, just maybe, he was choosing to cross paths with her for that touch between them, that electric touch that always produced tingles.

And he would do things to make her smile. He bought her a pregnancy T-shirt that had a tiny cowboy on a rocking horse on it.

"Chin up," he said when he handed her the shirt that blatantly announced her pregnancy.

"Chin up," she agreed. And he didn't pull away when she rested her hand on his arm.

At Thanksgiving dinner, surrounded by his cousin Rusty, Rusty's girlfriend and his maternal aunt and uncle, he actually laughed. And later, as he helped her from his truck, he reached out for her hand, held it longer than necessary then gave her a quick hug and a thank-you for making this holiday a good one.

He was trying. Really trying. But now, with his barriers breached, the pain felt like a constant bruise.

In his head he knew he was going through change and change took time. His self-image fluctuated between who he wanted to be and who he thought he was, keeping him off balance.

Deseré held him steady through it all, ignoring his short-temperedness and lapses into silence, welcoming his conversation when he could find the will to communicate.

He did his best to show her how much he appreciated her strength, how much he valued her presence, how much he wanted to be a man she could be proud of.

The week before Christmas they hung the border in the baby's room, pastel cowboy hats and boots. She had insisted he look through the limited selection available at the feed store with her and when he'd mentioned he liked it, she had declared it perfect. And when he'd brought down his old rocking horse from the attic, she had cried.

It had been a good moment as she had chattered about cribs and curtains until she'd started asking him questions about his childhood holidays.

Which was why now, two days before Christmas, he was carrying a sappy, sticky cedar tree over his shoulder as he entered the house.

Jordan hauled in the Christmas tree he'd bought as an apology to Deseré, hoping to make up for the hurt he'd seen in her eyes when he'd snapped at her that he didn't want to talk about holiday memories.

She'd mentioned it casually, talking about the oyster stuffing her mother had made compared to the cornbread dressing his aunt made. And when he'd said he usually spent Christmas Day catching up on end-of-year paperwork, she'd given him a sad, pitying smile.

He didn't need that. Didn't want that. Didn't need…

He'd been trying, really trying.

But need led to weakness. Need was a weapon to be exploited.

As he and his therapist had discussed, Jordan stopped himself from thinking those same old thoughts. Deseré had never hurt him, had never tried to hurt him. Deseré trusted him.

And he could trust her.

He wanted to be the man she needed him to be—like she was the woman he needed her to be. He wanted to have a future with Deseré.

All the hard head work he'd been doing was worth it when Deseré saw the tree and the box of decorations he'd picked up at the feed store.

As she hung the lower ornaments and directed him to hang the higher ones, Jordan felt like this was his first Christmas ever.

They drank hot chocolate while Ebenezer Scrooge did his thing on the television that played softly in the background.

"What do you want for Christmas?" she asked him.

He was nonplussed. How could he tell her he already had more than he could have ever expected?

So he shrugged and turned the question back to her. "What do you want?"

"You." She said it matter-of-factly. "All of you, heart, mind, body and soul.'

I want you, too, he thought back at her. But he couldn't say it, no matter how hard he tried.

After a few moments of silence she touched his arm, gave him a tremulous smile then walked away, with a big sigh echoing in her wake.

That sigh breeched his last barrier as no push or shout could have. Need engulfed him, need to make her world better. Need to give her what she wanted. Need to give him what he wanted, too.

A peacefulness settled deep inside him. Next time, and he knew there would be a next time, with Deseré there always was—next time would be different, better. Because he would be different. Better. The best he could be for her and baby James.

That night Deseré came to him, waking him from his dreams.

Her head nestled into his chest and he felt as if he was the one giving comfort instead of her. He felt very strong, very protective and very much her man.

She made snuffling, snuggling noises against his chest, noises that made both his mind and his body beg to hear what sounds she would make when they made love.

"Jordan," she whispered in the moonlight, "if you want to…"

She ducked her head back shyly as she ran a single finger down his chest, making his heart throb. That throb circulated through his whole body, coming to a peak deep and low in his solar plexus.

"I want to." His hand reached out, catching her wandering finger and bringing it to his mouth.

She ran her foot up his shin, making him tremble. "I want to, too."

He put his lips on her smooth, bare shoulder, where her oversize T-shirt fell away, and kissed up her neck, tasting the sweetness of her delicate skin.

He ran his hand down her spine, tracing the outline of that feminine backbone that kept him together when he needed her most. How could she be so soft yet so resilient at the same time?

"Saying no to you is the hardest thing I've ever done, Deseré." Using all his willpower, he commanded his hand to stop midway when all he wanted to do was cup her delicious bottom in his hand and puller her closer, protecting baby James between them.

"I want to make love to you more than anything in the world. But this is about more than me and you, Deseré. This is about James, too." He put his hand on her belly, feeling a tiny foot or maybe a hand move under his palm. "A child needs a steady father. A father he can count on. A father who will always be there for him, no matter what he does, no matter how he screws up. A father who will love him for exactly who he is and not with any preconceived ideas about who he should be."

Deseré sat up, dislodging Jordan's hand. "There are plenty of children who do just fine without a father like that."

"But James doesn't have to. I can be the kind of father who loves unconditionally. I know this because I already love your son that way."

He took a deep breath, continuing despite the tension he felt in Deseré. "The steadiness? I'm working on that part. Working on finding my balance, on being okay with who I am, on living up to my own expectations and not my father's. I'm learning that I can't please him and I have to be okay with that."

She covered his hand, which rested on her belly, and squeezed his fingers. "I know. I'm very proud of you for that, too."

"But always being there?" He pinned her with a look that seemed to try to see into her soul. "That's up to you. Will you allow me to be a father to your son? Will you allow me to be your husband?"

She needed more than for Jordan to marry her for her son. That's what his father had done for his mother and it hadn't made for a good marriage. That's what Santone had wanted to do with her.

Jordan wasn't Santone, far from it, but she wasn't his mother or her sister, either.

"You're a good man, Jordan Hart, but I'll only marry for love."

Deseré waited for the three little words that would complete them all.

He let out a sigh as he stared at the ceiling, absently tracing the outline of James's foot.

Just as she was drifting off to sleep she thought she heard Jordan whisper, "I love you, Deseré."

When she looked over, his eyes were closed and his breathing was deep and even.

Christmas Eve. It was going to be a long day.

Jordan headed to the ranch before Deseré stirred.

When he pulled up in his truck, Rusty came out of the barn to meet him, looking grim. "The buyer will be out late this afternoon to pick her up."

Jordan nodded. He was doing the right thing. Just because it hurt like hell didn't change that.

He walked into the barn and Valkyrie gave him a welcome whinny.

"It will be okay, girl. You're going to a good owner who will treat you right."

She nudged him and he scratched that place behind her left ear that made her give him dreamy horse eyes.

"It's got to be done. I can't think of any other way."

As if she understood, she nodded under his palm then nibbled the front of his shirt.

Turning away from her wasn't as hard as it had been to turn away from Deseré last night, but it was close.

With nothing but a backward wave at Rusty, Jordan climbed into his truck and headed for the clinic.

That morning, when Deseré came down for breakfast, she saw that Jordan had plugged in the tree lights for her.

It was the little things that showed her they were making progress and that encouraged her to be patient.

Just as she was trying to be patient about the arrival of baby James. Just a few more weeks, her doctor had said at her last check-up. Mid-January.

The Braxton-Hicks contraction reminded Deseré to call the billing department of the hospital to find out why her last check hadn't cleared.

With an office full of people, finding a private moment had been impossible until now.

She looked up as the judge and Plato laughed, as old men did.

Plato had come in earlier to have his vitals checked so he could get a refill on his high blood pressure medicine and the judge had come for a refill for his Viagra, which he now clutched in a brown paper bag.

The joy in the old men's voices made her smile, too, despite what the accountant on the phone was telling her for the second time.

She listened as the accounts manager thoroughly and slowly explained that the hospital hadn't cashed the last check because Deseré's account had been paid in full last week. They had put the check in the mail yesterday to mail it back to her.

"Who paid it?" The hang-up phone calls she'd been getting more frequently came to mind. Sinister chills ran down her spine.

"I don't know. Santa? It was paid in cash," the man on the end of the line said. "Merry Christmas."

Just as her belly gave her the slightest cramp, Jordan came into the office. He'd been doing that for the last several weeks, coming in on his days off, taking the load off her.

She had wanted to suggest he reduce her paycheck

but couldn't figure out how to pay ahead on the hospital bill if she did. And now it seemed she didn't need to worry about it.

But she was now worried for a different reason than money.

Was this paid hospital bill the work of Santone? Another way to claim he owned the baby she was carrying? That he owned her, too?

"Hey," Jordan said to her softly. "Are you feeling okay?"

She was achy all over and hormonal—which meant aching for Jordan's touch, aching for him to give her some release. Eight and a half months of being sexually on the edge would tend to make a woman a little testy, wouldn't it?

Add to that emotional state her tender feelings for Jordan, which he pushed away, and she was a hot mess.

She would like to blame it all on hormones but she had a feeling of dread that none of this would go away just because she gave birth.

The only way to get away from all her tumultuous feelings was to leave here, leave Jordan. And that made her feel more upset than any of the other emotions she was experiencing.

As the office got quiet, she realized she was listening to a dead phone line.

All the men were looking at the two strangers who had just pulled open the door, two strangers who stood there, staring at her.

But, then, one on them wasn't a stranger to her at all.

"Santone." She dropped the phone receiver. It clattered on the counter.

"Deseré." He took a step toward her but Jordan put himself between them.

Santone frowned. "If you'll excuse me, I'm here to talk to the mother of my child."

Jordan glared at him as if he were a bug he was about to squash then turned his attention to the other man. "And you are?"

The smaller man held out his hand with a card in it. Jordan took it.

"David Kessler. Life insurance agent."

"And your business?"

"I think Ms. Novak, Mr. Santone and I could use some privacy."

Deseré stayed behind the counter, feeling very safe with Jordan in front of her. "I'm among friends. We can talk about anything here."

The insurance agent looked worried then nodded. "I'm here to award the proceeds of Mrs. Celeste Santone's life insurance policy to Mr. Santone as the parent of her child. We just need your verification that your role is solely as surrogate."

He dug a sheaf of papers from his briefcase. "If you would sign this affidavit stating that Mr. Santone is the child's father and will be taking custody of the baby once it is born. There is a secondary policy payout you will receive once you verify you're the surrogate."

Deseré rubbed her back where baby James lay heavily on her kidney. "This is my child and he—" her hand quivered as she pointed at Santone "—is not my baby's father."

"Or course I am." Santone took a step forward but stopped when Jordan moved toward him.

Jordan looked from Santone back to Deseré with a look that was both hesitant and wistful.

At Deseré's nod, he looked the insurance agent

straight in the face. "I'm the child's father and Deseré is the child's mother."

"You're not." Santone's tone was so menacing, both Plato and the judge rose to their feet.

Quietly, Jordan asked, "I suggest you calm yourself in front of my fiancé. Would you like to do a blood test to prove your paternity after the baby's born?"

The insurance agent gave a deep sigh. "This is rather complicated, isn't it?"

The judge spoke up. "What would make it clearer for you, young man?"

The agent glanced down at the papers he carried. "The way the policy is written, if I can show that Ms. Novak isn't dependent on Mr. Santone for any of the expenses for the child, I can say she is not a surrogate but the child's mother."

The conversation she just had with the hospital made her feel light-headed. Had Santone paid that bill?

The judge asked, "Like what expenses?"

"Food. Shelter. Clothing. Hospital bills."

Jordan cleared his throat. "Either Deseré or I have paid for all those."

"Can you prove it?"

He nodded. "I have accounts at the grocery store and the feed store." His half-smile was crooked and embarrassed. "The feed store is where we've been purchasing maternity clothes."

"And medical bills?"

Deseré pulled her purse from under the counter and started going through receipts. "Here."

She thrust the crumpled receipts at the agent.

Jordan reached into his wallet and pulled out a folded receipt, too. "And this is from the hospital where I've prepaid for our son's delivery."

Our son. Pride clogged Jordan's throat as he said that. His son. Deseré had given him that privilege.

"So you claim paternity, Mr....?"

"Dr. Hart." He pulled his driver's license from his wallet and handed it to the agent. "Dr. Jordan Hart."

The agent checked the license and handed it back then cleared his throat.

To the room at large, he said, "The policy beneficiaries are listed as the parents and guardians of Mrs. Celeste Santone's child. Are you telling me that the child you are carrying, Ms. Novak, belongs to you and Dr. Hart?"

"Yes. He's our baby. Mine and Jordan's."

The world around Jordan seemed to pulse with a whole different light as joy burst so big inside him he felt every cell fill with incredible happiness.

He hadn't known, or even suspected, that love could feel this big.

"You lie. This man is not the father." Santone surged forward but again Jordan blocked his path to Deseré.

The agent sucked in his cheeks. "Your only option at this point, Dr. Santone, is to wait until the child is born and submit to a DNA test."

The judge picked up his cellphone and held it so Santone could see it. "Seems to me your business is done here. Do I need to call my boys with badges to escort you out of town?"

Santone shifted from foot to foot before he glared at them all and stalked out of the clinic.

As quickly as he could, Jordan went to Deseré's side, putting his arm around her in support. Calmness settled over him as she leaned against him, accepting what he offered.

Nancy walked in from the back. "Our last patient

just called and cancelled her appointment. Looks like we get to leave extra-early today. I think I'll go home and take a nap."

The judge and Plato both put on their coats and picked up their hats.

"Sounds like a good plan to me," the judge said as he shook his paper bag. "Merry Christmas, ya'll."

Jordan turned to Deseré. "A nap sounds like a good plan for you, too."

"For us, you mean?" Deseré challenged him.

Before he could answer, Nancy glanced at the two of them. "Go ahead. I'll lock up."

Deseré made her way to Jordan's truck, appreciating that he opened the door for her and helped her in. The step up into the cab took more effort on his part as he lifted her under both elbows to help her lift her baby bump inside. Why did she feel so much heavier today? She would have to pay more attention to her salt intake.

After he helped her with her seat belt and then started up the truck she said, "For a man who doesn't like to talk much, you had a lot to say back there."

He turned his focus to her, his eyes bright and sparkly with a hint of wariness in them, his lips lifting in the corners as if he'd just eaten a smile as he just said, "Hmmph."

"Hmmph is right." She crossed her arms, propping them on her stomach as she didn't have anywhere else to put them. "I don't know where to start."

Obligingly, Jordan turned down the radio that had begun to blare out a commercial for custom-made horse trailers and waited.

"Did you pay my hospital bills?"

"Yes." He stopped at a four-way stop sign but didn't move forward, even though no other cars were coming.

"Want to expound on that?"

"Not really."

She blew out a breath. "Do it for me anyway, okay?"

He blew out a breath, too. "Okay."

He put the truck into park, right there in the middle of the road. But, then, it was unlikely the big town of Piney Woods would suddenly develop a traffic problem.

He opened his mouth, closed it again and swallowed.

Deseré knew the pattern. Mentally, she counted to four and, as she expected, he started talking.

"I wanted to."

"How? I know your finances as well as I know mine and our last few months have been slow."

"I sold Valkyrie." His voice cracked when he confessed it.

"You *what*?" Another contraction grabbed her, this time strong enough to make her catch her breath.

"It had to be done." He gripped the steering-wheel. "I want to take care of you, Deseré. You and the baby. It makes me feel good."

"I don't know what to say."

"You don't need to say anything."

"Thank you. It's not enough—but thank you. You have all my gratitude."

"I don't expect thanks or gratitude." Jordan rubbed his hand over his face. "I meant it when I said I want to be part of James's life."

"Is Valkyrie gone already?"

He shook his head. "The new owner is picking her up this afternoon. She's a Christmas gift."

"Could we drive out so I can say goodbye?"

"Yes, we can do that." Jordan put the truck back into

gear and head for the ranch, realizing as he did so that having Deseré by his side as Valkyrie was trailered away would make the pain more bearable.

CHAPTER FOURTEEN

BY THE TIME they got to the ranch Deseré had to work hard to keep from squirming. Not only did she not have enough room but every time she moved, the seat belt tightened up, putting more and more pressure against her hard belly.

Rusty greeted them as they rolled to a stop.

As Jordan climbed out of the truck Rusty asked in a loud whisper, "Everything okay?"

Did he really think she couldn't hear him?

Jordan shrugged away his cousin's question. "Deseré came to see Valkyrie."

Again that stage whisper. "So you told her, huh?"

"Yes, he told me." She winced as her crankiness came through. But her back was beginning to ache and she had really wanted time alone with Jordan without Rusty to overhear.

Jordan came round and opened the door, handing her down as gracefully as the two of them could manage.

Rusty whistled. "Getting big there, huh, Deseré?"

Before Deseré could respond to that, Jordan gave him a hard stare. "I'm sure you have something to do that's not here, right?"

"Maybe I should check the oil levels on the tractor."

"Good idea."

And just like that, Deseré had what she wanted. Time alone with Jordan.

"Sun feels good, doesn't it?" He looked up at the sky full of cotton-ball clouds. "Typical Texas December day, warm and barely breezy. Shirtsleeve weather. It could turn cold and snow tomorrow, though."

"Weather talk always means you're avoiding something."

"Let's go and say hello to Valkyrie."

"Hello and goodbye." Deseré wanted to thank him again, to apologize for being the cause of his sacrifice, to make him feel better, but whatever she said would likely have the wrong results.

Male ego. Such a fragile and complex thing.

He held onto her elbow as she walked toward the barn.

"Hey, pretty girl." Deseré held out her hand and Valkyrie nuzzled it. "Thank you for doing this for me and for baby James." She sent a sideways glance at Jordan and was relieved to see he was nodding along with Valkyrie. He wasn't looking at the mare, though. He was looking at her.

Now was the time.

"Jordan?"

"Hmm?"

"Why did you tell them we were engaged?"

Jordan turned back to the stall, resting his boot on the lowest wooden rail of the stall. "Because I wanted it to be true."

"You want to marry me?"

"Um-hmm."

"Why?"

"The usual reasons."

"Could you give me a little more detail?"

"Because…" He took his foot off the bottom slat. "Because I want to be a good father to James. I want to take care of both of you. I want to hold you in my arms every night after we have sex."

"Wild and out-of-control sex?"

"If that's the way you want it."

"On Tuesdays and Fridays. But sweet, gentle sex on Mondays and Wednesdays and marathon sex on Saturdays."

"And on Sundays?"

"Potluck."

He seemed to be considering it. Finally he said, "I can do that."

She smiled at him. "I know you can."

He turned back to stare past Valkyrie. Deseré thought about letting her last question drop. But, no, she needed to hear it.

"Jordan?"

"Hmm?"

"Any other reason you want to marry me?"

This time, when he turned to face her, he put both his hands on her shoulders and looked straight into her eyes. In those dark, tender depths she saw the answer she was looking for.

She didn't have to wait that long before he said, in a deep rich voice, "I love you."

She let out the breath she hadn't realized she had been holding. "I love you, too, you know."

"I was hoping you'd say that."

"Then, yes." She shifted, too anxious to stand still.

"Yes?"

"Yes, I'll marry you."

He stood frozen, as if he was replaying their conversation in his head. She counted, one, two, three, four.

"I'd like that as soon as possible."

"But first…"

"Yeah?"

"I think you may need to deliver our baby."

Panic closed off every thought Jordan had.

"Are you sure?" he managed to put enough words together in order to ask.

"Pretty sure." She put his hand against her contracting belly. "I haven't timed them but they're getting stronger."

"When did they start?"

"This morning in the shower, but I thought they were Braxton-Hicks ones and ignored them."

Jordan glanced at his watch and noted the time while he guided her toward the tack room. "I'll blow up the air mattress."

"That would be nice." She grimaced as she said it. "Hey, I just thought of something. This way, we'll get a refund on the hospital payments, right? You can keep Valkyrie."

"I'd rather keep you."

"You don't have to choose. Tell the new owner sorry but we're keeping Valkyrie."

"We can talk about this later, okay?"

"Always later with you," she teased, taking the sting away.

The next pain hit but it couldn't dim her happiness even as she panted through it.

Jordan took her hand. "I would take the pain for you if I could."

"That's my cowboy." She grinned at him through her next contraction. "But I'd rather you laid me down and then caught your son."

And at midnight on Christmas Eve James Jordan Hart was born to two parents who loved him as dearly as they loved each other passionately.

* * * * *

A sneaky peek at next month...

Medical Romance™

CAPTIVATING MEDICAL DRAMA—WITH HEART

My wish list for next month's titles...

In stores from 6th December 2013:

❑ From Venice with Love – Alison Roberts

& Christmas with Her Ex – Fiona McArthur

❑ After the Christmas Party... – Janice Lynn

& Her Mistletoe Wish – Lucy Clark

❑ Date with a Surgeon Prince – Meredith Webber

& Once Upon a Christmas Night... – Annie Claydon

Available at WHSmith, Tesco, Asda, Eason, Amazon and Apple

Just can't wait?

Special Offers

very month we put together collections and
nger reads written by your favourite authors.

ere are some of next month's highlights—
nd don't miss our fabulous discount online!

n sale 6th December   On sale 1st November   On sale 6th December